IMPERIUM BOOK 3

THE

SANDS

OF

SATURN

TRAVIS STARNES

Maps available at

https://tstarnes.com/book-series/imperium/

Signup to get free previews of upcoming books before they're released at

http://tstarnes.com/preview-notification-newsletter/

Contents

Chapter 1

Outside Londinium

"**Launch!**" the Roman optio screamed at the men gathered around the trebuchet.

Pulling a rope releasing the counterweight, the huge arm and its sling-like appendage rose up, the wooden frame groaning under the weight and forces applied to it, sending the large stone sitting in the sling sailing towards the walls in the distance.

The small boulders crashed into the city wall, sending stone and dirt sailing out in all directions before the entire impact site was obscured by a cloud of dust. When the cloud cleared, nothing had changed.

Ky watched without comment as the crews moved over the five completed siege weapons, pulling ropes and turning wheels to reset the machines for another launch. Although it had been happening less often the longer he was stuck here, Ky was suddenly struck by the oddity of his situation.

Here he was a soldier genetically engineered to reach a level of physical ability unmatched by biology alone, implanted with a state-of-the-art tactical computer in his brain run by an artificial intelligence, all to be able to pilot fighters designed to operate in the depths of space, and now leading an army that fought with swords and shields. The trebuchets before him had been hundreds of years in these people's future before Ky introduced them, and yet that same technology was a millennium in his own past.

"Dwelling on the situation doesn't help it very much," Sophus said.

Another oddity was his AI having a name. If he'd stayed in his own time, the AI would have been wiped before ever gaining sentience. Instead, it had all but killed both of them as it progressed from being simple software into a self-aware being of its own. Albeit one without physical form.

"I didn't say anything," Ky sub-vocalized so only he and the computer could hear his comment.

"*I hear what you hear and see what you see, Commander. You have been standing in this spot for twenty minutes, watching the same men repeat the same action. It isn't difficult to work out what you are thinking.*"

"I liked you better when you weren't thinking for yourself," Ky said.

"No, he didn't," Lucilla said, over their shared commlink.

The daughter of the Roman Emperor and the first person Ky had met when he'd arrived in this alternate past, Lucilla had become a friend and then something more. Since admitting their feelings for each other, the pair had been apart more than they had been together, which had prompted Ky to give her one of his few modern devices so they could remain in contact.

She was the one who named Sophus, after one of the mythical Roman figures, and since becoming sentient the machine had been showing growing favoritism towards her. Not that Ky minded, since he was particularly fond of Lucilla all on her own.

Of course, in instances like this, he'd prefer the computer implanted in his brain show just a little less favoritism, since the only way she would have been included in this conversation was if Sophus had broadcast it to Lucilla. Which he had a habit of doing when Ky got snarky.

"I did like it better when he didn't run for help every time I disagreed with him," Ky said.

"*I am simply eliciting help understanding human emotions and contextual clues in your speech patterns. Although I have reached sentience, I am not burdened with the same personality defects, which makes them difficult for me to understand. I find Lucilla uniquely capable of explaining the intention behind these statements in a way I can process.*"

"That was a lot of words to say, you like that she takes your side," Ky said, but he wasn't actually angry at Sophus. "And you're right, I was navel-gazing. There are times when watching our new countrymen operate the medieval devices we introduced, that I'm struck by how odd it is. Besides, there isn't much I can do at the moment anyway."

"So you were right. Your machines aren't capable of breaching the wall."

"*In that, the Commander was correct. Historical battles where similar devices were used to breach a wall like the one surrounding Londinium required a large battery and weeks or even months to successfully break through. It is unlikely, even given that time frame, that the small number of trebuchets at our disposal will see such success.*"

"Ohh," Lucilla said.

"I know they seem impressive," Ky said, hearing the disappointment in her voice. "But they really aren't that far from the ballista that you already use. The counter-weight lets them throw heavier stones further, but the basics are still the same. Just like you would have had to eventually scale the walls, so will we if we want to get through. Especially if we want to do it before the Carthaginians can reinforce themselves."

"Then why haven't we done it? I thought our sources said we now outnumber the Carthaginians, at least the ones on Britannia."

"We do, but not by enough. I've gone over the numbers with Sophus and with my commanders, and they have enough manpower to make any breach we attempt extremely costly. We've managed to maintain the core of our forces in defeating two much larger armies, I'd hate to give up that experience now, when we have just the last city to take."

"So we starve them out? I didn't think we had time for that."

"We don't. We might have to go over the wall and accept the casualties, but I gave Velius and the other Legates five days to come up with an alternative plan that didn't wipe us out. They still have four days left. How are your Caledonians faring?"

While Ky took the bulk of the Britannic forces, including all of the Roman legions, directly to envelop Londinium to bottle up the remaining Carthaginian forces, he'd released both the cavalry and the independent Caledonian forces to secure the rest of the countryside. Ramirus's spies and the scouts they'd sent out had already told them that the Carthaginians had stripped the rest of the territory of soldiers as soon as word had reached them of their army's defeat.

Ky had hoped to both envelop the Carthaginians and catch those smaller units in the field so they could be defeated piecemeal, but as often happened, the victory left their forces almost as disorganized as the Carthaginians. It had taken almost a week to get his army moving south in enough force to make sure the Carthaginians didn't attempt the piecemeal destruction of his detached forces that he wanted to do to them. That had given the Carthaginians enough time to pull their men back.

Worse, it had also given them enough time to strip most of the countryside of food, or at least the food they hadn't already taken to supply the massive army the Britannic allies had just defeated.

That meant his planned sweep of the southern half of the island for Carthaginians had instead turned into an aide mission of sorts. There had also been the issue of sending the north men to help out the Romans who'd been living under Carthaginian rule for almost a hundred years. To them, it must have looked like a barbarian horde sweeping through on the heels of the fleeing Carthaginians.

Initially, Ky had been concerned by this, and it was only the need to keep the more disciplined Roman legions, who operated better in a siege environment, around Londinium, that had him sending out the Caledonians instead of the Romans to clear the countryside of hostiles. In hindsight, however, this might turn out to be one of the better decisions he'd made.

Ky had been very direct with Drest, the Caledonians' current commander, about the need to treat the locals well. It's also what had prompted him to send Lucilla with them. He'd hoped the presence of the Roman Emperor's daughter would make it clear this wasn't just an invasion of another foreign people. Thankfully, the Caledonians had handled themselves well and there had been only a handful of incidents, all swiftly taken care of by the Caledonians themselves.

As they realized these weren't new invaders but an unusual form of countrymen under the new Empire, the southern Romans had quickly begun warming to the Caledonians, helped in large part by the food the legions had liberated from the Carthaginian army and begun redistributing to the people it had been taken from.

In the long run, Ky thought this might be a good step in helping these Romans assimilate better into the new Britannic Empire, forgoing some of the problem spots they'd had with the Romans living in the middle of the island.

"Good," Lucilla said. "We've cleared almost all the way to the Western Coast. Word has started to spread ahead of us now, and we've even had a few villages come out to greet us with cheers, instead of hiding in their homes hoping we leave them alone."

"Good. Lartius and his cavalry have swept up and down the East Coast, so I think we've got the Carthaginians all bottled up in Londinium, which will make the next steps easier."

"The next step being ...?"

"First, we need to get as much planting happening as possible. We can't get any of the new farm equipment out here this season, since most of that is being used around Devnum or sent up to the Caledonians, but once we push the Carthaginians off the island entirely, we're going to have to put together a large enough army to take the fight to them. And we will need to feed that army."

"Why?"

"Why take the fight to them?"

"Yes. We have Britannia now. Why not just stay here and let them do what they want everywhere else?"

"Because they won't leave it at that. The army we beat was massive, and yet for the Carthaginians it was on the small side, and they have dozens more just like it. If they really put their willpower behind it, they can retake what we've managed to free. We were lucky they have been distracted consolidating their gains in Germania, which kept them from putting the full weight of their military against us."

"And your solution to their massive armies is to attack them?"

"*It is a widely accepted tactic that goes back to the earliest days of warfare. Attacking a stronger enemy where they are weak, continually keeping them off-balanced and unable to build the force to attack you directly is not a new idea. It is, in fact, a very old one,*" Sophus said.

"The only way our Empire survives is by ending the threat of theirs," Ky added. "Hiding on Britannia and hoping they go away will just play into their hands."

"Alright," Lucilla said. "So we need to get the locals planting."

"Spread the word that the Empire will be buying up any excess grain or foodstuffs they produce this year. They won't have to give up half their harvest in taxes like they did to the Carthaginians. Also, get the word out that anyone who wants to join the legions will be trained and given a good wage. We need to begin to replenish the losses we've suffered so far, and those we will lose retaking Londinium."

"I will."

"After that, tell Drest we are releasing any Caledonians that want to go home and plant. Those that want can stay and will have chances for glory in combat, but we need the Caledonians to begin planting just as much as we need the Romans planting," Ky said.

Talogren, the high chieftain of the Caledonians, had made it clear that the large number of warriors he had sent to help the Romans retake the island were on temporary loan and that, come planting season, he would need many of them back. Ky hated to lose what could be a third of his army, but he didn't disagree with Talogren's priorities.

"That will leave us much weaker," Lucilla pointed out.

"I know, but we need to be able to feed our armies, and soon we will have a lot more factory work that will need a workforce if we're to convert the legions into something that can challenge armies ten-fold their size."

"I will let them know," Lucilla said.

"Once that's done, leave the pacification of the region to the Praetorians. Send those Caledonians that wish to stay under arms to me, and then I need you to return to Devnum."

"You're sending me home?" Lucilla asked, sounding annoyed and a little angry.

"Yes, because that's where I'm going to need you. I will be sending three legions and most of the cavalry with you. We should hopefully be hearing from Llassar soon. We know the Carthaginians are on Hibernia, which hopefully means the people he is contacting will need help. We will offer our military assistance in exchange for a treaty with the Hibernians. My ultimate goal is to bring them into the Empire, which will give us control of both islands, give us both more supplies and more men to join the legions, and a strong homeland from which we can launch our assault on the Carthaginians. I am sending Velius with the released legions, and he will take them across if we get the word from Llassar. Until we get a faster form of communication between Londinium and Devnum, I need you there to help coordinate our forces. I've also already sent for Hortensius to come south so I can give him new designs and instructions. This next project will be very difficult and require much more vigilant work if we are to produce the weapons we're going to need to help secure the island. I need you with him so he can get quick answers to any questions he might have. I have a plan to shorten the time it takes to communicate without needing the two of us, but that will take time. Until I can get that set up, I need you there."

"Fine. Just tell me we aren't going to be separated for so long this time. I just got you back. I couldn't stand to spend months apart again."

"I will make it as fast as possible," Ky said.

Ériunia

Things had changed since Llassar had last been on the island. When he'd left, it had been poor and sparsely populated, much like his homeland, but there had been signs of new villages, along his trek from the Ulaid capital of Emain Macha to the coast when he'd finally been sent home from his captivity with the Ulaid.

Now, almost the reverse was true. Llassar had been cautious at first, trying to give any villages he came across a wide berth, until it became clear they were all burned-out ghost towns. All of the buildings not made of stone were cold ash and scraps of hide. The more permanent structures, mostly buildings used for grain storage, had entire sides knocked in, rubble filling the insides. Any traces of food or livestock was gone, as were all of the people.

He hadn't found any bodies, and what few skeletons he could find were already partially covered in plants and soil. Whatever happened to these villages hadn't been recent. Enough time had passed for scavengers and nature to hide what was left of the remains.

Lucilla had said there was word that the Carthaginians had made landings here, but he'd been under the impression they'd landed at the southern end of the island, far from where he'd landed. If they had gotten this far north, then there wasn't much of a chance the Ulaid would still be strong enough to join the new Britannic Empire Lucilla and Ky had created. That became a larger worry as he continued to find these villages as he got closer to Emain Macha.

He had just entered another village, after circling it once to make sure it was empty, and found it much in the same state as the others. This one, however, was much fresher. The wood was still cold, but he found first one, then five, then a dozen bodies scattered around. They had already past the bloated stage and animals had begun taking their tribute off them, but he could still make out clothing and even some wounds.

They were all peasants. No armor, not even the padded woolen armor worn more frequently by the Ulaid's conscript warriors, was to be seen. It was all simple tunics and breeches. The clothing of farmers and herders.

He stopped over one corpse that had been partially covered by a collapsed mud-brick wall, the debris keeping the animals from tearing at the wound sites like they did the others. Having noticed something on the other corpses, Llassar cleared off the bricks to see the body better, hoping to put something curious to rest.

He'd noticed the other bodies looked to have wider Ériu-style sword or ax wounds, not the spear or thinner sword wounds he'd expect if Carthaginians had been involved. Llassar was familiar with the weapons of the Ériu, partially from his earlier stay among them, but also because their weapons weren't far removed from the Caledonian-style weapons. At least those weapons the Caledonians had used before their alliance with the Romans.

One of the first things Talogren had done when the new Empire had been formed was to begin equipping his men with weapons made from the new steel the Romans were now producing. Roman weapons had always been of higher quality metal, but their new weapons were made from an even more superior material than before. A gift from Ky, Llassar had been told.

He was just finishing his inspection when a crunching sound behind him caused Llassar to stand and whirl around, his hand going to his blade, only to stop as he saw how vastly outnumbered he was.

Six Ulaid warriors in their thick-woolen, padded, knee-length coats stood before him, sword in hand, along with the small wooden shields the Ulaid liked to carry.

"Come to desecrate your kill," the leader, identifiable as the only man wearing a tough leather chest piece instead of the padded wool.

"I didn't kill these people," Llassar said in the Ériu language.

"A foreigner, on Ulaid land, kneeling over the body of one of our countrymen, and you'd like us to believe you didn't have anything to do with this?"

Llassar had never fully mastered the Ériu language. Its more guttural sounds, made at the back of the throat, had always been difficult for him to make.

"Look at these bodies. They have been dead for at least a week. Why would I circle back here, on my own, to look at people I killed a week ago?"

"You're a foreigner. Little of what you people do follows reason. Even if you did not kill these people, you are where you shouldn't be. Better to leave your corpse as a warning to others to stay away from where they are not wanted."

"I am here to see your king, Eochaid Sálbuide. He knows me. I have come to offer him help."

"He has been dead for five years," the man said, continuing to take steps towards Llassar.

"I haven't been here for some time. I spent two years at court, serving the king and his son Fergus. He will remember me as well."

"Fergus is not king either."

"Who is?"

"Conchobar."

Llassar remembered Conchobar. He was the son of a lesser noble and friends with Fergus. The two were younger than Llassar by several years, but already men. He remembered Conchobar as being clever, constantly outfoxing the hulking Fergus, who preferred raw power over everything else. It was surprising to hear he, not Fergus, was king, but that might prove useful. Llassar had gotten along with Conchobar much better than he had with Fergus, who he found to be a braggart.

"I know your new king as well. He will know me and will want to hear what I have to say."

"Sure he would," the man said, raising his sword.

Llassar considered for a moment pulling his own weapon, but it would have been pointless. He was a good fighter, but he could tell by the way they moved that these were seasoned warriors. Had there been just two or three, he would have stood a chance, but with this many, there was little chance he would survive.

Even if he did, killing the king's warriors was a bad way to start the conversation.

"Wait," Llassar said, holding up a hand. "Take me to Emain Macha under guard. Think about this. If the king does want to hear me out, how would he react to learning you killed me. If he doesn't, you can kill me there just as easily as you could here. If you're wrong, you could lose your position or even your life for angering the king. If you're right, you only lose a little time."

The man paused. Even to some born to the Caledonii, the Ulaid's method of justice had been harsh. Death tended to be the sentence for most infractions against the king, which always seemed to be a poor way to retain skilled men who made honest mistakes, but now it worked to Llassar's advantage.

The man stopped, considering. Unless a lot had changed in the last fifteen years, Llassar's description of what would happen in either case had been more or less accurate. The kings of the Ulaid preferred its minions to ask permission, even if that meant delaying an otherwise preferable set of choices. Those men who did take the initiative often found their necks stretched against the block when it was wrong.

"I guess we can kill you later," the man said, gesturing at Llassar with his sword. "Bind him."

Chapter 2

Londinium

"... Then what good are you?" Maharbaal yelled, inches from Caesius's face.

"You wanted to know what my father and his lackey were up to, and I got you that information. I even told you about their new weapons, not that you did anything with that information. I told you exactly how many men they had under arms and when they left Devnum to meet your forces. My spies told you everything you wanted. It was up to you to put an end to their forces and put me on my rightful throne. It was also you who screwed that up, losing an army five times the size of the Roman forces in an afternoon."

"I will have you gutted," Maharbaal fumed, spittle flying from his lips.

"How long do you think you'd last after I'm dead? I know you like to think you're some all-powerful ruler here on your island, but we both know who you answer to and we both know how little patience your Emperor has for men who can't do their duties. Now that you've all but given this island to this new empire of my father, I'm even more important to your Emperor than you are. I still have sources inside their territory able to pass along intelligence and maybe even designs or samples of these new weapons. All you have is a few thousand men, cowering behind your walls, slowly starving to death."

"No one's starving. Food shipments from Hibernia and Iberia continue."

"And yet your men still hide."

Maharbaal's fists tightened and, for a moment, Caesius thought he might have goaded the fool into actually doing it. The moment passed and Maharbaal's fists unclenched. For as arrogant and out of touch as the governor was, he wasn't completely brain dead. He'd survived the cutthroat world of the Carthaginian court and managed to get appointed as a governor of one of the empire's administrative districts. On the fringes of the empire, but their centuries-long battle against his own people made it a not insignificant one.

Caesius knew that Maharbaal knew he was right about how the Emperor would react to his having Caesius killed. They preferred to place someone controllable but native over every population they pacified and having the next man to wear the purple was as big of an agent as they could hope for. They would know Caesius being placed over his people would help keep the region under control, allowing them to redirect resources and manpower to other parts of their domain.

Plus, Maharbaal also had bigger things to worry about than one exiled prince. The city was dangerously low on soldiers and arms, and the shipments from Hibernia were not enough to offset the shortage. Caesius had read part of a message to Maharbaal when the fool hadn't been paying attention, and knew that a relief mission was being assembled in Africa, but that it would take some months to get enough manpower to retake the lost land.

Maharbaal was already in a precarious position. He'd done well to blame the loss on his general and appeared to have gotten the Emperor to believe him, but it was unlikely the governor could deflect another failure. And the Carthaginians had a well-known solution for dealing with failures that Maharbaal certainly didn't want to face.

"You," Maharbaal said, turning away from Caesius to one of his nearby aides. "Put guards on the storehouses and keep all of the food shipments that come in under guard. Confiscate all of the food you can from vendors and sell no food to vendors any longer. Begin distributing rations to people directly from the warehouses. Limit civilians to one-quarter of the standard soldier's ration. The soldiers themselves can maintain the standard rations. Go."

"It will take months for the supply convoy to arrive. You're not going to have enough food to keep soldiers at full rations while still feeding the populace," Caesius pointed out.

"I realize that. We still have work projects reinforcing the wall and repairing damage from the Roman's weapons and if we cut them off they won't have the strength to do the work that's needed. Once we make a list of essential workers, we'll cut off everyone not on that list, and keep them at minimal rations to survive."

"If they do anything to cut your shipments, by even a little bit, or your people slow down for whatever reason, you're still going to have to cut rations to your soldiers. When my sister and her fool come, and they are going to come, your men are going to be too weak to repel them."

Maharbaal's frown deepened. Caesius knew he hated him, but he was also in desperate need of good advice, and he had to know Caesius was right.

"Stop," Maharbaal yelled out after the retreating form of the aide. When the man returned to them, he said, "No rations to the civilians, unless they can show they are working on or they have been assigned to one of the work projects."

The aide hesitated for a moment, and then dashed off again.

"Now do your part. You have people out there. Raid the Britannians. Kill their commanders. Do something to show your worth or you can be added to the names of people not being fed," Maharbaal said, before turning and storming off.

Caesius watched him leave, contemplating. He was in a precarious position. He'd lost most of his informants, who'd been caught by Ramirus and his damn security forces. If he set those he had left on direct missions to counter his father's soldiers, he would lose most of them, and his remaining usefulness to the Carthaginians. He liked to think they'd keep him around to put into power when they retook the island, but he also knew they only wanted people completely loyal to them. Something no one would believe of him, no matter what he said.

He needed to be seen as helping the situation here, but he also still needed leverage. This city was going to fall, of that he was certain. He needed to be seen doing just enough to deflect claims that he'd stood aside during the defense of the city.

He also needed to start working on a plan to get out before the city actually fell.

Britannic Camp, Outside Londinium

" … and four-thousand, three hundred and twelve critically wounded, which includes everyone from non-mobile prisoners to those who will most certainly die in the next several weeks," Ursinus concluded.

After their defeat of the Carthaginian army Ky had pushed his commanders hard to cut off isolated detachments or fleeing survivors, keen to keep as many soldiers as possible from reaching Londinium and adding to their current manpower. They'd left a legion to guard the huge number of prisoners, but other than instructing Ursinus to treat the prisoners humanely, he hadn't given much thought to their disposition.

Now that the cleanup of southern Britain was complete and they'd pushed the Carthaginians behind the walls of the city, it was time to deal with the mess they'd left in their wake. Lucilla had begun getting aid and supplies to the Roman population abused for so long by the Carthaginians well in hand, but that left the huge numbers of prisoners they'd taken after the battle.

While the death toll had been catastrophic, Ky had managed to stop the battle as larger and larger groups began surrendering, keeping it from turning into an all-out slaughter. That had left him the problem of what to do with the nearly twenty-five thousand prisoners currently under guard, only a little shy of the entire force Ky had taken into the battle. Feeding his army had been a problem. Feeding them and the nearly thirty-thousand prisoners, counting the ones still being held from their previous battle, was going to be nearly impossible.

They had nearly doubled their territory with the capture of the land previously controlled by the Carthaginians, but planting season hadn't started yet and the Carthaginians had already stripped the land bare to feed their army. It would be months before they started producing enough food in these new regions to help offset the deficiency.

"You know my feelings on this," Ky said, looking at Ramirus and the four senators standing at one edge of the large table holding maps of the newly conquered region.

"We aren't recommending labor gangs," Ramirus said, reiterating the statement he'd made at the beginning of the meeting before asking Ursinus to list the current prisoner counts. "We understand that is forbidden under the anti-slavery laws that our new Imperial senate adopted, and we understand that you are against using prisoners in that way. We however wanted to make the scope of our problem clear before we started addressing our suggestions."

"Fine. I understand the scope of the problem and I will try to restrain myself until I hear all of your recommendations."

"The number of prisoners and our current food supplies aren't the only problems we face. Over the last hundred years, the Carthaginians have conscripted or eliminated many of the villagers who lived and worked in the re-conquered lands. The Carthaginians who later moved in and took over the land all fled with their soldiers behind the walls. While we now have all this land to grow food for our people, much of it is empty with no one to plant the food when the snows melt."

"Since Senator Opilio is here, I suspect you have recommendations on what to do about that," Ky said.

Opilio was the leader of what Ky had thought of as the farming block of senators. Theywere a handful of senators who represented mostly the farming interests, although that usually meant the large landowners, not the small yeoman farmers that provided nearly half of the food produced in the empire.

"I do have a suggestion, actually. Since much of that land was taken from our people who fled north when the Carthaginians pushed us back into the middle of the country, I think we should first allow their descendants to claim their re-conquered land. The remaining land we can auction off, allowing new opportunities to citizens willing to pay for it and revenue for the Imperial treasury, which has been sorely taxed of late by all of the new projects being introduced."

"For people reclaiming land, what if the people currently on that land didn't run? What if the descendants of former Romans, who didn't or couldn't escape north when the Carthaginians invaded, stayed? What if they were moved to new lands to work by the Carthaginians? A hundred years is a long time, and there will have been migrations. Children of those families might have moved to abandoned land and claimed it. We can't start alienating people we are bringing back into the empire right after freeing them."

"I've discussed this with the Emperor before coming down here, and he had similar concerns. This 'reclaiming' would only apply to currently unoccupied land. He made the point that we should make the same policy for land currently occupied by Carthaginians who chose to not flee to Londinium as we reclaimed the land."

"I agree with him. We can't very well call ourselves liberators if we are doing the same thing the Carthaginians did when they invaded. By my math, however, that will still not solve our problem. Without the slave labor that the Carthaginians used, we would either have to sell the land in very small parcels, or find the manpower to work that land."

Ky began to object again, before Ramirus raised his hand and said, "Consul, we are not suggesting we conscript the prisoners to do the work. Or at least, we are not suggesting we conscript them to do the work against their will."

"That sounds like a very fine line you are preparing to walk."

"We can't have men just languishing in prison camps every day. Idle men get into mischief. Especially soldiers," Velius said. "Better to keep them occupied."

"But only the ones that volunteer," Ramirus said. "This won't be slave labor. We'll offer more and better rations, which will matter, as we're going to have to start putting them on shorter rations now, if we don't want to have a major food crisis before the harvest. I know you said we needed to treat them humanely, and we are, but it's either ration them, or our own soldiers. There are just too many mouths to feed and insufficient food to do it with. We can also offer other amenities, like cots, beds, things like that."

"We aren't giving them those things now?" Ky asked

"We don't have enough," Ramirus replied. "We were barely able to cover our first batch of prisoners, and this group exceeds the size of that group several times over. We could give maybe ten percent of the camp those items, but that would create issues for every prisoner, while giving comfort to very few. We've also discussed the possibility of early release back to the mainland for those who put in a set amount of work. It means we'll have to fight many of them again, but I doubt we'll ever reach the bottom of that pool. That's only if the goods and food aren't enough to get men to volunteer."

"How will you control that many men?"

"We're working on that as well. Patrols of Praetorians, cycling men through farms in batches so we can watch them closer, requiring the families to hire guards or the like to keep them under control. We haven't figured out the details, but we will."

"Fine, see to it then, but make sure they understand they aren't required to do this. Volunteers only."

"There's something else," Velius said. "The Carthaginian general survived the battle. We found him this morning when surveying the prisoners. He was so badly injured none of his men could identify him. He only regained consciousness today."

"I see," Ky said.

"I had him moved out of the prison camp and to the command area of my legion encampment, for now. Under guard, of course. I thought you might want to talk to him, and I don't relish the idea of you walking into the prison camp, no matter how many guards you take."

"I would have been fine, but that was good thinking all the same. I think I will talk to him. You all carry on. You know what I expect and it sounds like you're doing your best to stay within those lines. Keep me apprised of what you decide."

"Yes, Consul," Ursinus said, slapping fist to chest in salute.

As the senior legate, the meeting had taken place in Velius's camp making Ky's journey to the place where the Carthaginian commander had been moved short. Besides the specialty tents like the one used as a mess hall or a medical tent, there were really only two-sized tents currently used in the legions, small two-man tents used by the average soldier and a much larger tent used by Tribunes and Legates, who needed the room to hold meetings with their subordinates. The Carthaginian commander had been moved into one of these larger tents, which probably meant a Tribune was somewhere unhappily sleeping in a two-man tent.

It was easy to tell which tent the general was in, considering the dozen men spread around the outside guarding it. Considering he had been unconscious since the day before and had been discovered with other severely injured Carthaginians, Ky assumed the guards were more to keep angry Britannians from getting revenge rather than fears that the general himself would escape.

Ky could feel the displeasure from Silo, the man currently leading his protective detail, when he ordered them to wait outside. While it was unlikely in the extreme that this injured man had somehow smuggled a weapon in with him, keeping it hidden on the off chance he was visited by the Britannian's leader, he understood their concern. The general wasn't asleep, but neither did he stir when Ky entered, continuing to stare at the ceiling of the tent, motionless.

"Hello, General," Ky said, stopping just inside the doorway.

"I will not answer any of your questions," the man said, continuing to look at the top of the tent, his expression focused and determined.

Sometimes, when dealing with his own people or watching his orders happen from afar, it was easy to forget how brutal and merciless this time period could be. While his own people, the ones back in the time he'd come from, could be equally heartless, the standards for how that manifested were much different.

Their people had known for centuries how ineffective physical torture was for obtaining information. While it would usually get a man to talk, the information supplied would often be at best worthless and at worst completely false or misleading. People under torture would say anything to get the pain to stop, often choosing to say what the torturer wanted to hear instead of the truth. Interrogators usually came in with their own notions of what the truth was and found it difficult to distinguish between what was true, but counter to their beliefs, and what matched their own pre-conceived notions but wasn't true. With torture, they would make the pain continue until they heard what they felt was right, regardless of its truth.

His people had abandoned physical persuasion for mind probes and psychology, both of which tended to give more accurate information. Of course, mind probes and psychological theory were both thousands of years away from the people of this time.

He knew his men hadn't questioned the general yet, so the man's response was probably more in anticipation of the expected torture, rather than fear that it would continue.

"I am not here to ask you questions, General. Or, I guess I am, but not in the way you think. I mostly wanted to see you and ensure you had everything you needed."

"Before you send in your torture masters!" the general said, a statement of anger more than a question.

"We have no torture masters," Ky said, pulling a chair, that had been placed at one side of the tent, next to the cot the general was lying on. "Do I hope to glean some information from you that might help us? Sure. But that is a side benefit. We know that you were brought here specifically to lead the army sent to destroy us, an army which no longer exists, its soldiers dead or in our camps, with your remaining countrymen on the island locked behind the walls of Londinium. I'm not sure what you could tell us about the situation behind those walls that we don't already know."

"You're the Roman commander?"

"We're Britannians now," Ky pointed out.

"I'd heard that. I commend you on your victory. I'd already heard of what happened to Zaracas when you faced him outside Devnum, but I wrote his loss off as incompetence. Now it seems I am either equally incompetent or I owe his memory an apology."

"Zaracas wasn't incompetent. A little foolhardy, having his men charge recklessly forward without holding back a reserve, but like you, he couldn't have known of the advantages we had over you."

"I don't suppose you'd tell me what those advantages are?"

"Sorry. No."

"Still, you suckered us in beautifully. I knew you were up to something when your men retreated, but I didn't recognize the full extent of the trap until you sprang it on us. I only wished I could have done something to save my men from your slaughter."

"There wasn't a slaughter. Once your commanders realized how badly the situation was going, they began surrendering. We put the surrendered men under guard, and they are currently in a prison camp while we determine what to do with them."

"So they aren't slaughtered yet."

"We are not Carthaginians," Ky said pointedly. "We do not kill our prisoners, mistreat them, or sell the camp followers into slavery. The non-soldiers we rounded up have been released to join your remaining countrymen behind the walls of Londinium. Those that chose not to have the option of being, eventually, returned to the mainland or becoming Britannian citizens, once they have completed enough service to the Empire to prove their fidelity."

"Clever," the general said. "Under the guise of mercy, you put more mouths for the Governor to feed, starving his soldiers sooner rather than later. What about my soldiers?"

"The soldiers, unfortunately, cannot be released while we are still at war with your people. To do so would simply mean facing the same people in battle again. You might have an unlimited supply of manpower, but you don't have an unlimited supply of seasoned commanders and men who know what to expect when fighting us. Better we keep those men under guard and unavailable to you. Don't worry. We won't be selling any of them into slavery or starving them to death. My commanders have strict orders to ensure the prisoners' safety until the fighting has ended and we can return them."

Bomilcar finally looked at Ky, "Then your people are unlike any I've ever faced."

"I don't know if that's true. We've talked to the people living in the areas your army passed through and some of your men have answered minor questions put to them, not under duress, I assure you. From the reports I've seen, I understand you had standing orders to limit looting and gave harsh punishments to any men who abused citizens or camp followers. That is very different from the other Carthaginian commanders I've faced. The first thing you asked about was your men's safety, another uncommon attitude from other Carthaginian commanders we've dealt with. I think you might be more like us than you are like the people you were fighting for."

"Your people haven't always been like this. From our reports, your lot was just as brutal. Maybe that's why your alliance with the northern barbarians came as such a surprise to us, considering how brutally you treated them before."

"True, but that's why it's important to be willing to change. If more of your people were like you, would we even be in this war?"

"It doesn't matter. We are at war. You are trying to kill my people and I am trying to kill yours. I won't help you in your pursuit, no matter how much you flatter my honor."

"Of course," Ky said, starting to turn for the door before stopping and looking back. "If you need anything, just call for the guards. They'll do their best to get you anything you need."

"Thank you," Bomilcar said, returning his gaze to the ceiling.

Chapter 3

Ky made his way from meeting the Carthaginian general to Velius's command tent. During the day, he had been out among the lines, making sure his men were on guard for any Carthaginian counterattack to break the siege and ensuring they had all of the supplies they needed. Ky guessed that, after their meeting about the Carthaginian prisoners, the legate was still in his command tent, reviewing the next day's orders with his subordinates.

On top of having a good mind for strategy and impressive personal bravery, one of the things Ky found most useful in him as a subordinate was his strong organizational and command skills. If merit had led the Roman legions prior to Ky's arrival, he would have been in command of all of Rome's forces instead of fools like Globulus and Eborius, both of whom fell beneath their impressive incompetence.

Aside from Lucilla, he might be the person Ky trusted the most to run things when he wasn't around, all of which was what led him to the legate's tent.

"Consul," Velius said, turning away from the map he'd been looking over.

"Our guest is very impressive."

"Really? I found him tedious. All he would say, over and over, was that he would not betray his empire. He assumes any privileges we give him are some sort of ploy to soften him up to speak to us."

"Is he wrong?"

"Yes. Well, no, it would be a helpful side effect, but we would do it either way."

"True, but he doesn't know that. The Carthaginians usually just massacre all enemy survivors, so it's doubtful he's had many opportunities to consider this from the other side."

"True. Still, I don't think we'll get much out of him."

"Maybe, maybe not, but we have to keep trying. Everything in Ramirus's reports says that he was one of the Carthaginian's premier commanders until fairly recently. Being shipped out to a backwater corner of their empire is a pretty big message of disapproval, and one-time insiders being pushed to the outside don't stay loyal for long."

"I don't know. Considering the size of the force and how big of an annoyance we must have become, this isn't as much of a step down as it once would have been. And he seemed pretty adamant about remaining loyal."

"True, but we have to keep trying. I think the Carthaginians will help us out, though."

"How so?"

"They have a bad tendency to blame the commander for failures and take outsized retribution for those failures, regardless if the commander is to blame for a loss. It's why they have so many leaders better at covering their own asses than actually leading armies, and probably what caused him to start losing favor in the first place. There's a chance they'll take some kind of drastic action, making him an example for other commanders. Even though they've made so many examples over the years, I'm not sure what they'd hope to accomplish doing it again. But it seems to be their way."

"And if they don't."

"Then we try something else. Isolation can break a man down, faster if it's seen as preferred treatment instead of a punishment. He'll get all of the negatives that come with isolation without being able to use stubbornness and resentment as a shield against it. We'll have Ramirus's more ... diplomatic interrogators continue working on the general. One way or another, we need to find out what he knows. Ramirus has decent sources on the continent, but most of what we get from Africa is second-hand at best. He has real information about the state of the rest of their empire, which will be important once we get past securing Britannia and start looking to the next step. Right now, we're blind to pretty much everything happening outside of Hispania or the Germanic coast."

"I'll make sure he's kept apart from the rest of his men."

"Actually, I'm going to be moving my flag to Ursinus's legion and I want you to send him over there. Sit down with Ursinus and make sure he knows how to deal with the general before you leave."

"I'm leaving?"

"Lucilla is headed back to Devnum tomorrow. I'm sending your legion, the fourth and the ninth legions with her, along with any Caledonians who don't return home. You're to hold outside Devnum until we hear from Llassar. His big play with the Hibernians is military assistance against the Carthaginians and any of the southern rivals they've managed to turn into client states. If he's successful, you'll need to be ready to get your men across the strait to make good on that offer. Llassar knows the people there, so I suggest you take his counsel seriously, but you'll be in charge of our forces. I need you two to work together to get the people there to at least sign an alliance with us and, if possible, get them to join the new Empire under the same terms as the Caledonians. Llassar knows what to do on that front, so work with him and get it done."

As he spoke, Ky could see Velius's expression change from one of displeasure, when he thought he was being removed from the final stages of the fight against the Carthaginians on this island, to excitement at the idea of running his own military action. It was a big step up for him as a commander, since under the previous senior legates, he'd gotten very little taste of independent command.

"I'll see to it at once."

"I know you will. When you get to Devnum, start working on securing the boats and logistics to get your men across as soon as they're called for. I have faith in you, Velius. Don't let me down."

Emain Macha

The throne room was just as Llassar remembered it, only smaller. It was still a large single room, its wooden timbers bent into a circular shape, making it unique among the places he'd been to. When he'd come as a younger man, Llassar remembered being astounded by the size of this one room, its curved walls seeming to stretch forever.

Of course, that was when he only knew of life among his people, whose largest huts could hold thirty men at best. Now he'd fought beside Romans, stood in their great forum which held two hundred men, well spread out among the benches carved out of marble.

He'd been impressed with the permanence of the building, its wooden walls and thick beams seeming like they'd last forever compared to the dried mud and leather of the buildings in Caledonia. The Romans had changed his perception on that front as well. Where his people built out of mud and these people built out of wood, the Romans built out of stone. He'd like to think his interactions with the southerners hadn't colored his perceptions of the world, but clearly, they had.

Now, this mighty capital with its architectural wonder seemed quaint, almost provincial. It was strange that it took crossing the straits to the land of the Ériu for him to realize his perceptions had changed.

That wasn't the only change he was expecting. When he'd been here last, Eochaid Sálbuide sat on the throne. A powerful man, his thick black beard making his dark eyes seem almost black, hooded under unruly eyebrows. He was a warrior king, much like Llassar's own liege, Talogren. Llassar had watched the king of the Ulaid fight with a giant axe, cleaving men in two as he led his warriors into battle.

Surprisingly, he was also a wise king. He ruled with an even hand, often choosing diplomacy and even guile over combat when it offered a better outcome. Llassar had been impressed enough by him that he even described his ruling style to Talogren, in hopes that his chieftain might temper his much more aggressive approach with some of the Ulaid king's methods. It hadn't taken, of course. Talogren was who he was, and Llassar couldn't fault the man for that. It was what drew him to Ky, who seemed to possess some of Sálbuide's qualities, although in a very alien way, different from the Ulaid, Caledonians, or Romans.

He'd been sad to hear of Sálbuide's passing. He hadn't been much older than Llassar was now, when he'd known him fifteen years before, and should have had many years left to lead his people. More surprising was the man who now sat on the throne, looking down on him.

Conchobar was as unique as Sálbuide, in his own way. He was not as huge as Sálbuide or his son Fergus, although not a slender man either. He was Llassar's age and the two had spent time together during Llassar's time here. The thing that stood out in his memory about Conchobar the most was how clever he was. In that, he was more like the old king than Fergus ever was, who was aggressive to the point of recklessness.

In some ways, Conchobar's ascendancy might help Llassar convince him to join the new alliance, although any plans he'd had of out-reasoning the Ulaid king were immediately gone. Conchobar was a smarter man than Llassar. There was no way he'd be able to outwit the new king, that was certain.

"I am surprised to see you, Llassar. I had thought when we released you back to your people, you had learned to keep to your own land and off of ours. Did you get lost again?"

"I didn't get lost. I came to speak with King Sálbuide. We've heard about your troubles with new invaders to the south and I was sent to offer him aide."

"King Sálbuide has joined his forbearers."

"I know, and I am sorry to hear about his passing. While I am surprised to see you on the throne instead of Fergus, my mission has not changed. I still bring an offer of help against your enemies."

"Fergus is a traitor. He sold his people out to Eochu Feidlech and his new benefactors. They slaughtered his father and our largest army, taking half of our lands with them."

"I am ... surprised," Llassar said.

That was an understatement. Fergus had been the jewel of his father's eye, and knew it. He'd always been loyal to his father, if a bit spoiled by the man's affections. Llassar could hardly fathom the idea of Fergus turning on the king.

"A lot has changed since you were last here. Old alliances have been broken and sons have betrayed their fathers, all drawn by promises of power and gold by these new people in the south. Which is why I find the timing of your arrival so concerning. We are beset on all sides, but have managed to hold off our rivals so far, and now you appear, a ghost from the past on the heels of their last failed assault, promising to help us out of the goodness of your heart. How do I know you aren't in league with Fergus and his new allies, sent to distract us or have us drop our guard?"

Things were worse here than Llassar had realized. He'd spent time with the Carthaginians sent to incite his own people against the Romans and heard their promises for himself. Things were different for the Caledonians, whose hold on their lands had always been precarious in the face of Romans who were better-armed and had larger armies. He'd understood why Talogren had allowed himself to be swayed by them, but he couldn't fathom why Fergus would have done the same. The Ulaid was the strongest kingdom on the whole island and he was set to inherit everything from his father. It made no sense that he'd throw that away to join the scattered smaller kingdoms and their foreign allies.

"We've dealt with these foreigners. They're called the Carthaginians, and they made us many of the same promises they made your people. Instead of taking them up on their offer, we joined with the Romans and pushed the Carthaginians back, almost completely off our island, in fact. It is because of them that I'm here at all. While I hold your people in high regard, I am not here out of love for them or the goodness of my heart. We are in a war for survival against the Carthaginians with our new Roman allies. To succeed in that war, we can't allow them to conquer this island and build up strength on either side of us. I am here because our interests align. Helping you is helping ourselves."

"You made an alliance with the Romans?" Conchobar asked, sounding genuinely surprised.

Llassar understood his surprise. Although the Romans and the Ulaid didn't interact very much, and then only through minimal trading, they knew about the long-standing animosity between the Romans and his people.

"From the outside, I'm sure it does seem unthinkable, but you've been experiencing a similar assault on your territory that the Romans have. They were desperate for assistance and looking for a way to fight back against the Carthaginians."

"I can understand why they'd want your help, but I can't understand how your people would willingly join them in some kind of alliance. You weren't being invaded, and had them as a buffer between you and these Carthaginians."

"They offered us concessions we couldn't turn down. Instead of constantly wondering if this is the year they push north with their greater strength and wipe us out, taking our land, we had the chance to join them as complete equals. We have as much of a say in the new Empire's course as the Romans do."

"And you thought we'd be as desperate as the Romans, willing to make concessions we might never have been willing to make before? You hope to make your new Empire overlords of my people, perhaps?"

"No. While I have been charged to offer you a chance to join our Empire, it would be as an equal member, not a subject. You would have an equal say in crafting the laws that govern the Empire as a whole and you'd maintain control of your land, as long as your laws fall within the bounds of the laws of the Empire. In return, we offer assistance in your battle to the south, in both men and material, right now, and more once the military situation is settled on our island. As a member of our alliance, you'll have access to new markets, a wider manpower pool, jobs for your people, and to new inventions that will change how your people live."

"Lies," Conchobar said. "You offer nothing more than the Carthaginians. At least they were honest with their demands that we subjugate ourselves to them. You come with your hand out, offering freedom, while holding a knife to our throats. Throw him in the dungeon."

"You're making a mistake, Conchobar. The Carthaginians will roll over your people and salt the ground you stand on."

"I would rather have my people die standing than live kneeling. Take him."

Chapter 4

Outside Londinium

Ky looked over Ursinus's reports. He'd liked the legate back when he'd been an optio, tasked with keeping Lucilla alive, but he missed Velius's ability to combine thoroughness with succinctness. In Ursinus's defense, he hadn't needed to oversee reports detailing the condition and disposition of several thousands of men when he'd been an optio. Scattered as the reports were, it was clear they had the Carthaginians well hemmed into the city.

With the departure two days before of Velius and three legions, along with over half the surviving Caledonians, most of whom were headed home for planting season, Ky's forces were down to just one-third of their previous strength. If he'd been the commander inside Londinium and he'd had any strength at all, he would have seen this as his chance to make a breakout.

Even if they were outnumbered, the enemy could have concentrated all of their forces on one or two sections of the Britannians' lines while Ky's men had to remain spread around the entire city, which ended up being almost an entire circle, split in half by the river, making reinforcing one part of his army from the other a slow and difficult task.

The Carthaginians had extended the walls far beyond what the Romans had built before abandoning the city and even beyond what the Romans in his original timeline would have built, at least according to Sophus's records.

The original wall had been on just the northern side of the Thames about three and a half kilometers long. The Carthaginians had added an additional wall on the crooked bend on the south of the Thames, allowing them to have a protected area to load and offload ships. Ky had patrols out to watch for ships coming down the river and archers ready to do as much damage to the resupply boats as possible, but the ones that made the trip at night completely blacked out made it difficult for his men to spot. Ky could have stood there and spotted them, since the dark wasn't an obstacle for him, but as the commander, he had other places he needed to be.

His men had been somewhat successful, turning back several small barges that had tried to make the run into the protected docks behind the Carthaginian wall. In the long run, it was a terrible position. If Ky had been in charge, he would have moved his soldiers to one of the southern port cities as soon as the invasion force was smashed, allowing for easier resupply.

Still, for now, it also meant Ky's forces were extremely spread out on both sides of the river, creating a supply headache for Ky as well, since he had to have food and essentials carted well west of the city and around, in order to resupply them.

Thankfully, as long as his supply columns stayed away from the walls of the city and had enough guards to protect them from bandits or opportunistic peasants, they were safe enough. His men had done a good job of scouring the countryside of all Carthaginians, but that only meant his supply lines were more or less secure. If the Carthaginians weren't going to come out to him, Ky needed to find a way to get his men into the city without getting a huge number of them killed. He and Sophus had gone through the problem multiple times, looking at both the southern and northern sections of the wall, looking at attacks down the river, through the only open section of the wall, and looking at massing their limited siege weapons on one small section to achieve a breakthrough, and none had a high enough chance of success. At least not one that didn't involve getting a large number of his men killed.

If that was the only way to do this, then Ky would order the attack, but he wanted to exhaust all other options before ordering a direct assault by men with ladders on the city walls. He'd ordered more trebuchets, but it would take time for those to get built and arrive, and he wasn't sure he'd be able to get enough to actually punch through the thick walls.

There was a cough at the entryway to his tent, causing Ky to turn. Hortensius, looking dusty and tired, stood in the doorway. For a man who spent all his time running the largest part of Rome's manufacturing, Ky hadn't seen him actually dirty before this moment.

"You look tired," Ky said, seeing the lines on the man's face.

"You look exactly the same, which considering the schedule you keep is infuriating. What I wouldn't give for your endurance."

"I don't think you'd enjoy what it took to have it," Ky said, flashing back to the surgeries and vomit-inducing medication he'd been subjected to when he'd first been selected to be a pilot.

"Probably not. You sent for me?"

"Yes. Now that the forges are going strong and the new mining operations have started, we can start looking at the next set of ideas and inventions I want to implement."

"Finally. You keep hinting at these things and I wondered if the day I'd get to learn about them would ever come."

"Some of this is going to be really extensive and difficult to understand. A lot of it you're going to have to take on faith until you see the end product."

"I've managed to make everything else you've given me work. I'm confident I can handle whatever this is."

"I am too, or I wouldn't be giving it to you, but I just wanted to prepare you. This is the key to the future of our military," Ky said handing a stack of scrolls over. "Everything we do moving forward, at least in the martial arena, is going to rely on this."

He had been working on these instructions even before the battle with the Carthaginians, since he knew this was the next step after they ended the immediate threat from the south.

"It's a mixture of some kind. Burned wood, brimstone ... and I don't know what this last thing is. I don't understand."

"I know. These things will seem insignificant and benign separately, but when mixed correctly, they can be devastating. I realized it might be confusing, so I had the men gather a small amount of the items days ago when I asked you to come down here, so I could show you the end result," Ky said, going to a table on one side of the tent and picking up a small covered clay bowl.

Setting it on the table, Ky removed the equally small lid, revealing a grainy, dark powder.

"This is called gunpowder. When lit on fire, it burns incredibly rapidly, releasing a burst of gas, fire, and heat."

Ky pulled Hortensius back from the table, lit a small piece of paper, and threw it in the bowl. The moment the paper hit the powder, there was a loud hissing pop and a bright flash that caused Hortensius to jump back, hands going to his eyes.

It was over almost as soon as it happened, causing the factory owner to look around the tent, to the bowl, to Ky, and back to the bowl in confusion and amazement.

"Go ahead," Ky said at the man's obvious curiosity.

Hortensius stepped tentatively forward, walking around the table the clay vessel had been sitting on, picking up its shattered pieces and turning them over.

"The powder is gone," he said in amazement.

"Yes. Burned up in an instant. That was a tiny amount. In large amounts, it can be used to destroy huge areas. In small, tight containers, built with metal strong enough to withstand the destructive power, the force of that explosion can be used to make terrible weapons."

"This is ... incredible. I've never seen anything like this. Such a tiny amount of black sand did ... this. Incredible."

"Like I said, it is the key to winning this war. It's how we will make up for the manpower difference we have with the Carthaginians."

"I am impressed with its ... potential, but I don't see how something like this can be used as a weapon. Maybe against walls or throwing barrels of this at the enemy."

"It's just the first piece of the plan. As impressive as gunpowder is, we don't use it in isolation. It is part of a larger weapon system that will, I promise, eventually make sense. But we're going to need a lot of gunpowder to make these weapons work, so we need to set up manufacturing to begin producing it now. I've written down instructions on the best ways to store the powder so that it remains dry, which is important for its use and safety. I've written down descriptions of how to properly mix the parts together. The end result will look somewhat different than what I had here, more like grains of spice than a powder."

"I recognize charcoal and brimstone, but I don't know what this last thing is. The words are, strange."

"The potassium nitrate. There is no Latin name for it, or at least not current Latin," Ky said. "For our immediate purposes, I've listed the exact location where we can mine small amounts, but these caves are going to be difficult to access, and I've added in a lengthy section on how to recognize what you're looking for. That might provide enough to get the process started, but unfortunately, it isn't going to be enough for what we need. There is a way to produce it ourselves, but it takes time. Even if you get started as soon as you return to Devnum, it will take a year for any of our efforts to produce the substance, and we'll have to continually be producing it to feed into our factories. I've included all the calculations for a staggered production schedule and the size of the facilities needed."

Ky waited for Hortensius's reaction when he read exactly what it would take to produce the substance themselves.

"You want us to collect what?" the manufacturer said when he finally got to that section.

Ky had been aghast himself when he'd found out what they had to do to create the potassium nitrate needed to make gunpowder in a pre-industrial civilization. It involved building what the medieval British would have called nitrate beds, which were prepared by mixing manure with wood ash and straw into a large compost pile. The heap was then covered from the rain and regularly moistened with urine, usually from horses because of the quantity needed. After a year, they could remove the soluble calcium nitrate, which could then be mixed with potash, which was derived from wood or plant ash, that they would also have to begin producing right away.

He could imagine the complaints of anyone who might have to work on the nitrate beds, since the smell was going to be something unbelievable, but it was what they needed to do if this was going to work. There was also an alternative Swiss method that was more passive, involving creating sandpits underneath stables, which would have a constant supply of urine from the horses above. The time frame on that one was the same and would help to add to their total output, but there weren't enough stables in either Rome or Caledonia to produce what they needed, and it would cause disruptions when the stables had to get dug out every year and reset, so it wasn't a replacement for the larger production nitrate beds.

Had they been in North America, or Spain, or even Italy, there would have been large natural deposits they could have accessed, but because of the wet nature of the British Isles, there had never been a significant source of naturally occurring potassium nitrate. Based on Sophus's records, this had been a problem for the British up until more modern chemical processing became available, and they had relied on many of the same methods, if somewhat less systematically than what Ky and Sophus were trying to set up.

This was also why Ky's plans only involved canon for now, since using what they could dig up from caves might be enough for limited artillery. They'd have to wait to convert the legions from their swords and shields to rifles until they had enough gunpowder to actually fire the rifles.

"I know it's disgusting, and it's not work people are going to want to do, but it's critical. The compounds we will get from these will be what ultimately ends the war."

"If you say it, then I believe it, of course; but I have trouble seeing how this, even as spectacular as your small demonstration was, will help us defeat the Carthaginians."

"I know, and for now you're going to have to trust me. Follow these directions to the letter, and I'll be able to put on a demonstration of what the weapons I'm having you build actually do. On that note, I actually have more plans for you as well," Ky said, handing over yet more scrolls.

"Interesting," Hortensius said after a long ten minutes of reading over Ky's written description of the design for a Galilean-style telescope, including the production of optical lenses for it.

Now that they had the forges running much hotter and with much more predictable temperatures using coke and coal instead of just wood, and the measurement tools he'd already introduced, he could start making precision glass, which was needed for telescopes. Since they could already make glass, even if it was too opaque and uneven to be useful as it was, this wasn't going to be a huge leap in technology like the canons and gunpowder.

"Using these looking glasses I've described, along with the stations at set distances and a series of flags, or lights at night, we can relay messages much faster than it would ever be possible using riders and runners. Once everyone gets enough practice, a message can travel from here to the Caledonians in a few hours. This system can also apply to ships, who will be able to communicate at a distance with each other, allowing them to coordinate better."

They were still a ways off from needing their own navy, but Ky was already eyeing the technology that would be needed, which was one of the factors that had led to him introducing this, rather than trying to push the Romans directly to an electric telegraph. While it was theoretically possible, using either a hand-cranked electromagnet or a voltaic battery; using the current technology base, it would require a lot more work to get up and running. They'd also have issues with insulating and protecting the wires over a long distance, since the Britannians didn't have the technology at the moment to process rubber, even if they could get the raw materials, which wasn't likely since the raw materials were on a continent that none of the locals even knew about. They were already working on operations in Ireland and Ky didn't think they were far from needing to look at the continent as their next step to countering the Carthaginians, so he needed something fast. The fact that this could also be used on ships was simply the thing that had swayed him to proceed with it over a telegraph.

"But how could glass allow us to see these distances?" Hortensius asked, noting the placement Ky had suggested for each tower station in the relay chain he'd drawn up.

"Again, you'll have to trust me that, if you follow the instructions, it will work."

"I trust you, but this is a lot. Will you be returning to Devnum soon? These are very thorough, but once we get started, I'm almost certainly going to need clarification and answers to problems that come up."

"I don't know. We are still working on a plan to take Londinium that doesn't devastate our remaining forces, prepare for the eventual Carthaginian response, and we will hopefully be operating in Hibernia soon. It's hard to say where I'll be. I am sending Lucilla back, both to help on the political front and to be there if you need assistance. She's much more involved in my planning and has some insight into these designs already, so hopefully, she'll be able to answer your questions, at least until we get the semaphore stations, that is the messaging stations shown here, set up," Ky said, pointing at the second set of documents he'd handed over.

"Good. Good. If she doesn't have the answer, it will be good to have her here with me, so she can relay my questions to you directly."

"What?" Ky said, trying to keep a straight face.

It sounded like Hortensius had suggested he knew about the transmitter he'd given Lucilla, which was impossible.

"Consul, I appreciate that you have knowledge of things we can never even imagine, let alone know about, and much of how we do things probably seems backward to you, but that doesn't make us stupid."

"I've never thought you were ..."

"I know. Not on purpose, at least. But this isn't the first time that you have suggested Lucilla has some special insight into your thinking to the point of acting as your voice when you aren't around. It was believable, to a point, when it was just in the political sphere, since at least she is familiar with that arena. This, however, is completely different. I have spent my life trying to improve Roman science, mostly to make money it's true, but I am still as close to an expert on our technical abilities as anyone in Devnum. Yet you would have me believe that you were able to explain all of this to her to the point where she would be able to answer any questions that might come up. Mind you, I'm not doubting Lucilla's capability, which I have great respect for, I simply call into question her experience in this arena."

Ky didn't answer right away. It was a valid question, and one he should have already prepared himself for. Hortensius was right, it made sense when he'd placed her as his proxy while he traveled north, since she'd already been training for politics under her father since she was small. He'd had to try and make the same arrangement here, since there was no way he could travel back to Devnum, even though they knew this was going to be harder to believe. He'd hoped that Hortensius would overlook the more unbelievable parts of the suggestion, but he should have been prepared for when the man hadn't.

"I should add that, last time, she did an amazing job answering a wide array of questions. Such a good job that I'd already thought maybe it wasn't just her natural ability and you preparing her to stand in your stead that allowed her to fill your place so well. Now that you've suggested this, I can't help but ask myself if something more is at play."

"Like?" Ky asked.

It wasn't that he didn't want to tell Hortensius about the transmitter. It was more that he couldn't think of a way of explaining it that made sense. He also wanted to keep its existence secret, since part of its usefulness was the fact that no one knew about it.

"That you have some way of communicating with her over large distances. I've heard from the soldiers that, somehow during the battle she knew exactly when you needed her side of the force to attack. Since it was mostly Caledonians, who have taken her as one of their own, the only thing I've heard is amazement at her ability to time the attack, and not questions of why you'd put someone not trained in military matters in charge of one-half of your forces to begin with. All of these facts together suggest you have some mystical ability that allows you to send her information regardless of how far apart the two of you are."

Ky was impressed. The logic was solid, but the idea was so far beyond the Romans' understanding that it should have been impossible for anyone born in this time to have made the leap to figuring out Ky and Lucilla were able to talk over distances. True, they believed in mystical forces that could let them explain away the more fantastical levels of technology, but it was still an impressive leap to make.

"It's important you don't tell anyone that this is possible. It gives us an edge that our enemies don't know about."

"I assumed as much, since you haven't told any of *us* about it, either. Although, it would make things easier if I could communicate with you in the same way."

"Unfortunately, it's not possible. It's not something that I can explain, but right now I am only able to communicate with her."

It wasn't that Ky didn't trust the manufacturer, he just didn't want to tell anyone there was an actual device that made this possible, since if word ever got out, it was something their opponents could look for, if they ever got their hands on her.

"How far does it work."

"Please, don't ask me questions about it. I am impressed you were able to work this out on your own, but it's important everything about it stays a secret."

Hortensius frowned, but assented, "I guess I'll have to live with not knowing. At least I know I'm not crazy for thinking about this."

"You're not. Besides, as soon as we get the semaphore stations set up, you're never going to be more than a few hours from an answer, even when she isn't around."

"That's true. I guess I better hurry back and get to work on this then."

"Good luck, my friend," Ky said, patting the man on the shoulder as he walked him out of the tent.

Chapter 5

After Hortensius left, Ky sat down at the small writing table he spent so much time at every day transferring the data in Sophus's databanks into something usable by the Romans, when Lucilla unexpectedly burst into his tent. He knew it was her the moment the tent flap opened without the normal introduction by one of his guards, since she was the only one his men allowed in unannounced.

"I thought you left with Hortensius?" Ky said, surprised she was still in the camp.

"He wanted to go close to the line and see the trebuchets in practice before we headed north. Velius tried to talk him out of it, since even out of the Carthaginian range, it can still be dangerous, but Hortensius insisted. He complained that he rarely gets to see his work in the field, and this was one of the few times he'd be close enough to the front line to see it."

"Tell me Velius sent a detachment with him?"

"He grumbled that it would slow the legions heading out, but he did."

"Just make sure he doesn't get too absorbed and loses track of time. We need these new projects started as soon as possible. I'd like to get the first canons in the field not long after we take Londinium. Ramirus says the Carthaginians will be able to have relief forces here in six months, which doesn't give us a lot of time."

"He knows."

"Speaking of Hortensius, he knows you and I can speak over long distances."

"You told him about the transmitter," she said, surprised.

Ky suppressed a smile. When he'd given it to her just a few short months ago, she had been astonished by it, treating the small comms unit like a magical talisman. Now she referenced it out of hand, like it was any other piece of equipment she used on a daily basis. It just showed how quickly someone could adapt to even the most radical technology, when given time and regular use.

"No. He figured it out himself. Not that you have a device in your ear, but that you and I can speak over long distances. He attributes it to magic, and I didn't dissuade him of it simply because the fewer people know about it, the less likely they are to look for the device."

"I told you he was brilliant. You underestimate him too much."

"He said the same thing. You're both right. I guess it's hard shaking the bias that my technology gives me; that I can't help but look at everyone who isn't used to it differently. I'm trying to stop it, however."

"Good. So what are we going to do about it?"

"Nothing. I asked him to keep it secret, but everything else should be the same. He's still going to come to you with questions, but you don't have to pretend you have to look through the notes I left you to get the answer. Try to have your conversations in private, but at least it makes it easier."

"I told you he wouldn't be convinced that you gave me information that you hadn't given him."

"And you were right, but it was the only reasonable explanation that I could come up with for why he could go to you for answers."

"*I still say you should give her the drone, so we can have access to the cameras and sensors on it to observe the progress of his projects. The tolerances for casting a canon are very slim. Any microscopic cracks or impurities could cause the weapon to rupture under pressure when it is fired.*"

Sophus had made the point several times since Ky decided Lucilla should go back to Devnum to act as a go-between for Ky and all of the projects they were about to start. The AI was convinced that it could alter the programming of the drone to use Lucilla's transmitter as a command bridge, but Ky wasn't convinced that was the best way to use the drone. He still believed he would need the advantage the drone gave them in combat when it came time to take the city. The legions had already suffered fairly high casualty rates, and they would lose any battle of attrition with the Carthaginians.

"I know, but I still disagree. We'll be there for the first test firing, and you can analyze the structure of the canon then. Besides, the drone doesn't have the senses to detect the kinds of impurities you're talking about. Hell, my optic sensors barely do, and there are a lot of flaws in the metal that we have no way of detecting no matter how we look at it. We just don't have the equipment for that. We're going to have to rely on more traditional methods of testing weapons for now."

The AI fell silent. Ever since it had gained sentience, Sophus had developed an attitude whenever its judgment was called into question. It had a bad habit of believing its data and logical processes were superior to human thought processes, and readily discounted things it didn't have, like intuition. It had a tendency to become snippy.

"I'm going to miss you," Lucilla said, putting her arms around Ky's middle and resting her head on his chest. "We keep getting separated."

"I know," Ky said, wrapping his arms around her in turn.

It was strange. He'd grown up in a society that didn't have much in the way of casual affection among unbonded couples, so he hadn't realized how much he'd been missing until finding Lucilla. Now he couldn't imagine living in a world without her touch.

"Once we've pushed the Carthaginians off the island entirely and we aren't in danger of being destroyed at any moment, I think it will be time for us to be married."

"What?" Ky said, releasing her and stepping back.

"I told you I was going to the Oracle to get blessings on our union, which I got before the raiding party took us captive. I don't want to have to hide what we have behind closed doors anymore, and besides, we aren't just any two people. There are a lot of eyes on us. Even if I didn't love you and want to be with you, it's still a good idea, politically. The Empire is still young and there are still a lot of people who aren't sure about it and especially about their new countrymen, on both sides. With my new ... status among the

Caledonians and with how both groups view you, it would give everyone something to rally behind."

Ky wasn't sure he believed that, but he was a soldier, not a politician.

"You really think the people would care?" Ky said, doubtfully.

"They would. I need to talk to my father about it, and there is a lot of planning that needs to happen, but when you've taken Londinium and the last of the Carthaginians on Britannia are dead or in chains, you and I are getting married."

"It sounds like I don't have much choice in this."

"You don't," she said with a smile. "There will be benefits in it for you, though."

She gave him a wink and swept out of the tent.

Ky took a few moments to let her words sink in before pushing his personal feelings aside to focus on his next duty for the day, even though the next duty was also one of his personal favorite parts of his position. He'd found the things he spent most of his time doing were administrative. Either facing the never-ending work of keeping tens of thousands of men in the field fed, focused, and active or the tedious transference of data from Sophus's database into a form men like Hortensius could use to move Rome into the industrial era.

He had spent his life prior to his sudden, unexpected trip into the past following orders, doing his job, and otherwise being a cog in the imperial war machine. He missed the simple camaraderie and unburdened focus he had from those days. Going out to the line to talk to the men was as close as he could get to his old life, and he treasured it. Of course, it wasn't exactly the same, since as both Consul and either The Sword of Jupiter to the Romans or a demon of war to the Caledonians, he wasn't exactly their equal.

Still, soldiers were soldiers, regardless of the millennia they served in, and there was a certain irreverence and commonality to it that Ky still got to participate in, in spite of his newly elevated status.

The men were in good spirits, even with the rather uneventful nature of their current duty. Except for Sepurcius's artillery men working the trebuchets, most of the legionnaires had very little to do except look at the walls of Londinium in front of them and wait for orders. The legions had stopped at long range for the trebuchets, putting them in range to pound the walls of the city, but outside the ability of the Carthaginians to reach them. The few break-out attempts early on had given the men some excitement, but it had been chaotic and uncoordinated, making the engagements limited. Since then, the legions had only to be enough of a threat to keep the Carthaginians penned up behind the wall.

The Britannians were enjoying the reversal of fortune, however. Especially the Romans, who'd been living under the threat of Carthaginian destruction for their entire lives. It was their chance to feel powerful and unstoppable, and they were reveling in it.

Ky had finished his circuit of the fifth legion and was heading towards the section of the wall held by the third legion when he came across the legates of both legions, who were in deep conversation with Ramirus, looking over maps spread out over a small portable table.

"Gentleman," Ky said, coming up on the group.

Ramirus had been looking in his direction, but hadn't said anything as Ky had approached, which explained the small smile the spymaster fought to keep under control as the two commanders jumped at the sound of Ky's voice.

"Consul," Ursinus said, saluting.

"Was there a council of war no one told me about?" Ky asked.

"No, sir," Auspex, who Ky had known the shortest amount of time of all of the legates, said. "We were just discussing deployments when Ramirus showed up and had some questions about possible assaults and the casualties we predicted. We would have informed you before we made any decisions, or if we …"

"I think he's teasing you," Ursinus said.

"Ohh," the younger legate said, looking down embarrassed.

"For that, I apologize," Ky said. "I was just walking the line and visiting with the men when I saw you three up here. So what was your answer about the predicted casualties?"

Ky already knew the answer, both from Sophus's estimates and because he and the legates had already had the discussion several times as they debated their next move against the Carthaginians. It was clear to everyone they couldn't just pound away at the walls with the trebuchets, waiting for a breakthrough and hoping their enemy wouldn't survive, but every plan they'd looked at involved too high of a price for the legions.

"The same as before. We can take the city, but a prepared defense like this favors the defenders and negates most of our unit advantages over the Carthaginians. We outnumber them by a large margin, but we're going to lose maybe as much as twenty percent of the men to do it."

"That's too high a price," Ky said. "We need to find another way of taking the city besides a full-on assault."

"Agreed," Ursinus said.

"Which is why I came to talk to the legates. I think I have an alternative," Ramirus said.

"Really?" Ky asked.

Ramirus was smart and had shown himself to excel at all manners of political and military analysis, but he wasn't a strategist. Ky respected his opinion but was surprised to hear he had one on this, since it was well outside of his expertise.

"Yes. I've been getting some messages from one of my contacts in town, trying to gather intel on the disposition of the enemy forces. We all know that they are currently still being supplied by means of the river. I know you're working on ways to put a stop to that, but for now, they've gotten small amounts of merchant ships and some fishing boats in and out. An upside to that is my contacts have been able to use these shipments to smuggle messages out to me, which means I have a fairly clear idea of the current situation inside the city."

The river was one of the only points of their plan for dealing with the Carthaginians that had not worked the way Ky and Sophus had intended. They'd already known that the trebuchets would not be effective, since the crews were still training on hitting stationary targets, which made hitting moving ships a tougher call. The ships were coming in stacked with hay bales along their sides and cover above to protect the rowers from archers, and the ships mostly came in at night completely blacked out, which made them even harder targets. Also, there was heavy tree cover along most of the river bank until the river reached the sea, that wasn't shown on the maps Sophus had in its databases, which complicated stopping the vessels short of the city.

They were in the process of sending one of the siege engines to the other bank to try and hammer at the city's port facilities in hopes of slowing its ability to resupply itself, but that was going to take time, since it required a fairly circuitous route without access to the bridge on the south bank of the city that the Carthaginians had destroyed when retreating behind Londinium's walls.

"It's helpful to know what we're facing and their supply issues, but it doesn't exactly get us inside the walls," Ky said.

"It might. One of my contacts owns one of the fishing trawlers that have been supplying the city's inhabitants. He also leases a warehouse on the far eastern end of the docks that he's been using to store supplies for his fishing boat and to offload and process the fish."

"And," Ky said, still not sure where this was going.

"His last message made it clear that the Carthaginians had stopped nearly all pretenses of internal security, as every man able to hold a weapon that isn't critical to supplying the city is being put on the wall in preparation for repelling the expected attack. That means, no one is watching the boats or the warehouses, except for when the governor's men come to take that day's catch to a central warehouse controlled and guarded by the governor's personal guard."

"So he's left unwatched. I'm still not seeing how this gets us over the walls without an assault."

"My plan involves the unwatched warehouse, and the fact that no one is watching the boats closely. When my contact goes out, he can go with a half crew, and return with a more than full crew made up of our soldiers, with their armor and weapons stored below. We do this every day, smuggling men into the warehouse, where they hide. This way, we can build up a force of a few hundred men that can attack from inside the wall while the rest of the forces assault from the outside. They'll be outnumbered, but they won't have to hold for long. Between their surprise attack and the chaos it will cause, it won't be hard for you and the rest of the men to get ladders up and climb over the wall the traditional way."

It was an interesting notion, although he was underplaying the danger that the men inside the walls would be in. They might outnumber the Carthaginians in total, but there were still almost five thousand soldiers inside the walls.

"How many men could we get in your friend's warehouse without being discovered and in a reasonable amount of time?"

"I think we could move as many as ten a day without it being noticed. He has a fairly large fishing boat, which means lots of oarsmen are needed. Most of the legionaries would have to work as oarsmen for the return trip, but that many shouldn't draw notice."

"That means if we sent men in every day for a month, we'd have three hundred men inside. That's a lot of men in one warehouse and a lot longer than I want to be sitting outside these walls. Worse, three hundred men aren't going to be enough to weaken the Carthaginian forces on the wall."

"We were just discussing that," Ursinus said. "We don't actually need these men to take a section of the wall. We just need them to punch a hole in the Carthaginian forces and keep the section of the wall we decide to attack free from reinforcements and in chaos. If, when we do launch the attack, we hammer all of the sections of the wall with lighter forces, we'll be able to hold most of their forces in place, or at least enough of them to allow five hundred or so men attacking from behind at the same point our main attack hits the other side of the wall to break through."

"That'll still be costly."

"If we don't go all out, and are just keeping them from emptying the rest of the wall, we should be able to keep the casualties low. The only point where we'll be in danger of serious casualties is the section where we are trying to break through. A surprise attack from inside the wall should be enough to counter that."

"So you think five hundred men is enough? That means we'll need a month and a half to sneak them into the city. That's a long time for these men to sit on their hands and be quiet, waiting for their opportunity to attack. And a lot of time for someone to notice them."

"His warehouse is fairly large and has access to several other warehouses, and he thinks he can keep them safe from being observed," Ramirus said.

"We're still talking about a long time for men to sit quietly, trapped in a small building," Ky pointed out.

"We'll have to pick the right men," Auspex said. "If we pick veterans known for staying cool under pressure and good men to lead them, I think they can manage it. They'll understand what's at stake if they're discovered."

Ky thought about it for a long time, long enough that the other three men started fidgeting with nervousness.

Finally, he said, "Make sure your plan is solid and your contact is ready to start receiving men, then do it. I want the two of you to draw up a list of everyone that is going, and I want to speak to all of the officers down to the lowest centurion and optio."

"Consul, I think I should go with them," Carus said from behind Ky. "This is going to be very different to the kind of duty these officers have done before. Keeping the men in check is one thing, but this entire operation is going to be under the noses of the Carthaginians, and one mistake will end the entire thing fast. We have to be able to adapt to the situation as it changes, and short of sending one of the legates or their tribunes along, I'm not sure the men selected will be able to adapt as needed."

Ky frowned. Carus was right about the need to adapt the plan to whatever the Carthaginians did. He had the ability to adjust plans on the fly that many soldiers didn't have, and he was nearly as calculating as Ramirus. He also was correct when he pointed out the other officers weren't capable to lead this mission, since he knew Ky wouldn't let the legates or tribunes do something this potentially risky.

One of the major strengths of the Roman legions was its ability to act in coordinated units instead of as loose groups of warriors like the Caledonians. A key to that cohesion was its officer core and the institutional memory they carried with them from battle to battle. He couldn't afford to send any of those men on something this risky.

His dilemma was that he couldn't afford to lose Carus either. Carus had trained with Ramirus on intelligence gathering, a skill that was in short supply, and had an extensive network of contacts inside the Roman and Caledonian military and governments, even though they were now allies. While he'd have Ramirus to fall back on if something happened to Carus, his loss would still be a severe blow to Ky personally.

"You know I'm right, Consul. Besides keeping the men calm, someone will need to deal with Ramirus's contact inside the town as well."

"Fine. You can go."

"Make sure the officers you pick know they are to coordinate with Carus, and he will be in operational control," Ky said to the two legates. "We also need to get enough civilian clothes that won't look out of place so that, if your men are seen, they don't draw attention. The armor and weapons are to be kept stored with them in the warehouse until it's time to start the attack."

The legates saluted and left with Ramirus to make plans. Carus, who was still technically one of Ky's guards, even though that position was to ensure him access to Ky and some amount of cover from anyone who might notice his regular presence, stayed where he was.

"I will be watching you and your men, and I'll send you a signal telling you the specific time for the attack to begin once we get closer. Leave your detail with Firminus and go coordinate with Ramirus. I want you to meet his contact before we start sending in men and I want you involved in every level of planning this. If you're going to lead it, I want to make sure you know it inside and out."

Carus, who was used to the fantastical things Ky did by now, didn't bat an eye at Ky's assurances about sending him a signal. Instead, the soldier and spymaster gave a salute of his own before rushing off to catch up with Ramirus.

Chapter 6

Londinium

"I don't care what the governor has ordered. Can you do it?"

"I don't know," the ship's captain said, looking around nervously. "We normally just make cargo runs to ports in Hibernia controlled by our people. If we were only going there, I'd say yes. Aside from the occasional collection of messages for the governor there to forward on to the emperor and his magistrates, he hasn't paid much attention to our trips since the first voyage. This is our first trip back to the capital, however. I can't imagine he'd accept handing me messages to deliver. He'll probably have his own man aboard, and I doubt I could keep you hidden from him on such a long voyage."

"I'll worry about him once we're underway. I just need you to get me on your boat that morning, before he brings you the message to send. I know him and his lackeys. They'll keep someone at the docks after you're handed the message until you're out of sight. I need to be in the hold and hiding before then."

"This isn't enough money!" the ship's captain said, weighing the bag of gold coins in his hand. "If they find out, they'll tie me to the bottom of my boat before having someone else sail her out. I'm not going to risk my life for this."

"The governor is done. Even if the emperor gets a relief force here before the city falls, what do you think's going to happen to the man who lost Britannia? He had the largest army this island has ever seen, *and* the second largest, I might add, and lost both to a force a tenth their size. I, on the other hand, am still an asset

50

to the emperor, especially now that they've lost the island. So who should you be more afraid of, a governor who's already dead, or me?"

"I ..." The man said, nervously, unsure of what to say next.

In a way, Caesius didn't blame him. While everything he said was true, for the moment at least, the governor still had more than enough loyal guards to do exactly what the captain was afraid of.

"You're loyalty to the emperor, by keeping me alive to assist in the reconquest of this island, will be rewarded. I will see that you get additional payments when we arrive. I take care of the men loyal to me."

With one last look past Caesius towards the handful of guards left to watch over the docks, the captain nodded his agreement.

"Good. The governor plans to send the message once the last ship that was sent to Hibernia returns, which should be in a week. I will be here on that evening to come aboard. Be ready."

The man nodded again before scuttling away like the rat he was. Caesius hated having to rely on someone so clearly deficient in both brain and spine, but this was the last real chance to get off the island before the city fell. He knew that, even if he survived the assault, he wouldn't survive captivity by his former subjects. Not after betraying them to the Carthaginians.

Emain Macha

Llassar wiped the drips of water off his face for the thousandth time, staring at the outline of the stone blocks above him, barely visible in the flickering torch light. His people had never built anything larger than a communal hut for gatherings and rituals, and even those were wood and thatch. He'd have liked to think that, had his people taken enough prisoners to need something like these dungeons, they would have built them better.

He'd have preferred being tied to a stake in the middle of the village or given a warrior's death in personal combat over this leaking, rat-infested cell. It wasn't so much the rate, or even the steady drip of water from what seemed like every inch of ceiling, that bothered him. It was more the quiet than the dark. It gave little for him to do but sit and stare, trying to make out details of his cell when the torch in the passageway flickered just right, giving at least some visibility of the walls around him.

Of course, if they'd just killed him, he would have failed at his mission. He'd been prepared for that. In spite of what he'd said to Lucilla, he'd been less than confident that the people here would be willing to deal with him. He had made friends, of a sort, when he was here before, but he'd still been a prisoner. There was enough of a history of raiding between their two peoples that an almost cultural hatred existed between them, not dissimilar to the cultural hatred that existed between his people and the Romans. Llassar had hoped that, just like with his people and the Romans, desperation would allow them to get over that hatred and come together for survival.

It had worked, to a point. He wasn't dead yet, which was why he wasn't surprised when a guard appeared at the door to the cell.

"Get up," he said, hand on his sword hilt.

In spite of the guard's rough shove as Llassar left the cell, the Caledonian was certain they weren't taking him to execute him. If they had wanted to do that, they would have done it earlier, and they probably would have sent more than a single guard. He was proven right when he was led into the palace, instead of into a courtyard or some other place suitable for a public execution.

Conchobar was on his throne again, looking sour. Llassar remembered the look from his previous stay. Conchobar may have been more thoughtful and clever than his playmate Fergus, but the two shared a stubborn streak that would have put anyone in his homeland to shame. The only reason the king would have pulled Llassar out of the dungeons for another audience was because he'd been forced to reconsider Llassar's offer. Knowing Conchobar, or at least knowing the young man he'd been years before, Llassar knew the only thing that would get him to reverse course was desperation.

Of course, that desperation had limits. Men like Conchobar had been known to let their kingdoms burn to save their wounded pride. He knew his people, or rather his new people, since thinking of the combined Caledonian and Roman people in the Britannic Empire still felt foreign, needed the Ulaid. He'd been sent to secure an alliance with them, which also meant not pushing them into destroying themselves before they could be of use.

"My king," Llassar said, taking a more formal tone than he normally did. "I am happy you've allowed me a second chance to explain my people's message to you. You know I am a warrior and unskilled in the language of diplomacy, and I think I might have given the wrong impression during my first audience."

"You say you don't speak the language of diplomacy, but you sound as if you share its forked tongue."

"Then I'll speak plainly. Your armies are outmatched. I know you had parity with the other kingdoms, or at least you did when I was here last. I remember the old king complaining of the uneasy truce with the Laigin, the Connacht, and the Erainn. We only recently heard of the Carthaginians landing on your southern shores, so I don't know how that has shifted the balance of power here, but I'm certain it has. I saw the destruction of Ulaid villages on my way here, before your men found me. In the days of the truce with the other kingdoms, that would have never been allowed to happen. I know you're not one to shirk your responsibility as king, which means it was allowed to happen because of an inability to stop it, instead of unwillingness. You're losing, Conchobar. Without help, the Carthaginians and their puppets will wash over you like the tide."

Conchobar didn't respond immediately. He stared down at Llassar, silently fuming, his jaw grinding as he fought with himself in his head.

One side or the other must have won the internal struggle, because after several tense and silent minutes, the king looked to the guards and ministers around him and said, "Leave us."

The speed at which the men fled the chamber, leaving only Conchobar and Llassar spoke to the king's power and authority.

He'd seen similar responses to Talogren and witnessed weaker leaders before his chieftain's rise to power whose advisors always hedged and wheedled when given an order, instead of obeying outright as these men had done.

"You were always too blunt for your own good," Conchobar said.

"I only did what you asked."

"So you did. You're right, though I hate to admit it. We're losing. The Carthaginians invaded in the south, taking Ivernis early on. The Erainn tried to fight them, but the foreigners were clever. They sent emissaries to all of the other kingdoms. The ones that came to us, I had executed right away, as did Labraid Loingsech. Unfortunately, Medb was willing to hear them out. Using her armies and the Carthaginian army in Ivernis, the Connacht defeated the Erainn. Crushed them, would be more accurate. Fergus had just been exiled and I was too busy solidifying my position to do anything about it, which left the Laigin on their own. With her new allies, Medb made quick work of subduing both kingdoms. She probably plans on betraying her benefactors at some point, once she's consolidated the entire island under her rule, but for now she's still their puppet."

"Your armies have not fared well?"

"No. You always said our metal was weak and brittle. I hated that, you know."

"I do know," Llassar said, thinking of their arguments as younger men.

Conchobar's pride had always extended to his people and he always took offense at the idea that anything his people did might be inferior.

"Medb isn't just using Carthaginian armies. She's armed her men with their weapons and armor as well. Half of our swords shatter or bend when brought against Carthaginian steel. When you showed up on my doorstep, we had just sent the largest army we've ever fielded against them. I just received word that our forces were completely routed. We don't have the men to stop them."

"We do."

"I don't want to become some kind of proxy for your war with them. I'm not going to be a Roman puppet any more than I'd be a Carthaginian one."

"I don't answer to the Romans. I am still a Caledonian and I still fight for my people. The new Empire we formed with the Romans, it's one of equals. We still maintain the laws in our lands and have an equal say in what happens to the Empire as a whole. While I was given instructions to offer you to become a part of that Empire, that isn't required for our assistance. Our only goal is to make ourselves safe from the Carthaginians and their plans to rule the entire world. That means pushing them off of our islands and out of our region entirely. For that to happen, we need help. Specifically, we need manpower. The only thing we ask in return for our help is that you pledge your people to helping us defeat the Carthaginians. After that, we are open to any form of treaty or alliance that both our people agree on, be it just for trading, or a military alliance, or you becoming an equal member of our Empire, with full autonomy to rule your lands as you see fit. Right now, we simply want to survive and defeat the Carthaginians."

Conchobar thought for a long moment, his hand resting under his nose, over his mouth, his brow furrowed.

"Tell me more about what kind of help your people can provide," the king said finally.

Outside Londinium

It had taken two days to work out the details with Ramirus's contact, and another day to work out how to get men on the ship without other ships finding out. Scouts had finally found a small inlet not far from the mouth of the river that the fishing boat could use to load men without one of the other ships seeing.

It had been a minor concern, since there were only a handful that braved the run out of Londinium each day, avoiding Roman archers and the one trebuchet still trying its best to hit the moving ships. Ky didn't want a chance witness bringing back news of the plan to the governor, both for the safety of the men already smuggled into the city and for the success of the plan itself, which was their best chance to breach the city without incurring large-scale casualties.

Ky had Ramirus get detailed descriptions of the warehouses to be used and had spent the better part of a day observing them using the drone. As best he could tell, they were being left completely alone. Ramirus had also been right when he'd said that there wasn't much foot traffic around any of the businesses near the docks. From what Ky could see, there were hardly any people in the streets at all that weren't actively engaged in some specific activity. Ramirus had heard that the citizens were being conscripted into a militia and were being forced to man the wall, which Ky imagined made those who hadn't been conscripted yet eager to keep from drawing attention to themselves.

The only problem with their plan, at the moment, was that Londinium and the Empire soldiers surrounding it were a good ride from the coast where the fishing boat would pick up the men. Although both his lictore and the legates had been less than thrilled with the idea, Ky had wanted to ride along this first time to see the handoff. As soon as he had, he saw a flaw in the plan. The Carthaginians might not notice squads of men leaving the line and heading east once or twice, but every night for a month and a half, someone would notice. Even if they sent them roundabout in other directions, someone might get curious. It was also a long ride for the men.

They'd agreed to find a spot to set up a small camp for the men selected to sneak into the city and a small security detachment, not far from where they'd be meeting the ship each day. There were other praetorian camps up and down the coast for the guards patrolling and watching for Carthaginian ships, so if it was maintained by the praetorians, anyone getting curious would at least find a reason for them to be there.

It was a day's ride back, which meant Ramirus had already returned to the lines outside the city, both to check on messages from his contacts and to work with the legates to get the men selected to sneak into the city ready to travel to their new camp.

Ky had expected that to take a day or two at the least, which was why he was surprised to see Ursinus and Ramirus riding out to meet them as he, the praetorian officers who'd be setting the camp up, and his security detachment returned to the Roman lines outside the city.

"Problems?" Ky asked as the men rode up.

"Yes. I just got word that the Carthaginians are going to try a break out along the river."

"That's insane!" Ky said. "They don't have the numbers to break through, and if they do, what then? Attack our lines from behind? Even down to two legions and the Caledonian forces that chose to remain, we have more than twice their number. What do they hope to accomplish?"

"I don't know," Ramirus answered. "I only know that one of my people floated a message to my man on the south bank two hours ago that the Carthaginians were armoring men at the west gate. It looks like a full phalanx."

"If they were going to try it, why not use cavalry? At least then they'd be mobile. Phalanxes are slow. We'll have plenty of time to converge on them, and if they did manage to break out, how would that many men on foot be able to do anything without support."

"I'm not sure they have very many experienced commanders left in the city," Ursinus said. "From the interviews we've done with the commanders, basically everyone with actual experience was with the army we defeated. This is probably the brainchild of someone desperate to be seen as doing something. What it does is present us with an opportunity. If we hit them right as they're coming out, we might be able to get through the gates before they can get their men back inside and lower them."

"That's a risk. As far as we can tell, they don't have any catapults in the city, since they sent them all out with the army just before winter, but they still have a good number of archers," Ky said. "Beyond that, fighting in an enclosed space like a gateway, especially one blocked by a phalanx, is going to be costly. We'd be eliminating our advantage of numbers for them."

"Any attack we do is going to be costly, but the gateway hurts them as much as it does us. A phalanx isn't going to operate in a gate like that. It isn't tall enough for them to get their spears all the way up, so rear ranks will either have to be more separated or their spears will be in the way of the line in front of them. That might work for one or two lines, but any deeper than that, and it will start to hinder them. Also, this isn't their front-line infantry. From what Ramirus has told us, nearly every unit with any level of training went out with the last army, and only a handful of stragglers made it back. Unless the governor plans on sending his guard force out, these are going to be poorly trained militia at best, or possibly some of the civilian population that the Carthaginians have been levying. Will we lose men? Yes. But if we're successful, it will be a lot fewer men than we'd lose storming the walls."

"They are correct, Commander. An assault as they're describing would have a higher chance of success than the current plan, with fewer points of failure."

"Very well then, let's do it," Ky said, for the benefit of both the commanders and Sophus. "Pull three centuries and stage them behind our line as close to the gate as possible. As soon as they are halfway out, I want at least five squadrons to hit them in the flank. As soon as they see the cavalry, they'll start to turn their line and get their spears set for the charge, so we're going to take casualties, but I think if we hit them fast enough, it won't be devastating. Either way, they need to hold the men there long enough for our soldiers to run across the open ground and engage. If we're lucky, our casualties will be light. Either way, we'll have their phalanx stuck in the gateway, blocking it. I also want to have a group of Caledonians ready to come in behind the legionaries to exploit a breakthrough. Once the phalanx is broken, their style of fighting will fit the chaos that will happen on the other side of the gate better than the legionnaires'. When they're through, we need to be ready to follow through with at least half of Auspex's legion closest to the gate. I want an overwhelming force inside in minutes after the gate falls. Do we know when they're going to attack?"

"No," Ramirus said.

"I don't think they'll try a night attack. If they stood a chance at all, they'd have to keep their phalanx tight and attack close to the river, where they don't have to worry about being rolled up on both sides. As it is, it's insane because we completely overlap them enough to completely circle them on one side, but at least it would be slower with only one flank exposed."

"But their commander has to be inexperienced to even try this, so they might not realize the same thing, which means a night assault is possible. Have the three legions, cavalry squadrons, and Caledonians stand ready. We'll release them an hour before dawn with fresh troops, that way if they do attack at dawn or sometime in the morning, our men won't be exhausted."

The legate saluted and he and Ramirus rode back to the lines to get the men assembled. If the Carthaginians were even fractionally intelligent, they'd notice the built-up Britannian forces facing that gate, and call the thing off once daylight hit. Of course, anyone insane enough to plan this crazy attack might not, either.

Ky had been gone all day and part of the previous day, which meant he had fallen behind on his work. While he left the actual running of the legions to the legates, he still had correspondence and messages to deal with as Consul, along with hours of transcribing of notes for Hortensius, Opilio, the Senator representing the farms and plantations, and the various mining operations on how to take the next steps in improving their operations and instructions he'd need to give them when it was time to begin the next phase of advancement.

While they'd worked out a schedule for introducing technology and plumbed Sophus's database on the best way to do that, Ky being the only one with a computer in his head capable of accessing that data meant they'd hit a serious bottleneck, since disseminating the data was limited to the speed of Ky's writing.

Ursinus's guess that they wouldn't try a breakout at night proved correct. There had still been no action outside of the city when Sophus alerted Ky thirty minutes before daybreak. Ky's best guess was that they'd try at first light, when the legions would only just be rising for the day. Ky had never understood that thinking, himself. Everyone knew it was the time people liked to attack, so if one was expected, there were always soldiers waiting for it, which negated the surprise element. True, they probably thought this time it was a surprise, but the thinking still puzzled Ky.

Everyone was assembled, with the cavalry up by the bend in the Roman lines as they curved with the bend in the city wall. The Roman lines were a little further than a third of a mile back from the walls of the city itself, close enough to see it, but mostly out of range of arrow fire and any smaller artillery like dart throwers they might have on the walls, hidden from plain sight.

The centuries and Caledonians were on the line facing the gate, the fresh units already making the switch for the ones that had kept watch all night. The men could see the distance they'd need to run, holding formation as best they could so they hit as one. It would take several minutes for the men to cross the open field and come to grips with the Carthaginians, which was going to be a long time for the cavalry riders to be in contact with spear-wielding infantry, but they'd have to hold.

As if on cue, as soon as light began to break over the field, the gates began to rise. There wasn't any fanfare or trumpets playing, but it was impossible for anyone looking that way to miss the gates going up and the long spears being lowered down to come through it. Once again, Ky marveled that anyone was going to attempt such an obviously doomed maneuver, but hoped they'd be able to exploit it and get on the other side of the wall before the Carthaginians realized their mistake.

Moments passed as one, then two, and then a third rank of men filed through the gate. They were compressed into columns ten men wide, which is just about as wide as they'd be able to march abreast and stay together coming through the gate, which meant it would take them longer than normal to get all of the men out. Ursinus, who had more field experience than Auspex, having been involved in both recent battles against the Carthaginians, had been left to decide the timing of the cavalry charge.

Thirty seconds ticked by and then a full minute with no response from the cavalry down the line. Another row marched out, and then another. Ky could feel Ramirus and the officers around him getting nervous. Ky had actually been more worried about the opposite problem of Ursinus sending the horsemen too soon. He was watching the gate up close, thanks to both his enhanced vision and the drone high in the sky, giving him two views of the gate and the soldiers marching out. The line of men was possibly much larger than the men around him suspected, as they were more used to seeing phalanxes arrayed for combat than transitioning through a gate.

Ursinus, who didn't have Ky's advantages, actually timed it pretty well. Ky saw the first horses cross the line when just over a third of the men were through the gate. They'd already started fanning out into a full battle line, which left an angle where the thinner line connected with the growing wider line, and the centurion leading the charge knew his business, smashing into it right at that angle. As suspected, the soldiers had noticed and brought their spears down to try and stop the charge, but there were too few of them to stop the charge entirely, and the horsemen cut through the line like a knife.

As soon as the first horseman had crossed the line, the signal was given for the centurions to charge. The Caledonians, who were already getting their blood up and looked like they might jump off early, thankfully held, which would give the legionaries time to hit the Carthaginians as a single unit.

The horsemen had strict instructions to not try and take the gate on their own, since once they got in the gateway, they'd be surrounded and easily cut down. They did have to come to grips with the Carthaginians, both to keep them from lining up with their spears and to keep them focused on the current threat until the legionaries got there.

The fighting was brutal and horsemen began to fall. More than Ky was comfortable with. The stirrups at least helped them stay on the animals as they swung across either side striking at the men below, but they were still being pulled down.

The Carthaginians themselves couldn't seem to make up their minds what to do. Some of the men still inside the city tried to run to their comrades' assistance while some of the men outside the city tried to run back inside, creating a traffic jam right inside the gateway. The men who'd already formed into position at least tried to fight as an organized unit, turning and trying to back away from the horsemen and to get their spears deployed. Whoever was leading them at least had some small unit tactical experience, because he'd almost done it, when the legionaries hit them from behind.

The portion of the phalanx that had deployed dissolved as they were attacked from either side. The cavalry began pulling back as the legionaries started forward into the gateway, pushing against the mass of men crammed into the small area, when the thing Ky nor his legates had predicted happened. The men on the other side slammed the heavy gate down, crushing any of their own men who happened to be in the way.

It was actually the only thing that had saved them from having the Romans break through the gate, but with so few soldiers left, Ky hadn't predicted they'd just leave those now caught on the other side to their fate. The Caledonians had finally caught up with the rest, and with their blood up and their goal blocked, vented their frustrations on the few Carthaginian soldiers still standing outside the walls.

It was a massacre. The centurion in command of the field force left the Carthaginians to the Caledonians and formed up across from the gate. Ky wasn't sure what he was trying to accomplish, since with the gate closed there was no chance they would get through, but it was a very human response. They'd been so close to breaking through, and it had been pulled away from them at the last second. While the last Carthaginians outside the wall were being slaughtered on the field, archers on the walls began to take a toll on the soldiers wandering in front of the wall, trying to figure out what to do next.

"Call them back," Ky said.

"They might ..." Ramirus started to say, before Ky interrupted him.

"They're not going to force that gate, and the Carthaginians aren't going to open it back up. We're just wasting men's lives right now. Call them back before we lose any more men we don't have to."

A trumpeter began to blow the signal for the men to retreat; they did their best to gather up their fallen comrades, most of who had been in the initial cavalry charge. It was going to cost more men, trying to rescue injured friends and bring the dead back with them, but Ky wasn't going to get in their way. He understood the way soldiers formed bonds and was sure he'd do the same thing in their position.

"Looks like we're going to have to stick with plan A after all."

Chapter 7

Devnum

"It's cloudy," Lucilla said. "I can't really see anything."

"Could you describe it being more specific please," Sophus said.

They'd been back in Devnum for two days, and Hortensius had been a whirlwind since their return. He'd already begun working on all of the projects Ky had given him; he sent men out to collect the necessary supplies for the gunpowder, began the first casting tests on the canon, and started producing the semaphore stations.

Of all the tasks he'd been given, the semaphore stations were the easiest. Ky had already marked out on a map where he wanted the permanent stations to be built that would allow messages to be transmitted between the major cities and the capital. The stations themselves were pretty straightforward and could be built using "volunteer" labor from the prisoner of war camps. The height of each tower depended on the height of the land it was built on, calculated by Sophus so that each should be able to see the next tower in spite of trees and obstacles. Some were a mere thirty feet off the ground while the tallest reached as high as the top of the Coliseum, the wooden frame designed to be sturdy even in the face of strong winds. Ky had devised a series of cables using Roman wire, which he'd also given instructions on how to strengthen using the new steel, and would be used to brace the tallest towers in all directions.

Most of the towers themselves, with their enclosed cabins and pulleys for raising and lowering flags or lanterns, would be finished in just a few weeks. The slower part of the project would be training the men tasked with operating the stations to read the code that Ky had worked out for them. The actual messaging wasn't hard since they could produce scrolls that identified what letter each flag combination or light sequence indicated. They'd also have to learn how to decode and encode those messages using ciphers. Lucilla's people had already been using the idea of shifting letters for other letters in a pattern known only by the people sending the message, but Ky had introduced a much more complex algorithm, using simple mathematical formulas that could be changed quickly, even automatically, based on the season or day of the week.

The instructions to do this were fairly clear, but they'd need to train several hundred men who would then be scattered across the countryside to operate each station, and they had to do it well enough to not make errors in their communications. Simple things could be figured out, but things like troop movements or questions of a scientific nature would require exact figures that could be easily ruined if a number was shifted accidentally. To reduce the errors, they had procedures to repeat and confirm messages, but men in the field often looked for shortcuts in performing their daily work, and she had no illusions that this wouldn't happen here.

The other, and more direct issue, was the looking glass that Ky had described. The stations were far enough apart that every station would need one, and more likely several, to see the message being sent. It was already clear the legions and most ship masters, as well as a large part of private industry, were going to be clamoring for these devices if they worked the way Ky said they would, so they needed to get into production right away. Unfortunately, this first attempt seemed completely worthless, which showed that even with specific instructions, creating things that none of the people working on it had seen before added new levels of challenge.

"I can see light through it, but not much else. It's much more cloudy than the glass I have seen used to make vessels and in some temples."

"I'm sorry, but for this to work, I need specifics."

"I know, but I don't know how to describe it in more detail for you."

"I will try and walk you through it," Sophus said.

The next two hours were some of the most frustrating of Lucilla's life. Sophus had her perform dozens of experiments, giving the most precise answers she could, sometimes doing the experiment over and over to ensure her answers were correct.

Just about the time she was ready to pull the small transmitter out of her ear and chuck it into the street, Sophus said, "I believe I have deduced the problem with this run of glass."

"Good, what is it?"

"The sand being melted down has too many impurities in it that are not being removed in the heating process. The instructions we'd originally given were in hopes that they could heat the furnaces to the point of removing impurities in the silica, enough that the lenses would be functional after grinding. That is what is used in more modern glass-making systems, but it requires the furnaces to have a stability in the heat that seems to not have been achieved yet. Since that isn't working, there is another method that can be used, although it will take more time. I will give instructions where to mine the quartz needed for the alternate method of glass making, as well as instructions to recognize it and to grind it into grains that can be melted properly into transparent glass."

Lucilla set down the cloudy glass and began writing down Sophus's dictated notes. She understood the importance of getting them right, but this went much faster when Ky did it, or at least she preferred it when she wasn't the one having to do the transcribing. She felt almost like a child again, doing her letters in front of her tutor, who would slap her knuckles every time she did something wrong. Thankfully, Sophus wasn't able to perform that part when she wrote a word wrong and had to go back to correct her error.

It was still very early on their timetable, but she had been hopeful that Hortensius's enthusiasm had put them ahead of schedule, and she was disheartened that this part of their work would be delayed.

Londinium

"Yes, Your Excellency," Maharbaal's aide said when he entered the room.

The man wore a close-fitting and highly adorned shendyt together with a tight-fitted inner rope making him seem impossibly thin. Maharbaal resisted the urge to roll his eyes, as he often did when dealing with his aide. The man was unfailingly loyal, which is why the governor had summoned him now, but his refusal to adapt to more lose fitting clothes and heavier outer garments that fit the dreary and cold weather of the Britannic isles had always baffled Maharbaal. The thin and tightly wound garments made sense in the hot African and Iberian sun, but here, it would leave a man shivering from the cold.

"I've prepared the message for the emperor. It is important you do not give it to any of his aides or lackeys. Find my agents there. They will ensure that, as my personal representative, you will be granted an audience to report on our dire situation. Some of my detractors might try to meet you at the docks to dissuade you or to convince you that they're working for me and to hand this over to them. Be vigilant."

"Yes, sire. I know the passcodes by heart. You can count on me."

"Good. They'd like nothing more than to see me fail, losing the island to the damned Romans and forced to scuttle back to court with my tail between my legs. You need to make it clear to the emperor and his generals how serious our situation is. Inform them that our final attempt to break out and take the attack to the Romans has failed. We are outnumbered and at the mercy of their new catapults, which outrange anything we have. Don't, however, point out that we've lost all of our siege equipment. Make it clear we must have reinforcements if we are to survive and reestablish our base here. I know there is an army on Hibernia, but their governor claims to be preoccupied dealing with the primitives there and says he is unable to send us any soldiers. A full relief army from home would be good, but at the very least we need the emperor to order Aradus to send at least two thousand men to us so we can properly man our defenses as we wait for the relief army. If not, the city will fall and the empire will have to re-invade this island. Remind his generals that, with the current activity in the east, they can't afford to divert the necessary men to retake the island and maintain our operations there."

The governor had covered these items with his aide already, and it was all clearly spelled out, although more diplomatically, in his letter, but Maharbaal was desperate. This posting was supposed to be the steppingstone for his career, allowing him to one day govern a province with real wealth and an opportunity to make a name for himself. Everything had fallen apart at the hands of the incompetents sent to lead his armies. If he didn't find a way to save the situation, he would be held responsible when he returned to Carthage.

He well knew how the emperor dealt with men that had failed. He'd thrown Bomilcar to the wolves, but that would not have been enough to appease the emperor.

"This next part is not in my letter. I need you to pass these instructions to my agents yourself. They are to begin spreading the word of the failure of the Roman traitor. They must tie his involvement to the emperor's decree that we work with him, being careful to not implicate the emperor in any mistake or error himself. There needs to be enough doubt in Caesius that the emperor has no choice but to single him out for this failure and hold him personally responsible while avoiding having any of Caesius's mistakes taint his own glory. I will make sure the coward stays and dies here at the hands of his people, which will make it easier to assign blame to him. It will take time for this to happen, so they need to start right away. If reinforcements don't come and I am forced to flee, the campaign to disparage the Roman must be well underway so that I am not made an example of as soon as I step off the boat. Do you understand what you must do?"

"Yes, Your Excellency."

Fool that he was, the man had played the game for a long time and knew how to operate at court. It was still a risk, since any man's loyalty had a price, one that was often paid by competitors, but Maharbaal couldn't go himself, so this was his only option.

"Good. Prepare yourself. I've sent orders for our most seaworthy ship to travel south as soon as the last supply shipment arrives from Hibernia with their dispatches. The man has been well paid, but don't trust him. Be wary of treachery."

"I will, Your Excellency."

"Then go. Prepare yourself. I think it is unlikely I shall see you before I return to Carthage."

The man bowed and left, leaving Maharbaal to fret alone over his future.

Devnum

"I understand it's how things are done in your village, but when in Roman territory, you must follow Roman laws, just like Roman citizens have to follow your laws when on Caledonian land," Lucilla said to the Caledonian applicant, standing before her father's throne, where she sat.

Ever since she returned, her father had been determined for her to throw herself back into the business of government. With her brother gone, she was the clear choice for his successor and he wanted her to have as much experience in the daily functions an Emperor had to deal with as possible.

True, it was out of the norm for a woman to inherit, but her marriage to Ky was a foregone conclusion at this point, at least to everyone but Ky, and his acting as consort would be enough to make her inheriting the position palatable to the majority of Romans. Besides, she wouldn't be just the Emperor of the Romans, but of the entire Britannic Empire, and she was one of the few leaders that both the Romans and the Caledonians would support.

"But that field was unused," the man said, not seeming to understand the problem.

"Because he was leaving it to lay fallow, but even if he decided to leave it unused for no reason, that's up to him. You are not allowed to use someone else's land without their permission. I understand this was an honest mistake and things are done differently up north, so I will limit your punishment to either paying for removing the planting or allowing the landowner to simply sell the harvest as his own, whichever the owner prefers."

"To fine a man for using untilled land is an insult," the man said, angrily.

To a degree, Lucilla understood his anger. For the Caledonians, at least before they came under the sway of the anti-slavery laws Ky had put into the foundations of the Britannic Empire, it was commonplace to sell anyone captured in a raid as property. As someone taken that very way and destined to be kept as a slave before Ky rode in and saved her, she was equally offended by their laws and traditions.

However, they'd agreed to let each people rule their own land as they saw fit, as long as it was within the limitations put in place by the Imperial Senate, and the average person who traveled north or south for profit needed to understand that. Their relationships with their neighbors would still be contentious until everyone got used to the idea of each member's independent sovereignty.

"I understand how you feel, and I sympathize. Think of it like this. Imagine that a Roman man married a Caledonian woman and moved north to live in Caledonia. Years later they have a child who grows up to be rebellious. The father decides he will not tolerate the child and says the child cannot inherit any of his property or live on his land any longer, and instead gives the land to his wife's sister's children. The child is then cast out, and must live as a beggar on the streets, asking passers-by for money. This is allowed in Rome. Should his neighbors be forced to live next to someone who would deny kinship?"

One of the strongest things in Caledonian culture was its kinship laws, which predated any actual written laws and provided a firm stance on how families were expected to behave. For instance, it was expected that families would care for and support their kin, keeping them from being a burden on the rest of society. The only people seen on the street begging were the poor souls who'd lost all forms of kinship, usually when everyone they could possibly be related to had died off, leaving them as the sole surviving member of their family. Considering kinship stretched multiple generations, this took quite a run of bad luck to occur and was exceedingly rare.

It was considered harmful to society as a whole to kick a family member out and no longer treat them as kin, to the point where there would almost be less of a punishment for killing the person, rather than making them a burden on society.

"No. Family bonds are unbreakable."

"Not in Roman lands. Would you accept a Roman going north and leaving children for the village to take care of?"

"No."

"It is the same here. We are all expected to respect and adhere to the rules of the country we are in. This is a rule here. Normally, taking another man's land would lead to some form of imprisonment or a larger fine, but I believe that while we all get used to the new way of things, leniency is deserved. There should be no punitive punishment, and the restitution I ordered was just to make the farmer whose land you used whole, so your actions did not cost him money."

The man was silent for a moment, and then grudgingly said, "Fine."

"Thank you. I know this situation is difficult and I know you meant no harm. May the gods grant their favor on you, and I hope you find the fortune you came here for."

The man just nodded and let himself be led away. Caledonians had their own gods and methods of worship, but they were generally accepting of the prayers of others, even if those prayers were to gods they didn't worship.

She took a breath and waited for the next petitioner, when a messenger, looking dirty and tired, was brought in instead.

"Optio," she said, noting his rank.

"With Amulius Tettius Velius's compliments, my lady," the messenger said in the formal language she'd had to readjust to now that she was back in court and not with the Caledonian and Roman soldiers.

"Is it from Velius?" she asked, taking the scroll from the guard who had, in turn, taken it from the messenger.

"No, my lady. This came this morning off of a boat from Hibernia, delivered by one of the barbarians."

"They aren't barbarians, optio."

"As you say, my lady."

Lucilla frowned but didn't comment on the man's characterization any further. It would take time to teach the Romans to stop seeing everyone not born in their lands as barbarians. There were still daily altercations between Caledonians and Romans, where a Roman, often without doing it intentionally, insulted one of their new allies. The frequency was, thankfully, slowly decreasing, at least in Devnum, thanks to a growing familiarity born by close contact, but it would be some time before Romans came to see the Caledonians as equals. Apparently, this slow acceptance wasn't extended to other foreigners.

Instead, she simply said, "Thank you for your prompt delivery. Return to your camp and inform Velius I will be out to see him today."

"Yes, my lady," the soldier said, slapping fist to chest before turning smartly and striding out.

The message itself was from Llassar, and the one she'd been hoping to see ever since he left for Ériu, as he had called it. The Ulaid had officially requested military assistance against Carthage and its allies pressing in from the south and were considering both a formal alliance and possibly even joining the Empire itself, on similar terms to its current members.

She was impressed. Llassar had made it sound like he was unsure of his ability to succeed when she'd asked him to travel across the channel that separated their two islands, but he'd managed to get everything she'd asked for, proving how valuable he really was.

"Call the members of the Imperial Senate together," she said. "There will be an emergency session in two hours."

Unlike how things had been before, when governors and the Emperor could more or less declare military action at will and only needed senate approval to establish new governorships or appoint new legates; the new Empire required the Emperor to get approval from the Imperial Senate before declaring war or attacking a new opponent. It had been one of the concessions her father and Ky had been forced to give to gain the agreement to establish what Ky called "a professional army."

Before the military reforms, legates and tribunes were political appointees, allowing certain blocks to maintain favors with military commands, a setup that had allowed for the recent insurrection. The recent insurrection attempt proved how dangerous that could be, but the senators had been hesitant to agree to a law that would strip them of that power, the Romans on the grounds that it was how it was always done, and the Caledonians because their military and political leadership had always done the exact same thing.

Ky and her father finally convinced them to give up the right to appoint commanders by giving them the sole right to declare war, which is why she now had to ask for their permission to proceed. They might have been at war with Carthage, but they weren't fighting the other Ériunia kingdoms, which made this a grey area.

She and her father had already discussed this and decided that it would be best for her, rather than him, to make the request. She had already spoken to the Caledonian senators, and more or less convinced them that aiding the Ulaid was necessary. Her father had been attempting to do the same thing with the Roman senators, and had gotten significant pushback from them. While the Caledonians saw the Ulaid as a peer, even if one regularly raided and fought against, the Roman senators harbored old prejudices that they were having difficulty letting go of.

After another stop to see her father and confer with him about their strategy of dealing with the Romans, she made her way to the rebuilt forum, which the Imperial Senate shared with the Roman Senate.

"Gentleman," she said after being announced and waiting through the traditional recitation of titles and virtues that the

Roman senators still insisted upon. "I appreciate you meeting with me on short notice to address a question that we must answer quickly."

"If this is about the barbarians, we already made our feelings about this clear to your father," Taenaris said.

Taenaris had been a loyal supporter of her father since the early days of his reign and had been the leader of the loyalist block of senators before the creation of the Imperial Senate. The first Imperial senators had been appointed, instead of elected, because of the need to get the government set up and underway and Taenaris had been her father's first choice as one of Rome's five allotted senators.

Oddly, the usually loyal Taenaris had become notably more prickly and independent following his appointment. She had discussed him with her father, who had seemed perplexed but generally unconcerned about the development, even though Taenaris was now the one giving the most pushback about sending troops to assist the Ulaid.

"Watch who you call barbarians, Roman," said Roti, a large, white-bearded Caledonian giant, who had been the leader of one of the northernmost tribes before Talogren appointed him to the Senate.

"I apologize," Taenaris said, clearly not meaning it. "Old habits die hard. My point is, we have our own issues and our military is already stretched thin. Yes, we've won a great victory, but the Carthaginians will be sending a relief army, one that they can land anywhere they choose along our coastline, and there is little we can do to stop it. We need every man we can spare watching the coast, giving the legions time to gather and counter their attack. I feel for the Ulaid, but their problems are their own."

All of the Romans began nodding their heads in agreement, as did one of the Caledonians, which was a bad sign. She couldn't fault them, at least not completely. They were afraid, the Romans most of all, and wanted to pull back and sit in a shell like a turtle.

"I understand your concerns, but that is the wrong choice. We've tried this before. We had men on our borders, guarding against an army that didn't need boats to send troops towards us, and they got within sight of the walls of this very city before they were stopped. The man who digs a hole to hide in often finds that hole looks a lot like a grave when the enemy finds it. We can't protect ourselves by hiding. The Consul has made it clear that his plan for stopping the Carthaginians is by taking the fight to them. For a hundred years, we have tried to ignore the Carthaginians to the south and simply protect our borders, *and it didn't work.* They still came for us. We are, right now, as safe as we have been in any of our lifetimes, and it's because we went to them."

"There is a difference between proactive and foolhardy. I don't hear the Consul talking about putting our legions on boats and attacking Africa itself."

"We're not talking about Africa. We're talking about an island barely a stone's throw across the channel that separates us. When they conquer the Ulaid and have laid claim to all of Ériu, what do you think they will do next? Do you think they will stop there? Or do you think they will use that island as a staging ground to get their armies safely across the sea and ready to invade? Being able to call for reinforcements a few miles from our shores is a lot easier than having to wait for troops to come all the way from Africa."

"Couldn't they come from Germania just as easily? Or Iberia?"

"Yes, and the Consul plans on taking the fight there, eventually. But we don't have allies who could join our fight on the continent, at least not that we know of. We do have those allies here, however. Rome is facing a manpower shortage. Even with the wondrous technology the Consul is bringing us, we do not have the manpower to stop the never-ending hordes of men the Carthaginians can send against us. We need allies, and there aren't many people left we can turn to who are not currently controlled by the Carthaginians. Letting the Ulaid be destroyed hurts our chances in the future and helps the Carthaginians. If you won't vote to send help because it's the right thing to do, vote to send help because in doing so, we help ourselves."

"Do we even have the manpower to help them without wasting our legions?" Sandilianus asked. "Many of the Caledonians who came south to help win the Battle of Venonis have returned for planting season. Our strength has been whittled down after several battles, and we've only been able to replace them with defecting enemy soldiers and ex-slaves."

She found it odd that the senator had picked up the name that had been growing among the common people for the victory that had allowed the Britannians to clear the island of the Carthaginians. Sandilianus had been the mayor of a southern town and the de facto leader of the citizens and businesses that had been operating closest to the Carthaginians for generations. She didn't blame the masses, most of whom had never ventured near the southern border to know how far the town of Venonis, which had been in Carthaginian control since her grandfather's time, was a half day's ride from the site of the battle. If anyone should have known that, it would be Sandilianus, although it was hard to go against the public consensus on things like that.

"We still have several thousand Caledonians under arms and the new men in the ranks performed their duties well during the battle. The Consul believes he has the manpower necessary to take Londinium and hold the coasts now. He specifically sent these three legions north so that they would be available to go to the Ulaid's aid, when needed. Considering how his strategy has worked for us in the past, I for one trust his judgment on this."

Sandilianus sat back down, chastised. She could see that, if reason hadn't convinced them, then at least appealing to their faith in Ky, would. For now, his name still had a magic air to it, able to sway men when other arguments would not. Of course, it only took one loss for his name to lose the power it enjoyed.

"This isn't the time for being timid," Lucilla said when no one else spoke up immediately. "We may have won a battle, but we are not out of danger. We still sit on the brink. If anything, our victory will force the Carthaginians to push even harder to destroy us. Their empire rests on the backs of conquered nations. They cannot allow Britannia to exist as an example for all of those subjugated people that the Carthaginian empire is not invincible. This is a time for boldness."

The senators went back and forth among themselves for another hour, discussing what it would take for them to vote to send the legions. It quickly became clear that enough of the men supported the action to make it a foregone conclusion, but she wanted a unanimous vote. The five Caledonians, along with two of the Romans, agreed outright.

It took time, but she was able to convince the other two holdouts that it was in their best interests to support the Ulaid. The major contention wasn't about actually sending men and arms to aid them, but about what would happen if the Ulaid asked to be part of the alliance.

The Romans were worried about diluting their power, which was always their concern and one of the things that almost derailed the forming of the Empire in the first place. Lucilla managed to convince them to deal with that when it happened, but if the Ulaid did ask to join the Empire as an equal member, she knew she wouldn't be able to sway the senators herself. She, her father, and Ky would have to take them on as a united front. They wouldn't have a Carthaginian army at their doorstep when that happened, and politicians tended to be short-sighted when it came to giving up power.

That was a problem for another day. For now, she had their agreement to send the three gathered legions to Ériu.

Chapter 8

Outside Londinium

Ky made his morning stop at the tent holding Bomilcar. The general was recovering well. Ky had been checking with the healers every day after seeing the general and had given specific instructions on his treatment. His injuries had been serious, but not life-threatening if treated appropriately, and if the healers avoided causing an infection. While they were following some of the new standards he'd introduced to the physicians in Devnum, he hadn't been able to introduce everything, and the healers were having trouble believing all of the science he'd tried to explain to them.

Through a combination of alcohol and regularly sterilized bandages, so far Bomilcar had managed to avoid any major infections, letting the body more or less repair itself. Without modern medicine, the general would always have a limp, since there was only so much a splint could do to set broken bones, but living with a limp was better than not surviving at all.

"Good morning, General," Ky said, entering the tent. "How are you feeling today?"

"Tired and in pain."

"Pain simply means you aren't dead yet," Ky said, stopping to look the general over, letting Sophus run what diagnostics on the man he could using Ky's enhanced senses.

While it could tell a lot, such as temperature, pulse, and respiration, it was a far cry from a medical checkup. It was, however, better than anything available using present-day techniques.

"Your fever is gone. That's a good sign."

The general gave Ky a perplexed look as he did every time Ky did something that should have been impossible, like being able to tell that the fever the man had been suffering while his body fought to repair itself had abated.

"Why do you continue to visit me every day? You haven't even asked me any questions. Why bother to treat my wounds?"

Carthaginians tended to let any prisoners they took who couldn't be used as slaves simply die, often of thirst and starvation, since they didn't believe in wasting resources on a dead man.

"Because you are our guest. An unwilling one, true, but a guest all the same."

"How are my men?"

"Doing well. As I promised, none have been sold into slavery or executed for following the orders of their leaders. Most of the non-critically injured have recovered enough to be moved into holding camps with the uninjured soldiers who surrendered, and are being treated fairly with food, clean water, and tents to protect them from the elements. The ones still in the hands of the healers are the most injured, and I'm sad to say many will probably die of their injuries, but we are doing what we can to make them comfortable until that time comes."

"I find it hard to believe you are treating prisoners as well as you keep saying."

"When you are better and can walk, I will take you on a ride around the camps so you can see for yourself. Some of your men are being used in public works programs, repairing homes and farms damaged in the fighting and helping build up our infrastructure, but this is only temporary. When this conflict ends, we will allow any of your people who wish to go home to do so."

"Do you really believe you can survive this war? Yes, you had a magnificent victory and you are a clever field commander, but my army was just a small fraction of the forces you'll be facing. You can't possibly believe you'll win."

"I can and do. Our victory in the field wasn't a fluke and yours was the second army many times our size that we defeated. As time goes on, we will be able to defeat even greater odds and I think things might not be as easy as your emperor believes it to be. As we continue to defy his attempts to conquer the world, others will see our example and will rise up against him. Your empire has been built on a foundation of subjugation. It is a house of cards, hollow on the inside. There are more people living as slaves than there are actual citizens of the Carthaginian empire. The day the people understand they outnumber their overlords, is the day the empire crumbles. Do I think we can defeat the entire might of the Carthaginian empire? Maybe. But I don't think we'll have to. Once we've taken out enough of its supports, the empire will collapse under its own weight."

"I see," Bomilcar said, looking away.

Ky left quietly, knowing that was what the general did when he didn't want to talk anymore. Ky was surprised he hadn't considered it. Did all of the Carthaginian leaders think their empire was on solid ground, unbeatable and invincible? How could they not see the danger at the heart of their own empire and its inherent weakness? It was one of the reasons Ky pushed for the ending of slavery in Rome. As the new Britannic Empire grew, it would be a rot that would have grown with it, setting his new people up to have the same vulnerabilities that the Carthaginians had.

Devnum

It was late in the day when Lucilla got back from the seventh legion's camp. She'd spent the past two days working with Velius and the other legates to coordinate transportation and logistics for getting the legions across the channel to Ériu and sending messages to their counterparts on the island for getting the legions landed and ready to fight.

It was clear this was going to take longer than she could have anticipated when pushing the Imperial Senate to move quickly. Velius seemed to take it in stride, which meant this was probably a common occurrence when moving large armies that the average person didn't see. Although she'd been involved in the training of the Caledonians over the winter while they prepared for the Carthaginian invasion, she hadn't been involved in the actual movement of troops, so she didn't have exposure to the logistics involved until now.

Thankfully, Velius and the other legates did have experience with it and seemed to think everything was going well, so she left the operations in their more experienced hands and returned to Devnum to the politics she did understand.

She was almost to her quarters in the rebuilt palace complex when one of her father's guards, who maintained watch on the entire palace complex and not just her father unlike her and Ky's guards, came towards her at a jog.

"Has something happened?" she asked, unable to keep the worried sound out of her voice.

It was hard not to have flashbacks to the insurrection, when her father's guards had barely gotten her into the main section of the palace before the revolting legionaries showed up in force with instructions to kill her, her father, and any officials they could find.

"No, my lady. Your father asked that we relay a message from Hortensius. He came looking for you earlier in the day, and asked that you come see him when you returned from the legions."

Lucilla gave a sigh. It wasn't really that late in the day and the sun had another two hours before it finished its journey across the sky, but she'd been going non-stop for days trying to make sure everything was in place for the legion's journey to help the Ulaid, including several long discussions with Ky that lasted well into the night.

While it was helpful to be able to talk to both him and Sophus, she could only do so when she was alone. Sometimes, she could clear a room to get space to hold discussions, but people would notice if this happened too often, so usually, that meant she had to wait until she was back in her quarters at night, with her guard safely on the other side of the door and out of earshot. Ky might have had some special ability to go for days at a time without sleep, but she was merely human and couldn't keep this pace up for long.

Still, her sleep would have to wait. Ky had entrusted her with overseeing the development of various inventions and she knew how critical they were to the war effort. Hortensius wasn't one to call for someone just so he could show off his latest success. If he asked for her, especially if he left a message with her father's guards for her to see him when she returned, then it was a safe bet that whatever he needed was urgent.

She made her way to the machinist's main factory, which also held a small room he used as his main office, her guards in tow. It spoke to the pace of the work happening across the Empire that the factory was still going full tilt. She knew Hortensius was running shifts throughout the night, but it was something else to see the factory still full of laborers, producing an impressive amount of noise.

She was also happy to see some of the projects were civilian in nature, including the new heavier plows made from the stronger steel Ky had already introduced, next to the military production. It was a sign of the security the people were starting to feel, now that they'd effectively kicked the Carthaginians off the island.

"My lady, I'm glad you came," Hortensius said, hurrying over from a huddle he'd been in with some of his foremen.

"It sounded urgent, so I thought it best I not keep you waiting."

"I wouldn't say it's urgent, but I wanted to get your take on the new works we set up outside of town for manufacturing this ... gun powder the Consul described," Hortensius said, pronouncing the alien words carefully.

She noted that the words weren't Latin and she had to admit it sounded strange to her ears as well.

"You moved the production out of town?"

"The Consul made it clear it was dangerous. I did a test with our first batch and I think, if anything, he undersold how volatile this substance is. I took a small batch out of the factory to test it, since he'd been so insistent that it was dangerous and it was amazing. I used a very small pile of the substance, although it was just the raw mixture; I didn't wet it down to make the cakes that he described later in his instructions. I still kept the candle far away from the powder, several hands span in fact, and whoosh, it went up instantly. I never touched the powder. If just the dust in the air from it that made it go up like that, we can't possibly have it near our other works or inside the city. It also means we can only work on it in the daylight with the windows of the building open for light. Any flame in the building is too much of a danger to our entire operation."

"But you were able to make it?"

"Yes, although the Consul was also right about how difficult the nitrates, as he called this new mineral, would be to procure. We've made an initial survey of the caves he identified for us, and they are going to be very hard to get into, let alone mine. However, he did point out where we could find another source until the nitrate beds we've already started building become ready, and it also presents a problem."

"How so?"

"Because the men are hesitant to do it. Have you ever dredged up the rotting straw and dirt under the floor of a stable? It's foul, as bad as anything I've seen working in the sewers. We were able to follow the instructions on how to treat the materials we dug up and my test showed it worked, but I'm going to have to pay the men more if we're going dig up every stable in the Empire."

"Are there enough stables? Will you be able to get enough to meet the production requirements?"

"No. If we can get the caves mined, then maybe, but only the short-term goals the Consul gave us. He also included where we can find some deposits near the outflow of the sewers, but I'm saving that as the absolute last resort, since I'm not sure I will be able to pay men enough to do that kind of work. I'm still not sure we'll get the amounts he mentioned we need to reach even after the nitrate beds start producing."

"The nitrate beds will produce a significantly larger quantity of usable potassium nitrate than they achieved digging up the floor beds of stables. The staggered staging of additional beds should reach the goals, although we included additional production overhead to counter potential shortfalls in the final conversion process."

"It should be enough," Lucilla said. "Ky worked out the numbers and is confident if you stick to the schedule he gave you, we'll be fine."

As they talked she and her guards followed him through the winding streets of Devnum, out through the city walls towards the river.

"Is it safe to have this out here? There are a lot of farms and most of the grain production using the new waterwheel designs are nearby."

"We put in a very large gap between the building and any of the other buildings, but we actually need the river to build the mills to grind the powder. We also need to keep it wetted down as we grind it, to reduce the dust, which means we need a large amount of water available, especially once production ramps up."

"We need to make sure people keep their distance, just in case."

"We've put up some signs, but if we start seeing people walking through the area, I'll put up more."

"Good," she said as he led her into the mill, where the work had stopped as the sun started going down.

It was well laid out and even with the men putting their supplies away, preparing to return to their homes, she could make out how the production flow would work. She had to hand it to Hortensius, he was one of the most organized men she'd ever seen.

She also couldn't miss the smell of bodily excretions coming from one end of the large building where he must have been processing the material they'd dug up from the stables. She'd at first thought the strips of cloth the men in the factory were wearing across their faces were meant to somehow protect them from the gun powder dust, but once the old urine smell started assaulting her nose, she was certain it was to keep them from passing out from the fumes. Her eyes were already starting to water, forcing her to cover her mouth and nose as best she could.

"It's pungent, I know. The worst parts of it we're processing outside of the building under a covering we erected, but that isn't sufficient for the later stages where we have to keep any rain from diluting the runoff before we can dry and separate the sludge. Once it gets to the sludge stage, we have to bring it inside so we can scrape off the nitrate layer."

"How do you stand it?"

"After a few hours, you kind of adjust. Not enough to breathe the air without a filter, but some. Another reason we need a good amount of water, in fact. The rags the men have over their faces help, but they work even better if they're wetted down, which means the men soak their face coverings every hour or so to keep them damp."

"It's awful."

"The contamination of fecal matter aggravates the process. The smell should dissipate once the process shifts to using product from the nitrate beds, instead of product dug up from under the stables."

Lucilla doubted it would help that much, since the urine smell was the thing she could pick out the most. The acrid stench felt like it was burning the insides of her nose.

"You shouldn't store the finished powder here," she said, gesturing at several barrels in one corner that she assumed held the finished product.

"We move the finished barrels to a warehouse in town. I know that defeats the point of moving the works out here, but we're building a warehouse even further out, away from anything that could be affected if it should go off, to store it in. We should be able to start moving product there next week."

"You're going to move all the gunpowder there?"

"Yes," he said, hesitant, hearing the tone in her voice that suggested it might not be a good idea.

"Correct me if I'm wrong, but if one of those barrels goes up, it will be enough to set off any other barrels stored in the same place, right?"

"Probably. That's why we're moving it so far out."

"Which is a good precaution, but if we run into a problem and that does happen, our entire gunpowder supply will be gone in an instant. You're already saying you don't think we'll hit the targets as it is, but we definitely won't hit them if we lose all of the gunpowder we have on hand at one time."

"That's a good point. I'll work out where to move everything so we never have that much in one place."

"While not putting other factories or citizens in danger, in case it goes up. There are a lot of wooden buildings in town, enough that fire is a serious danger. Remember the damage caused when the rebels burned down the warehouse holding the arcuballista?"

"I know. It will be complicated, storing it that far out, especially since I have to put a guard anywhere I store it. If you think the insurrectionists caused damage setting fire to a warehouse, imagine what they could do with a barrel of this."

"That's very true. I know this will be challenging, but I have faith you'll be able to get it done. How soon until we can test fire the cannon?"

Cannon was another word she'd never heard until recently. Ky might be purposefully reshaping Roman technology and society, but he was also inadvertently reshaping their language along with it. Already she and Hortensius were using these words regularly, to the point that it was starting to not even feel strange to say them. Once these items got into wide use, especially military items, the words would quickly become part of everyday language.

"Not for some time, I fear. It's not that different from making a bell, which we make on small scale for animals and ceremonies, but the cannon's shape requires increasing the size causing significant issues. More importantly, small cracks in a bell doesn't mean the bell can explode, killing everyone around it when it does. The pressures the Consul described mean any flaw can cause a massive failure. We built a mold, but our first test had so many pits and imperfections it was worthless and we melted it back down."

"Do you need any assistance?"

"I almost certainly will, but I haven't finished working out how to implement the notes we already have. I think I know where some of the problems are, and I have some ideas of how to work them out, but knowing how these things go, I will almost certainly not solve everything and will need help getting back in the right direction."

"I'm available if you need to ask me questions," she said, giving him a look.

She knew he understood that she meant either to pass messages along to Ky to get him the answer or, if they could find a private place to talk, holding a conversation directly with her acting as a translator of sorts.

"I will, of course, let you know. If you would, please convey to the Consul what you've seen of our works and let me know if he has any input on the situation. I know you've had a long day and you want to go get some sleep, so I appreciate you taking the time to take a look at the new shop layout, and especially your advice on how to store the powder. I can't believe the mistake I almost made by putting it all in one building."

"You have a lot to pay attention to Hortensius, and you are doing an amazing job, especially considering the sheer volume of new ideas you're being expected to absorb."

"Thank you, my lady," he said with a bow.

Chapter 9

Ériunia, Southern Ulaid

Llassar swayed on the back of his horse, watching the ragged army move down the hillside below and into an open plain to face their enemy, resisting the urge to smirk at the sudden change in his situation. A little over a week previous, he'd been in a dank dungeon, trying to ignore rats and water dripping from above, and now he was one of only a handful of men on horseback, riding with the army's commander and his 'officers.'

Calling this an army was a stretch, even by Caledonian standards. It was a ragtag force of seasoned warriors, farmers, and anyone else Conchobar's guard could round up and force into the depleted ranks. The fact that he'd been given a horse as a sign of respect, and to make up for throwing him into a dungeon, was sign enough of how badly they were faring. Horses had, apparently, become a precious military resource after several devastating losses, including their largest horse breeders and grazing lands.

"Now you will see our men in action," Guaire, an Ulaid general who also happened to be one of Conchobar's lesser cousins, said.

Llassar doubted it, seeing the contrast between those men and the Carthaginians. Dozens of Carthaginian phalanxes, packed in tight squares, their spears bristling in the sunlight, flanked by a similar ragtag group of warriors as those being fielded by the Ulaid were waiting. The Ulaid might have been able to show something if they were only facing off against the warriors from Connacht or Ivernis, although even that would have been a stretch now that the loss of so many of their actual warriors had forced them to conscript people who'd barely even held a sword before.

Against a trained Carthaginian army equipped with steel-tipped swords, hardened leather armor, and metal breastplates, they stood no chance at all. It wouldn't have done to actually point that out, however, so Llassar only nodded in acknowledgment.

Llassar could appreciate the simplicity of Guaire's plan, sending his army headfirst into the opposition. His people had fought more or less the same way since his ancestors' time and until he watched Ky and his legates use maneuver and position to defeat huge armies with a fraction of their force, he'd never seen anything wrong with that plan.

Unfortunately, the Ulaid couldn't seem to hold to even this simple plan. As they aligned against the Carthaginians, Llassar had expected them to slowly move forward, reserving their strength until the last moment, and then charging as a single group to increase the impact.

Instead, as soon as they hit the plain, the Ulaid began their charge, every man running full out, the faster ones quickly outpacing the slower ones. Llassar just shook his head. It was foolish. They had a long open expanse of ground to cross and the Ulaid would be exhausted by the time they got there. Their leaders, what few followed the army down onto the plains, didn't seem to do anything to try and stop them.

The Carthaginians weren't even moving, although they lowered their spears into position, ready to attack. Even the Carthaginian's allies held their ground, which Llassar knew would be hard on them, since warriors like that would have their blood up and it wouldn't take much to get them to countercharge.

The Carthaginian allies finally launched their attacks a few minutes later when the Ulaid got close enough. The Carthaginians continued to hold their ground, probably happy to let their allies waste their men on this battle rather than losing men of their own. To their credit, even exhausted, the men who made it across the field first held their own against the Carthaginian allies, at least for a moment, with as many of them going down as the Ulaid's own men.

Numbers told the story, however. There were too many of the Carthaginian allies and not enough of the Ulaid, half of who turned to run as things started to turn against them. The assault quickly turned into an all-out rout, with the enemy hot on the Ulaid's heels. The Carthaginian forces hadn't even had to move. They just stood there and let their allies mop up the last of the opposing forces.

Everything in Llassar's being told him to ride down and show these people what a real warrior could do, but he hadn't gotten this far by being foolish. Guaire and the few other Ulaid still on the hilltop turned and began galloping away, leaving the men to their fate. It was a pathetic display and one he thought Conchobar would be ashamed to hear about, but there wasn't anything Llassar could do to help that wouldn't lead to his death. The only way he was going to help was to be there to coordinate between his people and the Ulaid when the Britannic legions arrived.

It was with no small measure of shame that Llassar turned his horse and followed after the fleeing Ulaid leaders.

Outside Londinium

Another large boulder crashed into the wall, about a third of the way up, and remained there, impacted into the wood and brick structure, but not able to push past the earth berm that had been pushed up the other side.

"The men's aim is getting better," Ky said as an aside to Ursinus, who stood behind him on a small rise, watching the two trebuchets on this section of the line pull their ballasts back so the men could load another projectile.

"I'd hope so. They've been firing away every day for weeks now, not that it's done us any good. Jupiter knows, we've probably made it stronger with all the boulders we've left embedded in the walls," he said, gesturing at the boulder that the machines had just left behind.

"It won't matter in the long run. The logged rounds won't affect the men trying to go over the wall."

"I don't understand why we don't fire over the walls. We have the range, and even with all the practice the men are getting, a lot of shots miss the city and end up in the dirt. We'd at least kill a few of their soldiers and maybe actually cause some damage. I know we're trying to avoid causing collateral damage, but we're taking a city. We have to accept some collateral damage. When we storm the wall, there's going to be damage anyway."

"We have to rule these people once we kick out the Carthaginians, so collateral damage does matter, but that isn't why I don't want the men to fire over the wall. We're never going to cause enough damage with this little artillery to help us get over the wall, so where we fire doesn't actually matter all that much. Destroying large swaths of the city in exchange for killing a handful of soldiers doesn't gain us enough to make it worthwhile, especially when you remember our actual goal is to amass men inside the city. If we create a lot of rubble and destruction behind the wall, it will slow our men inside the wall when they begin their assault, which will make it easier for the Carthaginians to bottle them up well short of the wall, which would make them completely ineffective."

"Then why even bother with continuing to fire at the walls day and night?"

"Because if we are just sitting here, not doing anything, they'll start to wonder what we are doing. They know we want to get into the city, and even their commander, as inexperienced or incompetent as he seems to be, would wonder if we are up to something. We need to keep their attention fixed on us, so they don't start looking for our real plan. A better commander would know that what we're doing is pointless and we'd be forced to send in regular assaults on the wall, getting men killed, to keep him focused. I'm hoping we'll be able to get away with just these trebuchet shots and won't have to waste men's lives on a diversion."

"And you can tell that we're doing enough?" Ursinus asked.

It wasn't accusatory or doubtful, but asked in earnest. Ursinus had been one of the first people in this timeline to fight alongside

Ky, and he'd had a curiosity ever since to understand some of the things Ky was able to do.

"I can. My little bird allows me to see the men on the other side of the wall. No troops have moved off their side of the wall and there is no troop or guard movement through the city, which there would be if they were hunting for something. They've actually been concentrating their forces on the sections of the wall we've been hitting with the trebuchets, which suggests they are taking the bait."

When speaking in Latin, instead of talking to Sophus in his native language, he sometimes had to find exchange words, because the concepts were so foreign. Sometimes, if it was something the Romans would have to interact with regularly, like gunpowder, it was easier to introduce the word into their vocabulary. But the Romans wouldn't reach the point of independently operated drones in even his extended lifespan, so it wasn't worth the effort to explain what a drone was. It was easier to find something comparable and just go with it. All Ursinus needed to know was he was able to look down on the city from above, and Ursinus had witnessed him doing that before and got the gist.

"I guess you know what you're doing," Ursinus said.

"I hope so," Ky responded.

Londinium Docks

Carus stepped off the boat and onto the dock and wondered that this crumbling place, with piles of trash and refuse in the street and buildings crumbling from lack of maintenance, was the city his people had been trying to retake his entire life.

A guardsman walked past the end of the dock, and Carus had to avoid turning his head or acting suspiciously. Dressed in rough, and extremely itchy, tunics like that worn by common Carthaginian laborers, they looked just like any of the other people unloading boats or otherwise working on getting what little food they could into the city. Carus couldn't help but notice the group of guards around a wagon onto which a pretty significant amount of the food was being loaded. If he had to guess, the food, which was enough to feed a dozen families for a week, was all heading to the governor and his cronies. It was typical of what he'd heard about the man, who had little regard for human life, regardless if they were citizens supposedly under his protection or not.

Since there was nothing he could do about it, Carus turned his back on the scene and headed towards the warehouse the shipmaster had indicated as they pulled up to the dock, leading the other nine men with him. Each carried an empty box to look like they had a purpose, since the shipmaster couldn't afford to give away food, even to help them.

The inside of the building was totally packed with Roman soldiers, all wearing the same tunic he was wearing, their armor being kept in crates along the walls of the warehouse until it was time for the fighting to begin. Ramirus had thought that if guards did stumble into the warehouse, they might be able to bluff their way out, saying the soldiers were refugees or some such, hopefully preserving the plan.

The men were doing a good job of being calm, holding hushed conversations, and generally keeping quiet. So much so that, if Carus hadn't known the warehouse was full of soldiers ahead of time, he wouldn't have known at all. Of course, that was easier during the day, when laborers were unloading ships and offloading into the warehouses. It was harder at night, when the city settled down to sleep, but the combination of the sound of water rushing by in the river and the occasional boom from the direction of the city wall when another boulder smashed into it, helped to hide any noise, as long as it didn't get out of hand.

Carus was doubly impressed since he knew soldiers. They were, by and large, not a particularly subtle or quiet bunch, and some of the men had been crammed in here for weeks, with nothing to do and less and less room to stretch their legs as the warehouse filled up.

Carus was a little concerned by the lack of space. Soldiers crammed into such a small place couldn't move around much, which meant they wouldn't be at their best when it came time to get down to the business at hand. He'd turned around to head back out of the warehouse and find Ramirus's contact, and almost ran into the man who was coming inside.

"This building is getting very full," Carus said.

"I know, but I wanted to get as many of your people here as we could at first. I have two more warehouses we can use, but both are smaller and further into the city, which means there's less background noise at night to hide the sounds of the men."

"That makes sense, but the men need a little room to move around, or they're going to be useless on the final attack. We need to shift some of these men to the smaller warehouses. If we send a third of the men in here and split them between the two warehouses you have, leaving enough room there for the men to have a little room to move about, will we have enough space for the rest of the men coming behind me?"

"No, but I should be able to get at least one more warehouse that its owner has been trying to sell me. I've been putting it off because it's not as well located to either the city or the docks and because I don't have the money on hand to buy it."

"Speaking of money, Ramirus sent this for you," Carus said, pulling a small bag that had been tied around his arm and under his tunic and handing it over.

The shipmaster opened the drawstring and shook it, letting the gold pieces clink against each other.

"If I spend this on more warehouses for your men, my reward for helping you will be all gone."

"Talk to Ramirus, he'll make sure you're well taken care of."

The man looked skeptical, but said, "I will."

"I saw the guardsman out there. Have any of them poked around the warehouse or asked about the men you've been bringing in?"

"No. The only thing they seem to care about is getting the governor's cut of every shipment and taking whatever graft they have from businesses that are still operating. They were always greedy, but the worse things have gotten, the larger their greed has become."

"Are they pressuring you?"

"Yes, and because I'm bringing in your men, my boats seem to have larger crews than they actually do, which makes them think I am more prosperous than I am. They are taking almost half of my shipments every day, thinking they're only taking a third."

He wasn't asking for a handout again straight out, but Carus could read between the lines. He'd known men like the shipmaster and had no doubt that if the man thought he could make more money by selling the Romans off to the Carthaginians, he'd do it in a moment and still take Ramirus's money beforehand. The only thing keeping him from doing it now was the certainty that the Carthaginians, at least here in Londinium, were doomed.

Since he couldn't actually tell the man what he thought, Carus only said, "Talk to Ramirus. If we pull this off, he'll make sure you're very well taken care of."

Devnum

"... then we will be forced to tax every Roman business that operates on Caledonian land that sends its money back to owners in the south instead of investing in the areas they profit from."

Lucilla had to mentally push back the yawn that threatened to escape. She knew this was important, but the bickering over taxation rights had been going on for the better part of an hour and this was the third time she'd heard this exact point. Worse, she was mostly just a spectator today. Although her father had asked her to handle the vote on troop deployment to Ériu, that had been a tactical move because of her relationship with the Caledonians, which he thought would give her leverage in the discussion.

That same relationship caused problems when it came to disputes between the Caledonians and the Romans. Even though she was a Roman citizen, several of the senators had already accused her of favoritism toward the northerners when trying to mediate disputes between them in the Imperial Senate. True, she had a fondness for them, but still considered herself a Roman at heart. She always tried to be meticulously fair when it came to the dealings between them, but that was a hard thing to prove, which is why her father had decided to keep handling the senate sessions personally.

His reasoning made sense, but it also meant she had a passive role in these debates, which took away most of their interest. She realized she'd let her mind wander again and had missed everything that her father had said in reply as Taenaris, the nominal leader of the Romans in the Imperial Senate, who'd switched places with the Caledonian who'd been speaking in the center of the forum.

"If our northern countrymen can hold to that, then we accept those terms."

"Are you questioning our word?" Bredei, the Caledonian who'd been yelling earlier, said angrily.

"Of course not, but your people are still getting used to following the decisions made by their representatives, or are you forgetting the incident at Trefaldwyn?"

Bredei mumbled something but sat back down as Taenaris had scored a point. Lucilla loved the northerners and found their blunt to-the-point nature to be refreshing, but she had to admit a lot of them still struggled with the idea of republican democracy. For the bulk of their history, the Caledonians had been used to a more direct form of rule. Talogren's Caledonian League had been novel when he'd first put it together, which is how he'd made the northerners a true threat to the Southern Romans for the first time since the two cultures had clashed.

For the bulk of their history, every northerner had seen themselves as only a member of whatever tribe or village they'd grown up in, and saw everyone else, even neighboring tribes or villages as foreigners. The idea of someone far away having the right to bargain and negotiate for their rights and responsibilities had never even crossed their minds. They believed in a direct form of democracy that allowed everyone not only a voice in every decision, but the expediency of being able to kill or exile a leader they felt no longer made the right choices for them.

While that had a simplicity to it, it had also limited the Caledonians from ever having the power to protect their homes and families from larger, more organized, groups. Which was how Talogren had been able to gain power in the first place. Now, many of those villages, particularly more remote ones that had less frequent contact with either the central villages of the Caledonian League or their new Roman countrymen, were having trouble adapting.

There'd been several instances of entire villages trying to break away or simply ignoring rules they didn't feel like they had to follow, so she understood Taenaris's point, although he could have been more diplomatic in the way he made it.

"I have confidence they will do everything in their power to ensure all sides hold to the compromise. Now, I believe you had some new business you wanted to discuss," her father said, moving things along.

"Yes. I wanted to address the increase in immigration that's started happening. While we've always had a trickle of people from the mainland make their way here, it had mostly been traders and the like. Over the last month or so, that trickle has become a flood of people from Iberia, Germania, and Scandia. The Roman Senate has requested that, since this is one of the areas the Empire has authority over, we do something about it. The coastal cities are already starting to feel the strain of these additional people on public works and it could become a serious problem if left unchecked."

Lucilla noticed the Caledonian senators nodding in agreement, which was an indication of just how big this influx of immigration must be to have them agreeing to anything Taenaris might say.

"This is a good thing, isn't it? Haven't we been discussing the problem of not enough men for the legions and not enough workers for the factories and farms?" Lucilla asked.

"We have, but these aren't men in their prime, they're families left to fend for themselves after their men were drafted into the Carthaginian legions. It's old men, women, and children. They've heard that Britannia is a safe haven from the Carthaginians and came here with only the clothes on their backs, and not much else. They are having trouble making it out of the villages where the captains who take the last of their valuables in exchange for passage dump them. Some of the families find work, but these are mostly small fishing villages that aren't able to support so many refugees."

"Even the Scandi?" Lucilla asked.

The Scandi were the people on the other side of the narrow sea north of Germania. While not many Romans had seen Scandia, they'd been in regular contact with the Scandi people who made up a lot of the traders they dealt with. Since they'd never been conquered by the Carthaginians, they were the most direct source of trade for the free peoples still living on Britannia and a conduit to markets further east.

"No. The Scandi immigrants are mostly traders and a few craftsmen that have moved their families here, hoping to take advantage of all the money the Empire is spending and to have faster access to some of the new goods that have been released commercially. Hortensius said the factory owners that are focusing on civilian goods are starting to see a lot of demand, enough that it might make sense for factories working on government contracts to switch over when they finish up with their current contracts. That will bring problems of its own, but Hortensius was planning on bringing that to your attention separately."

"I'm still not sure I see the problem. One of the reasons we made room for civilian manufacturing was because of the money it would bring from outside of the Empire and the new tax revenues that it would create, since most of the sales are of things covered by the patent tax the Consul created. The army is still short on supplies across the board, especially when considering the material being taken by the legions to the Ulaid."

Patent was another new word Ky had introduced that, at least in the halls of government, had become so common that none of the senators seemed to even notice and she barely thought about it before saying it.

"We did, and when it was just an influx of traders, that was fine. The families coming here and settling with them, and the refugees from Germania, are a different matter."

"What do you want us to do? We've had immigrants in the Empire for as long as we've been in Britannia, and that doesn't even count the large non-citizen base of slaves that existed during that time. Before coming to Britannia there were more non-citizens than citizens in Rome. Why, now that we're an Empire made up of multiple cultures, is a non-citizen base a problem?"

"When we were in Italy, it was easy to distinguish between citizens and non-citizens, even citizens and slaves. That isn't true now. I am not saying this to insult our Caledonian brothers," Taenaris said with a nod to the group of senators, who started to shift at the hint of insult. "But it is harder to distinguish who is and who is not a Britannic citizen. While you haven't brought it before us yet, I know you have offered the Ulaid a choice to join the Empire as an equal member, which would make it even harder. Much of the work we need done is in critical industries and these people are largely coming out of Carthaginian-held areas. We are opening ourselves up to saboteurs and spies, both of which could take from us the advantages that have allowed us to survive so far."

"Do you want to keep them from coming here? Are you asking for the Praetorians to patrol the shores, rounding up refugees and putting them back on boats for the continent?" her father asked, speaking up for the first time since the subject changed.

She hadn't meant to take over, but her father spent all of his time with senators and government officials, and didn't walk among the average people. Neither did the senators, even the Caledonian ones, who were just as classist as their Roman counterparts. One of the benefits of spending so much time with Hortensius in the factories and among the legions was it let her see the lives of the workers they were discussing in a way that the men in the room didn't.

"That would be a mistake," she said, heatedly. "We need people to work in the fields, feeding all of our armies on the march. We need craftsmen and unskilled laborers working on the dozens of public projects, and in the factories and mills creating both military supplies and civilian goods for sale both here and abroad, to bring in the money to pay for this war. Across every part of the Empire, both in Caledonia and in Rome, the thing we need the most is bodies, and this is the answer for that."

"No. We aren't blind to the needs of the Empire. We just want to ensure that the people coming and working in these critical industries, or joining the legions, have a stake in the Empire."

Her father put his hand on her arm, stopping her reply, and asked, "What are you proposing?"

"We aren't going to kick any of these people out. We know as well as anyone what it's like to live under the thumb of the Carthaginians and would never send anyone back to live that oppression. However, these refugees and transplants will put additional pressure on the Empire, which we are obligated to address. Under the power granted to the Imperial Senate over citizens and the Empire as a whole, and its goal to facilitate the movement of those citizens across the member states, we plan on passing a law placing a tax on all non-citizens. The same law will introduce a path to citizenship for them, either by a member of that family serving in the military or holding a government position, through work in a critical industry and with the backing of their employer, or by a fee paid to the government. Once they become citizens, they will no longer have to pay the tax and will have all the rights and privileges of any other Britannic citizen. We believe this is a good compromise, as it provides us with extra manpower and protects the Empire."

"What do the rest of the senators think of this?" Lucilla asked.

"We are all in agreement, my lady," Bredei said from the benches.

"That seems fair," her father said. "Please have the law drawn up and we will review it at the next session."

Lucilla was fuming but sat quietly as her father and the senators finished up the rest of the day's business. Finally, she and her father left, heading back toward the palace.

"Why did you give in to them?" she asked as soon as they were away from the senators. "Some of the people thinking about coming here will think twice when they know about this foreigner tax and what it will take to become a citizen. This is a mistake."

"I don't think it will chase off as many as you feel it might, but even if it does, we had little choice. This is what it means to be Emperor. The average person may think the Emperor can do whatever he likes and answers to no one, but you can't be that naive. You're going to be doing this one day, and you have to realize that a governing body like the senate is the only way to make our Empire work. Being Emperor is as much about knowing how and when to compromise as deciding what is best for the Empire. Today was a time for compromise."

Lucilla didn't answer right away. Her instinct was to disagree and argue with him, but she'd learned that when her father gave these lectures, it was best to think on it rather than relying on her first instinct. She might decide in the end that she was right, but she didn't want to make the mistake of ignoring his advice out of hand. That had been one of the first lessons her father had taught her, and it had served her well.

Chapter 10

Outside Londinium

"Consul," the guard said, in a loud whisper from outside the slightly opened tent flap.

Ky had told them they didn't need to do that, but this early in the morning, it was probably hard for them to conform. Most of the men they would guard would be asleep at this time, and even the calmest of commanders could be difficult to deal with when waking them up from a deep sleep.

Ky's guards knew he didn't normally sleep, not in the conventional sense, but they still acted like they were bothering him. He was sitting in the center of the tent, allowing most of his body to shut down into a near sleep-like state while he discussed the problems Lucilla had come across in the design of canons with Sophus. He was putting it off, but he was going to have to make a trip to Devnum soon, if only to quiet the AI and its increasing agitation over not being able to see the problems with the forging itself.

Ky opened his eyes and gave the guard a wave that he could let whoever was outside in, as the rest of his body began waking up.

"I'm sorry for waking you, Consul," Ramirus said, ducking through the flaps.

"I wasn't asleep," Ky said, certain that Ramirus knew as much of his sleeping habits as his guards.

"I just received the latest package from my contacts inside the city from Marius, the ship captain, and it has some information I thought you'd want to see."

"Has he had any more information about the men he's taken inside the city?"

Ky had been watching the docks as much as he could, accounting for the need to check the walls for unusual movement and occasionally charging the drone, but a camera feed from above didn't tell him everything he needed to know.

"They've started putting men in a second warehouse. He said they haven't been noticed by the guards, who've had their own problems to worry about. Everything is on track."

"I see," Ky said, not buying how calm Ramirus was about the dangerous position they'd put those men in. "What news did he bring?"

Ky had always been more of a soldier, used to facing his enemies head-on, so maybe he was just less accustomed to these kinds of covert actions, the unknown being more comfortable for him.

"One of my people in the governor's residence got a look at the last messages he received from their base in Hibernia. It included an update of reinforcement coming from Carthage."

"Are they going to be here early enough to upset our plans?"

"No. The message was to inform the governor of a delay in the reinforcements and instructing him to take whatever precautions he needed to take in order to hold the walls until they got there."

"I'm sure he took that well."

"Probably. He's temperamental, so it's not hard to imagine his reaction to being told to do the impossible."

"That's good news though," Ky said.

For Ramirus to show up this early, Ky had been expecting bad news, not a notification that they had more time to take the city than he'd originally planned.

"The delay is good news, but the reason for it isn't. It seems the emperor has decided we are a problem after all. Instead of shipping in border soldiers from the continent, most of whom would be conscripts, based on the numbers of captured soldiers from the last two armies that have asked for amnesty, they've pulled several of their veteran phalanxes from Persia and are bringing them west. We're not going to be facing men who will panic when they get surrounded. These are the men who crushed the Parthians and tracked down most of the Berber tribes that had gone deep into the desert. They're going to be backed up by line troops out of Africa and Sardinia. At least a hundred thousand of them, according to the message my source saw. They're planning on sailing them right into the city, but from the way it was written, if my source's description is accurate, they're prepared for a land invasion, if it comes to it."

Ky frowned. Part of what had allowed him to win the last several engagements was a reliance on the inflexibility of the Carthaginian phalanxes. While that was true of the fighting form as a whole, Ramirus's intelligence reports had painted a different picture of the units fighting out in Persia. They'd had to adapt their tactics to deal with the eastern horse archers, and they'd done it successfully.

Bomilcar was a good general, but he'd been handed substandard tools to work with. The ambush Ky had set up for them had been a difficult situation to overcome, but the lines holding the Carthaginian army in had been thin, out of necessity. Where Bomilcar's soldiers broke once the general and his command group went down, a veteran army would have pushed on. Had they kept at it, there was every chance they would have broken through his lines, which would have led to a very different outcome.

Against a veteran army, it would come down to simple numbers, and even if they added the Ulaid into their ranks and got men transferred back in time, which was doubtful considering what they were probably facing in Ireland, the Britannians would still be mightily outnumbered. It also meant they couldn't allow Londinium to still be in Carthaginian hands when they arrived. A large, veteran army with a solid base of supply from which to operate, would be impossible to defeat.

Eventually, they'd have to face that kind of army, but Ky was putting that off until he managed to get enough firearms into Britannian hands to properly counter the numerical disadvantage.

"Alright," Ky said. "At least we know what's coming."

"I heard a rumor that you've been working on a design for a new ship. Is there any chance those can be finished and ready by the time the Carthaginian fleet gets here?"

Ky suppressed a frown. He trusted Ramirus completely, but he hadn't discussed the ships with anyone yet. The only way Ramirus could know what Ky was working on was if one of Ky's lictore had told him, and that was a problem. Ky had become lax around his guards, although he was pretty sure he hadn't let them over-hear his discussions with Lucilla about Sophus. There were some things even his closest allies weren't ready to hear about, yet. If he couldn't trust his guards, he'd have to be more careful about keeping things close to his chest, or at least being away from anyone who might be able to see what he was working on.

"I saw the edge of a scroll the last time we met," Ramirus said, clearly reading Ky's face. "I just saw a few words, but it mentioned ship designs. Considering what you've got Hortensius working on now, it isn't a hard leap."

"I see," Ky said, at least happy to hear his men hadn't talked behind his back. "No. I won't have the new plans for Hortensius for another month at least, and we need to find people with the practical skills to work on the project with him. Hortensius is a smart man, and he has a lot of experience with all kinds of manufacturing, but building a ship is completely different from running a foundry. We'll also have to find crews capable of han-dling the new ships. Neither Romans nor Caledonians have much experience sailing beyond simple fishermen or merchants who make the short hop to the continent. Nearly all of our trade further out is done by foreign ships with crews from somewhere else, so we don't have a lot of experience to draw on. So no, we won't be able to meet their fleet with one of our own. One day maybe ... but not in this timeline."

"Then we're in trouble."

"Maybe," Ky said, thinking. "Maybe."

Londinium Docks

Carus made his way towards the docks through the throng of people trying to buy what food they could before curfew. The men were now spread across three warehouses, and it was becoming a problem. A guard had been poking around the third warehouse, looking in through the windows, and had seen his men inside. Luckily Carus had been on hand and made sure no one would ever find that guard again, at least not before the city fell, but this was just the beginning.

Men, mostly guardsmen, were starting to disappear on boats that went out fishing and never returned, probably making their way to Hibernia or the continent. They could see the writing on the wall and had the money to buy, or the ability to threaten their way to, a secret passage out before the city fell. The governor had decreed that all loyal subjects should stay and help defend the city, but loyalty was in short supply in a city under threat.

A lot of these men had decided that, if they were going to be forced to flee, they were going to take enough with them to set themselves up when they got wherever they were headed. The city guard wasn't a position that tended to pay well beyond the obvious benefits of having a little bit of power in a society where those at the bottom had none, making it an easy decision to use that power to take what they needed.

Crime in the city, and theft specifically, was at an all-time high, which was why there was a curfew in place. The problem was big enough that Carus, who went out of his way to never talk to anyone, had heard about it.

In general, he didn't care that much about the problem, since most of the Romans had been pushed out of the city years ago to make room for Carthaginian transplants, but it was becoming a problem for his mission. All of the homes owned by people without connections to someone able to do something to stop it had been ransacked, which left businesses the next target of opportunity.

Warehouses were starting to be emptied by guards whenever they got a chance, which is how the unfortunate guard ended up stumbling into a warehouse of armed soldiers. He'd been looking for something to steal and got significantly more than he bargained for.

They'd been lucky so far, but their luck wasn't going to hold out, and it would take just one guard getting away, or a few more disappearing, before they'd be discovered. Which is why he was out looking for Marius. Ky had the men watching as well as they could, but only he and one optio spoke Phoenician, and the optio would never pass for a local. There were few enough Romans in town that if forced to speak to a local, they'd instantly draw attention to themselves. Since the men were spread over three warehouses, there was no way Carus could keep watch on all of them even if he tried.

Carus was hoping that Marius would have one or two men who could keep watch and alert them if anyone was snooping. The original plan had been for all of the Romans, including Carus, to stay out of sight and only move about in the dark if they had to, but the curfew messed up that plan which is why Carus found himself at the docks in broad daylight trying his hardest to not attract any attention to himself.

Walking with his head down to try and avoid drawing anyone's attention is how he almost ran into Caesius.

"Watch where you're going, idiot," the would-be emperor said, pushing hard against Carus's shoulder.

Carus looked up in surprise, making direct eye contact with him. Carus had met him multiple times in his position as one of the Consul's guards, and once before that during a review of the troops. Thankfully, Caesius rarely paid attention to people he thought were beneath him and he seemed to take Carus's look of surprise as a result of being pushed, and not recognized.

The moment passed and Caesius walked on, towards one of the larger boats moored at the docks, paying no more attention to the altercation. Carus's hand drifted to a hidden knife under his tunic, his first thought to get rid of the traitor once and for all. It hadn't gone unnoticed that Caesius had no guards with him, making the man vulnerable. The moment passed and Carus pulled his hand back. There might not be any guards with him, but there would be enough witnesses that the killing wouldn't go unnoticed and would draw undue attention to their operation.

Carus watched the man board the boat with barely a nod to the fidgety-looking captain and disappear below decks before putting the episode behind him and focusing on his original goal.

Marius was at his ship, as expected, doing some kind of repair before his nightly run, and was rightfully surprised to see Carus in daylight.

"Has something happened?" the captain asked.

"Yes. A guard stumbled across one of the warehouses. We were able to take care of him, but only because I was outside the building when it happened. We probably won't be that lucky next time. We need to figure something out before it happens again."

"Ohh," he said.

It wasn't the reaction Carus hoped for, but one he expected. The captain knew his job, but this was well outside of his experience. He was doing this for money and a chance to survive when the city fell. It had been a decent plan, but the warehouses had always been the weak point in the plan, and he didn't seem to have an idea of what to do next.

"We need to get the men consolidated in one warehouse."

"There's too many to put in one warehouse," the man said, unhelpfully.

"Yes, I know that, but it still needs to be done. Think. Is there some way we can get the men out of these various warehouses, hopefully before this whole plan falls apart completely?"

"Well," the captain said after looking off towards the water, thinking. "They brought in a lot of refugees before the city gates closed for good. Mostly Romans whose families worked with the Carthaginians and didn't think your people would treat them kindly when they liberated the ground. They've been held in the western part of the city, but two days ago the governor started registering them so they can be put to work doing public projects or repairing the walls. Notably, he isn't housing or feeding them, so if they're not on a work detail no one pays much attention to them, as long as they show up for work."

"How does this help us? We need to keep the men together for when the time to assault the walls comes. Having them spread out across the city helping build the defenses will make it impossible to pull off the assault, and it still doesn't help us with the men still inside the warehouse being discovered."

"The way they're tracking who's been registered to work is by handing out clay marks with the governor's seal, so these people can pass through the city to their assigned work sites. I have a friend whose working on enrolling refugees for the work details. He can get some of your men these marks without putting them on the official rolls, so they won't actually be assigned duties, but if they're wandering around outside, it will give a reason for it. A lot of these people are country people who speak only Latin, so it would give them a reason for not speaking the language if they're stopped by any guards. It doesn't keep the guards from trying to look into the warehouses, but it will allow more of your men outside to keep an eye on the place and possibly deal with any guards that might stumble onto them."

"It will have to do," Carus said.

It wasn't the solution he was looking for, since enough disappearing guards would still be a problem, but it helped. They didn't have much longer to wait, and it wasn't like Marius had a hideout somewhere else, away from the guards, to stash hundreds of men.

Carus just hoped it would be enough.

Emain Macha

Llassar had been back from the battle for just over a day, but the remains of the army continued to stagger in. Conchobar had been furious over the loss and had words with his cousin, barely stopping himself from having the man arrested for treason against the kingdom for his waste of the dwindling number of soldiers the Ulaid had left.

Llassar stayed quiet throughout, but he had to wonder why the king was so surprised by the loss, considering their original army had been routed and it had been made up of seasoned warriors and not farmers and conscripts like the latest one. The moment Llassar had seen it, he'd been certain he knew what the outcome would be, although he'd still been obliged to go south with it, since it wouldn't do to tell a future ally their army was pathetic and not worth following.

What surprised him wasn't the outcome of the battle, but the fact that the Carthaginians and their local proxies hadn't followed up on their victory by marching directly on Emain Macha. The kingdom was already in a precarious state and the former king's son was still in Connacht under the protection of Queen Medb. From the outlay of forces in the battle, it seemed like she was the leader of the two kingdoms that had allied with the Carthaginians, which meant she should have been able to take their army north and put Fergus on the throne. That would have, more or less, given the Carthaginians the entire island. In the hands of proxies, but that's how they governed most of their conquered lands, so it would have suited them just fine.

Instead, they'd gobbled up some villages, and then stopped short of the capital. The Ulaid didn't seem to have a version of Ramirus and his army of informants spread into every corner of the world, so they had no information on what was happening south of the areas their scouts could get to. Llassar didn't hold that against them, since until joining with the Romans and finding out just how valuable information like that could be, he'd never really heard of that kind of thing. The closest his people had ever come was one of their people having a cousin or acquaintance in a village they were fighting, who'd occasionally get them information if they could. Since joining the Romans, he'd found the information they always seemed to have on their enemies invaluable and mourned the loss of it now.

If he had to guess, it might have been logistical in nature. From what Ramirus had been able to tell him before he left Britannia, the Carthaginian's foothold on this island was fairly small, with their main focus still being the pacification of Britannia. The local kingdoms, especially the southern ones, were poor and they'd already been struggling to keep themselves fed the past several years, which is why the better organized Ulaid had been able to stake their claim as the most powerful kingdom in Ériunia. That meant that the Carthaginians on Britannia, who had all of the lands south of the Romans under direct control rather than being held by a proxy, had been supplying the armies sent to conquer Ériunia. With that support suddenly gone, and worse, their having to help supply Londinium, keeping their army fed might be a problem.

If he had to guess, they'd probably have to start relying on the people they'd conquered in Germania to feed their men, which meant the food had to travel further. The Carthaginians, like the Romans, were terrible sailors using oared boats that even his people's fishing boats could often outmaneuver, so longer shipping time could create serious issues in delivering food, which would then have to be marched halfway across the island to get to their army.

That was all a guess, of course, since all he knew was what the Ulaid scouts had been able to report to Conchobar, which was that the Carthaginians only advanced a mile or so, mopping up most of the injured Ulaid from the brief battle, before stopping. They'd ransacked a few villages nearby, but otherwise were waiting in the same spot, not moving.

While that was confusing, it wasn't what brought Llassar onto the steps of the meeting hall that served as the king's palace. A rider had come in early that morning, reporting that the Britannic forces had begun landing and the first group of them, mostly cavalry, would be riding in shortly behind him. Conchobar had his men put together a hurried welcome, with what guard he had in the city lined along the main road from the gate at the city walls to the great hall, where Conchobar, his wife, major advisors, and Llassar stood waiting to greet them. The Roman legate was getting a significantly better welcome than Llassar had, but then Conchobar hadn't realized the lifeline he'd represented when Llassar had first shown up.

The legate hadn't taken much time to get there. The last of Conchobar's advisors had barely shown up in his spot when the city gates opened and Velius, along with several dozen other armored men on horseback, came riding through the front gates. In spite of his bias towards Caledonian warriors, he had to admit the Romans made an impressive sight. Although, to be fair, they weren't all Roman. One of the men, wearing standard legionary armor, meaning he'd actually joined the legions as opposed to fighting alongside them, was a warrior Llassar had known for years. There were a couple of others that had the look and bearing of Caledonians, although they too were wearing legionary armor, making it hard to tell. What he didn't see was any of the Caledonians dressed in their normal attire, which must have meant Ky had only sent Roman legions and none of the Caledonian forces from Britannia.

Part of him wished the Consul had made a different decision, since the Ulaid fought more like Caledonian warriors than Roman legionaries, but he didn't know all of the factors that would have gone into making that decision. Other than a brief message informing him that the Imperial Senate had agreed to send help, he hadn't been able to ask any more questions or find out what was happening back in Britannia. Having watched Ky and Lucilla, who had advised him, operate, he trusted them to make the best decision they could.

"Greetings, great king Conchobar," Velius said when he pulled the reins to stop in front of the steps.

It wasn't quite the normal greetings someone from Ériu would be given, but the king didn't call it out. It wasn't that far off either, and Llassar wondered who'd advised Velius on how to address his new hosts. He'd found the legate to be a decent man the few times the two had spoken, but he was a typical warrior and not one given to flowery language or diplomacy.

"I am Amulius Tettius Velius, legate of the Seventh legion and commander of the relief army sent by my Emperor, Titus Flavius Germanicus, to assist your warriors in throwing the Carthaginians off your island."

He was definitely coached, Llassar thought as he translated this to the King.

"Welcome, Amulius Tettius Velius. My men will see to your soldiers. Please come inside, so we can discuss the situation and what your men can do to help."

Velius visibly relaxed when Llassar translated Conchobar's words and it became clear there wasn't going to be a lengthy back-and-forth greeting with flowery words that many of the Romans seemed to prefer.

Conchobar didn't waste any time, turning and heading inside, leaving his aides to show Velius, and any of the men who'd accompanied him, the way. After giving brief instructions to the man next to him, Velius dismounted and came up the steps, stopping in front of Llassar and clasping arms with him.

"It's good to see you," Velius said. "I was happy to hear your mission was such a success."

"It almost wasn't and you're not going to like the situation that prompted them to pull me out of the dungeon they threw me in and agree to let us help. Things here are not going well."

"It can't be any worse than our last confrontation with the Carthaginians."

"The Carthaginian forces are a lot smaller, but you'll be doing this mostly on your own. The Ulaid army has been almost completely crushed. Those soldiers you rode in with makes you the most heavily armed forces between here and the Carthaginians."

"Well, let's go in and see what kind of deal we can make," Velius said, gesturing towards the doorway.

At least the legate was taking it in stride, although Llassar had done his best to warn him about the poor condition of most of the warriors he'd seen on the island. He still expected some help from the Ulaid, especially once they were armed with whatever weapons Velius had managed to bring with him, but the legate was a good commander and understood the pointlessness of complaining about a situation instead of figuring out how to make it work with what he had.

"How many men have you brought with you?" Conchobar, already seated on his throne, asked as soon as they caught up to him.

"Three legions, just over twelve thousand men. As long as we can come to an agreement on an alliance between our people, we are prepared to march south as soon as my men are all ashore."

"Although Llassar has already told us about your offer, I would like to hear from you just what it is your people require in return for your help?"

"Only that our soldiers remain under our command, although we will consult with you and your commanders on goals and strategies, and that, once your island is clear of this threat, you send men to help us in our battle against the Carthaginians when we call."

"Does this include just on Britannia, or beyond that?"

"We would like for you to be with us when we take the fight to the Carthaginians on the continent and Africa, but my Emperor understands you might have reservations about that. He would agree to have your men remain behind, freeing up Britannic soldiers from otherwise protecting our homeland for the battle against the Carthaginians."

"And for that, you'll fight with us?"

"Yes, that and the establishment of regular trade. The speed at which we're expanding our military to fight the Carthaginians requires a lot of supplies, and we'd like the ability to buy those from your people. I know even with that, it seems like too good of a deal, but from our point of view, it is worth it. A Carthaginian base this close to Britannia would make it impossible for us to have a base that is secure enough to launch an assault against the continent. We'd also leave Insula Manavia as your responsibility, since it currently has a Carthaginian base on it as well. We understand you have good relations with the people there."

"We trade with them, but they are closer to the Caledonians and I believe there are some blood relations between them."

"He's right," Llassar added, saying the sentence in both the Ulaid languages and Roman, so both men would understand him. "We have dealt with the people there, mostly through trade, for several years."

"Then we'd ask that you work with the Caledonians to help them recover from the Carthaginian's rule and establish trade with them," Velius continued, addressing Conchobar. "Most of the Caledonian warriors will be with us, so we'd still ask that, if the service of your men is limited to only the Britannic isles, you deal with that problem. We will see to it that your men are armed with the best weapons and equipment we can produce to help them in that fight, and I've brought a shipment of our latest weapons with my forces. We'd welcome any of your men to fight alongside us as we march south, although they would have to be under our command for the time being."

"How many weapons and how much equipment will you give us?"

"If we form only a simple alliance to deal with the Carthaginians here, then just the shipment I brought with me. This includes almost a thousand swords, shields, and our new arcuballista, which I believe your people will find useful. If we manage a more comprehensive agreement, then as much as our factories can supply."

"That would mean becoming another part of your Empire, yes? We don't have any interest in becoming a Roman colony," Conchobar asked.

"You wouldn't be. You'd be equals, just like the Caledonians. You would have an equal say with all other members of the Empire and you'd have complete control of your kingdom. Any Caledonians or Romans who came here would have to follow your laws, just as any of your people would have to follow Roman or Caledonian rules if they migrated to Britannia. Talk to Llassar. The Caledonians have prospered since our agreement was completed, and you would too. Beyond military support, you'd have financial and technical support to help rebuild after we secure the island."

"I don't know," the king said, leaving a long pause. Finally, he said, "It doesn't matter what we agree to if they destroy us."

"We won't let that happen," Velius said.

Chapter 11

Devnum

Lucilla made her way into one of the several smaller amphitheaters that had sprung up across the city as it grew and the new workers began demanding entertainment. The men, and it was all men, already assembled there looked nervously towards her as she and her guards made their way down the steps towards the center stage area.

Their nervousness was why she's picked a place out of the way and small, rather than the large original amphitheater, the forum, the Colosseum, or worse, her father's audience hall, for this meeting. These people had been pulled in from the small coastal villages where they'd been gathering since making it to the island by Praetorians, which would have been a frightening thing for refugees. She didn't want to frighten them further by having them brought into a place designed to inspire awe.

"Good morning," she said once she reached the stage, speaking loud enough for the forty or so men to hear her, but trying to keep her voice as neutral as possible. "Does anyone here speak Latin?"

Two of the men raised their hands, while the rest continued looking confused and worried.

"Do you speak the languages of any of the other men here?"

"Yes," the man with blond hair and striking blue eyes said.

"Some," the larger, darker-haired of the pair said.

"Good. Since so many of you are from different places, this is going to take some time. Could you talk to your fellows? I speak many languages, but I need to know what everyone speaks, so I know how to address them directly. I could use your help getting them to just talk to me for a few minutes until I can work out the correct language. After that, we'll get to the point of why you were brought here. None of you or your people are in trouble. You were only brought here to give us a little information and then you'll be sent back to your people."

Hearing they weren't going to be harmed outright, the men relaxed and started working with her to get each of the other men in the crowd to talk to her enough for Sophus to work out the languages that needed to be translated. She'd spent time with the voice in her ear, learning to follow the translations and respond without long pauses in between. It was harder than she thought it would be since it sometimes required her to listen and speak at the same time.

Thankfully, unlike her, Sophus was able to follow dozens of people talking at a time and could supply her with the bits she missed. Sophus wasn't always great at figuring out who she needed to talk to at a given time, because it couldn't see who was speaking, but they'd been working at it diligently every night, especially since the senate session where the issue of refugees had come up.

The Senators made pronouncements about how to deal with these people, some of whom weren't refugees at all but traders and businessmen, without ever talking to any of them to find out what they wanted or were even capable of doing. At some point, she'd have to go back and try to get something less inflexible put in place, since this wouldn't be the last group of refugees they'd have to deal with, but first, she needed to talk to them, since decision-making without information just led to bad decisions.

In the end, she was able to divide the men into three groups, refugees who were fleeing the Carthaginians and couldn't go back, people from regions that had submitted to but weren't controlled by the Carthaginians, mostly from northern Germania, and traders whose stay in Britannia would be temporary, mostly made up of Scandi.

The easiest group to deal with were the true refugees from Iberia and southern Germania, people whose leaders had either collaborated or been executed and their communities integrated into the Carthaginian machine. These people had no real hope of ever returning home and mostly liked the idea of becoming Britannic citizens, which would allow them to more or less resume their lives.

"What if, one day, your homelands were freed? Would you return there and try to rebuild?"

"Yes," one man said.

"It depends on who freed it and if they intended to stay. If they're no better than the Carthaginians, what would be the point," said another.

"No. There's nothing to return to. All of the men of fighting age have been taken for the army and half the women have just been taken. There's nothing left to return to."

Those three statements more or less made up the responses from the others, not that it mattered. She didn't know Ky's plan yet for dealing with a freed territory. If they did take the continent, it was a lot of land, more than they could effectively control, and even before the Carthaginians there hadn't been a lot of centralized control. Germania had been, at best, a series of loosely bonded tribes, and at worst a series of warring tribes. The landscape had changed, but they wouldn't be making deals with just a few kingdoms. It would be hundreds of alliances, some of which would make other alliances impossible. And even if they did make alliances, they'd never have the manpower to patrol and defend all that land.

"For those of you who wish to stay, the senate has recently passed a measure allowing you to become citizens if you join critical parts of the labor force or the military. We have lots of need for bodies in both of those fields, so all you have to do is ask and you'll have employment needed to get your citizenship. For those that don't want to stay, and just want a place to keep their families safe, we have plenty of work for you too. If you aren't going to become citizens, then you're going to have a tax placed on you, to help support our legions which are keeping the island clear of Carthaginians and safe for you. Don't worry," she said when the men who'd indicated they would probably leave as soon as their homelands were freed started shifting. "The work we have pays well, and you'll do better, even paying the taxes, than you did under Carthaginian rule. Besides, helping to support the legions is also helping to free your homeland, since at the moment our forces are the only ones pushing the Carthaginians back. Since you won't be swearing fealty to the Empire, you will remain under extra scrutiny, but we will try and keep it from interfering with your lives."

"What about us?" one of the Scandi asked. "We have no interest in working in factories or joining your army."

"That's a good question. Your people are not, yet at least, being threatened by the Carthaginians. One day you will be, since the Carthaginians have made no secret of their desire to conquer every part of the world, but you've remained largely untouched by their wars. How do you think your people would feel about allying with the Empire, to keep that day from ever happening?"

"We wouldn't," the man said, without hesitation.

"That seems short-sighted."

"Don't get me wrong, many of us, especially those that sail into areas controlled by the Carthaginians, can see what you mean, but if you think Germania isn't a unified whole, you will find that my people take autonomy to a whole new level. Our homeland is mountainous and most of our villages are along the coast, and none of them cooperate in anything that could be considered a single nation like you or the Carthaginians. You'd have to make deals with each village independently."

"That's disappointing. Still, we welcome you and your people who want to stay here, although you will have to pay the same tax as the other non-citizens. In return, there will be even more new goods that I think you'll have little trouble finding markets for. There is a lot of money to be made over the next few years, if we can survive the Carthaginian's attempts to reclaim the island. If we don't, then there won't be another civilization capable of standing up to them in our lifetimes, and when they do come for you, there won't be anything to stop them from doing to you what they've done to the rest of us. Something for you to think about."

The man appeared to listen but didn't say anything else. She spent the next hour talking to each leader, finding out how many people they had in their group, and where their interests lay. Few of them cared about having to pay a tax if there was ready work and they had a temporary safe haven from the Carthaginians, and even more indicated they'd be willing to do more, if need be. The sticking point was the various Scandi, each operating independently from the rest.

The people from Germania had a reason to fear the Carthaginians. Even those whose villages had submitted hated their overloads, and by and large, it seemed doubtful they'd become spies or saboteurs for their former conquerors. The Scandi were here for the money. Those that didn't see the long-term danger from the Carthaginians, or didn't care, would see the profit in working for their enemies. Romans and Caledonians weren't sailors, and they needed the Scandi markets for raw materials and as a place to sell Roman goods for shipments to Asia, most of which remained untouched by Carthaginian greed. The money they brought in helped fund the war effort, either directly through taxes or by keeping the factories with government contracts in business long enough to fulfill them.

Eventually, the senators would realize their idea to tax those who didn't want to become Britannians wouldn't stop some of the more entrepreneurial Scandi from taking advantage of the vast wealth the Carthaginians were bound to offer for information on Britannia's new technologies and its military movements. When the senators did realize it, she was certain some would act rashly, without realizing how much they needed the mariners.

That was a problem for tomorrow. For now, while these people wouldn't solve Britannia's manpower problems, they could offset it a little. Today, that was enough.

Outside Londinium

"Come to pester me again," Bomilcar said, in his now daily greeting.

The first few times it had been almost hostile, but as Ky had continued his visits, the statement had begun to become more joking than serious. Normally Ky played into it, hoping the slowly building friendship, even between men who could never be friends because of their competing allegiances, would allow the Carthaginian general a reason to give into his personal feelings rather than sticking to stoic loyalties.

Today, however, he had bad news to deliver.

"My people intercepted a message this morning that had information I thought you should know. There isn't a good way to break this to you, so I'll just say it. Your family, including your extended family, was seized by the emperor and executed."

"What? You're lying."

"I'm not. From the notice we intercepted, the government has declared that you are to blame for the loss of your army. They say they have information that you were in league with us and led your men into a trap to help us defeat them and take over the island, in exchange for money and titles. It also says some of your family were found to be in on the plot, which made all of your family suspect, making all of their lives forfeit."

"That's not true," Bomilcar said in disbelief.

"I know it isn't, but your empire has now lost two armies to us. The refugees that have started pouring onto the island are a sign of how people are taking to the news of your loss. We've also heard that several villages in Germania have revolted, maybe thinking the empire has gotten weak. Your emperor has to have a scapegoat to explain the loss, and they've decided it's you. I know this might seem like a trick, and I have no way of proving it to you, but you know your empire. Is this the kind thing your people would do?"

The way the general's face fell told Ky all he needed to know. He could see the realization that his brothers, his wife, and his children were all dead. Several times in their conversations, Bomilcar had talked about them, since that information didn't betray the empire. Ky wasn't sure how far they would have gone, but surely any of those relatives Bomilcar was closest to were all be dead by now.

"I'm so sorry," Ky said. "I know it's little consolation, but I am sorry. Your family didn't deserve this."

"Thank you," he mumbled.

"A death warrant has also been signed against you. If you return home, you will be taken into custody and executed."

Bomilcar just nodded.

"Is there anything we can do for you?"

The general didn't answer, just shook his head no. His body language signaled his defeat. Sitting on the edge of the thin cot he'd been given, his shoulders slumped, like he was curling into himself.

Ky patted his shoulder and left the man to his grief. Bomilcar knew the people he served and, having led several of their expeditions, he had to have seen some of the ways the Carthaginians treated people, but it was impossible to ignore their cruelty when it was directed at you and your family.

Devnum

It was getting dark, but Lucilla had one more thing to do. She normally ended most days checking in with Hortensius, to get progress reports on his work that she could pass on to Ky, but she'd missed the last several days.

Since speaking to the refugees, she'd traveled with some of the men she'd interviewed to the nearest port where they'd been gathering to see their people. She was happy to see the locals had taken good care of them, finding places for them to stay and keeping them fed while the authorities figured out what to do with them. She'd had Hortensius talk to several of the other factory owners and found jobs for the group she visited, so her trip was to escort them back to Devnum where they could start their new lives.

That had taken the better part of four days, which hopefully meant Hortensius had a lot to talk to her about, which is why she decided to make her end-of-the-day stop, even though the sun was already going down. She was less than a block away when she saw someone, she thought it was Hortensius, come running through the large front door of the factory. He was part way out of the door when the building exploded.

She'd never seen anything like that before, short of when Ky had fired the weapon he carried. Everything seemed to become as bright as daylight, the light causing her eyes to hurt, followed by an ear-shattering boom. Then the wind hit. The air was hot, like standing next to one of Hortensius' forges and the wind was stronger than the worst storm she'd experienced, the force of it almost taking her off her feet.

Thankfully, they were outside of town, and Hortensius had constructed numerous small warehouses, separated by large distances the thought being that it was enough space to keep the fire from spreading from one to the other. That hadn't taken into account the ball of fire that exploded through the roof, spreading fire in all directions as flaming debris rained down.

"Go get help," she yelled to her guards. "We need to get these fires out before the other storage buildings explode. Hurry."

Her ears were ringing, and she was having trouble hearing after the boom, which was mostly why she was yelling, since if she couldn't hear, neither could her guards.

"You're not going any closer," Cynwrig said, grabbing her arm as she started forward to check on Hortensius.

"He's hurt."

"I know, and we'll check on him, but we aren't going to risk you. If these other buildings go up, you'll be injured. Stay here."

Modius and Cynwrig ran towards the still burning remains of the factory while another guard ran towards town to get the fire watch and people to help put out the fire, while a single guard stayed back with Lucilla. All she could do was pace, waiting for more people to arrive to help her handful of guards trying valiantly, but futilely, to put out the fire and worry about what this was going to mean for their preparations.

Chapter 12

As the sun came up, she was back in the city, still smudged from the ash that had fallen on her for hours. It had been a close thing, but Hortensius's precautions had worked and none of the other buildings had gone up in the resulting fires. Hortensius was another matter. He'd been unconscious with blood coming from his ears and nose when Cynwrig and Modius dragged him clear of the structure, his clothing scorched black from how close he'd been to the heat of the explosion. He had just been lucky enough to be thrown clear by the blast of hot air, which Sophus had called a blast wave and over-pressurization, words she didn't recognize, rather than be engulfed by it.

She stayed at the site, directing the firefighting efforts, for several hours after the manufacturer had been put in a cart and taken to the physicians. Losing the factory was going to set them back, but they hadn't lost any of the finished gunpowder that had already been moved out, so it wasn't a complete disaster. After they had discussed taking precautions to limit the danger of the gunpowder accidentally igniting, Hortensius had a series of buildings built, or purchased, outside of the city for holding the gunpowder. The buildings next to the factory were just for holding the gunpowder until it could be moved to the more spread-out buildings, usually holding only a day or two worth of production, so even losing the closer buildings only cost them a day or two of production.

Of course, they didn't know what caused the explosion, but the fire in the warehouse that held the arcuballista made this occurrence suspicious. The senators had been worried that the influx of refugees could be a way for the Carthaginians or people who still supported the failed insurrection to get agents inside the Empire's critical works, where they could have the opportunity to damage them. Most of the people working in the gunpowder factories didn't really understand what it was for, but they knew it was destined for the military and the level of effort the Empire was putting into it. She ordered the praetorians to double the guards on the warehouses around town, just in case.

Regardless of the cause, the loss of the factory and the raw materials that had been gathered there was going to be a problem, especially the nitrate, which they were already having trouble collecting. The biggest loss of the night, however, was Hortensius, whose death would set the Empire back in every area of its technological expansion. There were other inventors and manufacturers in the city, but none that matched Hortensius in his ability to quickly grasp and work out how to turn Ky's instructions into reality. His loss would be devastating.

That was why, despite being awake for almost twenty-four hours and exhausted after the excitement of the evening, she made her way to the valetudinaria, a series of buildings near the center of town for treating the most injured soldiers from their battles with the Carthaginians. Although Hortensius wasn't a veteran, he was critical to the war effort and the valetudinaria had the best collection of medics and healers in the city.

While she agreed with bringing him here, she'd had Sophus in her ear long enough that her faith in current medical treatment was shaken. In her visits to wounded soldiers, it had pointed out places, several times, where the healers were doing things that would ultimately make the soldiers' wounds worse. Between herself and Ky, they'd been working on correcting a lot of these issues, although not without pushback from the physicians, who were still incredibly slow to adopt any of the suggested changes.

In spite of their resistance, they had been making progress and death from diseases that set in after the healers' treatments had lessened. While the progress had been amazing, Ky was still not happy with how long it was taking and the lack of success in the apothecaries in developing treatments. That again showed how critical Hortensius had been to the Empire. There was no person like him in other industries like farming, shipbuilding, or alchemy. Before Ky's arrival, developing something like gunpowder would have gone to the alchemist instead of a factory owner, but Ky had decided that it was critical enough they needed someone like Hortensius leading its development, and since Hortensius was, so far at least, one of a kind in the Empire, it had gone to him, even though the combining of elements in precise measurements to create a new mixture was somewhat out of his element.

Ky had said several times that, eventually, the apothecaries would come up with medicines that could cure many of the diseases men were still dying from after receiving injuries on the battlefield, but for now, they were limited to what he called 'more general cures.' This had mostly been a strong push for cleanliness when dealing with wounds. Things like boiling bandages and instruments before reusing them, scrubbing the hands vigorously with a lye-based soap that burned the skin and then not touching anything else before touching the wound, and regularly cleaning wound sites.

To his credit, in the places where this was being practiced, which included the valetudinaria, since he could get the military to force the medics to follow his policies, the instance of infections after setting bones or removing debris was significantly lessened. The medics at the valetudinaria, at least, were starting to learn from experience and stopped fighting so hard against Ky's decrees.

Lucilla made sure to visit the tents and buildings of the valetudinaria every few days, when she was in Devnum, to try and cheer up the soldiers, and every time the smell of the place hit her like a slap in the face. A mixture of rotting flesh and harsh lye from the soap made her eyes burn a bit as she pushed through the tent. As the daughter of the Emperor, she had made trips to see injured soldiers even before Ky's arrival, and she had to admit the smell was at least better now, although the air hadn't burned as much before the introduction of the new soap Ky had instructed the apothecary to make. Then, the smell had been almost entirely that of pus and decaying flesh, so at least the acrid smell of the soap covered some of that up.

With one of the physicians in tow, she moved through the tent greeting several recovering soldiers, who she had met on her last several visits, before arriving at the back of the tent where they had put Hortensius. He looked bad. Bruises had already started to appear across his face and neck, and probably elsewhere covered by his tunic and a blanket.

"How is he?" she asked the physician.

"Alive. His breathing is bad. As he sleeps it comes as a rasping sound. I have seen this before when a man has been kicked by a horse or when items have fallen on a man's chest. Sometimes they recover, but often they begin coughing and suffocate."

"Is there any treatment for this?"

"No."

She had addressed the doctor, but she was actually asking Sophus, since she knew her own people couldn't do much for a person whose chest had caved in. She had seen a man kicked in the chest by a horse, the force strong enough to cause him to die right there, gasping for air. His chest had been almost concave, bending inward, like the bones had been warped and bent in. She couldn't see any evidence of that here, so she hoped there wasn't anything actually pushing his chest in, keeping him from breathing.

"There are treatments, but none that are possible at this time that wouldn't increase the risk to the patient. From an acoustical analysis, I believe the blast at the factory was not large enough to cause air embolization or pneumothorax, as most of the blast was directed upwards thanks to the series of concrete barriers built around the building to cause just such an effect. Being outside the building allowed him to be spared the brunt of the over-pressurization. The body can heal most of the damage, but the lungs need to maintain oxygen to give the body time for that to happen. Without imaging devices, it's impossible to tell what level of damage he has received, but the physician is correct, in that his breathing is labored and suggestive of internal damage. Theoretically, it is possible to build a device that could introduce low levels of oxygen into his respiratory system, simulating proper pressurization and allowing him time to recover. The device would have to be manually operated, which will be difficult and time-consuming, but it should allow his system time to heal itself. For the burns, they should continue to apply clean bandages wetted with a highly diluted vinegar solution."

She listened to Sophus describe the device that needed to be built and realized the irony that Hortensius was better qualified than anyone to build the device that would be needed to save him. She kept a neutral expression on her face, staring at her friend, as she tried to work out exactly how to draw what Sophus was describing.

Finally, she straightened up and said, "For now, continue doing what you're doing. Make sure any bandages used to soak in the vinegar solution are first boiled and allowed to dry clear away from any other items before they are applied. For his breathing, I will have a device I want you to build and will instruct you in the proper use of it. It will require someone to operate it constantly for all hours of the day and night, but I will find men to operate it under your guidance and pay for them myself."

"What does this device do?"

"It very slowly pushes air into his chest, keeping it inflated and working while his body heals itself. It might not work, but it will increase his chance of survival."

The physician looked skeptical, as they often did when being told of a new life-saving method that went counter to their training. Ky, at least, they could accept. He'd been sent down by the gods, after all. She, however, was 'just a woman.'

"I will be leaving one of my guards here. You will build this device exactly to my specifications, and you will keep it operating at all times until I give you permission to stop, or he regains consciousness. Is this clear?"

She didn't raise her voice or yell, but she'd learned to speak with a command voice from her father, and only used it when she needed to be taken seriously. She used it now, and saw the man take a step back in spite of himself.

"Cynwrig. Stay here and make sure they do as I instructed."

The look her guard gave her made it clear he wasn't thrilled about being left behind, but he only said, "Sure."

Unlike the Romans, who treated her with formality, Cynwrig never said 'my lady' or added honorifics when speaking to her. He often incurred Modius's ire when he addressed her by name or 'little bird,' the Caledonian nickname she picked up, but she didn't mind. She liked the way that he, and the other Caledonians, treated her with more informal respect that was often more genuine than the performative respect used by many Romans.

She picked him to stay behind because she knew how he and her other Caledonian guards felt about her. Not that she distrusted her Roman guards, but for this, she wanted an enthusiasm that the Romans generally couldn't duplicate.

Since she was in the city, she returned to the palace to draw the instructions for the device, since it would take a continual back and forth with Sophus to ensure she drew it correctly, and there wasn't any other place that would guarantee she'd be left alone and out of earshot so she could talk to herself.

After almost two hours of painstakingly writing instructions and drawing diagrams, she handed the instructions to Cynwrig, who assured her he could find trustworthy men to operate the device. She trusted him enough to do a good job getting the device built and keeping it operating that, after handing him the instructions, she was finally able to get some rest after the long, disastrous evening.

Outside Londinium

"You sent for me?" Ky said as he entered the tent assigned to Bomilcar.

The general was looking better. According to his guards, he had been able to get out of bed several times, moving around unsteadily as his body slowly healed. Ky had been happy to hear about the man's recovery, but even more satisfying was the man's request to see him.

Although Ky visited him nearly every day, this was the first time the Carthaginian had reached out to see Ky and he took that as a sign that their relationship might be at a turning point. While he liked the man and thought he was a solid military commander, what Ky wanted most of all was insight into the Carthaginians.

So far, he'd guessed their movements based on what the Romans could tell him about the Carthaginians they had dealt with on the island. That insight wouldn't be helpful once the last of the

Carthaginians were expelled, however. Ramirus had some sources outside of Britannia, but not nearly as many as he had here, which left them in the dark about how the Carthaginians might respond to moves by his people. Bomilcar had not only been a high-ranking general, involved in numerous campaigns, and from a family with a long history of service to the Carthaginian Empire, he was the only one that the Carthaginians had wronged to the point that he might be willing to use his knowledge to help the Britannians.

Although their reasons for making Bomilcar their scapegoat were obvious, Ky wondered if they'd ever considered the possible side effects of their action. They knew their proclamation that Bomilcar had been in league with the Britannians was a lie, but did they realize that the murder of his family might lead to the very thing they'd accused him of?

It had been several days since Ky had given the man the bad news, and since then the general had not spoken a word, leaving Ky to take both sides of the conversation on his next visits. Ky had worried that the news and his own failure to defeat the Britannians had driven the man into some kind of fugue state, since he'd all but gone catatonic, barely even registering Ky's presence during his visits.

This request to see him was the first sign of life they'd seen since he'd shut down, which made it all the more surprising.

"You're going to have trouble with the northern walls. I ordered them fortified before we marched out, including adding anti-ladder precautions," Bomilcar said, not making eye contact as he spoke.

"That's interesting, but do you understand what you're doing?" Ky asked.

Although he'd been working for this moment since his first visit, Ky understood a soldier's loyalty. Between Ramirus and the drone, he already had good information about what was happening inside Londinium. His intent with Bomilcar went further than just intel for one city. He needed the man ready to walk away from everything he'd believed in, not just give up some information in a fit of anger.

"I am betraying my allegiance to the empire; but in my defense, they betrayed me first."

"You know by siding with us, you're becoming exactly what they accused you of. They will find a way to take revenge."

"I have no one and nothing left I care about, and I'm not doing it just because of their betrayal. I'm not a fool. I've served the empire for a long time and I've seen the things that we've done. I accepted them, because that was where my family's allegiance lay, but I never liked what we did. They have killed everything that kept me true to them, in the name of saving face. If I can't honor my family name, I can at least keep my personal honor by finally standing for what's right."

"You understand this doesn't mean my people will accept you with open arms. You led an army intended to crush us. I know you would have treated the towns you captured fairly, but the men who came behind you wouldn't have, and my people won't see a difference between you and them."

"I know, and I'm not asking them to. I just want to help put right some of the things I ruined in my life by serving the empire."

"Very well. Then I will gladly accept your help."

"About the walls ..."

"It's alright. We don't plan on going over the walls."

"Really? You're going to let the city stand? You have to know they'll keep your men engaged or harass your supply lines as long as the city remains, and it gives the empire a place to focus on and a base of supply if they can open a pathway to it."

"We aren't going to let the city stand. Within a month, the city will fall."

"If you aren't going to go over the walls, how are you going to take the city?"

"Unfortunately, here is where the not trusting you part starts. I know you're captive and have no way of sharing the plans with anyone, but for now, I'm still not going to tell you. Once it's over, I'll let you in on how we did it. Fair enough?"

"I guess this is going to be harder than I thought."

"You'll manage. Now, about the armies on the continent ..."

Ky spent the next several hours trying to get as much information out of the general as he could. Much of his information would be out of date by the time they were able to exploit it, but things like supply routes would be harder for such a large, interconnected empire to change quickly. As for the rest, he'd get the information to Ramirus, and make the general available to him. He had confidence that the Spymaster would be able to make use of the information.

"... the praetorians are still investigating, so no word if this was an accident or deliberate."

"You said you had guards on the factory."

"I did, but only two since we also had to have a guard on every warehouse as well. It wouldn't have been that hard to get around them."

"I'm still not sure this was the act of the insurrectionists. The gunpowder is wildly volatile and even keeping open flames out of the buildings and the windows open for ventilation, it would only take one spark to set it all off. The most likely culprit is the grinding wheel itself. That is the downside of using the water wheel for both water and the mechanism to turn the grinder, if you cut off the water flow, it will stop flowing before the water wheel is locked down. Hortensius likes a tidy factory and when the wheel stops turning, the water doesn't wind down the drainage channel and pours onto the floors instead. He might have cut the water flow before turning off the water wheel to keep that from happening, which would stop the water flow while the wheel would continue turning for a few minutes. It's just a guess and there are twenty or thirty other things that could have caused a spark. There were factory workers, people loading and moving the barrels. Any of them could have spilled gunpowder or left some exposed."

"It seems like a stretch," Lucilla said.

"*I think what the Commander is getting at is very few people knew of the project itself. He never explained to the people working on it what it did, other than it was combustible, and the workers in the factory were well vetted. It is doubtful any insurrectionists would know about its military application and go after it to hurt the war effort. Especially when there are other, more immediate targets to strike, like the forges working on weapons for the efforts in Ériu."*

"Also, the gunpowder would have gone up instantly when a spark was thrown inside. There was no real way to set it off covertly. I guess someone could have thrown a torch in through the window, but you were looking right at the building and didn't see anything. Hortensius was just outside the building when it went off, and you saw what it did to him. It knocked down everything within a pretty wide radius of the building. You even said you felt the force of the wind from the explosion, and you were still pretty far away when it happened. I find it unlikely anyone who got close enough would have come away uninjured. Did you find anyone around the building that shouldn't have been there?"

"No, we didn't find anyone."

"It was smart moving the factory outside of town, and even smarter spreading the finished gunpowder over separate locations. It means we don't have to start over completely."

"That was mostly Hortensius. I only pointed out how dangerous it was to keep it in the city. He was the one who thought we should keep it all separate and made it happen."

"How is he?"

"I don't know. He's breathing better with the machine Sophus had us build, although he hasn't woken up yet."

"From Lucilla's description, he seems to have avoided the worst possible outcomes from the explosion. When they were building the new factory, I'd recommended the building be designed with blast diversion in mind, to redirect the force of any explosion upward, which helped keep most of the overpressure from hitting him. Barring brain injury, he should be able to recover with the assistance being provided, as long as positive pressure can be maintained to give his lungs time to recover."

"Good," Ky said. "Losing him would really set us back. None of us have the practical experience to turn our theories into actual processes here and now."

"I know, and I'm sorry," Lucilla said.

"For what?"

"You left me in charge of running this, and I almost got Hortensius killed."

"Nonsense. Even in societies that are used to working with gun-powder, accidents sometimes happen. You made sure we didn't lose everything and took sensible precautions. We need to rebuild the factory. He had people do it once, so have them rebuild it the same, but maybe reinforce it more than before. Talk to his foreman. Once it's back up and running, see if he can manage to keep the production going. Hopefully, Hortensius trained his people to run things without him holding their hands."

"I'll take care of it," Lucilla said.

"You're doing good work, Lucilla. Sometimes we have setbacks. Don't take it to heart, alright?"

"I'll try."

Chapter 13

Outside Londinium

"I think we're about ready," Ky said to Ursinus and Auspex, as the three looked at a map showing Londinium, with the positions of their legions and the Carthaginians mapped out.

"So, we wait for Carus to take the wall, and then we attack? What happens if his men can't take it?"

"Actually, no. The wall isn't the target. The gate is."

"What?" Ursinus said.

"We moved siege equipment across from the northern wall and we've been focusing our fire on that section. We've all but told them that's where we're going to attack, so they've done the most sensible thing. Stationed most of their men, and what looks like all of their actual soldiers there. The gate and wall around it are being manned mostly by conscripts. In practice, that makes sense. The wall is close to the water and extends into the river. The ground is less solid and won't work well for ladders, and above the gate is solid, so there isn't anywhere for soldiers to climb onto and fight their way down. They believe, probably rightly, that we can't get through the gate. We even proved that when we backed away from our assault on it last month when they tried to rally, instead of trying to force our way through."

"Was that always the plan?" Auspex asked.

"No, but the plan needs to change. One, we have information that the northern wall has been strengthened and fitted with structures to make attaching ladders to it harder, or at least easier to push over. Two, the shifting of forces to the northern wall has only just happened. It changes the math of what we're up against. With the forces on the north wall, it would be tough for Carus and the men we have there to break through enough to make our assault successful, especially with going over the wall being harder."

"If the plan is changing, how will Carus know?" Ursinus asked.

"I'll be able to tell him. What we need to do is get ready for it. We need to shift troops to be able to throw the bulk of our forces against the gate as soon as it goes up. I want you to leave a few centuries spread thin to make sure no one goes over the wall in the other direction and escapes. Since they won't do any good inside the city, I want the cavalry to operate as a mobile force to reinforce any part of our thinned-out line that gets assaulted. Once they push the defenders out of the way, Carus and his men will set up a line to keep the gate clear until our men get through. Unlike the last time, I want the Caledonians to push through first. Since Carus will already be there with a base of support to operate from, the Caledonians will be better suited for the street fighting. As they clear areas, I want the legions to push out from the gate, pushing up each avenue. The more Carthaginians we can trap against the wall, the better."

"If we shift all but a few centuries across from the gate, won't they see us and shift their troops again?"

"They would, which is why we need to obscure our assault. We still have the design for those smoke pots we used outside of Devnum to stop that first army. I want you to put together a bunch of them now. We should have the supplies on hand, if not, we need to send riders to get what we need quickly. I want to start laying down a thick layer of smoke in front of our line, starting with the north end and going all the way around. It'll tell them the assault is coming soon, but they know it's coming eventually, so that doesn't matter so much. We'll have to keep the smoke going for days, and I know it's going to be a bad assignment for whoever you give it to, but it's important we keep the pots burning until we've moved all the troops and begun the attack. I've already mapped out the placement of the pots, which should keep the layer of smoke solid enough even if we get some unexpected weather."

Although he didn't have satellites to access anymore, Sophus had been able to put together a forecast based on readings taken from the drone flying at its furthest range and what data it could get from Ky's enhanced senses. It wasn't a sure-fire forecast, but it was enough for him to feel confident there wasn't going to be a sudden shift in the weather that would make the smoke ineffective. There were indications that a major system was building and there would be a weather front coming in sometime soon that would hamper the assault, which was one of the reasons Ky ordered the attack to start now.

They were sending the last shipment of soldiers into the city that evening, although Ky wasn't planning on sending a message with them just in case they got captured. He had other thoughts on how to alert Carus to the change in plans.

Devnum

"My lady," Faenius said, from outside the audience chamber.

She had just finished the last set of audiences for the day, continuing to deal with the growing pains of integrating Romans and Caledonians, with the added burden of problems created by the immigrants, as both the Roman and Caledonians were having issues with the mostly Germanic immigrants who had begun moving to Devnum and other cities looking for work.

"Faenius," she said, standing from her seat. "I thought you were near Londinium?"

"The Consul asked me to come back and help investigate the destruction of the factory and Hortensius's injury. Since the factory is a critical part of the war effort, he wanted me to make sure the investigation was thorough and for me to double check our security efforts around the other factories and warehouses."

Lucilla sat back down and frowned as Faenius approached. Ky had been pretty insistent that the destruction wasn't caused by saboteurs and was probably an accident, so she couldn't figure out why he'd sent the head of the praetorians back to supervise the investigation.

"Did he tell you he thought it was sabotage?"

"No, my lady. He said that there had been a fire, Hortensius was injured, and that you had the local commander conducting an investigation of the scene. He wanted me to double-check the investigation and make sure all critical sites were secured, just as I said. Did he not send a messenger ahead of me?"

"He did not. I'm sorry, I didn't mean to question you, I was just surprised to see you. I appreciate you being here and helping with this. Have you made any progress?"

"I have, my lady. I am pretty confident there was no sabotage. My men, both of whom have recovered from their injuries, had done several sweeps of the area and one of the city patrols had made a circuit of the outskirts of the city a little under an hour before the explosion. None of them saw anything out of place. The last shift of workers had left a little before that patrol's circuit, so the area was all but empty. Your guards also reported seeing no one but Hortensius and the guards assigned to the building just before it caught fire, and no bodies were recovered from the scene. Furthermore, when Hortensius requested the local commander assign guards, he specifically cited how combustible the material he was working on was, which is why he wanted to move it out of the city in the first place. I'm confident that there was no sabotage. This was an accident, although until Hortensius regains consciousness, I'm not sure we'll be able to say what the accident was."

Ky had already convinced her that it wasn't sabotage, which made sending Faenius to her confusing. Maybe he wanted her to have peace of mind or to be sure himself, but either way, no one seemed to think this was sabotage. If she had Faenius here, though, she might as well take advantage of him.

"Fine. Thank you for your thoroughness. While you're here, I need you to double-check all the security arrangements on the places holding gunpowder and, when it's rebuilt, the factory. We can all see now how volatile this stuff is and the damage it can cause. While this might not have been caused by saboteurs, it will give anyone paying attention an idea of what can be done. Whatever danger of sabotage there was has now increased exponentially with this accident."

"At your command," Faenius said, bowing.

Lucilla frowned as he left. Part of the reason she'd been so hesitant to accept this was just an accident was the extreme measures Hortensius had taken to ensure exactly this circumstance wouldn't happen. If it was an accident, then all of those precautions had been for naught. It brought into question how they could ever use this stuff safely. Once it was in use, it would have to travel with the legions, where they'd have a lot less control over its storage than in a warehouse, where the barrels could be checked and where open flame near it could be controlled.

Ky seemed convinced this was the thing that would help them defeat the Carthaginians, but she had trouble being as sure.

Ériunia

Velius looked through the spyglass, as Hortensius had called it, and marveled at the invention. He knew Ky had the ability to see things at extreme distances and while he knew this wasn't how Ky did it, he imagined this was how the Consul must also feel having this capability. The men cresting the far rise weren't so clear that he could make out individuals, but he could work out the basic formations and get an idea of the numbers of men he was facing.

He knew most of this from his scouts, who'd been shadowing the Carthaginian army as it began its forward momentum after weeks of inactivity following the Ulaid's last defeat. Seeing it for himself, and being able to make decisions immediately instead of waiting on messages and scouts to get back to him, would be a huge help in battle.

The manufacturer had apologized for this early crude version and promised there would be better versions as they refined the glass-making technique, but Velius was happy with what he had.

He was less happy with what he saw heading toward him. The army was larger than Llassar had indicated it would be, and the portion of local warriors to Carthaginian phalanxes was larger than he'd indicated too. Waiting for local fighters instead of marching to Emain Macha didn't make sense, but it looked like that's exactly what they had done. In comparison, Velius had three weakened legions, since there hadn't been enough replacements to make up for their losses from the last battle, nor time to train or equip the new recruits they did have.

Although the locals were an x-factor, a larger army worked in Velius's favor, since they tended to stack deeper than his own formations. The larger force meant there wasn't going to be an envelopment, or any other tricky maneuvers. Worse, they knew he was there, and were holding on a rise and it didn't look like they were going to move. It gave them the high ground, but he couldn't ignore them or leave them at his rear as he marched on the Carthaginian allies.

He still had some surprises for them.

He slid the spyglass back into its case and turned to the other two legates saying, "Move the men forward, with the seventh in the center. Curl the line, but don't overextend. Most of your legions will be facing locals. They won't have the discipline to stand firm, but they're going to press you hard. If they're anything like the Caledonians, they're going to be dangerous one-on-one. Remember, unit cohesion will be the thing that saves us. Keep your back centuries ready, listen for the call, and watch for signals from my command."

Both men saluted and rode off to their forces. Turning to his current cavalry commander, Velius had a moment's regret. Lartius had been moved to an independent command in charge of a new, entirely horse-mounted force that had remained with the Consul outside of Londinium. For what he wanted, he really needed a more experienced commander than Lartius's replacement, but he had to use who he had.

"I need you to keep their mounted units hemmed in and the locals from getting around to our flanks. Press hard and then disengage. Remember your training exercises and how maneuverable you are. Use it to your advantage."

The commander saluted and rode off as well. Velius watched as the legions started forward in a steady line and wished he had been allowed some trebuchets. The enemy was infantry-heavy, which meant they had very few archers, which was good. Already arrows were starting to fall among his men. The casualties were light, but as the attacking force, there wasn't much he could do to return fire as they marched across open land.

He was proud of his men. They ignored the projectiles and maintained a solid front all the way across, the three legions looking to the untrained eye like a solid wall. Doing this across uneven, rocky ground, was harder than it seemed, but also critical. If one legion, or cohort, or even century, got ahead or behind the rest, it would make gaps in the line, allowing the enemy to push into it and put flanking pressure on the units to either side. This kind of training was why he wasn't worried about the local fighters on the flanks of the phalanxes as much as he was the Carthaginians in the center.

The arrows slowed and stopped as his men began their climb up the slope. It wasn't steep, but the Carthaginians still had the high ground, making it harder to get past the long spears stabbing down at them. The men held their shields high, but too many of those spearheads, pointing at a downward angle, stabbed over shields, catching men in the head and face. Legionnaires started to go down in twos and threes, with the rear ranks pressing forward to fill the gaps.

The front made contact and solidified, with the legions beginning to push hard into the phalanxes. The Carthaginian allies were starting to swarm, trying to wrap around their flanks. Aelius was doing well on the right, his outer cohort curling to refuse its flank while maintaining good cohesion with the units next to it. He expected nothing less of Aelius, who'd been a legate almost as long as Velius had been and had been in every major battle with him since this new campaign started. Vibius, who'd spent the last several years on the border, was struggling. He should have had more experience with this style of fighting, but he'd been fighting raiders, not large formations.

A dangerous depression was developing in the center of his outer cohort that, if it continued, would cause the cohort to be split from the rest of his command, where it could be swarmed and that would tear the group of men to pieces.

"Gordianus," he said to his second in command. "Signal Micon. I need him to swing his mounted units back to hit the left flank hard, right behind where Vibius's units are being engaged. They need to charge and break, and then do it again, until the people hammering that outer cohort back off. He needs to relieve the pressure, and he needs to do it now."

Gordianus went to find the signalmen who hoisted up the new signaling flags, one of the many changes made by the Consul that they'd adopted. If Micon, the new cavalry commander, was paying attention, it would be easier to see than it would be to hear the horns they'd used before, the sound of which was often drowned out by the sounds of the fighting around them. They'd trained using the signal flags extensively, since its introduction, so they should be able to recognize the signals, if they saw them. That was the part they were having more trouble with, especially with the cavalry, which didn't grind to a halt when it engaged, but was continually moving.

Seeing the center line solidify, Velius said, "Signal all three legions. Back ranks to begin firing."

It was time to show the Carthaginians their little surprise. Although it had been long enough since their last battle for word of the arcuballistas to get out, not many Carthaginians survived or remained uncaptured after the battle where the weapon was introduced, and it was uncertain how well word filtered from the forces on Britannia to here.

Although he had his own small force of archers, unless the opposing force was large enough, they were only able to fire before the units engaged. Worse, when he was the attacker, such as he was here, his units would be in range of the enemy's archers before his archers had the enemy in range. That was, however, standard.

142

Something every military had to deal with for centuries. It's why, while they had their place on the battlefield, he'd never seen archers turn the tide of battle. They just weren't effective after the opening phases of the battle. After that, they were basically left with firing on other archers, as his men and the Carthaginians were doing now. With as spread out as the archers were and the indirect nature of their fire, both groups would run out of arrows before either gained an advantage.

The arcuballista had changed all that. Lighter and smaller than the ones his people had used before, with a stronger more durable pull, they could be fired directly and carried by men in the line. Before Ky's arrival, the legionaries would carry one or two javelins that they could hurl at their opponent before the lines met, in a kind of opening salvo. While this was an advantage to a phalanx, which couldn't engage until they reached spear range, a legionary was only able to carry one or two of the javelins, and they had a limited amount of range and penetration power. Many ended up bouncing off of shields or armor, or only causing minor damage that didn't put the enemy out of commission.

During the last battle, they'd given most of their limited quantity of arcuballistas to civilian auxiliaries. The legions had been so thinned out trying to contain the massive army they faced, that they wouldn't have had the manpower to use them anyway. In the two months that had passed since their defeat of the Carthaginian army and clearing the countryside, the factories had continued to churn out the weapons at a growing pace. Now each legionary was given a weapon, which was light enough to wear clipped to a harness on their back, and rugged enough with the new steel parts to mostly survive any pressing from the men behind them when engaged in battle.

The centuries on the front two lines left theirs strapped, so they had their hands free to move in and relieve their fallen comrades. If the situation was right, however, the centuries deeper in the lines wouldn't be engaged right away, waiting to be moved in as reinforcements or for orders to spread out or pivot to meet some other threat. If the landscape was right, this allowed the men further back time to unfasten their arcuballista and fire directly at the engaged enemy that was too close for normal archers to do so.

143

If the ground was more or less flat, this wouldn't work, but if either his force or the enemy had any kind of high ground, it allowed his men to fire into the enemy force. Unlike their old javelins, these bolts had the ability to go through shields and armor with little problem, and a man could carry a lot more of the small bolts the arcuballista fired than they could carry javelins, allowing them dozens of shots each, instead of just two.

Considering the rolling plains of this region, Velius had known the terrain would be right to use this tactic and had prepared the men for it ahead of time. As he watched, the second and third cohorts of Aelius's legion, and one cohort from the two on the flanks, pulled their weapons and rested them on their shields which made excellent firing platforms for the men, since they were stopped.

At first, the Carthaginians didn't seem to realize what was happening, as men began falling. They might have thought the Roman archers were firing into them. Although it was dangerous and caused a lot of deaths by friendly fire, it wasn't unheard of, especially as units were getting overrun or were largely outnumbered. The Carthaginian commander may not have even realized what was happening until his left flank began to waver. Although there were a lot of Carthaginians, enough that even entire cohorts firing away with arcuballista wouldn't be enough to swing the battle their way, Velius's battle orders had directed all of the men to fire at only the left flank of the Carthaginian army.

"Signal to hold fire," Velius said as that side of the line began to waver.

The damage was done and the front centuries were beginning to push past the front rank of Carthaginians. Already, men in the rear of that flank were beginning to rout. Once they did, he needed Aelius on the right to pursue them and the rear cohorts of his legion to extend right, to keep the more intact phalanx in the center and left from extending into the space their comrades vacated.

It worked almost as well as it had in training, with the Carthaginians breaking just as the Roman fire began to sputter to a stop, the men re-slinging their arcuballista, picking up their shields, and beginning to press forward. The Carthaginian left flank took a few steps back and then broke, losing all cohesion.

The problem with a phalanx was that the long spears were only an effective weapon when massed together. A single man with one of the spears facing a man with a shield, nearly as tall as he was, and a gladius was a dead man. While the legionary might have problems with more individualistic warriors, like the Carthaginian allies, those people had already started to break and bend in towards the Carthaginians when they'd been unable to get around the side of Aelius's forces, caught between the Romans and the Carthaginians. When the more solid Carthaginians began to run, so did their local allies.

The Carthaginians veered further to the right as they ran, away from their allies, creating more space until it suddenly became two separate groups the Romans were facing.

"Signal Aelius, tell him to … never mind," Velius said.

Seeing the Carthaginians and locals on his side of the line lose all cohesion, Velius knew the ninth legion would have no problem in mopping up the runners, which meant they could spare some men. He was about to order Aelius to break off a cohort and send it back towards the remaining Carthaginians, who were now boxed in on three sides as the seventh and fourth legions began slowly working around its flanks. Aelius had seen it too, however, and as Velius began to give the order, he saw two cohorts held and then turn around, reforming into tightly packed units, marching towards the rear of the Carthaginians.

Their commander must have seen it too, because almost immediately he tried to get his men to begin backing up, withdrawing in good order from the pocket that had begun to close around them. It didn't work. Either his men were too engaged to obey his orders or too poorly trained to execute them. He only managed to get his men back less than a full body length before Aelius's two cohorts slammed into his rear. The slaughter was near total, as the Carthaginians refused to give up, choosing to insanely fight to the last man.

Things didn't go much better for the fleeing men. The cavalry, freed from trying to protect the fourth legions' left flank, tore after them, riding the running men down with abandon. Some of the enemy, probably the locals more than the regular Carthaginian soldiers, escaped, but it wasn't more than a handful.

Velius had taken casualties, but not as many as he'd expected and the victory was near as total as any in Roman history. True, it wasn't up to the scale of some of the Consul's victories, but he was sent by the gods and Velius was just a soldier.

He still had work ahead of him to clear the island, but this was something to be proud of. He'd eliminated any immediate threat to the Ulaid and completely crushed a foe with minimal causalities.

It had been a good day.

Chapter 14

Londinium

Carus made his final round of the three warehouses his men were allocated between, his impatience growing, carrying a crate that he'd been moving from warehouse to warehouse, giving him an excuse to check on his men. The last of the men he had been expecting had shown up two days ago, which should have meant they were ready to launch the assault. And yet, there had been no word from the Consul or anyone else since the last soldier came through.

The senior legionnaire had known they were the last group to come through and passed the word to Carus that he had all the soldiers he was going to get. Carus understood not sending a note with instructions on what would happen next. It wasn't worth taking the risk of the soldier carrying that information being caught, so he was glad the Consul hadn't made that mistake. He knew Ky had something up his sleeve to let him know what to do next, but he had no idea what that would be, he just wished it would happen soon.

He was almost to the warehouse close to the docks when Marius showed up looking ... puzzled.

"Is something wrong?" he asked, since the fishing boat captain was heading directly towards him, with that strange look on his face.

"I ... something happened on my boat."

"What? Was one of the guards ..."

"No, nothing like that. There was a voice, or something, coming from the ship. I was the only one on board and I checked everywhere but couldn't find anyone. It almost sounded like it was coming from below, but there wasn't anything in the hold and the water line was clear."

"It could have been someone hiding underwater."

"I don't think so. The voice wasn't ... human. It was like a demon, or something, was speaking, and it was saying your name."

"Show me," Carus said, already walking toward the dock, forcing the captain to catch up.

Once at the boat, the captain refused to go on board. He stayed at the end of the dock, as far from his boat as he could get while still being able to see it, while Carus continued on. Nothing looked amiss at first glance, although he thought he could occasionally hear a slight hum in between the sounds of water lapping against the hull.

Giving one last pass over the deck, Carus headed into the hold beneath where the rowers sat and where the soldiers had stored their armor during the trip into the city. As soon as he was below deck, cutting some of the sounds of water, he could hear the hum, which sounded like it had gotten louder.

"Hello," he said out loud when nothing or no one jumped out at him.

After a beat, there was movement at the end of the hold, coming out from behind some barrels. He recognized it. It was the small disk with a glowing circle underneath that reflected off the floor. It was thin, almost like a plate. He'd watched the Consul throw it in the air several times, although neither he nor his fellow lictore had asked what it was. He'd just assumed it was one of Ky's magical tools, like the weapon he carried that melted stone.

"Kaeso Vedius Carus. Do not be alarmed. I have a message from the Consul."

"Are you alive?"

It probably wasn't important and any message, delivered at this moment, was probably about the upcoming attack and important, but he couldn't help it. The voice came from the device but seemed to resonate from all around it.

"That is a difficult question, but the device in front of you is just a tool that I am speaking through. It has no communication receiver, so the Consul isn't able to speak to you directly. I was able to adapt the telemetry system to interface with the onboard broadcast speaker normally used for playing recorded messages to speak with you."

None of those words meant anything to Carus, but he got the gist. The thing said he wasn't in this disc, and it was just a tool, which he understood, at least. Something, although not the Consul, was speaking through this thing and could apparently hear him, although the metallic voice was like nothing he'd ever experienced, sending chills down his spine.

"You have a message from the Consul?"

"The city defenders have settled into a routine. Although the men on the north wall rotate out for meals to keep the wall fully manned, the other walls, including the west gate, are undermanned enough that for meals, they have to take men away from the gate to eat. They also have no kitchen facilities near the gate, except for a house commandeered nearby for their use. Although officers go to that house for meals, the conscripted soldiers must walk around to the center of the north wall where the other conscripted soldiers are forced to take their meals. When they do this, the force at and near the west gate falls to approximately two-dozen soldiers. They are almost entirely conscripts, poorly trained, and likely to flee at the sight of trained soldiers."

"So the Consul wants us to attack the west gate?"

"Correct. The north wall is a more defensible position, the assault of which would lead to extensive casualties. The Consul has been staging the lines to make it appear as if the attack will come against the north wall, which the Carthaginians seem to believe, as they have been shifting their better-trained soldiers almost entirely there, weakening the other walls and leaving mostly conscripts and junior officers to defend them. The Consul believes this will be a less costly target for our attack. His orders are for you to take your men at the appointed time, march quickly up the main thoroughfare and assault the gate, raising it and forming a defensive perimeter to ensure it remains clear long enough for the troops he has massing on the west side to cross the ground and attack the city."

"How will I know it's mealtime?"

"This drone has to return to recharge, but the Consul will send it back to the largest warehouse where you normally sleep. Using the telemetry

circuits like this puts more power through the system than it is rated for and shortens its lifespan, so there will be no audio confirmation. Instead, look to the north rafter, which is blocked off from view except at the extreme south end of the building. I will flash the guide light three times in quick succession, which is the signal that it will be time to march out. Have your men armored by first light, so they are prepared. It is critical you move quickly up the main thoroughfare and get to the gate before they can get troops to you, as it is unlikely you will make it the entire way before someone raises the alarm. They will not be able to form full phalanxes in the limited space of the streets around the gate, which should give your men an advantage."

"I understand, and I'll be watching."

Ériunia, Northern Connacht

It took the better part of a day to round up the soldiers and get the wounded on wagons back to the temporary fort his men had built on the coast, where his messengers could cross back to Britannia and they could receive supplies. Now that he was completely out of Ulaid territory, he had to use a significant portion of his cavalry to secure his supply lines, which was going to deprive him of their use in the next battle, but there wasn't much choice in the matter. One of Ky's early pronouncements was that they not strip the countryside bare as they marched through, instead paying for what they needed as they went.

Velius understood the concept. They were trying to free these areas and they needed the locals to support them, joining the ranks as soldiers or, at a minimum, providing intel on the Carthaginian movements. It would be hard to convince people to switch allegiances if you were taking everything they needed to survive. So far, it had been working, but it did make their foraging significantly harder and increased the importance of the supply lines.

They were finally on the move again, or had been until they stopped to dig out temporary headquarters, a precaution he had his men take every night when in hostile territory. It ate up a significant amount of time and the men grumbled every evening when they stacked shields and picked up shovels, but he'd seen what happened to legions that failed to protect themselves. It also allowed a small force to man the temporary barricades, letting the bulk of the men sleep through the night, which meant he had a better-rested force each morning for sustained marches and, more importantly, fighting.

He had just finished riding the fortifications that enclosed the three legions when a commotion near the temporary front gate drew his attention. The guards didn't sound the alarm, and as he rode closer he could see the banners of the Ulaid and the standards of their king, and sighed. Although they'd crushed the leading Carthaginian army, they still had a lot of work ahead of them to clear the island of hostiles. Most of the Carthaginian allies still had fully intact armies and the Carthaginians still had a fair amount of troops themselves, all of which had to be dealt with before Velius could take his army home. True, none of them could match the size of the last two armies sent against Rome, but they still outnumbered his three legions.

He had better equipment and better tactics, but that didn't make them invulnerable. Rushing in like they were unbeatable was a good way to get routed, and he had a bad feeling that was what his new allies were going to push for. Being a legate was as much about politics as it was fighting, especially in the Roman military prior to Ky's reforms. Politicians, even kings and emperors, always wanted things faster, so they could show their success. They often had little patience for war by strategy and movement, wanting only battles and victory. If he could achieve a victory by maneuvering his men into positions that forced the enemy into surrendering without losing a man; he'd take that over a battle, any day.

Still, politics were what they were, and he had to keep relations with their new allies on a good footing. Ky's ultimate goal was to bring the Ulaid into the alliance, adding their manpower and natural resources to the Empire, hopefully giving them a strong enough base to stop fighting defensively and take the war to the Carthaginians. That meant Prime Legate Amulius Tettius Velius had to play nice.

"Your majesty," Velius said, as he pulled up in front of the procession. "Welcome to our camp. I'm sorry about the lack of a proper reception. Had we known you were coming ..."

He spoke slowly, the language of the Ulaid finding its way into his mouth with some difficulty. Although it was very similar to the language spoken by the Caledonians, which he was still working hard to learn and was far from being fluent in, there were enough differences that he was finding it difficult to learn.

"Nonsense," the king said, interrupting him, sounding a lot more convivial than he did the last time Velius stood in front of him. "I just wanted to see the men that won such a great victory. You told me you would defeat our enemies and end the threat to my people, and you did that in a spectacular fashion. If my observers with your army are correct, you absolutely crushed the rebels and have chased all of them off of Ulaid land."

The Ulaid who'd traveled with his legions and had come to see their king were smiling ear to ear at their king's praise, in spite of only acting as observers and 'advisors' and not participating in the battle at all. His men, or at least those within earshot, looked on stoically, not sharing in the revelry. They were veterans of the Battle of Devnum and the Battle of Venonis.These men knew that they weren't done by a long stretch, and the hard work of taking the cities and capitals of the Carthaginian allies still lay ahead of them. Although he was sure the Consul would find a way to take Londinium without a great loss of life, for mere mortals the siege and sacking of a city was a costly business, and there were several major settlements, all of which had fortified keeps, that had to be taken before they could say the island was truly pacified. Many of these men would die before the campaign was done, which meant they'd miss the celebration.

"If you will follow me to my tent, I'd be happy to assist you in any way I can," he said to the king, before turning to one of the aides. "Find Llassar and have him meet us."

Although Velius was pretty sure the king didn't speak Latin, he must have heard him say Llassar's name, which meant they'd have an interpreter, which is probably why he didn't continue the conversation as they rode through the camp, soldiers beginning to gather along the main avenue to see what the commotion was about.

Either the messenger found Llassar easily or the Caledonian had seen the procession and guessed where they were headed, because he beat Velius, the king, and his entourage to the tent.

"Welcome to our camp," Llassar said as Velius led the king into the tent. "I take it news of the victory already made it back to Emain Macha."

"It has. As I said to Velius, when you promised to take care of the rebels, I didn't expect success this soon."

"It was a good victory, but we still have a ways to go," Llassar said, noticing the frown on Velius's face as he translated Conchobar's statement. "It is unlikely they will meet us in the field head-on like that again."

"Which is why I am here. Although I did want to see the men who won this great victory, it isn't the only reason for my visit. Knowing that you have more fighting ahead of you and that you can deliver the victories you promised, I wanted to make sure you had our entire support and my people were playing their part in freeing our land. In this vein, I have begun recruiting more soldiers for the effort. Now that we have the first shipment of the weapons you promised, we are prepared to take our place in the vanguard of your army, showing our enemies what it means to come for the Ulaid."

"I am happy to hear about the support and that our weapons shipment arrived on time. I think that ... uhh ... perhaps ..." Velius said looking at Llassar, his brow furrowing as he tried to compose his thoughts and find a way to say what he wanted to say without creating a diplomatic incident.

Llassar, apparently, had different ideas. Although he spoke in the Ulaid dialect of Celtic, Velius was able to follow along. He'd always found understanding easier than speaking, and wished he spoke the language well enough to participate. Not that he didn't trust Llassar, considering the work he'd done so far for the Empire, but the Caledonian tended to be less diplomatic than he should be at times. And this seemed to be exactly one of those times.

"What the legate is trying to say is he doesn't trust your men to lead the attack, considering their previous performance."

"Llassar," Velius said warningly.

"What do you mean?" Conchobar asked, his smile fading.

"I mean, in every engagement, your men were defeated. Badly. It wasn't just the weapons. Your enemies here have roughly the same quality of weapons as your men, but were able to beat them in several engagements, even before the Carthaginian soldiers arrived. All it took was numerical superiority."

"That is how war is," Conchobar said, sounding equally confused and annoyed. "The army with the most troops wins. Yes, you won a victory here, but you had about the same number of soldiers, which is why the better equipment made a difference. With our men, we will outnumber each of the other kingdoms' armies, which will give us victory."

"Unless they bring their armies together," Velius said, although Llassar ignored him, continuing on his own point.

"Do you know that the Romans beat a Carthaginian army four times their size just a few months ago? Not only defeated it but destroyed it, killing tens of thousands of men and capturing many times that number. You haven't seen them in action, I have. I fought them as their enemy and I fought with them as their ally, and I can tell you their organization and discipline is what makes them such an unstoppable force. Before we joined together to form our new Empire, I thought the same way as you. Warriors fought combat as individuals, each victory a glory to their ancestors, showing their strength and ability. I thought, if we ever managed to get enough people together to face the Romans, who fought as cowards behind their shields, we'd show them what we could do. Now ... I think we would have been slaughtered."

"So you don't think we'd win against the Connacht, the Laigin, or the Ivernis? We have fought them off before and for generations we've been the power on Ériu."

"One, they are being supplied weapons by the Carthaginians. Maybe not quite as fine as the Roman's ... or I should say our, since we are now countrymen, new steel, but still better than what they had before, making the difference between you a lot less. And two, before you were fighting them one at a time, *and* they were fighting each other. Now, every kingdom left on this island has rallied together against you. You are still outnumbered, unless you can somehow defeat each army individually, with the rest waiting for you to finish with their allies before they attack. You will also have casualties in each fight, whittling down your forces. Now, look at what the Britannic legions achieved. A fraction of the wounded you would have had in a similar victory. The reason for that isn't material, it's training."

"So what are you saying, you don't want our men? I thought you wanted us to join this alliance, so you could add our manpower to your own. Now our men are too poor quality to be worth fighting with."

"No," Velius said, beating Llassar to the response, although sticking with Latin, forcing the Caledonian to translate again, and hopefully keeping the Ulaid king from becoming so insulted he kicked them off his island. "We definitely want you as part of our alliance and need your warriors to join our legions if we are to have hope of taking the fight to the Carthaginians and ensuring they never invade either of our islands again. But, we need to be able to integrate your men into our units, instead of being two separate forces fighting in the same direction. We have experience working with warriors such as yours in their own units, but under our command and working towards our objectives, so that is an option. Ideally, we'd like to begin training some of your men to integrate them into our legions directly. If you look at some of the forces here, you'll see that, although they wear the same uniforms and fight in the same way, they are a mixture of Romans and Caledonians. True, there are more Romans than Caledonians, but that is because our alliance is new, and it takes time to train men to fight in our system."

"You let your men fight like this, instead of as true warriors?" Conchobar asked Llassar.

"Those who want to. I know it seems like they've surrendered their honor and lost all chance at personal glory, but I've fought against them and I can tell you they are difficult to defeat. We never managed anything beyond hit-and-run against scattered forces. Most of our men felt like you, and fight in their own units, and have plenty of chances for glory, with the added benefit of winning more than we lose. Ultimately, I think your and my way of waging war is a thing of the past. If you want to win, you'll listen to them."

Conchobar thought for several moments, then shrugged and said, "I'll think about it. We still have to find men who are able to fight."

After Llassar translated, Velius said, "We look forward to working with your men and appreciate any that choose to fight with us."

Kings do not, as a rule, like having their commands ignored or turned down, and Conchobar was no exception. Velius could see the man visibly rally as he pulled himself straight to make his next pronouncement, which the legate knew he would need to find some way to accept, allowing Conchobar a way to regain some of his monarchial dignity.

"My son has accompanied me on this journey. He has recently come of age and has yet to find glory in combat. This war against my kingdom is a war against my household and it is fitting that a member of my house has blood in this fight. I am going to leave him with you so that he can gain experience in battle and lead my people to victory."

Velius almost wished he'd agreed to the first command, so he could argue against this one. Allowing a unit of locals, most of whom would be farmers and laborers at this point, would have at least given him people who'd more or less follow orders. A prince, however, was much less likely to listen to anyone. He didn't know Conchobar, so he didn't know how he raised his son, but he'd seen men like Caesius, who thought they knew everything simply because of their birth. Even before his treason, Caesius was a petulant, demanding fool who thought he knew more than anyone around him. That was the last thing Velius needed to deal with right now, and also something he had to accept in the name of diplomacy.

"We'd, of course, welcome your son," Velius said, and then hesitated. "As with your men, we ask that he understands he is under my command while he travels with the legions."

"Of course," the king said, thankfully not sounding offended. "I want you to show him how your people fight and hopefully give him a chance to win some glory of his own, as long as his personal guard accompanies him."

"We welcome him and his men," Velius said.

That could have gone worse. Now he just had to deal with a princeling, keep him from getting himself killed, and let him find glory, all while fighting the Carthaginians and their local allies.

Chapter 15

Londinium

The sun had been up for over an hour and Carus had spent the entire time staring at the corner of the warehouse ceiling, waiting for the signal to begin the attack. He'd spent the night going to each warehouse, getting the men armored up and ready. Since they didn't know when the attack would start, all of the legionnaires had been standing ready since daybreak. After weeks of waiting, doing nothing, the men were keyed up, but holding ready to attack was draining. He hoped the signal would come soon. The longer men held the duller their senses would become.

He was doing his best to stay focused, but his mind had started to wander as he sat there waiting and almost missed the signal. The small flying disk was back, in the small nook at the north end of the warehouse like the voice said, a faint blue light strobing off and on. Although he'd been looking in that direction, he'd missed it coming into the warehouse and when the light started flashing, but he didn't think it had been going for long.

"Let's go," he said, loud enough to be heard by most of the men in the warehouse.

It was still early morning, but the docks were already bustling, with the ships preparing to head out for another day of fishing to feed the city. Marius, having been warned about what was coming, had left at dawn, which was earlier than normal for him, but not so much so that it drew attention.

Carus was in the third group leaving the warehouse, behind the vanguard of his force made up of his most senior fighters, whose job it was to keep the way clear and not let them get bogged down in street fighting, and the rear guard, who actually left the warehouse first. Their job was to spread out and clear out any guards or anyone else who might cause a problem, and to follow behind after the warehouse was emptied. The rear guard would repeat this action at the other two warehouses, fanning out and keeping the area clear as the men hiding in the warehouses spilled out and joined the force moving quickly toward the gate.

Carus had gone over the plan multiple times throughout the night. There were a lot of moving parts and a lot of places where something could go wrong. That was what worried him about this plan, since a lot of it relied on junior officers keeping the men focused on individual tasks, instead of groups operating as a single unit like they did in normal combat.

Things started off well, however. The reaction of the people around the docks was instant, with screams and shouts coming even before Carus made it outside. By the time he and the second group of soldiers cleared the warehouse door, the bodies of guards around the docks lay scattered, many with their weapons still sheathed, taken completely by surprise at the sudden attack.

They moved up the main road towards the gate at a jog. As they passed the first of the two additional warehouses holding his men, more legionnaires joined his group, pouring out of the warehouse, filing into the rear of his unit as it continued past, never breaking stride. His rear guard fanned out, protecting them as the warehouse emptied, but as far as Carus could tell, they hadn't even been needed.

The streets were empty, although he could hear commotions on the smaller streets running parallel, which probably meant a warning had already gone up. He expected to see some guards, but aside from those at the docks, there hadn't been any in sight, yet.

He doubted their luck would hold all the way to the gate.

Outside the City

"It's time," Ky said to Ursinus.

The legions had been up since dawn, preparing as silently as they could, although there was no way to hide the sound of thousands of men equipping themselves and forming up in lines, which is why Ky had ordered the two cohorts left behind to face the north wall to make as much noise as possible. It would ruin the surprise that an attack was coming, but that would have happened anyway. At least this way, the city's defenders might hold to the north wall, assuming whatever was happening at the city gate was just a feint or a distraction.

"Is Carus on the move?"

"Yes," Ky said, looking towards the city but actually watching the feed from the drone, which had left the warehouse and was currently high above the city. "They have just passed the last warehouse where he was housing legionnaires and they are making progress toward the west gate. So far, they have had minimal resistance, but there is a force of city guards moving parallel to them, but I think they are waiting on more men before they try to attack."

"Is he in any danger? Will they stop him from getting to the gate?" Ursinus asked.

"Everything is a danger at this stage, but I don't think so. He has flanking guards setting up walls along each alley they pass, leapfrogging each other to keep them from getting hit in the side, and maintaining a solid rear guard. The Carthaginians closest to his force are outnumbered and I doubt whoever's leading them will throw them directly into the path of our soldiers, since they would just roll over the token resistance. No, the street layout favors our way of battle, funneling any force trying to hit them

160

down narrow alleys, making it hard to overwhelm them short of the open space at the gate."

"Has word gotten to anyone on the north wall?" Ursinus asked.

It was the only legitimate chance the Carthaginians had to stop Carus. There weren't enough guardsmen inside the city to stop him anywhere but in the gate's open area.

"They'd have to shift soldiers from the north wall to the gate to have any hope of holding it, and I don't see any evidence of that happening. The men who'd filed out for breakfast are starting to hurry back to their command, but they're slow about it, and most are headed back to the north wall, hopefully thinking our attack on that part of the wall is imminent. The commanders and senior soldiers from the gate who'd gone for breakfast are on their way back, but unless something drastic happens, Carus will beat them there."

"Good."

"Get the Caledonian commander ready. As soon as the fight at the gate starts, I want them in motion so they can clear the gate the moment it opens. They know their routes and assignments, but make sure their leaders keep them focused. Then get with your men and get them ready to follow the Caledonians in. And Ursinus, I *don't* want you going in with the vanguard. You are to stay rear of the front line, is that clear? The outcome of this isn't in question, and I don't want to risk losing you for it."

Ursinus didn't seem pleased by the pronouncement, since like all soldiers from his time, they'd been taught real commanders lead from the front, but he accepted it, giving Ky a firm nod before heading to his units.

Inside Londinium

Carus could hear the sounds of fighting behind him. This was the second attempt by the city guard to cut his force in two, attacking down alleyways from the north. The first one had been a concentrated assault down a single alleyway that his men had pushed back, only losing two legionnaires while killing almost a dozen city guardsmen.

Although he wasn't worried about the guardsman breaking through his line, since they were generally poorly armored in leather or without armor, carrying only medium-length swords and no shields, he'd still doubled his defenders covering each alley, giving each group a layer of three rows formed into a standard shield wall. None carried spears or arcuballista, since the narrow and winding streets gave little room for ranged weapons, but they knew how to operate as a unit, their gladius stabbing out every time the guardsmen got close enough while their heavy armor and shields made it difficult for the guards to get a hit in.

Peeling off more men for his flankers and a rear guard would leave less for the actual confrontation at the gate, but he needed to make sure his men arrived as a single unit and didn't get bogged down in street fighting. The disk thing that passed the Consul's orders had made it clear that speed was the most important thing in this assault, and Carus had taken that to heart.

Finally, the gate was in sight! It had been less than ten minutes since the assault had kicked off, although it felt a *lot* longer than that. The men by the gate were armed in a similar fashion to the city guardsmen, although they at least were wearing metal armor. The standard Carthaginian phalanx didn't work well in a city, so they'd put aside the thick walls of spears they normally fought with, switching instead of small, round shields and swords about half again as long as a Roman gladius. This was actually good for the Romans. The danger of a phalanx was the almost hedgehog nature of them when they were tightly packed.

Against a phalanx, a cohort had to go in with shields held up, with the main job of the front-line soldiers being to push the phalanx spear points up, trying to keep them from pushing into the lines of legionnaires and killing the men behind them. Without the spears, they were more vulnerable, in addition to being outnumbered.

As soon as they cleared the buildings and were into the open area, Carus shouted, "Front rank, fan out."

The men already knew what to do, and reacted as soon as Carus's order rang out, splitting and moving to the sides, to keep anyone from coming in on their flank. They were only one row deep, which would leave them vulnerable in the early stages, until the men further back caught up and followed their orders to fill in the gaps.

As soon as the front ranks cleared to the left and right, leaving an open space for the men behind, Carus shouted, "Charge."

The men all sprinted forward, the front rank with their swords sheathed, holding their shields with two hands and their shoulders pressed against the layered wood. Their job was to hit the opposing men in the front as hard as they could, hopefully knocking them back. They did their job. The Carthaginians were not in a tight formation, and, being almost entirely conscripts, they began to break as soon as the Romans got close, meaning they were half-turned or hit from the rear, sending them into the ground, where they were stabbed as the soldiers behind the front line passed over them.

The gate guard folded almost instantly. One or two men tried to fight, but they were struck down quickly. It wasn't without cost. Almost a dozen Romans were down, including one from the flankers facing north, where Carthaginian reinforcements suddenly appeared, too late to keep Carus from taking the gate, but still making the situation precarious. Thankfully, his men knew their jobs and a second rank on that flank was already filling in as more and more of his men cleared the buildings.

"Get that gate up," he ordered the men closest to the gate.

He could see the Caledonians, thundering across the open ground towards the gate. The Consul had timed the charge well, and they'd hit the wall almost at the same moment as his men had the gate out of the way.

"Optio, take your men up those stairs and begin clearing the Carthaginians off the ramparts on the wall. Stop on the other side of the gate and prepare for a counterattack. They're going to send men along the wall any time now."

The optio nodded and took three contubernium up a set of stairs on the left of the gate. Until they were on top of the wall, their shields would be a hindrance, but hopefully the poor quality of the defending Carthaginians would work in their favor.

The last of the conscripts, who had been pushed against the gate, were slaughtered as the gate came up and the Caledonians came pouring through. The Caledonians swarmed through the Roman line, slamming into the Carthaginians who were running to secure the gate. However, Carus knew their lines were going to be spread out as they came through the gate in waves, which meant he needed to prepare for a counterattack.

"Form up," Carus said, moving behind his men as they formed a perimeter around the gate.

North Wall

"What?" Maharbaal shouted, the messenger shrinking back from the anger in his voice.

Although he'd visited the walls often in the early days of the siege, worried that the Romans, or whatever they called themselves now, were going to attack, as the days stretched into weeks, he'd stopped, falling to the tedium. There had been a moment when he'd thought there was a way out of this nightmare when his officers swore they could break through the line surrounding his city, but the incompetents had wasted even that opportunity.

He had only started his trips to the wall again when it seemed like the assault on the city would begin soon. The Romans had started burning something all along their lines, hiding their soldiers behind a wall of smoke, and their strange catapults had increased their fire, constantly hammering the walls. Thankfully, the improvements ordered by that fool Bomilcar had at least been good, and the wall was holding. He could only hope that the defenses that were added on the outside of the wall, would make ladders or other siege equipment for getting soldiers over the wall useless.

Of course, the wall could also be holding up because the Roman's new, strange catapults seemed to be wildly deficient. They had a longer range than his, but instead of moving their lines a little closer so they could get their shots over the walls, hitting inside the city, they seemed satisfied letting the rocks bounce off the wall or harmlessly plowing into the ground in front. All those rocks had begun to pile up, which made getting over the north wall even harder.

Seeing the impediments, he'd started feeling better about their chances to survive at least until the messenger arrived to report a large Roman force at the western gate.

"The gate is open and the Romans are inside the wall," the messenger repeated his report, taking a step back as he did.

"How did this happen? Where are the men who were guarding that gate?"

"I don't know, your excellency."

"Is this a feint? Are they going to attack here or not?" He demanded, turning to the officer closest to him.

Officer was a strong term. There were hardly any trained soldiers left in the city, and he'd only been the commander of the city guard before everything had fallen apart.

"I don't think so, your excellency. I think this is the attack."

"Then counterattack. Send the men guarding the walls to take back the gate and get it shut."

"But my lord, if we empty the walls, there won't be anything keeping the Romans outside the walls from coming over."

"They're already over the walls, you idiot. If we don't take that gate back, the whole city will fall. Just do it before I find a new commander."

The man blanched and backed quickly away before turning and running to carry out his orders.

West Gate

"Get your men moving," Ky said unhelpfully.

He knew Ursinus had his men moving, and the only reason they hadn't passed the gate yet was that the small entryway created a bottleneck, and they needed to wait for the Caledonians to clear the other side before the legions could begin moving in.

His urgency came from the action on the north wall. As the Caledonians made their way through the west gate, Ky had sent a messenger around to the line facing the north wall, standing the trebuchets down and putting out the smoke pots. The haze wouldn't clear for a week or more, but if the battle reached the north wall, he didn't want an errant shot causing friendly casualties. They might have initially thought the warning about Britannians inside the wall was a mistake or a diversion for an attack aimed at the north wall, but even the inexperienced and incompetents couldn't miss what was happening when the small, but consistent, barrage that had been going on steadily for a month finally stopped.

He could see through the drone feed that men were starting to move off the north wall. Even being thrown in piecemeal, as they were there, the Carthaginians would outnumber the total of Carus's force and the Caledonians. True, they couldn't mass all at once, even in the open area around the gate, but that would then work in their favor as more legionnaires made it through the gate and engaged, keeping the Britannians from outnumbering and surrounding the Carthaginians. They still had a small window, if they moved fast, to dislodge the Britannian's foothold at the gate, but that window was closing, and Ky wanted to close it faster by getting his men through the gate as quickly as he could.

"We need to send more men up on the wall. The Carthaginians on the north wall are coming along the ramparts. Our men are going to be outnumbered very soon and won't be able to hold on for long."

Ursinus rode off without responding, shouting orders to a century nearby that would be through the gate shortly. Ky rode towards the city surrounded by a sea of legionnaires. So far, everything was going according to plan, which was always worrying, but it did sometimes happen.

North Wall

"Show them what we are made of," Maharbaal said as the men made their way along the wall toward the sound of fighting. "Take the gate back and throw the invaders outside the city. If you die, take three of them with you. We will make them bleed for their insolence."

The men weren't exactly buoyed by his speech, but they moved towards the sounds of fighting. He sent more men along the top of the wall, since that was still their best chance to regain the gate. If they pushed the Romans to the other side of the gate on the upper ramparts, they could cut the pulleys and trap part of the Romans outside and part of them inside.

Not that that was likely to happen. The Romans were more heavily armored and better trained. Sure, the ramparts negated the quickly growing Roman numbers and put his men on an even footing, but on an even footing with them, his men would lose.

"Go," he commanded. "Fight to the last. Your lives will live on in the songs of the empire. I'm with you men," he said while backing away from the wall.

"Get me to the docks," Maharbaal said to his personal guard as soon as the soldiers were out of earshot.

If the Romans were inside the city, then the city was already doomed. He might not be able to go back to Carthage, but he could at least escape to the bases in Hibernia or Manavia. It would take time to rehabilitate his name and he'd have to be careful in shifting the blame for the loss of the city, but at least he'd be alive.

West Gate

It took Ky several minutes to work out what the small group that had broken from the north wall toward the dock was doing. At first, it confused him, since the Carthaginians had finally realized this wasn't a feint or a tactic and that they'd completely lost the gate and had every other position in the city exposed. Every Carthaginian soldier Ky could see from the drone's elevated position was headed towards the west gate, trying to get it closed and keep the Britannians on the other side. The citizens were doing the opposite, trying to get to the east gate, moving away from the battle.

The small group that had been by the north wall was the only soldiers he could see not converging on the gate, and it was pretty clear where they were headed, since they were moving against the flow of everyone else in the city. It had to be either a move of desperation or whoever was leading the fifteen or so men knew something, because as soon as Carus's men exploded out of the warehouses they'd been hiding in, the captains of every ship that was seaworthy had unmoored and headed downstream for the open ocean and safety. Even Captain Marius, who had every reason to believe he'd be safe if the battle ended in the Britannian's favor had refused to stay in port, since battles tended to be chaotic and messy, and often ended badly for everyone who remained.

With the chaos and buildings in the way, it took Sophus almost a full minute to get a shot of each of the men heading toward the docks. Although Ky had never met the man in person, they'd been able to identify him on one of his few visits to the north wall, following him long enough to be sure they had the right man. If he was going to the docks, it probably wasn't just a 'Hail Mary.' He seemed like the kind of man who'd keep a bolt-hole ready just in case. There was an off chance that the guards he would have placed at the docks to ensure his means of escape remained in port were killed by Carus's men on his initial breakout from that area, but Ky couldn't rely on it.

Although his capture wasn't essential to this victory, since he would have almost certainly lost any power he had once the island he was supposed to govern fell, Ky didn't want him to get away. The man had a lot to answer for and was a likely rallying point for future attempts to retake the island.

"Stay here," Ky said to his guards.

Although the Roman line wasn't being pressed and they were making good headway towards the north wall, where the bulk of Carthaginian soldiers were still coming from, Ky was going to have to fight his way to the docks. He knew his guards were loyal and would follow him, but they would be surrounded and several would almost certainly die. Besides, he wasn't planning on taking a route they could follow.

"Consul, you ca..." Carus, who Ky had made his way to and was standing beside, started to say when Ky took three long strides and leaped over the heads of the line of Romans and the Carthaginians trying to push them back.

Even for him, it was a tough jump, but he made it, grabbing onto a wooden brace at the edge of the building he'd aimed for and pulling himself up onto the roof. Men fighting below on both sides stopped trying to kill each other and watched, mouths opened as Ky pulled himself up onto the roof and began leaping from rooftop to rooftop like some kind of bipedal gazelle.

"Commander, this is a mistake," Sophus said, even as it laid out a guide path along the rooftops for Ky to follow. *"Without your flight suit, you no longer have the protection of your shielding. One-on-one, you may not be in significant danger, but there are at least fifteen guards with the governor and the area around the docks is not clear of hostiles. It is likely you will be surrounded, making it impossible to see all of the*

targets in order to adjust motion assist and apply predictive patterning to their likely actions. I cannot keep you safe in that environment."

"Use the drone," Ky said, letting out a slight 'oof' as he landed hard after a particularly long jump to cross an alleyway. "It will allow you to see the entire combat area."

"Commander, you are fully trained on both the reconnaissance drone and my capabilities and should be aware that no function exists to allow the drone's camera footage to tie into my tactical systems."

"That was you before you achieved sentience. Stop thinking like a computer and start thinking like Sophus. You were designed to tie a fighter's sensors into your tactical systems to map a three-sixty combat area stretching out a tenth of a light year. We're only talking about five hundred meters, where one side is waterfront without any threats."

"If given appropriate time, perhaps I could ..."

"You have about thirty seconds. This is happening one way or another. I have faith in you," Ky said.

Sophus fell silent and Ky hoped that was a sign that the AI was putting all of its efforts into doing something neither it nor the drone had ever been designed to do. He wasn't as pessimistic as Sophus, however. For one, he would have the element of surprise. He was moving faster than anyone on the ground who'd seen him take the first leap could have followed and the people running towards the west gate might have heard something or even seen a flash as he leaped from building to building, but it is doubtful they would work out exactly what was happening. And the governor and his guards had absolutely no way of knowing he was coming. He'd be on them before they had any warning, giving him a lot of time to even the odds before they could react. From there, if he could get his back to the river, Sophus should be able to keep all the combatants in sight, even if he didn't manage to tie into the drone.

He could see the docks and, through the drone, the position of the governor and his entourage, who were getting close to a small ship that Ky had, at first, thought might be out of commission. It had some kind of netting on one side and looked to be under repair, but as one of the governor's guards, who'd run ahead appeared, a man had come from below decks and begun cutting the netting away, revealing an undamaged side of the ship. He had to admit, it was a clever masquerade that had fooled even him into overlooking the ship as not being sea-worthy.

Although Sophus hadn't said anything, the AI was still working, as it predicted the governor's path and plotted where Ky should jump from to land in a position where he could dispatch the maximum number of men the fastest.

Ky pulled the gladius he carried, but hadn't used since the first battle outside of Devnum, as he leaped from the edge of the roof, arcing high and dropping down, landing directly behind the guards bunched behind the governor. One of the guards, perhaps through some form of intuition or seeing a flash of movement from the corner of his eye, looked up just as Ky neared the ground, his mouth forming an O in surprise. Ky's sword flashed out diagonally as he landed, separating the man's head from his shoulders.

The moment Ky touched the ground, he was in motion. His sword stabbed out, piercing through the breastplate of the guard on his right as his left hand shot out, gripping another guard around the neck, his engineered muscles wrapping around the man's windpipe and pulling. Both men dropped, gurgling, one's lungs pierced by steel while the other's hands went to his neck, blood pooling through his fingers.

The guards and the governor finally realized that something was wrong, as two more men went down. The guards reacted with admirable speed, hands going to swords, while the governor froze in place, not that the guards' response would save them. Ky brought his sword down on its reverse trajectory from the last swing, taking a man's leg clean off, while his foot shot out, slamming into a guard's chest, sending him hurtling back at speed into the man behind him, the kicked guard's crushed ribs turning him into a dead weight on his fellow guardsman.

The governor just stood there as Ky whipped around him, moving with inhuman speed, a deathly blur cutting through the guards like a buzz saw. The governor finally got his wits back, turning and running towards the boat as Ky finished off the last of his guards.

"*Danger behind you, Commander,*" Sophus said, as Ky took a step towards the governor to chase him.

Looking behind him, Ky saw nearly two dozen soldiers, who had been making their way toward the west gate, turning towards him at the sight of Ky's lorica segmentata, the Roman armor still the standard among the Britannic legions, and the bodies of the Carthaginian guards spread around him. Ky took a breath, realizing he wasn't going to get to the governor and subdue him before the soldiers got to him.

Ky's hand shot out, sending his gladius cutting through the air and taking the governor off his feet as the blade sunk in his back to the handle and sending him skidding across the wooden dock.

Reaching down and picking up two swords dropped by the governor's guards, Ky turned, readying himself for what had to be done next.

West Gate

"Step," Carus shouted.

As one, the legionnaires in front of him collectively took a step forward, pushing the soldiers facing them back, their gladius stabbing forward. Carthaginians fell, some stumbling over the bodies of their fallen comrades, others at the tips of the Britannic swords. The line had pushed forward two blocks from the west gate, the ranks filling out to hold the alleys and doorways. Carus knew it was precarious. They were overextended, making a large pocket into the Carthaginians, who were still pushing hard to try and do something to stop the Britannians.

The last he'd seen, the Caledonians were making good progress towards the north gate, although their casualties were going to be much higher than the men trained to fight as a single legion, but they were working their way around the wall, which left most of the Carthaginians between them and Carus's now overextended legion. He'd already sent a runner to pull one of the cohorts left across from the north wall to circle around and help extend the line, but that would take time he wasn't willing to give. The Consul had made his reckless run deep into the city. He may be formidable, but Carus had seen first-hand that the man wasn't invulnerable. He was, however, essential to the Empire's long-term chances for survival, which meant he had to be protected.

The legions were already down to just four rows deep on each side, and he was about to order that thinned to three rows, so that they could extend another block into the city.

"Step," he said again, and the men pushed forward.

Thankfully, the pressure on the front started to let up as fewer and fewer men joined the melee, but he still couldn't let up. There were still attacks up and down his line, although it wasn't clear if the Carthaginians were now trying to push the Britannians back, or just trying to escape the city. He hadn't heard from the cohort on the east gate, but he knew they were holding position, keeping anyone from leaving that way. If given the option between chaos in the west or a formed and prepared line on the left, Carus knew which he would take.

"Step," he called again, and again his men pushed.

This continued for what seemed like an eternity, the Carthaginians either being slaughtered by the men behind the front row or forced to take a step back from the Britannians. Although they'd been fighting for hours, Carus recognized the ground that he'd passed through early that morning and knew he was near the docks. His men were down to just a single row, with the legionnaires having to push in tighter if a man fell, since there was no longer a supporting row behind them to take the spot of a fallen soldier.

He was so focused on trying to watch the entire line, since all of the officers were spread more or less evenly back to the gate, that he almost missed that the men had stopped fighting. There were no more Carthaginians in front of them, although the noise of battle still rang out from off towards the north wall. Looking beyond the front rank, he saw the Consul, holding two of the longer Carthaginian blades, covered in blood, looking like a demon sent from the depths of the underworld.

The volume of bodies around him, the edge of which the legion-naires had stopped at, was staggering and made it hard for them to move closer to him and retain their footing.

"What took you so long?" Ky said with a smile.

Chapter 16

Walking through the city, the damage wasn't as bad as Ky had feared, and most of that was centered around the west gate where the bulk of the fighting had been.

Thankfully, despite being where the battle started and, at least part of it, ended, the docks were in good shape. Although the Emperor had already decided to keep Devnum as the capital of the Empire, there was little doubt in anyone's mind that Londinium would eventually reassert itself as a major center for trade and commerce. Its river-borne trade and road connections to major southern ports were why both the Carthaginians and the Romans, before they'd been forced to the north of the island, had based their capitals there in the first place. Its docks were a key part of that and would be helpful in bringing in supplies for rebuilding the damaged portion of the city.

The population wasn't as lucky. Thanks to the governor's decision to keep nearly all of the food for himself and the soldiers, the population that had come into the city for protection had been all but starved for a month, and legionnaires conducting a survey of the city for survivors and looking for soldiers in hiding had found the bodies of more than a few families that had starved to death unnoticed in their homes.

Ky had ordered food supplies brought in, but they were running into problems there as well. Between feeding the legions now spread over two islands and the large number of prisoners they'd managed to acquire, food supplies were starting to run low and the harvests were still months away.

Prisoners were less of a problem. To keep his men fighting to the last, the governor's lieutenants had spent the previous months drilling into their heads the brutal ways they could expect to be treated by the Britannians if the city fell. Although Ky couldn't see how they could have possibly believed some of the tales that were communicated to him, they clearly had, as the bulk of the city's garrison had refused to surrender, choosing instead to fight to the last man.

Although Ky didn't like the idea of slaughtering any enemy when their situation was hopeless, this time it cost the lives of hundreds of more Caledonians than necessary, which he very much regretted. Part of him thought that, if he'd been there instead of chasing down the governor, he might have been able to make a difference and save a lot of lives, but he knew that was just a soldier's guilt talking.

Although he hadn't yet been able to introduce things like debriefings or after-action reports, that could help the officer corps learn from battles and pass that experience to the next batch of officers, he did spend some time interviewing the men there personally. From everything he could tell, the men had fought well and hadn't taken any undue risks, or at least, no undue risks from the Caledonian point of view. Unless he'd been prepared to kill every Carthaginian single-handedly, it was unlikely the death toll on their end could have been any lower.

In the end, there were less than a hundred survivors from the Carthaginian forces, and most of those were Carthaginian conscripts, laborers who had migrated to Britannia for a chance at prosperity on their empire's frontiers but had ended up as cannon fodder. While the low number of prisoners meant there weren't as many mouths to feed, these were the exact people that were agreeing to walk away from the Carthaginians and become Britannian citizens instead, since all they were looking for was a chance at prosperity.

"I understand you're having a supply problem," Lucilla said in his ear as he made his circuit of the east wall, to see how that side of the town fared through the siege.

"I see Sophus has been talking to you," Ky said.

Although he valued the AI's input, which had been invaluable in keeping him alive, it had developed a habit since gaining sentience of telling on him to Lucilla if it didn't like a decision Ky was making. It was an annoying development, to be sure.

"Only because we have been dealing with the same issue here and I've been working on some solutions that might help."

"I'm glad to hear it. We did a good job getting the harvest in before winter, but the increased size of the legions and all of the prisoners are starting to take a toll. I'd hoped the Caledonians would be able to help blunt some of that, but they saved less than we did. I don't suppose the Ulaid have supplies we can buy from them?"

"No. In fact, that's part of why I've been working on this problem already. Velius has asked for supplies of food, clothing, and medicine for the civilians there, since entire villages have been wiped out by raiders, brigands, and the Carthaginians."

Ky sighed, pinching the bridge of his nose. Thanks to his altered biology and the medical nanobots swimming through his system, he didn't get stress headaches, so the gesture was more of a habit he'd picked up from the locals than something to relieve actual pain.

"That sounds less like a solution and more like a compounding of the problem."

"It isn't my solution, just an explanation of why I've been working on one."

"I see, then what's the solution?"

"I've been talking to some of the Scandi traders, and I think we can get them to begin bringing food shipments here on their return voyages after taking our finished products to the eastern markets to sell."

"Scandi isn't exactly a major food producer. As I understand it, near the end of winter they have to get a lot of their food from external shipments themselves. I find it doubtful they'd have much excess to sell on to us. Even if they did, we're also buying up all the raw materials for the foundries we can, and pound for pound, they'd make more money on those shipments than they would on foodstuffs. I'm not sure how much we can rely on the charity of Scandi traders to give up profit in order to bring us food."

"I wasn't planning on appealing to their charity. I was planning on appealing to their greed. The new, stronger steel, along with heavy plows and arcuballista, although we are allowing only a small number of those to be sold, are in high demand in the northern and eastern ports, so we've put a high tax on them. My thought was that we reduce, or even eliminate, that tax if they agree to allot at least fifty percent of their hold space on the return journey for foodstuffs, which will also not be taxed. While they still make less money on the food, eliminating both the export and import taxes will change that math enough that I think we can get them to agree to those terms."

"That's a good idea, but it doesn't solve the other problem. The Scandi don't have an excess of food to sell us, and neither do most of the free Germanic tribes. The Carthaginians are the only ones with that kind of harvest, and we've already told them none of our products may be sold into Carthaginian markets, and that we'd cut them off from our ports entirely if we find out they have been selling to them."

"Apparently, they have an Asian port in the east that's accessible to them that leads to a lot of grassland and tribes that have excess food to sell. Now that the ice is thawing, it's accessible and close enough that it can be profitable for them to buy from those markets."

That was a good point as well. Although Ky had not forgotten about the Eurasian ports on the Baltic, the tribes that lived there in his timeline did only small-scale trading with the people from Scandinavia and were more often a market to sell finished goods into rather than a source of raw materials. He'd assumed the changes in this timeline, which had led to tribes pushing into Roman lands hundreds of years before they should have, would have also destabilized the region as a whole, leaving less organized villages and conglomerates to trade with.

That was a problem he needed to get over, thinking of these regions as they were in the original timeline instead of investigating the situation as it really was now. It wasn't hard to do locally, where he could see, or at least get regular reports, on conditions and determine where those changes had a direct effect on him. It was much harder to do for faraway places. Even Ramirus, with his far-flung net of spies and sources, knew little beyond Europe and the Mediterranean. He knew cultures existed and some goods still made their way from China and India, or what would be China and India in Ky's timeline, but not much else beyond that.

The Carthaginian control of the Middle East meant that only their agents made the difficult trek through the traditional trade routes, and sailing technology hadn't developed to the point of allowing boats to circle the Horn of Africa and take the long way around. What information Ky did have came from the Steppes tribe - Scandi pipeline, which was much less reliable than traditional trade routes, at least with information.

"That's interesting. Do the traders you've spoken to say they'd be interested in that option?"

"They do. They wanted to skip paying any export taxes now, and they aren't happy that, instead, we've told them we'll give them a credit for it once they bring in the foodstuffs, but everything they're saying is hedged with "ifs" and "maybes," as far as what food is available to import. They'll get over it and do it though, I think. Money always wins out."

"Good. Good," Ky said.

"Now that that's settled, let's talk about you putting yourself in unnecessary danger," Lucilla said, her voice getting much more serious.

Devnum

Lucilla paced in her room, equal parts bored and annoyed. Bored, because she'd been stuck here all day and annoyed because she had a lot to do, and this was wasting too much time. She'd had multiple meetings scheduled for the day, not the least of which was a trip to the foundry, where several of Hortensius's assistants were trying to keep up with his vision and staggering workload to continue all of the projects he had going. She couldn't fault them for how hard they were trying, but none of them had the overall picture and foresight that their boss had, and every project was falling behind.

She'd visited the gunpowder works, temporarily in a comman-deered wheelhouse that they quickly expanded with a covered area for production, and that, at least, was moving along more or less as it had. The actual process, once they got it down, wasn't difficult, just dangerous. Thankfully, because of their need to keep the moisture levels regulated, the nitrate beds had been located elsewhere and hadn't gone up with the explosion. Likewise, steel production had more or less settled into a process that the fore-men could maintain for a time without Hortensius's help.

The semaphore towers, new glass works, and cannon produc-tion, however, all still needed the manufacturer's input and direc-tion, and were falling far behind schedule. For the glass works, thankfully, Hortensius had found an artist who'd been doing glass, had some talent for it, and had been running with the ideas given to them by Ky. He just needed to be focused and reminded that the end goal was the lenses he was making. That much, at least, was within Lucilla's abilities.

The towers were also being erected in spite of Hortensius's absence, but he had made alterations to the plans shortly before his injury for the next series to be built. She'd spent the last several days visiting the construction sites of the first towers, since they were being built on Ky's original plans. The original plans called for basically a large platform with pulleys that would allow the operator to raise and lower a series of flags on one of six branches that extended up above the tower, designed to be visible from the towers next in the series.

Hortensius's new design still had the pulley system, but had an added setup where the pulleys had additional connections, and ro-tated around. This would let one person "load up" the message, so the next series of flags could go up quickly. Lucilla was concerned that if the operator raised the flags too quickly, the person looking at it through one of the 'telescopes' that Ky had described might miss the message. She also wasn't clear on the changes in the pulley design, which looked like an attempt to keep the flags from jamming in the mechanism, but seemed over-designed to her. She did like that it was designed so that lanterns could be raised or lowered in the place of flags for use at night, and it looked as if the lanterns would never turn over, always keeping the candles within upright.

He'd also added a wheel that allowed the platform to turn, that extended down into the tower, so that the operator would turn with it, allowing one tower to point its flags at more than one destination, since to gain the full effect, they needed to be looked at straight on, so the person seeing them could work out what flag they were looking at. This allowed for a station to be a "node" as he called it, splitting a line of stations to go different directions or cross without having to have multiple stations put in.

The explanations made sense, but it all seemed over-engineered and complicated, and the men in charge of having them built had questions she couldn't answer. Sophus tried, but her descriptions were sometimes not good enough for it to determine what the best answer was. Originally, she'd thought to just put it aside and get the first few towers built and then wait on Ky to come and see the changes for himself, since Sophus could see through his eyes and finally understand what she had been describing.

That had also been her plan for the canon factory. Even when Hortensius was mobile, they were getting close to the point that they had to have Ky there to inspect the finished molds and first test castings. It had been made clear to her numerous times how important it was that there be no impurities or imperfections of any kind, which was fine, except the imperfections could often be so small as to be undetectable by the human eye. From where she stood, looking at the one piece that had been finished, it looked good to her, but without Ky's ability to examine it fully, she was at a standstill.

Ky had another solution, since he thought it would be a couple of weeks before he could make it back to the capital, and he didn't want to wait that long. The evening after the victory in Londinium, he had dispatched a crate to her under guard, which had arrived that morning. Inside was the small disk he called a drone that he sometimes sent into the air to see things at a distance or from a different vantage point. Sophus said he could alter its firmware, whatever that meant, so that it could operate the drone using her comms device, similar to how it operated the small devices Ky had put into her body to help her stay healthy.

Unfortunately, she had to be wearing it for the comms unit to be active, Sophus had no idea how long the alterations would take, and she had to stay near the drone because of something Sophus called 'signal degradation.' All of that was why Lucilla had been forced to stand in her room and wait while some kind of light on the bottom of the thing occasionally gave off a faint blue light, and then promptly went dark again. While this was an indication that at least something was happening, that was the only thing to tell her she wasn't wasting her time. Sophus hadn't replied to her or connected her to Ky since they started this process. Although the only time that had happened before was when Ky had fallen into that unwaking sleep, she was pretty sure that wasn't the case now.

Of course, it didn't help relieve her boredom and frustration, and the gods only knew what her guards thought she was doing all day in her rooms by herself.

"I have finished," Sophus's voice suddenly said, breaking the quiet.

She'd been pouting, yelling, holding both sides of an argument where she played out yelling at Ky and Sophus for wasting her day, when its voice made her jump in surprise. She turned towards the device, which was now hovering a foot from her at eye level.

"Finally, can you ... ohh."

"It is pleasing to see you, Lucilla."

"You can see me?"

"I can. More importantly, this unit has the sensor suite necessary to do a full check of the cannon molds, although it is advisable to move everyone out of viewing distance before we activate it."

She found it an odd sensation, looking at this thing hovering in front of her while hearing Sophus's voice in her ear. It was hard to not think of this thing as Sophus while talking to it, so the voice coming from another location was a bit disconcerting.

"Good. It's late, but we can at least go to the foundry, since it's still running. Will you float behind me, or ..."

"I am not inside the drone, simply controlling it through your comms unit. I believe it would be best to conceal the drone until you get to the foundry and have the building completely cleared, before releasing it onto the shop floor to examine the molds and first castings. Although you've seen the drone before and have had time to adjust to my presence,

it is possible that technology this advanced will cause disruptions among people with less exposure."

"You're probably right. Do I need to put this back in that crate, or ..."

"No. The crate used to transport it here was a precaution to keep it away from prying eyes. The drone itself is able to compact itself for storage, which is how the Commander is able to put it in a thin pouch in the leg of his uniform. I can give it a command to shrink to storage size, which is a little smaller than the palm of your hand."

"I could put it in a coin purse," Lucilla suggested.

"That should suffice, although it is important that no one takes that purse or it becomes misplaced. While it is unlikely you would be targeted by thieves, given the guard that follows you, it is still important to be mindful."

"I have a purse that hangs around my neck when I wear ceremonial robes, since they don't have drawstrings or belts to attach a coin purse to. It is smaller than the normal coin purse, but it should be large enough to hold something as small as you described and it can open very large if need be."

"That should be sufficient," Sophus said.

As she found the coin purse and prepared to leave, Lucilla was just happy that they were finally ready to move forward.

Chapter 17

Ériunia

Velius watched the Ulaid troops sacking the city below him and frowned. Although a lot of other Romans had disagreed with the policy, one of the things Ky had done that Velius had been happiest about was the declaration ending sacks of conquered cities and the penalties put in place for those who participated. Conchobar was going to have to lead these people if they managed to conquer the island for him, and people whose homes were demolished, possessions taken, and wives and daughters sullied were unlikely to be loyal citizens.

He'd made a plea to Guaire, the commander of the local forces under his command, but the king's cousin had ignored him. He understood why the man thought he couldn't keep his soldiers from their rewards since, unlike the Britannians, the bulk of what a soldier could earn after being conscripted was through sacks and the sale of captured men. If the Ulaid did end up joining the Empire, they'd be forced to change their ways, but until they did, there was little Velius could do to stop them.

He'd made a big deal out of the Ulaid being allowed to govern their territory and how they wouldn't just be simple vassals under Britannic rule, which meant in cases like this, he was mindful of how far he could push them. He'd already pushed the king hard to keep soldiers under his direct command in combat, something neither the king nor his commanders had been pleased about.

Thankfully, none of his soldiers, not even the fairly recent Caledonian recruits, had tried to join in on the plundering, and all held to their positions either guarding the outskirts of the city or remaining in the fortified camp Velius ordered built every night.

"It's glorious, isn't it?" Cormac, the king's son, said.

Velius turned to look at the prince, resisting the urge to shake his head. The boy was barely into his manhood, not yet gaining the muscle and stature that he surely would in time, given his father, which seemed to be a collection of all the worst traits of both young men and less civilized societies. Cormac seemed to enjoy pointless cruelty for its own sake, was a braggart given to boasting the achievements of others, regardless of the part he played, and continually asked about more aggressive, and foolhardy, tactics during Velius's meetings with his commanders.

The commanders, at least, ignored the boy, understanding that Velius had little choice but to let him be present at the war councils. Rome had similar problems with an emperor's son butting into military policy until fairly recently. Ky's new policies pushing merit over position might have started taking hold in Britannia, but they were completely unheard of in places like this.

"No, it's not," Velius said dryly, looking past the boy to Llassar as he prepared himself for the lecture he was being forced to give yet again. "You're going to be expected to govern these people. You're going to ask them to produce the food your army needs to feed itself and the weapons it needs to fight. You're going to need them to be loyal, so that you don't have to divert large parts of your army to pacifying territory you already vanquished. How loyal would you be if your new rulers allowed your women to be assaulted, your precious few valuables taken, and your home to be burned."

"It's what will make them loyal. They will fear us and know what could happen if we are forced to come back and teach them another lesson."

Velius refrained from pointing out that his father's army hadn't taught them anything and wouldn't be in the position to sack the city at all if it wasn't for Velius and his legions.

Instead, he said, "You should look to your own histories, Prince, since your family is an example of the very thing I'm talking about. Your father was not the next in line for the throne, and the man that was is still out there, leading armies to recapture it. Your father fought to remove him from power and put in a rule that was more just for your people. You should ask yourself, is there someone like your father out there, plotting revenge for the unjust way they must feel they are being treated?"

The prince fell quiet, although Velius couldn't tell if it was because the message got through or if he was just sulking.

"It's going to take at least a day to get them back in order and on the march again, unless you're thinking about leaving them behind and continuing to our objective without them," Llassar said, from the other side of the boy.

"No, we need to take them with us. In this kind of state, it's going to be hard for the cavalry to distinguish them from the bandits that have been plaguing the border kingdoms, and we're already stretching our lines of communication thin enough without losing horsemen to confusion, deciding if a group in the distance is friend or foe. This isn't a particularly large city, so they should burn themselves out, or at least the town out, by this evening. We'll send in teams to round up anyone who hasn't made it back to the camps in the morning, and then be on our way towards the coast."

"They'll be exhausted. It will slow down our progress all day tomorrow to keep them with us."

Velius thought Llassar was probably right, but there wasn't much he could do about it. He'd learned a long time ago it was better to accept the reality of a situation and plan accordingly than sit wishing the situation was different, wasting time.

"Like I said, there isn't much we can do about it. We have some time. As far as we can tell, the Carthaginians have forced their allies to pull all of their forces to the south to protect Inverness, which is the only port large enough to receive supplies and reinforcements, and they don't look to be moving north. Best guess, since taking us head-on didn't work out great for them, they want to let us come to them this time. They probably have something planned for us and they've given an all-or-nothing ultimatum to their allies, forcing them to all but abandon their capitals and join in that plan."

"If they've left their capitals unguarded, shouldn't you take this opportunity to wipe them out, so they don't have anywhere to turn to?" the prince asked, looking annoyed that Velius and Llassar were talking over him like he wasn't there.

"What would be the point?" Velius asked. "By themselves, they aren't a significant threat beyond raiding. Hell, you wouldn't have needed us at all if it was just them. Until they got the backing of the Carthaginians, you were able to keep all of the kingdoms in check. They all hated your people, but even banding together, they weren't able to come for you, until they got help."

"What's your point?" Cormac asked.

"My point is, they aren't a threat. At least not on their own. We gain nothing spending the time diverting to their cities so we can sack them. In fact, you lose something for the same reason we shouldn't be sacking this place, but even ignoring that, it's a bad idea. Right now, the enemy is sitting still, waiting on us. Yes, it allows them to come up with a plan to fight us, but it also means we get to choose when and where we attack, to some degree, since they're not going to want us circling around behind them. If we sit and wait, they'll start moving. Our scouts are good, but two moving forces add extra uncertainty to the situation, and uncertainty isn't something a soldier wants. If I was them and I found out we were out here sacking cities, I'd move to hit us while our forces were divided."

"They need to be taught a lesson," Cormac muttered, just loud enough to be heard, but not looking at either Velius or Llassar.

"Your father left you with us to learn, Child," Llassar said, leaning over and grabbing the reins of the younger man's horse. "If you can't listen, we can't teach you anything, and we might as well send you back to your mother's skirts."

"That's enough, Llassar," Velius said.

He could appreciate the tough love approach Llassar was taking. It was his preferred technique with the legions, where they regularly had to turn willful young men into soldiers capable of following orders. A young princeling, on the other hand, had to be treated differently. Beyond growing up believing, and being told, that they were better than everyone else, he'd seen enough of the young man's father to know he'd spent his life receiving this approach. If he was still this way after that, then being firm with him would never bear fruit.

"If you want to win wars, you have to think like a soldier and not a brigand. We're not here to teach these people lessons. We're here to win a war, which means defeating their armies and forcing their leaders to submit to peace under our terms. If you lose sight of your objectives, you'll lose sight of your enemy, and they will make you pay the price for your inattention."

Waving one of his aides over, Velius said, "This foolishness has gone on long enough. See if you can find any of their commanders and tell them if they can't get their men in line in the next two hours, the legions will leave without them. We have a war to fight."

Devnum

It had taken a little experimenting, but she had figured out how to secretly store the 'drone,' as Sophus kept calling it. At first glance, it had seemed small enough, but it was too large to fit through the opening of the pouch and, while it was very flexible, it couldn't be folded in half to be shoved inside.

She'd eventually worked out a way to attach it to the pouch using a pair of hair clips and several small lengths of leather strip, all of it tied tight enough to keep it from falling, as long as she didn't start running or doing some other fast movement.

The sun hadn't gone down yet, but it was getting late in the day when she got to the foundry that was working on the cannon. The men working that day didn't mind getting let out an hour early, especially once she told them that they would be paid for the whole day, including the time they didn't work because she'd made them stop. Thankfully, this was one of Hortensius's shops, which he ran under the philosophy that well-treated workers actually produce more and better-quality products than workers toiling under the whip, so she didn't have to deal with foremen objecting.

She did have the foremen wait outside for her, in case she had new instructions, which they were less pleased with, since the idea of a short day sounded as good to them as it had to the workers, but they complied, waiting with one of her guards while the rest secured the building to keep prying eyes away from it.

Although she'd been in the foundry many times, it always stunned her how hot it was inside and how brutal the conditions for the workers must be. Even though the furnaces were now only glowing embers, no longer being stoked, and the air outside was still crisp with the last days of winter not far behind them, she could feel sweat instantly begin pooling on her neck as she began walking through the large building.

They'd finished the latest casting of the test cannon almost a week before, which had been pushed to one side of the building, waiting for Hortensius's sign-off when he recovered. Helpfully, the foremen had also moved the molds for casting it close by, so both could be examined. She'd been surprised the first time she'd seen the cannon, discovering that it had been made out of bronze rather than iron or steel. Bronze was rarely seen outside of decorative metal working anymore, because of how much weaker it was than even the steel they'd been able to make before Ky's appearance. It was generally considered a metal for a less civilized time, so she hadn't expected to see the coppery-gold appearance of the cannon the first time.

Sophus had explained that the bronze cannon was lighter and more likely to crack rather than shatter if the metal failed, making it less deadly for the men using it, while still being strong enough to generally stand up to the gunpowder they were producing, but she was still doubtful. The large, metal balls they were producing to fire out of it were also of lower quality, being simple cast iron rather than more refined iron or steel. This was apparently because of weight and speed of production, and she could at least understand not wanting to spend a lot of time and money on something that would be launched at the enemy and probably never recover.

Looking around and confirming the building was empty, she reached inside her tunic and loosened the drone, pulling it out and holding it in the palm of her hand.

"We're alone," she said out loud to Sophus, who had no way of knowing what was happening while the drone was compact like this.

The drone instantly expanded, becoming wider and more ridged, and leaped from her hand so lightly that it surprised her. She thought there might be a push-off against her hand, like when a bird would take flight after loitering on your finger or arm, but there wasn't. It just went up, as if by magic, which she still wasn't convinced wasn't the case. Ky kept assuring her it was technology, but she couldn't even imagine a technology that would allow for something like that.

The drone circled the cannon slowly, stopping for long minutes here and there. There wasn't any indication it was doing anything other than just floating there, but she waited silently until the disk finally finished going over the cannon and mold and came floating back to her.

"Although there are still issues, the progress is impressive and I believe it will not be long before a usable production model is achievable. An admirable success."

"So, what needs to change?" Lucilla asked.

"The mold still does not have the precision needed to properly cast the cannon. I know Hortensius used the measurement guides that have been working for the current weapons, but the tolerances needed for this are much more exacting and have less room for variations. We might need to reproduce the measurement equipment used by this facility or adjust them to be more precise, and most likely there needs to be additional training for the men using them to adhere specifically to those measurements. I won't know until I examine the tools being used, but my guess is this is more a case of the men deciding things are 'close enough' rather than a fault with the tools themselves. The issue here is the mold itself and not the cannon, which is well formed and from my measurements adheres precisely to the mold, although it could use more polishing and shaping once the metal cools. Other than the mold, which needs to be recreated, especially the cavity for the borehole, which is much too small to allow for the current horizontal borer to be properly shaped. If steam power was currently possible, we could achieve the force needed to shape the metal from a more solid starting point, but even with the metal slightly heated to allow it to be more malleable,

the water-powered bore is not strong enough to get the cavity properly shaped, leading to the walls of the cannon being much too thick. Since switching to a new form of power isn't feasible in the time we have available, especially since it can't both be perfected and produced in quantities to be useful, the simplest adjustment is to increase the initial bore cavity, leaving less metal for the bore drill to have to remove."

"Is there anything that can be done to the drill to make it work better?" she asked, looking at the long device that could be hooked up to the gears coming off the waterwheel that the factory was built around to give it power.

"Not that's feasible with the current technological base. There is a need to advance to steam power soon, especially before we advance to rifling, which will need steel rather than bronze which can't be cut by this low-powered drill, but for now, this is passable."

Lucilla didn't know what rifling was, but she could understand the need for a stronger drill. Although she hadn't understood much about metallurgy a year ago, the time she'd spent working with Hortensius going over steel production, cannon development, and the myriad of other things Ky had left in her charge, both when he'd been injured and after he'd sent her back to Devnum to supervise these activities, had given her a solid base of understanding of how these things worked.

She knew, for example, how much stronger steel was than bronze, which would make it impossible to cut using the drill driven by waterpower. A large man could dent and shape it with a hammer, something they wouldn't be able to do with steel, and the foremen were already complaining about the difficulties they were having with cutting into the metal. She'd heard both Sophus and Ky refer to a machine that could do what the waterwheel did, but with much more power, but she still didn't understand what that was, exactly. The name they'd called it made it clear that it used steam, but how scalding water vapor could apply more force than a rushing river was beyond her.

That was for the future when Ky was back in Devnum and heading these projects. For now, the drone had done its job and pointed out where the flaws in the cannon were, and how to correct them. She told the foremen they could go home and that they would have to begin recreating the mold and recasting the cannon in the morning, when they'd be given new plans and instructions on what needed to be changed. They'd already recast the cannon numerous times in their attempts to perfect the technology, so they didn't seem bothered by having to start over again. If anything, they seemed happy to have someone giving them specific instructions again, instead of having to do it on their own without Hortensius's guiding hand.

She spent the next several hours, well into the evening, in her rooms, writing up the plans to Sophus's specifications, the drone hovering over her shoulder so the usually disembodied voice could watch what she was doing and make corrections and alterations.

Outside Devnum

"What's the point?" one of the men gathered around the small table said. "The Carthaginians are gone and, if what you said is accurate, Caesius has sailed for Africa. There are too few of us and there is no one left to come to our assistance."

The home, which had once been the center of a large, landed estate, had begun to look more worn than it once had. The landowner, who'd refused to sell off his slaves when word of the anti-slave laws began circulating, had been forced to sell much of that land to the new freeman farmers that had begun popping up over the last several months. The government had paid him when they'd taken his slaves, but only a pittance of what he believed they were worth and not enough for him to make up for having to pay some of the same people who used to work in his fields for free a wage for the exact same labor, cutting into his profits every week.

"There are still a lot of us loyal to Rome and ready to do what we have to to bring our Empire back to what it was. If we rise up, the people would see it and rally to us. There are too many of us for them to stop."

Decius shook his head. He'd heard this sentiment for the last several months, as he smuggled himself from one supporter's home to another, trying to rally support for some kind of action while staying one step ahead of Ramirus's men, who'd never given up trying to find him even after they murdered his son. These people were mostly angry because they'd lost something to the Emperor's lackeys, either slaves or business when the Empire enacted its slate of new laws, business prospects when the new Britannic Empire was formed, cutting off most of the lands to the north as a possible point of expansion, or through direct retaliation when they'd dealt with the barbarians, who wanted to pretend they were civilized people. As someone who'd lost more than just money, he could sympathize with their pain and was forever indebted to them, both for their kindness in hiding him and their willingness to fight for the cause, but he was starting to see a troubling pattern.

They'd decided that anyone who disagreed with their hatred of the Emperor and his lackeys was, by default a supporter, and not someone they wanted any contact with. This had started to include anyone who worked on government projects, took government contracts, or even had a family member in one of the legions. The more extreme they got in their stances, the more isolated they became from anyone that didn't agree with them. They started to only hear people who thought like they did, which gave them a sense that most of the 'real' people in Rome were on their side.

Decius had traveled the city, never staying in one place for long, and often he wasn't able to turn to people like the landowner or the other men gathered here, because they'd started to draw attention to themselves. Dealing with only other disaffected citizens, and being vocal about it, had put them on the spymaster's lists. More than once, Decius had been forced to find new lodgings at the last minute after learning that the supporter he was planning on staying with was suddenly under surveillance. This meeting had taken more than a month to set up and he'd been forced to all but threaten several of the members to keep to themselves leading up to it, to make sure Ramirus's thugs didn't kick down the door in the middle of the meeting.

Decius knew that, while there were people like them out there, the group wasn't as large as these men believed. Even when they did have a much wider base of support, including the support of two full legions, their attempt to take Rome back had failed. Since then, the immediate threat of Carthaginian invasion had ended, and people were starting to see some of the benefits of all the imperial spending, which meant there was significantly less support now than there had been in early winter. If they rose up, they would be crushed. Easily.

Of course, these were true believers, and none of them would hear a word he had to say if he tried to bring them back to reality. Instead, he needed to get them pointed in the right direction, to at least put their foolishness to good use, before they ended up in one of Ramirus's cells.

"I couldn't agree more, if it were only the new 'Consul' and his thugs," Decius said, making sure to use derision on the Consul's title, since he was at the center of all of their anger. "But things are different now. We aren't just dealing with the praetorians or Ramirus's men. Besides the Caledonians, who are now everywhere you look, the Emperor's daughter has begun bringing in Iberians, Germanians, and all kinds of wild men from the continent; bribed with jobs and promises of becoming citizens just like you and me. If we stand up, who do you think all of these barbarians will side with? No, we need to be smarter. We can't just take to the streets, putting the palace to the torch. If we are going to strike, we must be smart about it."

"What would you suggest?" the landowner asked.

The man was angry and looking for some way to vent against what he felt were injustices committed against them. Decius had to be careful. While there was no way someone like Ramirus would find his way of speaking 'appeasement to the government,' the landowner and some of the men like him had become too extreme. Anything short of civil war sounded to them like giving in to the Emperor.

"We need to be smart about how we hurt them. Taking to the streets and dying would accomplish nothing. They would sell your home to some northern barbarian and your family would end up working the fields you once owned. I'm willing to give my life, but only if it hurts them enough to make that sacrifice worth it. Caesius is out there, trying to rally support for us. Yes, what you heard is true, he was forced to flee the island when the last safe refuge for him disappeared, but he won't stay gone. He will come back to take his rightful place as soon as he's able to. What we can do is help him make that day come sooner. It may look like they are winning, but that's an illusion. The Emperor's legions are still badly outnumbered. We've all seen the new factories going up across the city and I'm sure by now some of you will have heard about the devastating fire at that new one outside of town. We all know the Emperor's new 'Consul' is the man actually behind these, and clearly, his daughter is in charge of them while her demon lover is out of the city. What we can do is make sure these weapons never make it to the legions, leaving them vulnerable when the Carthaginians return to free us."

"How do we do that?" he asked, this time sounding interested, instead of sarcastic.

"We kill her."

"My son-in-law is working in one of the factories. Hortensius was in, at least for a little bit, every single day, before he got injured, making sure everything was running right and that the foremen knew what they needed to do. Lucilla is making the rounds, but not nearly as often as Hortensius did, and from what I hear, she's mostly just asking questions. If the factories can keep running without him, how is killing her going to stop them."

"Because there isn't someone like her to take her place the way she took Hortensius's. Yes, she isn't around as much, but from what I hear, production is already falling behind, so clearly, his absence is having an effect. If she's gone, they'll have to find someone else to take over, and it's doubtful that person will have either Hortensius's drive, or her connection to the 'Consul,' who's the person really behind all this anyway. Better yet, it might force him to come back to Devnum, giving us a chance to get to him."

"That's interesting," the man said.

"How would we get to her?" another man asked. "She's protected by guards at all times."

"She's been meeting with these immigrants from Germania regularly, and indications are she'll be meeting with them again.

Immigrants she has spoken to are moved to other locations and replaced by others who are strangers to her and permitted to get close to her. She's also touring some of their camps, which allows people to get even closer to her. There's an opportunity there."

From there, the men started running with the idea, allowing him to take a step back. They were brave; he had to give them that. Most of the men were willing to give their lives if it meant hurting the people they hated, but they hadn't thought about what would happen after that. Ramirus would tear their lives apart, finding anyone they associated with that might harbor similar feelings.

Regardless of how successful these men were, this entire group would be in cells shortly after their attempt. Killing the Emperor's daughter was worth their lives, saddened by it as he would be. It also meant he would have to leave very soon and lay low again, at least for a while.

Chapter 18

"How are you feeling?" Lucilla asked, looking down at Hortensius, who stirred at her voice.

"Thankful to be alive," he said, his voice croaking. "I hear you played some part in keeping me alive while I healed."

"Only a small part," she said, knowing he'd understand, since he knew she could communicate with Ky, and he was ultimately the source of the knowledge that helped keep him alive.

"They let me look over this breathing apparatus you had them build. It's got some interesting components, although I can see a few places you could have made it better. Not needing someone pumping on it day and night, for one."

"We were limited on time, although I'm sure the physicians wouldn't mind if you perfected it. I imagine it could be used in the future by people who can't afford to pay for an army of workers to always be available to keep air flowing."

"Maybe," he said, looking thoughtful. "Maybe."

"Did they give you any indication of when you can go home?"

"They want me out today. Apparently, now that I'm awake, they want this bed for someone else."

"And when can you come back to work?" she asked, then realized how that sounded. "Not that I want you to rush your recovery, but I'm a poor replacement and I feel like I'm drowning just trying to keep up with a fraction of your workload."

"Which makes you sane," he said, letting out a laugh that halfway through turned into a cough. "Your luck isn't that good, unfortunately. My chest is doing better, although it hurts every time I breathe. They said they had no treatment for it, apparently, the Consul's last conversation with them included taking away most of their cures. They think it could heal on its own, but they

197

wouldn't actually promise anything. I thought maybe the Consul could tell me differently, but until he makes it back, I'll have to live with it. Unfortunately, I might be limping forever. They want me to keep off my leg for a while longer, so that's going to slow me down, which means I'm going to need your help a while longer. So, no one here could tell me. How much damage did the fire do?"

"Explosion," Lucilla said, the strange word still feeling awkward in her mouth.

"Clap?" he asked, understanding part of the word she said, which was oddly the first thing she'd said when she'd heard Ky use it the first time.

"It's the word Ky used to describe what happens when the gunpowder goes off. You probably didn't hear it, since you were so close, but it kind of did sound like a clap, although one that was done by the Titans. As for the damage, the whole building is gone. The only reason you survived was because you were outside when it happened. It threw you through the air like thrashed straw."

"Sabotage?"

"No. Probably an errant spark set it off."

"We're going to have to make new safety procedures."

"We already have, although you're welcome to check my work. Thankfully, we only lost a little product, since everything but the supplies needed for one day's production was stored off-site. It slowed us down a little bit, but we already have a new factory running, so we're only a little behind on our goals."

"See, you hardly need me."

"Nonsense. The only reason everything is still running is because you trained your men well, and they've carried on. We've made progress on the cannons, although you're going to have to remake the molds, and we've almost got the new docks built so we can start construction on the ships Ky has described. We're falling behind on the semaphore stations and we have questions about some of your modifications, but we were able to make good progress on the looking glasses."

"Again, I don't see what you need from me."

"That was all the good stuff, now let me tell you the problems we've been having," she said, pulling up a stool next to the bed and settling in for what was almost certainly going to be a long conversation.

Southern Ériunia

Velius frowned as he watched the legions marching past him. Progress had been much slower than he'd hoped, to the point he was concerned the Carthaginians and their local allies would begin trying to outmaneuver him, instead of holding until he got in range. If he was able to threaten their supply lines or get on their flanks, they'd be forced to move, allowing him to choose the field of battle. If they came directly for him, they would get to pick where the fight happened, and if they were smart, they'd find a spot that negated some of his advantages.

That was partly why he was trying to push his men south as hard as he could, to get into the southern coastal plains, where the trees thinned out, giving his cavalry room to maneuver. The Carthaginians were almost entirely infantry, with very few mounted soldiers. His greater weight in horsemen coupled with how maneuverable they were, allowed his men to hit the Carthaginians on the flanks and from behind, which would force part of their force to turn and address the threat. He didn't have enough cavalry to actually cut into their forces, but if his men kept hitting and moving away, always targeting different spots along the Carthaginian line, they could cause havoc and confusion that would help negate the Carthaginian manpower advantage.

Right now, he was still crossing through passes between mountainous regions and down into a forested area that limited his visibility and gave very little opportunity for his cavalry to run free. If the fight happened here, it would be a contest of infantry, which would not work in Velius's favor. Worse, the heavy tree cover would also hamper the advantages the arcuballista they brought, since the range would be too short to concentrate their fire on one section of the line like he did in the last battle.

From what his scouts had reported, the Carthaginian force was huge. Maybe not the size of the one they had fought to win control of Britannia, but still several times greater than Velius's army. It appeared to be mostly locals, with the Carthaginians making up a small fraction of the fighting force, which would help, since they seemed to be as undisciplined as his allies, but if the Carthaginians **did** maintain control of them, the numbers were still too far in their favor for Velius to take them in a straight up fight. Or at least not without getting torn to shreds doing it.

No, to win this, he needed every advantage to maneuver. Although he wouldn't be able to make a specific plan until he knew what kind of ground he was dealing with, he was most likely going to have to split his already outnumbered force and find a way to hit them from multiple directions simultaneously. Without Ky's ability to signal a separated force, that would be difficult, but it wasn't unheard of, and his men had been training for just this kind of thing on the days they stopped to allow their supply lines to catch up.

But first, he had to get out of these mountains and forests. His men were moving at a brisk pace and would already be clear of the mountains and halfway through the forests below if they weren't being slowed by their local allies. Three times, he had to stop when the Ulaid allies decided they needed to sack a nearby village, simply because it was on the land of one of their enemies. In every case, they were small, poor farming villages that couldn't have had much to take anyway, and yet he'd lost a day at each one trying to get their leaders to get them back in line and on the march. Even on the march, they were slow and lumbering, treating the campaign as some kind of holiday instead of a fight for their very lives.

Having been in one of these fights very recently, he couldn't understand why they weren't taking it seriously. Maybe it was because nearly every man sent by Conchobar to fight with them was a conscript and not a soldier, or maybe because most weren't aware of how badly their kingdom had fared to this point, but either way, what Velius really wanted to do was leave them behind. As fighters, they'd be all but useless, and he'd have to focus more on keeping them out of the way of his legionnaires than on how to properly use them. It was sad that most would die before the campaign was over, but that would be something for the Ulaid to deal with. Velius had been sent to push the Carthaginians off this island and keep them from being able to launch new attacks on Britannia, and that was what he was going to do.

Maybe, if they decided to join the Empire, they'd be able to add men to the corps that could be trained as real soldiers. As men, they weren't a complete loss. In general, they had bravery and a willingness to fight. What they lacked was discipline and training, things not valued by most of the kingdoms on Ériunia.

His thoughts were interrupted when a rider came charging up the slope towards them.

"A messenger from the scouting parties," one of Velius's aides said, recognizing the man.

"Report," Velius said when the man rode up, looking tired and saddle worn.

"The Carthaginians are on the move. Their army began pulling out two days ago, marching north. They've begun pushing our scouts back more aggressively, making it hard to get a good read on them, but we've started seeing some additional forces coming from the east, joining the main body."

"Carthaginian phalanxes?"

"No. Locals, but a good number of them. Well over a thousand they think, although it's hard to get a good read on the real number. The optio in charge of the eastern scouts didn't want to send his men deeper into the area they've started cordoning off. The locals aren't friendly and we've had to dodge villages and farmers to keep from having our locations fed to the Carthaginians."

"Sensible. Ride back and inform them to track the Carthaginian forces as best they can, but don't take unnecessary risks."

The messenger saluted and turned his horse to ride back out. It was likely the man was already exhausted, but they were all going to be tired by the time this was over, so he'd just have to do the best he could.

"Why keep them back?" Llassar asked, watching the man go. "It's worth losing some men if it tells us their position."

"I don't think they're going to go north of these mountains. This is the first Carthaginian army I've seen that is made up of more local units than phalanxes, which means they are running short on their own men. It's probably why they pulled all the way back here, instead of trying to intercept us like the previous army did, and why they've had their allies all but empty their own territories."

"That couldn't be popular with their allies. To them, a victory is sacking a city and running off with plunder and slaves. Hell, before joining your people, we hardly ever fought large battles like you keep doing. There would be a few battles, some sacks, and then everyone would back off and the war would be over. Sometimes territory changed hands, but not often. This way of war is different from what they are used to."

"Which is why they're moving now that we're clear of the mountains. They can't just wait for us forever, so they're going to bring the fight to us."

"So, what are we going to do? If they're coming for us and we can't run and can't take them head-on, it doesn't leave a lot of options for us."

"I don't know yet. Hopefully, I'll think of something clever."

Devnum

"Are you sure you're well enough?" Lucilla asked for the thirtieth time that morning.

She had predicted Hortensius wouldn't make it two weeks lying in bed, resting while he recovered. It turned out that was wildly optimistic, as the manufacturer started making noises almost immediately and twice the woman Lucilla hired to tend to him at home had to chastise him to get back into bed after he tried to hobble his way out of the house.

Finally, Sophus came to the rescue and described a design for a wheeled chair that he could use to move around while still letting his leg rest. Weirdly, Hortensius had heard of that before.

202

Apparently, there were records of the Greeks making something like that a long time ago, and from time to time, someone dug it up and tried to recreate it. He was at first very dismissive of the idea, because everyone who had tried to recreate it ran into the same problem.

Roman roads and even buildings weren't exactly flat and free of obstructions. The best-case scenario was a dirt road that had been worn flat, but those became impassible when it rained, which is why the most critical areas of town had more or less flat stones pressed close together, forming an artificial surface. This was fine for carts and the like, whose large wheels moved across the small gaps in the stones without much issue, but it didn't work for the smaller wheels that would have to be used on a chair with wheels. Apparently, someone had once tried to use a wider wheel like a cart, but that had made the chair almost impossible to move.

Sophus had thought of this, and its suggestions were enough to almost make things worse, since Hortensius wanted to go straight to the foundries to inspect the developments. It took time, but Lucilla convinced him to be patient and let his foremen have the first shot at making the chair, and he could have a more active hand once he was mobile again.

The thing that got him most excited was another advancement in steel. It was apparently a big advancement, although Lucilla didn't really understand what the excitement was about. According to Sophus, they'd already advanced to making something it called Wootz steel. She made the mistake of asking what that was, only to cut Sophus off after ten minutes of explanation she couldn't follow at all. The change was in the process of heat treating the steel a second time, making it able to bend slightly and return to its original shape. It apparently wasn't as good as something called 'spring steel' but it should work for his chair design.

The steel was what got Hortensius excited. Apparently, a steel that could bend slightly under heavy pressure, instead of breaking when it passed its tension point had all kinds of implications for building, both in weapons and tools and in making buildings themselves.

For now, they were limiting it to a single design Sophus had called a 'leaf spring' that looked almost like part of an eye in the top and bottom facing towards each other, where they connected together in a stronger, non-bending piece of metal. After she explained it to Hortensius, using Sophus's words, the manufacturer instantly got the idea and was already making notes for several of his assistants to begin working on it.

The downside of all of that was that Lucilla had to remain in the foundry for almost the entire week, overseeing the production of these leaf springs. She was there so often that the workers had even started adapting to her occasionally clearing the workshop floor, to allow her to deploy the drone so Sophus could see the project firsthand. Its close observation of the production meant that they hadn't needed to start over numerous times like they'd had for the cannon, since Sophus had been able to identify errors and problems while they were still able to be corrected.

That week's worth of work had resulted in Hortensius being pushed down the street by an aide, his leg supported straight out in front of him, successfully being kept from jostling or becoming further injured by the chair that bounced with the ground while he stayed more or less stationary. Although she was still having trouble believing that he wasn't causing himself more injury, Hortensius was having the time of his life.

"Absolutely, my lady. This is simply amazing. Wait until we adapt this for carts to carry people. Imagine being able to ride on one without being thrown this way and that as the wheels bounce in ruts and divots. Or having half of a shipment of goods end up broken by the rough transport from the ports. I tell you; this is going to change shipping completely."

"It probably will, but first we should focus on things we can use for the progress of the war."

"Right. Right. The docks have come along nicely. I have to commend you on your work."

"That was mostly Lucan's doing," she said.

Shortly before the accident, Hortensius had settled on Herius Gratius Lucan to handle the shipbuilding project. Although he wasn't the most experienced of Britannia's very limited supply of shipbuilders, he was the most flexible and most likely to adapt to the proposed changes. Having spoken to him numerous times, Lucilla found him stubborn, obstinate, and questioning of everything she suggested. She couldn't imagine how bad the other men were for Lucan to be their best choice, but she trusted Hortensius's judgment. Although it had taken browbeating and the occasional reminder of their relative positions of power, explanations of every single thing that needed to be done, and reminders of who was paying for this project, he had made excellent progress.

The new "dry docks," which Ky sometimes called a slipway, weren't all that much of a problem, since they at least followed the general pattern of how Romans built ships. The main difference was that these were built to be permanent. Rome had built very few ships in the last hundred years, relying mostly on people like the Scandi for what limited maritime trade they did. Of the ships they did build, most were small fishing ships built on the beaches by villagers. The handful of larger ships they had built were all one-offs, with temporary frameworks and scaffolding built at the edge of the docks, so the boat could be pushed into the water when it was finished.

The new, built-in docks, designed so that when finished, the ship could be released into the water down a ramp, were similar to this, except that there was what almost looked like a warehouse around it with permanent scaffolding that could move into place as the ship was built from the keel up.

Its similarity to the traditional Roman methods had allowed the dockyard to go up fairly quickly, and within just a few months they had the facilities to build up to five ships simultaneously, which seemed like overkill to Lucilla, but Ky had promised they would be important as time went on.

No, the real problem had started as she handed the plans of the new ship to Lucan, who thought everything about these tall ships, with their large and weirdly shaped sails and no placement for rowers was wrong.

"And he's started constructing the first ships," he said as they entered one of the covered buildings where a ship was being built.

"Mostly. There have been ... disagreements."

"Yes, Lucan can be stubborn. I'll talk to him, but honestly, in this area, you're going to have to continue being highly involved. I can understand some of the changes the Consul is introducing, or at least the long-term implications of them, but this is well outside of my expertise, and I wouldn't know how to answer his questions or concerns."

"I was afraid you might say that. I don't love being called an 'idiot child' every other day."

"Don't take it to heart. Lucan is like that with everyone. He doesn't have the patience to follow social norms or niceties, which is why he's so rarely used on large-scale projects. Those of us who know good work, however, know what he's worth."

"I'll figure out a way to deal with him. Besides, he's not the worst part of this project. These ships are costing a fortune to build and the Senate has yet to accept that they are a necessity."

"I don't know about being a necessity for war, but if the figures for what these ships can carry is true, they will do wonders for our trade. Although they're going to be limited on what ports they can go into, since many of our docks are built for much shallower drafted ships. They couldn't go into Londinium, for one."

"Ky's already taken that into account. He's still primarily interested in how they'll do carrying troops and supplies, but he figured once you and some of the merchants heard what they could do, you'd be interested."

"I am, although that brings up another problem. From my understanding, reading over the Consul's notes, these ships are going to need a skilled crew, with specialized knowledge of sails, rope use, and the like. I also saw a mention of maybe even putting the cannon we're developing onto these ships, although for the life of me, I can't imagine how that would work. Not with the way ships move up and down with the waves. I guess … Sorry, too many things in my head at once. What I meant was, until it was outlawed, rowers were predominantly slaves and their most important skill was a strong back. We're going to have a problem finding anyone who's worked a large, deep drafting sail-driven ship before, let alone enough people to put on one of these."

"I actually have an idea how to address that," Lucilla said. "There's a chance we have more people available to us with experience sailing ships than you realize."

Chapter 19

Lucilla was once again in the forum surrounded by leaders of various immigrant groups, although this time most of them hadn't traveled as far. The praetorians had made good progress getting all the people still landing on their shores out of the small fishing villages that couldn't handle them and to some of the larger cities, where the need for labor was still outpacing its supply.

A sign of that success was also in how many more people were there than had attended before. Part of that was because the immigrants weren't gathered up in villages, where they could elect one person to serve as their representative, and instead were starting to be more spread out among the cities. Since they came from all over Germania, and now even points further east, they weren't a predominant single, or even series, of ethnic or cultural groups either, meaning smaller groups needed to send spokesmen if they wanted to be heard.

Everything started off well. Most of the immigrants were happy to swear allegiance to Britannia, forsaking a return to their homeland and had started integrating into society. There'd been some issues with housing, and the western part of the city had already begun expanding as more was being built. So far, her father had left that up to private industry, which was buying up land from farmers, some of whom wanted to move south where new land was available in the former Carthaginian territory and others that had had difficulty adjusting to the new reality without slaves. They were being paid well for the land, with the businessmen buying the property and bidding against each other, all of them seeing an opportunity to make money off of these new citizens.

It hadn't happened yet, but her father's agents had several conversations with these businessmen to find out how they planned on making money from people with very little to their name. Some had a plan to sell it to the immigrants, taking payment over time, with interest taken with each payment, while others were setting themselves up as landlords, renting the apartments or houses out. The reason there was so much competition to buy up property and set up these new homes was because part of the agreement for citizenship required joining the legions or working in critical industry, meaning all of these new citizens were guaranteed to have some sort of steady income.

Nearly all of the properties being built were three-story insulae Each multi-unit building had eight small single or multi-room domiciles on the top two stories, with shops for rent on the ground floor, which made sense. There wasn't enough land for villas or small single-family homes, and even with their new employment, these people wouldn't make enough to afford anything like that in the near future. At the rate they were going, Devnum was going to grow half again in size by next year, which was a startling rate of growth, especially considering there were a lot of abandoned and destroyed homes in Londinium and other cities that had, until recently, been controlled by the Carthaginians.

Of course, that only seemed incredible because she was here and could see the changes firsthand. Other cities, both up in Caledonia and along the border in mining towns, were growing just as fast, since they had as much need for manpower as Devnum did. She was certain once business began to expand south into the reconquered territory, those cities would also see significant growth, since the influx of immigrants didn't seem to be stopping any time soon.

The one thing her father did was warn the businessmen investing in this expansion not to take advantage of these new citizens. They knew these people had little choice but to accept whatever deal they were offered, since there wasn't housing for them inside the city and they couldn't very well go back to where they came from, making the immigrants a tempting target for exploitation.

That was the first topic Lucilla discussed with them, after greeting them and learning a little bit about the now more diverse group of immigrants being represented.

"We've petitioned the Imperial Senate and asked both the Caledonian leadership and the Roman Senate to pass laws limiting the amount of interest these developers can ask for the new homes being built. It will take time, but we will try and protect you from being taken advantage of. I wanted you to be aware of what we are doing so you can pass it on to your people and tell them to be patient if a deal you are being offered seems wrong in some way. We will continue to try to support you as best we can by maintaining some of the communal homes outside of town so you have a roof over your heads until we can get laws passed protecting you from unfair exploitation."

The influx of refugees had been so great that they'd been forced to erect temporary buildings or tent cities outside of town, mostly in the areas where the legions had camped over the winter, to give the immigrants and their families a place to live until they could figure out better housing. They'd also instructed the praetorians to set up similar facilities in other cities that were seeing an influx of immigrants from the continent.

"What do we do if we think someone is taking advantage of us? We appreciate your people giving us a place to live, but we want a place of our own. We want to start our new lives. We have sworn allegiance to the Empire and are working in what you called 'critical industries,' doing our part to help our new country. Living by your charity makes us as reliant on you as we would be on our new landlords and any unfair deal they give us. We just want to live and work."

"I understand that, and I do not want you becoming reliant on the Empire for your ability to live. It's why all the places we assigned for you to stay in, *are temporary*. We are not putting in permanent buildings to house new immigrants, because it is in our best interest to get you integrated into society as quickly as possible. That being said, we don't want you to feel pushed into taking a deal you know is bad for you, just because you don't want to accept charity. I'm not asking you to wait until we get a law passed protecting you. I'm just asking you to make sure your people are careful about what deals they take."

"How do we do that? We did not have to worry about borrowing money or paying money for a home to someone else where I came from. How would we know what is fair or not? And how would we go about doing something about it if we find out it isn't fair?" another man asked.

"That's a good question. We are going to have a few clerks from the Imperial Treasury making stops at the temporary settlement camps every week, where they will spend the day answering questions about what is considered reasonable and if a deal is unreasonable. If you have been offered an unreasonable deal, report it to them. While legally we may not be able to pressure these businessmen into doing the right thing, many are also working on government contracts that are making them very rich, which gives us additional ways to remind them of their responsibilities as a citizen of the Empire. We will speak with these builders and lenders and try to convince them to offer you something more in line with what is considered reasonable or normal in the Empire. If we can't, we'll let you know and you can choose to look to other builders, wait for the new laws mandating fair treatment to pass, or take the deal and move on with things. Ultimately, it is your decision what to do, and if you are anxious enough to start your new life and, knowing the fairness of the deal you are being offered, decide to accept it, then we, of course, will not stop you."

Next followed a series of questions about specifics of deals they'd already been offered, even though none of the housing was up yet. That part wasn't unusual or suspect, and Lucilla already assumed much of the new housing would be sold or rented before they were finished, but she wasn't prepared to answer most of those questions. All she could do was promise that she would pass the questions on to some of the clerks being assigned to investigate refugee claims and make sure they'd get back to them with the answer.

In the end, she was pretty sure many of these people would end up taking deals regardless of how fair it was without waiting for government oversight, partly out of a desire to get on with their lives, but mostly out of fear that if they didn't, someone else who was more desperate, would take it first, and they'd be left in the settlement camps.

She tried to explain to them that eventually they'd find places for everyone, and no one was going to be left in the camps long term, but scared people in new environments often made decisions against their own self-interest and had trouble listening to advice that required ignoring that fear. As she said, she wasn't going to stop them if that was what they decided, although it was going to create future problems for the Empire as a new impoverished class began to form. It wouldn't be slavery exactly, but it would be close to it, where wages barely kept up with workers' debts, putting them further at the mercy of the people they were indebted to.

That, however, was a problem for another day. All they could do was try and protect them as best they could, get them out of the settlement camps and off government support, and into the factories and legions. Hortensius had been mobile for only a handful of days and he was already looking at half a dozen new projects to start, forming new partnerships with other manufacturers and factory owners to increase production as export demand for Britannian goods increased. They needed to increase their workforce, and they needed to do it now, not at the leisure of the senate and their negotiations.

As the meeting started to wind down, she found the spokesmen for several Scandi groups and asked them to stay behind.

"We appreciate you inviting us to these things, but we have none of the same concerns as these people," one of the spokesmen said as the other immigrant leaders left. "We are just here to trade and make money and aren't looking to buy property or integrate into your Empire."

"Yes, I understand that, and honestly, I didn't invite you to this meeting to talk about those things. I just had to get their concerns out of the way before we could speak. However, I have been told that some of you have been moving your families here. That is a lot more permanent than just setting up shop as merchants."

Several of the men looked at each other. Lucilla was surprised at their naiveté. They had to know her people were paying attention to their movements, both to keep track of the kinds of products being shipped in and out of the Empire and to keep an eye out for Carthaginian agents posing as merchants that might be trying to hide among them.

"Only a few, and mostly those are for the men arranging for shipments and working with the local businesses."

"I'm not criticizing; just pointing out that trying to say you're only here loading up ships isn't entirely true. You're all paying the required taxes, so we aren't asking you to become citizens or for anything more than you are already doing."

"Then what exactly did you need from us?" another man said, getting to the point.

"Right now, what is the heaviest loads you can carry, and how far can you reasonably go to transport and sell those goods?"

"It depends."

She had actually expected this answer. Although the Scandi didn't get to what her people used to call Mare Nostrum before being forced north away from its shores, and now generally just called the Middle Sea, since it was between Italia and Africa, they did sail on the Germanic Sea, which had some similarities. From what she'd been told, the Germanic Sea was almost as calm as the Middle Sea and had the added benefit of having land closer to most points than someone sailing from Italia to Africa might have. That meant that any of their ships in the Germanic Sea tended to be smaller and often oar driven, much like the boats Romans currently used for short hops to the continent. They also used similar fishing vessels to her people, usually shallow single mast boats, sometimes with a handful of rowers for the larger versions that had to remain close to shore, away from the larger waves that would swamp them.

What she was interested in were the larger ships that sailed across the sea north of Britannia and skirted the edge of the ocean south to Iberia, with their large single sails and higher sides that kept them from getting swamped in the high waves that often sank smaller Roman ships.

"I'm asking about the ships that sail the ocean that is west of Scandi and south and west of Britannia, not the smaller boats your people sail on the Germanic Sea."

"The largest ones can carry ten thousand of your amphorae."

Before she started working on this project, that would have sounded significant, since the largest ships she knew of, even back before the loss of Italia, would have carried closer to five thousand amphorae.

"What if I told you we are developing ships capable of carrying fifteen or sixteen thousand amphorae and are designed to move even with almost no wind or travel against the wind, and maps that show far islands and accurate land features to take you from here to the very bottom of Africa and around to Asia, including ways of telling north and south and your exact position even if you are several days sail from land."

"I would say you must be in contact with the gods or you are insane. A larger ship I can imagine, although something able to carry those weights would be hard to handle. Traveling into the wind, telling direction and position that far from land, impossible. I've been on the water my entire life and I've never seen anything like that."

"We could teach you. It would open a world of possibilities for you. Some of it would require tools we have to design, but the knowledge, once you learned it from us, would still be there. You'd learn new ways of building ships, new ways of sailing ships, and knowledge of the world you've never dreamed of having."

"And you want to give us this knowledge out of the goodness of your heart?"

"No. But we would be willing to trade for the knowledge. We do not have men with sailing experience like you! Our ships founder on the open water and our sailors never get out of sight of land. While almost everything about these new ships is new, from the way they're built to the way they're sailed, I'm told that the fundamentals by which you sail your ships are similar to how these would be sailed. We're prepared for several possibilities. Best case, for us, is some of your people agree to sail for us, under a Britannian banner. Worst case, you stay and train, or help train our people in the sailing of these ships ... after learning of the new developments, of course. Plus, we will show you how to make your own. There are variations that we can offer, but the upside is that you will have access to new technologies that allow you to sail far from land and carry more cargo, while we gain assistance in training our own sailors. Then again, perhaps some of your people will decide to sign on as part of our new navy. We will have ships armed with weapons you have not heard of or dreamed of. These ships will ultimately be tasked with patrolling and protecting ships traveling under friendly banners, making the trade in waters we control significantly safer."

"Nonsense," the old sailor said. "We've seen your people and their boats. You might have impressive new tools to sell, but nothing I've seen suggests your people know enough about boats to allow for all of this. If you had the ability to do this, why wait to do it now? And if you can make all this, why can't you train your people to sail them?"

"We can, but it will take time to build the ships and we can't start training them until the ships are finished. Your people have a head start. They can learn faster, and we don't have enough people to train as it is. Our first goal is to train a group, who will then train others, and we're hoping to shortcut that process with people who already know what they're doing."

What Lucilla didn't want to say was they only had one person who had any idea how this all worked. As it was, they were going to lose Ky for some time as he trained the first group that would go on to train others. Considering all the projects they had in the air, they needed to make that absence as short as possible.

"And you want us to believe you'd just give us all this new technology for only training your people?" another man said. "I came here to make money. I'm not here to get involved in your war. We're happy with the arrangement we have right now, thank you."

With that, the group started to file out, except for one of the youngest men, who stopped in front of Lucilla.

"I'm interested," he said.

Lucilla couldn't help but notice the smirks several of the men leaving gave the younger man, although if that was because they thought the young man was making a mistake listening to Lucilla or they thought Lucilla was making a mistake taking someone so much younger than them seriously, she couldn't tell.

"Good. If I could ask, how many ships do you have working for you, and how many men?"

"We're the smallest group here, with only three ships total, but my men are all experienced. Some have sailed as far south as

214

Carthage, before your war with them, and we recently made a run up the North Sea, around the top of Sviariki, which included three days sail away from land, navigating by the stars alone."

"Those other men seemed to find humor in your agreeing to stay. Is there a joke I am missing?"

"My father was a sailor and knew most of them. He died just as I came of age, and instead of selling my boats to them or to one of my father's men, I took command myself. Most of the men who'd worked for my father left to go to men like Hakan and Dag, but some stayed with me and I've been able to recruit others to crew my boats."

"You'll probably have to dock your boats for a time, at least while your men are learning how to sail these new ships and then training enough of our people to train the next batch, so you can go back to your normal business."

"That will become expensive for me. Without my ships working, I won't be able to pay my men."

Lucilla recognized his tone. He wasn't complaining. He was bargaining.

"I guess you are a merchant after all," she said with a smile.

Southern Ériunia

The rain was coming down in sheets and had been doing so for a day and a half, turning the dirt tracts that the Ériu called roads into muddy rivers that bogged down the men, the horses, and the baggage train. They'd gone from an average of twelve mille passus per day, already incredibly slow compared to how his legion marched by itself, not encumbered by the slow pace of the Ulaid, to below five a day now.

Worse, it might drop even more if the rain didn't stop, since his baggage train couldn't even keep up with the five mille passus a day. He could just have the men carry enough food with them to make the rest of the march to the coast, but the horses required a lot of feed and if they had to rely on grazing, they would lose just as much time, since they couldn't just release them to graze overnight, at least not with the enemy patrols about.

"Tell me we have good news," he said to Aelius, who came riding up to him.

The ninth legion was in the lead, which was normally where Velius liked to have his legion, but he wanted to stay close to their local allies so he could prod them along as much as possible. The only other option would be to put the locals in the middle of the Roman column, but considering how strung out they let themselves become, that would only make his army's disorganization worse. At least this way, he could keep the three legions together if things went badly.

"Unfortunately, no," Aelius said, pulling his horse up short. "The scouts have lost sight of the enemy completely."

"How is that possible?"

"The Carthaginians have finally figured out how to screen properly, apparently. They've basically put their entire mounted force as a screen. We've already lost several scouts and we still can't catch sight of them. Their screen has pushed out far in multiple directions, so we don't even know what direction they're headed in and only have the barest idea of where they are, based on where their screen is. Worse, our scouts have had to give their screens more room since the rain started. Between the low visibility and the poor condition of the ground, they've gotten lost in this mess and gotten mixed in with the enemy horsemen several times. It's turning into chaos."

"But we think they're still coming to intercept us, right?"

"They couldn't answer that, but I think so. Our last sighting had them heading this way and their screen is on the move, so we know they haven't stopped. It's going to be impossible to maneuver to keep from slamming straight into them though."

"Dammit," Velius said, resting his chin in his hand, thinking.

"Should we stop, set up a defensive position, and let them come to us?"

"No. They have local guides who know this region while hardly any of our Ulaid friends have traveled this far south and we couldn't find any who recognize this region. If we stop, they'll be able to get around us without much problem."

"So, we keep moving forward and hope this clears up?"

"What else can we do? If we try and turn around to make it back over the mountains, they'll hit us in the rear for sure."

"I know but stumbling forward feels like a mistake."

"I know, but I can't think of anything else that wouldn't be a bigger mistake. Push out several centuries on either flank, close enough so they don't lose contact, but far enough to blunt any attack long enough for us to get our forces concentrated."

"If we do get hit, they will get ravaged."

"I know, and I hate spending their lives so meaninglessly, but it's better than your entire legion getting ravaged. We will stop early tonight to give the men extra time to strengthen their protection. I know some of the men are complaining, but I want each legion to build their fortified camp every night. No exceptions. If we don't know where they are, they could easily hit us at night."

Aelius frowned, but saluted and rode away to follow his commander's orders.

Chapter 20

Devnum

"So what do you think?" Lucilla asked Valdar, the young shipmaster, as they walked away from the docks crowded with workmen.

It was drizzling and the streets were all mush, but Lucilla had insisted they still go out. The rain had started days ago and had been off and on, which meant she needed to take what chances she could to get outside and observe some of the projects. Today, it was a tour of the new ships under construction followed by a visit with some of the Scandi families living outside the walls of the city.

"I think I have never seen a ship built like that before. We always build from the keel up, but you've started with the frame of the ship, which is massive, by the way. You also aren't overlapping the boards, but are fitting them together, which I have never seen. While it's amazing how precise your boards are, cut to exactly the right length, I can't figure out how you will keep them watertight. We seal our ships, but the seal doesn't hold well enough to keep planks pressed edge to edge from leaking."

"I don't know much about shipbuilding, but the man who designed these said that this is using something called a carvel construction as opposed to something he called clinker construction, which I think is the one you use, with the overlapping boards. He said that the ship would be less flexible with the carvel construction, allowing for multiple masts with large sails, also allowing it to be more stable in the rougher waters of the ocean, and that is why the ships can be longer and broader."

"I get that they draft deeper than our ships and have larger holds, but I'm having trouble seeing it hold the volumes you were suggesting."

"These won't. These are smaller ships called caravels ..."

"From the type of construction you mentioned?" he asked, interrupting her.

"I think so. Again, I'm just telling you what I was told about them. Like your Scandi friends said, my people aren't generally good on the water, so I never spent a lot of time learning about seafaring. Anyway, after we finish these, the next set will be something called a carrack, which will be similar in construction, but larger with higher sides. Beyond carrying capacity, the caravels will have a much more shallow draft than the larger carrack, although not as shallow as some of your current ships, they'll be able to sail into the wind more, and will need smaller crews. Beyond their speed, the main reason these were chosen to be built first is the need for a smaller crew, since manpower is our biggest concern at the moment."

She was getting this from Sophus only a little faster than she could repeat it, and didn't understand everything she was explaining. Valdar, on the other hand, seemed to follow along well and apparently found the explanations exciting.

"That all sounds impressive, although I still have trouble seeing how ships like this would move well in the water. We have to be careful of overloading our ships, because our sail won't give enough push for them to move well even on windy days. The weight of these ships alone would be the same as one of our smaller vessels half-loaded, before a single piece of cargo is put aboard."

"It will make more sense when you see how we have changed the sails. There is also something called a rudder at the back of the ship, which is very different than the steering oar you currently use."

"Seeing how different these ship hulls look, even half completed, I'll have to assume you know what you're talking about and all of these changes are with a purpose."

"I appreciate your trust," she said.

219

They were headed into one of the camps set up for the Scandi near the docks, but outside of town. Beyond not having housing for all of the sailors currently staying in Devnum, because they had decided to not become citizens, there was a concern about having this many foreigners walking around the city. She thought it short-sighted, since they were relying on the Scandi for nearly all of their trade, and would continue to be reliant until they built up their own fleet of ships.

Several members of the Roman Senate had been stirring up trouble of late, making noises about infiltrators and saboteurs coming mixed in with the other foreigners, which had been driving up tensions. The Germanics had managed to escape the brunt of the distrust. Although that might have been partly due to their swearing loyalty to the Empire, Lucilla was pretty sure the main reason none of the allegations stuck to them is how widely they'd started integrating with everyday Romans.

Most of the Germans had chosen not to join the legions, which was expected. Men of the age to join the military would have already been conscripted by the Carthaginians, so what was left were men too old, too young, or too infirm to fight. The variety of work in the factories, from working the nitrate pits to weaving and textiles, to farming and foundries, made for a wide range of jobs that needed different levels of physical ability. Several businesses actually preferred the older workers who had more experience and needed less training over the younger, stronger workers, especially in the more technical fields.

This had caused the immigrants to disperse widely among the farms, mines, and factories, putting more Britannians in contact with their new neighbors. Regular contact with immigrants seemed to go a long way toward breeding familiarity and keeping people from being afraid of them.

The Scandi, on the other hand, didn't integrate with the population and had refused to swear allegiance to the Empire, making them automatically suspect. The growing distrust among the populace caused the citizens to be upset and put the Scandi in more danger, which had ultimately led her father to 'suggest' the merchants set up outside the city, near the river, where they could live, coming into the city docks each day for work. In an effort to keep the merchants, who were really the lifeline the Empire was relying on to supply it funds for the ongoing war effort, the Emperor had created several public projects to build up a semi-permanent area that would be set aside for the Scandi's use just outside the city wall, and have the praetorians post guards to the entry into this area for their protection.

Although Lucilla generally agreed with this idea, Sophus said that the same thing had been tried other times, with mixed results, and warned caution at keeping them isolated for too long. Apparently, other places that had set up these separate compounds for groups considered outsiders to the city sometimes ended up a scapegoat for anything the people inside the city feared, which had led to massacres and violence.

Lucilla hoped that wouldn't happen here. Unlike the places that Sophus described, the Scandi were still adamant that their presence was temporary and that they had no plans to become permanent residents.

In spite of the growing mistrust, she found the Scandi she stopped to speak with friendly, especially the families who were living in the makeshift camp, waiting for the foreign sector to finish being built.

Finishing up her conversation with the group of families she had stopped to talk to, she walked on to the next tents. People were excited, although mostly because of all the people following after her as she visited with each group, since it was unlikely that most of these people actually knew who Lucilla was.

She stopped at the tents as older men, women, and small children, along with a handful of men, gathered around to see what all the fuss was about. If they were anything like the other groups she'd stopped to talk to, the men were mostly sailors visiting with family members while their ship was in port loading up for its next journey.

She'd just started asking an old woman, who looked to be the matriarch of this clan, which was how the Scandi family groups were organized, trying to get a better sense of what these people were looking for or needed while they were in Britannia or their thoughts on staying here in general, when one of the few men in the group pushed forward.

He didn't have the look of one of the sailors visiting family while their ship was in port, but was younger than the rest of the old men she'd seen, most of whom continued on the ships until the harsh conditions killed them.

She'd just finished her question when he screamed 'death to traitors' and lunged forward with a knife that suddenly appeared in his hand. Her guards reacted quickly, but she'd ordered them to stay back while she interviewed the families, not wanting the women and children to be frightened, which put all of them several steps away from the threat that suddenly materialized in front of her.

She saw Modius's sword plunge into the man even as she fell, a burning pain in her side where the blade had pierced her.

"Ky," she managed to say, hoping Sophus could hear her, before she dropped to the ground, overwhelming exhaustion overtaking her.

Londinium

"We need to figure out another source," Ky said to Auspex as the two watched a ship unloading at the docks. "I know the Carthaginians let their stockpiles run low, but our supplies are already low until the harvests come in. I know they were keeping supplies away from the people, but the governor and his cronies seemed to be doing alright. What happened to their food supplies?"

"Nearly depleted. Had the siege gone on a few more weeks, they would have had to go on rationing as well."

"They had half the island under control for almost a hundred years and we know they brought in tenant farmers to work the land. What happened to the food stores? It's not like they were overpopulated before, and once they started conscripting the pop-

222

ulace into their armies for the final push against us, they had even fewer mouths to feed."

"We've been hearing rumors from the handful of ship captains that stayed behind that, at least until they lost at the Battle of Venonis, they were shipping out every bit of food and fodder they could get their hands on to Insula Manavia, probably to feed the army they sent over to Hibernia. All of the soldiers they sent here leading up to Venonis ate a lot of what was left. Their shipments had already started to cause some famine before we pushed the rest of them behind these walls. As word has started to spread about our relief efforts here, people from the surrounding countryside have started coming into the city to get food for their families. That's why we're having such a problem meeting the demand."

"What about the fishing boats? The Carthaginians had been supplying their soldiers almost entirely off of what those boats brought in."

"Most are gone. As soon as Carus launched the attack, those that could get to the docks did so, sailing with whatever crew they could get their hands on. Most never came back and we can only assume they went to Manavia, Hibernia, or the continent, since none of those boats could have made the ocean crossing to get back to Africa. Regardless, if they were coming back here, they would have. As of now, we only have two ships able to go out each day, and that isn't enough to put a dent in the demand."

"What about the Scandi merchants?"

Ky already knew the answer from talking to Lucilla, but he was frustrated at his inability to do anything about the situation. She'd had to pay almost double for what food they were willing to bring in, since it took up a lot of space they could use for more profitable cargo and there wasn't much to be had from the tribes that would trade with them anyway, meaning they had to go all the way to the Asian ports on the Baltic Sea for what little food the Steppe tribes, currently controlling that area, could muster.

"Only one ship has come in so far with food supplies, but they were directed here from Devnum and couldn't tell me if there would be another one," Auspex said, getting equally as frustrated with his inability to answer Ky's questions.

"That's alright, it's not your fault. We're going to have shortages until the harvests start coming in. I know you're going to hear complaints, but try to ration out the food as much as possible. Since the legions here aren't going to be involved in fighting for a while, we should put them on rations too. You're going to hear some grumbling, but spread the word as best you can that this is temporary. We're getting as much land as possible planted and we should have plenty of food once we hit the summer. We just have to survive for a few months. I'll send word to the Emperor that we should probably put all imperial workers and the senate on rations too. Seeing their leaders undergoing the same hardships will help keep hungry people from doing something stupid."

"There's still going to be grumbling."

"I know. Just do the best you can and we'll keep trying to bring in more food."

"Yes, Consul," Auspex said, saluting and heading off to continue his overseeing of the relief supplies.

Auspex really was doing the best he could and, unless something went very wrong, Ky was pretty sure they wouldn't have any wide-scale starvation before the harvests came in. The men were unhappy, but they'd deal with that. They'd been on the defensive for so many generations, that they'd convinced themselves that victory on the battlefield would solve all their problems. They now had to learn that victory brought a whole new set of problems and tended to solve very little in the short term. Hopefully, this would be a good lesson for the battles to come.

He was just preparing to make his way back to the governor's palace, which had become their temporary command facilities, when Sophus's voice brought him up short. Although the AI's tone was the same as it always was, Ky could almost feel the desperation in its voice as it began speaking.

"Commander, you must return to Devnum. Lucilla has been attacked and is critically injured," Sophus said.

Surprised, Ky froze in place.

"What happened?"

"She was touring the Scandinavian merchants' camps, trying to understand the needs of the merchants' families and gauge response to the

merchant quarter being built on the outskirts of the city when a man stepped towards her and stabbed her."

"Is she alive?" he asked, his imagination suddenly showing him his worst fears.

"She is, but her condition is critical and I am concerned that one of the local doctors might attempt to treat her, compounding the problem."

"I thought her guards knew she had some protections not common to other people and were told not to take her to the medics if she was injured."

"They were, but I left her comm open and can hear discussion among them about what to do, and that option has been brought up."

Ky was already moving through the streets in a blur, trying to get to a horse, silently cursing their inability to get the semaphore stations set up. He, or any messenger he could send, was limited to the speed of the horses they could ride. A semaphore message could have made it there in less than an hour, but they'd left that project as a lower priority than the cannon or gunpowder, and Hortensius's injury had put it mostly on pause except for the towers closest to Devnum. Lucilla was his only link to the city, and with her incapacitated, there was no way to tell anyone there anything for at least three days.

"If she was stabbed, why is she unconscious?" Ky asked, the realization that she shouldn't be incapacitated suddenly coming to him.

With an injury like this, the victim usually retained consciousness until blood loss overtook them, but even if an artery was cut, that would take a minute or two, and it wouldn't matter what Ky could say or do if it were true. Sophus had said critical, however, and not mortal, and the AI rarely minced words like a person would, so Ky doubted it was that.

Since most of the other wounds Ky could think of would have also left her conscious, Ky didn't understand why she couldn't at least hear him and pass on instructions to her guards.

"The injury damaged her kidney, causing a severe amount of internal bleeding. In order to limit blood loss, I had the nanites currently in her system induce a comatose state to slow her heart rate. Although I have managed to increase the lifespan of the transferred nanites, it has been some time since the ones she had were replaced, leaving too few to

conduct repairs quickly. They have begun to seal off the injured areas and slow the rate of internal bleeding, but the add-on effects of what bleeding has already occurred will cause additional complications that will take time to heal. It would be best to maintain her in this state until most of that healing has been done."

"Why ... wait," Ky said, grabbing a horse from the gates of the city and mounting it.

He'd left his lictore behind, and knew his sudden disappearance would cause a panic, since no one would know why he'd suddenly run out of the city, riding north out of town.

Stopping at one of the guards by the gate, Ky said, "Tell my guards when they get here that I must return to Devnum, and they are to follow as best they can. Have them tell the legates to continue relief efforts and I will send messengers with additional instructions."

The centurion, who'd looked stunned by Ky's sudden appearance and theft of one of the horses left there for the guard's use, looked shell-shocked as Ky rode away. He felt for the man, who would be grilled hard by Ursinus when word of Ky's sudden departure reached him, but Ky couldn't wait to give more detailed instructions. Thankfully, they had set up a few messenger relay stations, so Ky could ride the horse hard and switch out at each station. Besides allowing him to move quickly and not stop until he reached the capitol, it would make it easier for his lictore to reach him as quickly as possible. They wouldn't be able to ride day and night, even if they got fresh horses, and would eventually have to stop and rest. He trusted Sellic, Strabo, and Carus to keep from killing their own men in a pointless effort to catch up to him.

"Then why keep her comatose? If the bleeding has been stopped, that should be enough to keep her alive and conscious until I get there."

"The external bleeding has been stopped through the localized administration of coagulants. The internal bleeding has slowed but hasn't completely stopped yet. There aren't enough nanites to quickly repair the ruptured organs. My estimation is that it will be several hours before all of the most critical tears are closed off and the focus can shift from stabilization to more thorough healing. Unfortunately, the blood loss was rapid enough that her blood pressure dropped to dangerous

levels. *I have assigned some nanites to extract more fluids from other parts of the body and convert them into plasma, but they are having difficulty traversing with such low blood pressure. Without someone nearby who can administer intravenous fluids, or orally introduce fluids, it is difficult to keep her alive and conscious at the same time. Slowing her system is the best way to keep her stable until you can reach her.*"

"Once we get her fluids and replenish her nanos, she'll be alright though, right?"

"*She should be, although it will not be immediate and I would suggest having her remain in a comatose state until her kidneys, lung, and heart can be repaired.*"

"Kidneys, lung, and heart? I thought just her kidneys were injured."

"*There was minor damage to her right lung as the blade was withdrawn. It is difficult to be precise, but from the reports from the medical nanos and the sounds analyzed during and after the attack, I believe the attacker was pulled down as he was removing the knife, causing it to slice up as she fell down, widening the wound channel and bringing the blade into contact with the lower portion of her lung. Although it does not seem severe, the comatose state will help keep the lung from ripping any further until it can be repaired.*"

"How long will she have to remain unconscious?"

"*That is unknown. I will remind you, Commander, that we are using nanites designed for your system in her, which severely limits their capabilities. They cannot, for example, generate tissue that her body would not attempt to reject, so it must mend cuts together on the molecular level, and then let her body repair itself. Once that is done, the nanites can remove much of the residual scar tissue, resulting in limited long-term damage. That process, however, means that some steps must wait on her natural recovery time.*"

"Make sure you don't keep her under so deep that it seems to observers that she is dead. Other than feeling a pulse or breath, they have no way to determine if a person is alive or dead. I don't want someone burying her or doing anything else drastic, thinking she was killed in the attack."

"*Yes, Commander. That has been considered. I am continuing to use audio signals through the comm to surveil the area around her and have* used the nanites to simulate a more significant level of consciousness, to ensure her protectors know she is not dead."

"What does that mean?"

"I've simulated both a more prominent pulse and breathing, although since it is clear the people of this time don't know how to check those things accurately, I have also used the nanites to vibrate her vocal cords, producing sounds roughly similar to a moan."

"Be careful with that. The idea of possession is still common. I doubt you could make similar sounds to her, and if it is too different, it might provoke a negative reaction."

"From their responses, I believe the ruse worked, although your advice is taken. I will try and limit the use of that technique except when absolutely necessary."

"Good," Ky said, pushing the horse to go faster. "I'll be there as soon as I can. Just keep her alive."

Chapter 21

Southern Ériunia

It was getting dark. The rain had finally let up that afternoon, but the roads were still awful. The army had slowed to a crawl, barely covering a couple of miles every day, and Velius was starting to think they should just set up a fortified camp and wait it out until the roads dried. The only problem with that was he didn't want to get hemmed in by the Carthaginians who could easily surround them. The greatest strength of the legions over the Carthaginian phalanxes was their mobility.

Right now, his line could outstretch at least the phalanx part of the opposing army, which would leave it exposed. The Carthaginian allies were both less of a problem, because of their lack of organization and tendency to charge straight in, and more of a problem, because of their sheer numbers. Numbers he could deal with, but again, only as long as they were mobile. Which at the moment, they weren't.

"It's getting late," Gordianus, the seventh legion's second in command, said. "If you want to fortify the camps, we're going to have to stop soon."

He was right, Velius thought, although it was hard to tell, since the rain had blocked out the sun for days, with the only difference in day and night being gradations of darkness. Velius had been pushing it, hoping to get just a little more distance, even though he knew better. With this kind of ground and the men's feet sinking ankle-deep in mud, they were actually working harder than they would have had they marched miles longer on dry ground.

He needed them rested. They'd moved into the envelope the enemy scouts had created, to the point that his lead elements had even seen some of the enemy horsemen. His cavalry pursued them, but they were locals and knew the land better than his men. Velius could feel them out there, but none of his allies had been this far south before, meaning they were blundering around in the dark, blind. If they could hit the coast, at least they'd have something to key off of, but until then or until the rain let up, allowing his men to be mobile again, all he could do was crawl forward a little at a time.

Still, that didn't mean he should be taking stupid chances.

"Alright, let's call it a day. Send word to the fourth and ninth legions, I want more distance between each camp. At least half a mille passus between each camp."

"Is that wise?" Gordianus asked. "With that much distance, if the enemy does find us, they can get in between our camps, and cut us off from support."

"Yes, but if we're all together, they can surround our entire force, which completely negates our advantages while playing into theirs. They have a large force, but not enough of one to cover that much distance."

"They could surround each camp in turn," Gordianus pointed out.

"They could, but they'd have to split their forces up. They couldn't easily support each other and they'd have to fight with parts of their forces in two directions. It puts them in a weaker position than if they had us all grouped together."

"As you say," Gordianus said.

Velius knew this was his way of saying he'd follow orders even though he didn't agree with them, but Velius could live with that. Gordianus was a good man, but he had trouble seeing the entire battle-scape, at times.

"Make sure they set up the towers and watchers," Velius said.

The towers were a new touch and he'd already heard some grumbling that it was pointless. When the camps were next to each other, a messenger could travel with news faster than the shuttered lanterns could blink their coded signals, and the men up in the towers were closer to the rain and wind, making for an uncomfortable night. He'd looked over the Consul's plan for these towers before he left, and even without the new spyglasses, at half a mille passus, they could transmit signals faster than any messenger could run and without the chance of the message being intercepted.

Of course, maybe all his precautions would be for naught. Best case scenario, nothing would happen and they'd be on the move again in the morning. If something did happen, however, Velius at least wanted to be set up so that the battle would be in his favor.

Devnum

It was after midnight when Ky rode into the city, almost knocking over the city guards as he blew past them. The men were startled but recognized the Consul enough to get out of the way, instead of intercepting him. Sophus had heard enough to know Lucilla had been taken to her rooms in the palace, since there wasn't much for the physicians to do. With her wounds closed up, miraculously from their point of view, they couldn't do much beyond force-feeding her honeyed water and hoping she'd recover on her own.

That, at least, wouldn't do her any harm and the nanites could use the glucose in the honey as they fought to repair her systems. Ky had other concerns. In the two days he'd ridden, stopping only long enough to exchange horses, her condition had started to deteriorate. The few active medical nanites she still had in her body were barely able to keep the internal bleeding under control and hadn't been able to address any of the damage beyond the bleeding. Ky's hurry was because the stabilization they had achieved had been very temporary, and that window was quickly closing.

Her lungs were still not able to get enough oxygen into her blood, causing add-on effects that, if left unchecked, would cause damage to other organs, including her brain. Worse, her kidneys, where the most serious damage had happened, were not processing and cleaning fluids, causing a rise in her potassium levels, weakening her heart, and creating fluid retention, which had caused her arms and legs to begin swelling dangerously.

Most troubling, the over-taxed nanites were beginning to fail. There were few enough left in her body as it was, and it wouldn't take much more before she reached the point of no return. Medical nanites were powerful tools, but they had limits and without having modern surgical techniques and organ cloning available, there would be no hope of bringing her back.

Seeing his face, her guards moved quickly to get out of Ky's way before he trampled them in his rush to get to her. As he burst into her room, he was completely focused on her and the information that started to flood across his vision as Sophus finally got into range of the altered nanites in her system and got full readouts instead of the simplified ones it had been limited to through the comm. Ky barely noticed her guards as they followed him into the room, ignoring all of them as he knelt beside her bed.

They were curious but unalarmed. He didn't blame them. On the outside, she looked peaceful, like she was sleeping. They had no way of knowing the battle that was raging inside her body, or how badly she was losing it.

Ky leaned forward, pressing his lips firmly to hers. Sophus had already collected as many nanites as Ky could spare without inhibiting future replication and had altered them for her system, encasing them in a molecular shell to keep his system from seeing them as invaders that had suddenly appeared. Ky's kiss, while being full of love and worry for her, was also the delivery method for this bundle, which tumbled into her system, its shell instantly being ripped apart by several of the nanites Sophus had ordered to stand ready.

"Are we in time?" Ky said, out loud, which was unusual even for him and a sign of the stress he was under.

"Consul?" Modius asked, unsure what Ky meant, or even if he was talking to them.

"I believe so, commander. The damage is extensive and the nanites are not functioning at the same level of efficiency as they would for you. However, I believe the damage done is completely reversible. You will need to stay nearby her for some time so that I may have direct control over the repair. You will also need to reduce your physical activity so that more resources are available to produce additional medical nanites. I will have to push the ones just delivered into her system beyond their capabilities, and they will burn out, meaning you will need to donate more to her recovery. She will also need to remain comatose for the time being. It could be several days before we can wake her."

"I'm not going anywhere. Anything you need, just tell me," Ky said, subvocalizing this time, before turning to one of her guards. "My lictore should be a day or so behind me. Make sure they know where to find me and inform the Emperor where I am if he needs me. For now, I will be unable to leave her side, but she will not be harmed if anyone needs to come speak to me."

Her guards looked at each other as Ky settled in the chair next to her, seemingly to do nothing, and backed out of the room. He knew his actions probably seemed strange to them, barging in, kissing her, and then proceeding to do nothing while refusing to leave her, but there wasn't any way he could explain it that would make sense to them.

He sat in silence, watching a data feed that Sophus provided him giving updates on her condition and responses to the nanites, but this wasn't a quick process and everything was in Sophus's metaphorical hands, so he was mostly consoling himself rather than actually doing anything useful.

"Perhaps your time would be better spent working on updating the instructions I have compiled for the various projects."

"Probably, but as long as she's in this condition, I can't concentrate on anything else."

"Why not? You know what is being done for her and as of now, you know there is nothing else you can do for her. Losing focus because of her condition seems a poor allocation of your time and resources."

"I know it probably seems like that to you, but people aren't made that way. We worry over things we know we can't affect, mostly because there isn't anything we can do about them. If there was, we'd worry less since we'd have something to do."

"It seems inefficient."

"I know. Just consider it one of our many peculiarities. It comes with being human."

"I see," Sophus said, falling silent.

Ky sat, one hand resting on her shoulder, still as a statue, for almost an hour. It was still too early to tell if the new nanites were going to be able to reverse all the damage, and he spent most of that time referencing Sophus's files, trying to understand everything the AI was doing. He had rudimentary training in emergency medicine given to all pilots, but that had assumed the patients would all be augmented to the same physical level Ky was., What Sophus had done so far for her protection, and what it was doing now, was well beyond what any of the nanites had been designed for. Even if Ky had more training, he wouldn't have understood what was being done. No one but Sophus could understand what the data he was seeing actually meant.

Almost an hour later, Ky was still sitting in that same position when the door opened unceremoniously and the Emperor strode in unannounced. Ky was so focused on watching the data that at first, he didn't register the Emperor's presence.

"Your Majesty," Ky said after several long heartbeats and stood. "I'm sorry, I was distracted."

The Emperor's eyes first went to his daughter who, from all outside appearances, seemed completely unchanged, laying in the same place she had been the last time he'd been in this room.

"Can you help her?" he asked.

His voice wasn't that of a man of power, a leader of a new Empire with thousands of subjects at his command. It was that of a father, worried for the life of his child.

"I think so. I'm doing what I can, but it will take time. She was severely wounded and the repairs to her body's systems are not easy."

"I know as well as anyone the miracles you can perform. It's just hard to see her like this. I was hoping ..."

"I know," Ky said as the Emperor's voice trailed off. "While your poisoning was serious, it hadn't had a lot of time to damage your body beyond the sickness it created, unlike what the blade did to her."

"Thank you for coming. I still don't know how you managed to get here so fast, since we only sent a messenger to you yesterday, but I'm glad you're here. The healers told me that, although her wounds healed miraculously, most people who enter the wakeless sleep rarely come out of it, and to not get my hopes up."

Ky didn't have a response for that, since nothing he said would make sense. Gunpowder, telescopes, and steam engines he could explain to them. They might seem magical, but they followed the processes of the observable world. Seeing inside a working body was impossible for the people of this time, leaving them to devise all kinds of miraculous or fantastical explanations for why people sometimes got sick and died. He could tell them about viruses and bacteria all he liked, but there was no way for them to understand what that meant, since they couldn't see them.

"Can you ... how much of your attention does her treatment take? I don't want to distract you from your treatments of her, but if you are able ..."

Ky was actually impressed. He knew the Emperor cared for his daughter and he was clearly concerned for her condition, but in spite of his personal tragedy, he still had an Empire to run and he hadn't forgotten it.

"I am, although you probably know more about what is happening than I do," Ky pointed out.

"I doubt that."

As far as he knew, Lucilla had never discussed with her father their ability to speak over long distances, although considering the multiple times he or she had responded to something happening to the other before word could ever reach them, it was very possible he hadn't needed to be told to figure it out.

"Alright, maybe not more, but as much. We're behind on a lot of projects, although with Hortensius's recovery, or at least being mobile again, I understand they're all underway again. I'm most anxious to get the semaphore stations up and running, including the temporary, mobile ones I want to send over to Ériu. The king's last message sounded like he might be considering joining the Empire, which would go a long way to improving our supply issues. With some of our advancements in farming, their yields could well exceed their needs, producing enough to help cover our shortfalls here and feed the legions when they move on to the continent, but only if we get the crops in the ground soon."

"I don't know if we can rely on that happening. Even when we do finish conquering the island for them, they're joining the alliance will take time. More than it did for us to form it in the first place, since they won't have the pressure of an invading army to defeat like we did. I'm also not convinced our victory is as assured as you are. Velius is still young for a legate and this is his first independent command. We've received very little word about Velius's progress south, especially once he passed the mountains, and I hear the weather has turned against him."

"Have faith in Velius. He's a good man."

"I hope you're right," The Emperor said.

Southern Ériunia

Velius sat in his tent, unable to sleep. He knew he should be resting, since tomorrow would be a long day of either marching or fighting, but he had the feeling he always got before a fight, and it was keeping him awake.

The last report from the scouts included multiple contacts with Carthaginian allied scouts. From the locations of the contacts, Velius was almost certain their armies were close by and the odds were good they'd confront each other in the morning, once both armies started marching again.

He was just going over, for the thirtieth time, his options for such an engagement, when a tremendous shout started from what sounded like the northwestern edge of the camp. There wasn't a doubt in his mind what it was. The enemy army was out there and knew the area. They wouldn't just be stumbling around in the dark. The Carthaginians weren't idiots. They'd been taught time and again that the Britannians' superior tactics could beat them, even when they were massively outnumbered. The easiest way to get around the Britannians' strategic skills in the field would be to hit them in camp, when the men were asleep and their arms stacked. Which is why Velius insisted on having a full cohort in armor and ready to fight, rotating through in three-hour blocks as a reactionary force. His commanders thought he was being absurd, since it meant they'd have to spend more time in camp to still give everyone enough rest to march the next day, but Velius had insisted.

The noise was steadily increasing, with screams and yelling, along with the noises of a battle reaching through the rest of the camp as men began to awaken and react to the attack.

Velius was halfway into his armor when an aide rushed into his tent.

"Alert the commanders. All cohorts are to report to their pre-assigned positions."

They'd planned for this and done drills most nights so the men knew what to do, even though they were exhausted. Finally armored, Velius ducked through the opening of his tent, almost running into Gordianus, who had been about to duck into his tent.

"What's the situation?"

"It looks like their entire damn army. Hundreds are pouring out of the woods every minute."

"The defenses?"

"Holding, for now. The ditches are really slowing them down and the men are starting fires by using their arcuballistas to shoot it into them, although in another thirty minutes, there'll be enough bodies in the ditches that they'll be able to just walk over their friends' bodies."

The defenses included two trenches dug around the circumference of the camp with stakes at the bottom of each, a set of angled stakes in the rise between the two trenches, followed by a wall of larger, solid logs sharpened at the end, hammered deep into the ground. It was time-consuming to set up and take down each day, but today it would pay off for them.

"Have we signaled the other legions?"

"I just came from the signal tower. They are not under attack, yet. It looks like the enemy only had a rough idea of where we stopped for the night and are only coming from the northwest. The first contact was only a hundred men or so, and is only now building, so my guess is they stumbled into us and are concentrating on where they know they have made contact. Between the clouds blocking the moon and the heavy trees north of us, they've probably been as much in the dark about our location as we've been about theirs."

"It won't take them long to start wrapping around the camp, trying to find a weak spot in our defenses."

"Or at least cut us off. The other legions are already gathering their men to set up lines on either side of our camp, extending south."

"No. Signal them to not come towards us. I want both of them to march south a mille passus beyond where the ninth camped, and then split up, one cutting east and one cutting west. I agree we're about to be completely surrounded, but if they fight like the Caledonians, they'll just pile in wherever there's space instead of setting up proper offensive lines, so they'll be completely massed, at least until our defenses break and they can collapse in on us. I want our other legions to circle wide around us and then come back, one from each direction, hitting the armies surrounding us from either side."

"That could take hours, especially with the ground like it is."

"I know, although they'll manage better off the main roads, where it hasn't been torn up from having three legions marching over the same ground. Tell them to push as hard as they can. If we can catch them between us, we can end this right now."

"What about our allies? They were camped north of us and must be engaged by now."

"There's nothing we can do for them. If they listened to my suggestion, they'll have some kind of defensive position set up, and hopefully can hold out long enough for our counterattack. If we try and march out to save them now, we'll just open the hole the Carthaginians are looking for and get us all killed. Now go. Signal them."

Gordianus rushed off to the signal tower, to get the message sent. Velius hoped he was in time. The last thing they needed now was to compress all three legions in together. With Vibius and Aelius still mobile, they had a chance.

The north end of the camp was chaos as men continued to file into lines. With his men hemmed in, they were easy targets for the arrows that began to rain in on them from the tree line the Britannians had created when they cut down trees to make the clearing for the camp. The fortification was keeping the Carthaginians at a distance for now, but it also meant there was enough separation that the enemy archers could fire with impunity, and spread out to cover the entire perimeter of the camp. The Britannians didn't have the manpower to allow for a steady loss of men and continue fighting.

"Testudo formation," Velius called out to the commanders nearest him, and heard the command shouted down the line.

The men, except those in the first row, began raising their large shields over their heads, creating an overhead covering, protecting the entire ten-man deep line from arrow fire. There had been some alterations to the version of this maneuver his men had used before the introduction of the arcuballista. With the shields lifted up over their heads, there wasn't room to draw a bow and fire from this formation, so it was generally used for getting close to a wall or fortification where arrows were a problem. The new arcuballista changed all of that. Previously, it hadn't been a widely used weapon, because its range was well short of a standard arrow and because it didn't have the stopping power to get past shields or even some armor.

The new version the Consul had introduced had a longer range, although still less than the bows used by trained archers, more importantly, it had significantly more stopping power. Instead of holding their shields up, the front row angled them slightly, just as they did on the battlefield, using them as a firing platform. This did open up a wider gap in the testudo, but being able to fire back was worth the added risk.

Initially, the rate of fire from the Carthaginian forces didn't slacken as the testudo formed, but after a minute their rate slowed down drastically. This was because after the Britannians in the front line fired their arcuballistas they were able to continue firing without reloading as arcuballistas were passed forward to them

239

ready to fire. In addition, the Roman archers and even some of the dismounted cavalry, neither of whom could benefit from the testudo's protection, had gotten into the game and begun to add their fire to slow down the Carthaginian advance.

Carthaginians were still getting to the wall. Although the gaps in the logs were too narrow to allow a man to slip through them, the men were able to get a handhold on individual logs and begin pulling them. Velius's legionnaires did their best to target these men first, but it wasn't working. As they began to surround his fortress, the Carthaginian allies, who made up the bulk of this assault so far, had started to get the logs to move in the soft ground. They couldn't pull them out entirely, but they could push some forward and some backward, widening the gaps and allowing men to pass through. As they did, the men in the legion front ranks closest to the breakthroughs had to sling their arcuballistas and pull their gladius to fight back, which slowed the rate of fire.

The defenses had kept the enemy out of the camp for just under thirty minutes. First one, then two, then a dozen holes appeared in the wall, allowing men to pour through the gaps and begin engaging his lines. They hadn't done so without a cost. A thick carpet of bodies covered the perimeter of the camp, not that it stopped them. Like the Caledonians, their personal bravery was something to admire, even if it did make it harder to pass down lessons their armies had learned in the past in training or institutional memory.

The one benefit of their breakthrough to the Britannians was that the arrows from the tree line began to stop, or at least move deeper into the camp.

"Form lines!" he yelled, the command again rippling down the line.

Although the men were already in line, they knew what the command meant, transitioning out of the testudo formation and back into their standard battle formation as more and more of the fortification was pulled down. It was dark and he couldn't see the entire perimeter, but in every section he could see, men were fighting, pushing the line hard. They were now exactly where Velius hadn't wanted them to be, hemmed in without any maneuverability, where the enemy could smash into them, beating his force into paste.

"Get any auxiliary forces, including scouts and cavalry, armed and ready to fill any gaps or holes that appear. Except for the men on the message tower and a few messengers."

It was dark, but the tower would also work well as an observation post, giving him at least some idea of what was going on. The relief force wasn't going to do well on the line, but it was all he had.

"Any word of the other two legions?" Velius asked Gordianus.

"No. It's been an hour. Even if they left as soon as you sent the message and haven't encountered the enemy, it should still be some time before they can get around the enemy and attack. With the ground the way it is …"

"I know. I know," Velius said, and then pointed off at a section of the line and looked at one of the tribunes nearby. "That section's about to fold. Pull the back century from the next cohort and reinforce it."

The man rode off and Velius went back into action. With the arrows no longer falling and his men no longer in the testudo, the back lines were able to reengage with their arcuballista. There still weren't enough of the enemy, but between what they could get on target, the mounds of bodies and the still-standing parts of walls and barriers, the flood began to at least abate a little, making it manageable for his men, as they stopped being pressed backward.

They were still losing men at a steady rate, and attrition was becoming a problem. Even picking up the shields of the fallen men, the cavalry and camp followers who were being thrown in as replacements weren't lasting long, and he was quickly running out of reinforcements.

An hour passed and his men, exhausted by the continued effort, were faltering. Several had just collapsed where they fought, unable to continue the fight. Even with the arcuballista and barriers, more of the enemy had become engaged with the entire fortification under pressure as more and more men tried to find a place to fight. The only thing that had saved his legion from collapsing so far was the sheer number of bodies, some of his men but mostly the enemy, creating a new wall that the Carthaginians and their allies had to climb over to get to his men.

Even as he thought that, another section nearby began to collapse, its rear rows now either non-existent or filled with wounded, who could do little more than press back against attempts to push past the front row. When several legionnaires went down at once, the weakened rear went with them, creating a hole that the enemy began exploiting.

With no reserves of any kind left, Velius pulled his sword and charged towards the breach, yelling, "Follow me."

The enemy, almost as exhausted as his men were, must have thought they were clear of the Britannian line, because they seemed surprised when Velius, the few guards that he hadn't been able to send off as reinforcements, and his aides slammed into them.

It had been years since Velius had been engaged in this level of fighting, but he still remembered the moves, his gladius stabbing out, catching men unprepared. Without a shield in his hands or being part of a century, packed together in mutual defense, this was a fight more suited for the men he faced than for himself. Thankfully, in addition to being surprised, the men were as exhausted as his troops, with the first two he met barely even reacting as he slashed through their guard. Realizing the danger in front of them, their resolve returned and the fight got harder. One of his aides went down, an axe embedded in his skull and Velius felt a hot sear as a sword thrust he deflected still managed to score along his side, opening up a shallow but painful gash.

Velius cut down the man who cut him, but more were starting to fill the breach, which his tired legionaries were having trouble stopping. Five, then ten, then fifteen men launched themselves over the low wall of bodies separating the two armies and came at them, trying to push past Velius and his officers to tear open the line once and for all. Velius stiffened, preparing to meet the onrushing men.

Everyone, him included, stopped, their heads whipping to the west, at the sound of a trumpet call. Velius couldn't see it over the mound of bodies in front of him, but the sound could only mean one thing. The ninth legion had finally arrived.

Chapter 22

Devnum

After four days of sitting silently next to Lucilla, Ky took his first steps out of her room. His guards had arrived a few days before and were standing watch alongside her guards outside her room.

After the first day, which had been very tense as Sophus tried desperately to fix her most critical injuries before her body reached a point of no return, things had started to improve. That morning, the AI told him that it was certain now she would live. She'd have to remain comatose for a few more days to help the injuries heal faster, but most of the major damage was corrected, and what was left could be done by nanites controlled by the comm unit, which meant Ky wasn't required to remain next to her to aid in her healing, any longer.

If it was up to Ky, he'd remain next to Lucilla until she awoke, but Sophus reminded him how short on time they were and that there was still much to do. Lucilla had done an admirable job running everything while he completed the conquering of Londinium, and he'd received enough messages from Hortensius while he stood vigil over Lucilla to know the manufacturer was back at work again, but there were some things he would need to do if they were going to have everything ready before the Carthaginians arrived.

So, he'd allowed Sophus to cajole him out of the room, even if it was only going to be for a few hours. Ky still planned to spend his nights sitting next to her bed, allowing Sophus more direct access if he needed it. Also, because he couldn't bear the thought of being far from her while she was like this.

He felt bad about forcing Hortensius, who was still healing, to meet him at the foundry where the cannons were in production, since he was still in the wheelchair that Sophus had designed for him. As medical equipment went, it was a vast improvement over anything of its type, and there were apparently a couple more already being produced for injured soldiers who were unlikely to ever walk again. They were, however, not perfect and tended to still jostle the user around, which could be fairly unpleasant if they were still recovering.

He had little choice, however. The cannon would be needed *soon*, and they'd need more than just one working test unit, which meant they needed to begin actual production now.

Although he'd been following the progress through Lucilla's reports and Sophus had been able to use the drone's sensors to get a more detailed look at everything, it wasn't the same as Ky seeing it for himself.

As soon as Ky entered the factory, Hortensius came trundling down one of the walkways, being pushed by one of the assistants. Ky had seen him with Hortensius, before.

"Consul, it's good to see you. I'm so sorry about Lucilla's injury and pray to the gods every morning for her swift recovery."

"Thank you. Her recovery is looking good and she should be up and around soon. How are you feeling?"

"Then my prayers have been answered. I am doing better, although the healers tell me I will need to remain in this confounded thing for weeks more, and constantly chastise me for not getting enough bed rest."

"They're probably right," Ky said.

Although they needed the manufacturer working, he liked Hortensius and did want to see the man recover. Without the nanites that he, and now Lucilla, had protecting them, he still had a long road to recovery. Knowing the man, however, Ky knew he wouldn't have any better luck than the physicians in getting him to slow down.

"Bah," Hortensius said, waving the thought away. "Let me show you what we've got. We finished the molds and the latest test model of the cannon two days ago, following Lucilla's instructions. We also made some adjustments to the measurement bases that she suggested, and some alterations to the drill, based on some of the things she said. It was almost as if we had to recreate the entire process from the beginning, so hopefully, we are closer to the result you two are looking for. Although I will say after all that work, we can't tell any difference between this one and the previous version. I know you and Lucilla are judging them based on things we don't really understand, but to me, they're identical."

"I know, and I appreciate you incorporating all the changes even though it seems pointless. I promise that they are necessary for this project to be successful. Now, let's see this new cannon. Hopefully, this is the final test version and we can actually begin production soon."

Hortensius led Ky down to the far end of the factory, where the mold and cannon had been set up for him to examine, much like they'd done for the last version with Lucilla. Ky made a slow sweep across both the cannon and the mold, slowly circling them as Sophus collated the data on them. The drone had excellent sensors, but even without having to use the cobbled-together connection for Sophus to use it, they still weren't up to the standard of Ky's artificially augmented eyes which, as a combat pilot, were the most advanced in use in the empire of his birth.

"The material is still not to the level of strength preferred, which will make it more difficult to switch to a steel cannon that can accept rifling, but for the technology we currently have available, this should be fine."

"I'm not seeing the same imperfections in the pour that you reported observing with Lucilla the last time. Has that been corrected?" Ky subvocalized.

"I believe so. The new mold has been created much closer to the required tolerances, which has limited pooling during the casting stage, allowing a more even structural integrity as the alloy cooled and hardened."

"Will it withstand the pressures of firing?"

"If we were using more modern forms of gunpowder, no, it would not. However, with the early-stage black powder currently being developed, yes. This should be sufficient. There will most likely be failures, since it is infeasible to check each cannon in the same fashion, but an advantage

of using bronze is the failures will not be catastrophic. It is something that will have to be addressed in later models as we progress to the rifled steel versions of the cannon."

"What about the barrel? Last time, you told Lucilla it had problems."

"It is surprisingly good and much closer to the required tolerances than I believed we would be able to achieve with current technology. Even using bronze, which is much softer than steel, the horizontal borer does not have the necessary power using water-turned gears. Until we introduce steam-driven power, which is more consistent, reliable, and can generate a higher cutting speed, these will be limited to final shaping and polishing rather than cutting, which will limit the scale of ammunition and charge packs available to us."

"If it's that ineffective, how is this 'surprisingly good' in comparison to what you saw before?"

"One of the flaws in the last test platform I observed was sagging in the borer as it worked further into the barrel, causing a slight variance from the base of the barrel to the end, which will cause a loss of pressure on one side of the projectile as it is fired, causing a shallow arc to be added into its flight trajectory, which would greatly limit the range. This variance was slight enough that it is unlikely to have been visible to the standard human eye and was included in the notes that Lucilla handed Hortensius's foreman on the last inspection."

Ky found himself nodding along as he looked down the barrel of the cannon. He was using the same sensors as Sophus, but he didn't know what the AI had been looking at specifically to see the change. To him, it read as being surprisingly straight and smooth, considering the technology they were using.

"These look good," Ky said after one last circuit of the mold and cannon. "We need to set up to test fire it, just to be sure, but if successful, we should be able to put these in production."

"Excellent. We are still having some trouble with the extra bracing Lucilla asked us to add to the horizontal borer, but I think we should have that figured out soon."

"From what I can see, what you've done already has gone a long way to fixing the problems she saw on her last visit. I'll have some additional notes for you tonight about what we need to do for the test, specifically the fuses and the sewn canvas sacks that we will fill with measured amounts of gunpowder. These charges will both allow the cannons to fire more rapidly and ensure we don't load too much propellant into the tubes, which could cause over-pressurization, rupturing the cannon. We also need to build the carriages the cannon will sit in, as well as a method for changing its elevation reliably when aiming it. That is, more or less, simple carpentry and blacksmithing similar to what your people are already doing, so it shouldn't require any major retooling."

"If it's as simple as you're suggesting, then hopefully we'll be able to do the test sometime next week."

"Good. We're going to need these soon, and we're going to need enough to stage them at each of the possible points where the Carthaginians might land, since we probably won't have more than a day's notice from the time we first sight them."

"I understand. These are my top priority. Once we test them, I believe I can get enough produced for you in time. The gunpowder will be trickier and it's unlikely you'll have more than twenty shots to any cannon, if I'm right about the number of cannons you want. We're still producing more, of course, but it will probably be another nine months before the nitrate beds start producing enough for us to really increase production."

"I understand. Do your best. Where are we on the other projects? Last I heard, we were far behind schedule on the semaphore towers."

"We're making better progress. We've got work crews augmented by some of the forced labor from the prison camps out building at least the basic structures for each tower now. We're leaving the more complex parts to my teams, but since they now only have to add the winch and pulley system and new braces for flags and lanterns, it should take them only a few days at each tower to get it functional. I believe we'll have the first chain to Londinium completed within the week."

"Good. Good. Be prepared to send teams over to Ériunia to begin building a signal system there as well. If they decide to join the Empire, I want to be ready to get to work with as little delay as possible."

"I'll see to it."

"Thanks. I want to get back to Lucilla, but please let me know if you have any questions."

Emain Macha

Llassar rode into the Ulaid capital for the third time and found the experience very different than his first two. Instead of being led in chains or riding ahead of men fleeing into a city cowering in fear of an army at its doorsteps, he was welcomed into the city as a conquering hero. Or at least the group he was with was welcomed that way.

The prince, who Velius had sent back with Llassar so he could report to his father, took all of it as a sign of his people's love for him, and was basking in their shouts of admiration and strips of red cloth being thrown at him from the people lining the street to the central meeting hall.

Llassar knew better. They were celebrating being alive and this was their first opportunity to see soldiers, even the small number that had ridden with him and the prince, returning in victory. Llassar knew that people could be fickle. They might have a loyalty to his father, who they had recognized as their king for more than ten years, but princes came and went. All it would take was one defeat or bad harvest for their cheers to change into shouts of anger.

Still, he did prefer this welcome to the other types.

The king was again waiting on the steps as the party rode up to the meeting hall. The prince, seeing his father, leaped off the horse and jogged up to meet him.

"I hear we have won a great victory."

"Father, you wouldn't believe it. The fighting was like nothing I've seen before. We were surrounded on all sides. Our enemies were dying under our swords which created giant mounds of their corpses that their friends had to crawl over to continue the attack."

"Our swords is it?" Conchobar said, with a smile at the young man's enthusiasm.

"Yes. Our swords. I was with the legate and his officers as they directed the fight when there was a break in the line. He'd already sent in all of his reserves and there was no one left to stop the break from becoming a route, so he charged in, and the rest of us followed. I killed two men myself."

When the king looked past his son to Llassar, Llassar said, "We told you there would be danger in having him with us and you insisted he needed to see war firsthand if he was to lead your people one day. How was he to do that without ever fighting? The boy did well."

The king made a face, but Llassar didn't back down.

The prince interjected, "You should have seen him. While I was fighting the men that I killed, Llassar killed seven men. Several of them he fought two at a time. You should see the Romans ..."

"Britannians," Llassar corrected. "They may all dress the same, but many of those soldiers were Caledonians, not Romans."

"Yes, Britannians. You should have seen them fight. They were a wall that the Concani, Vodiae, and Velabri warriors smashed into and died, over and over. The Britannians had dug out these long trenches around their fortified camp and they killed so many men that the trenches were full of them so that the men behind them could just walk over the bodies. It will take generations for the southern kingdoms to be able to field an army again after this victory."

"You'd be surprised how fast a nation can get new men under arms, even when losing thousands in a single defeat," his father said. "But I am pleased to hear of the victory. Let's go inside, and you can tell me more about our great victory."

They followed the king into the meeting hall that served as both his throne room and as a place for the leaders to meet. For now, it was empty of anyone but the king, his guards, the prince, and Llassar's party.

Settling into his throne at the far end of the circular room, Conchobar asked, "Now tell me how things stand. My son has fawned over the valor of the Britannian soldiers, but what of our warriors?"

The prince frowned and looked away from his father, which was a good indication of what had happened to them.

"They had decided against setting up a fortified encampment as Velius recommended and his legions use. They also didn't put out guards to watch for an attack and were caught unaware when the enemy broke from the trees. We left the morning after the victory, so I don't know the full extent, but my understanding is that the losses were significant."

"I see," Conchobar said.

"I am sorry you had to lose so many men, but this is a lesson that my people had to learn very quickly, and I hope yours can, too. The world is changing, and it will continue to change very quickly over the next several years. The days of wars being won by whoever had the strongest warriors is over. To win against armies like the Carthaginians, you need an organized and well-trained army, and the armies must know when and where they should fight, not just charge directly into the opposing army, with whoever runs out of men first losing."

"So you keep telling me. So where are we after this victory?"

"The Carthaginians were never involved in the last battle at all. They set their allies on us while moving the last of their phalanxes into the port they've been using as a base of operations. Their local allies have all but melted away at this point, having lost the bulk of their armies, they've returned to their capitals. The port the Carthaginians have been using isn't even really a port, from what we've been able to garner from our prisoners. It has a single dock that the Carthaginians themselves installed and there are no walls around the city, it's a poor position to defend. They split from their local allies as soon as we crossed the southern mountains, so they've had time to build up the city's defenses, but there hasn't been enough time to do much beyond adding simple wooden barricades and trenches. With the way the phalanxes fight, that isn't enough to counter our larger force. If I was them, I would be trying to evacuate my remaining men, especially since they still have an island nearby under their control to run to, but it's impossible to tell what they will actually do. In any event, I don't believe Velius will have much trouble taking the port, which just leaves your rebel kingdoms to deal with, which we will leave to you and your armies."

"You're removing your forces? What if the Carthaginians come back?"

"That will be difficult. They've lost their hold on Britannia, which means they have just the island the Romans call Manavia as a base to operate from, and I believe the Consul has plans for dealing with that as well. Once that island is under our control, any Carthaginian forces will have to come from the mainland and be supplied from there. They'd have to bypass Britannia to come for you, which would leave them vulnerable. I don't think they will make an attempt to retake your lands without first trying to reclaim their lost lands on Britannia."

"What about the rebel kingdoms? My armies are all but destroyed. I can't reconquer those lands without your armies."

"With all due respect, that is not our problem. We offered to help you free your land of the Carthaginian invaders and did so, losing many of our men in the process. We welcome continued trade between our people and the aid we have already provided will go a long way to re-equipping a new army, but that is as far as you wanted to go when we first discussed an alliance between our people."

"This is about becoming a member of your Empire and submitting to your Roman Emperor. You think you can blackmail us into submitting?"

"I do not, nor am I asking you to. We came in the spirit of friendship and spent Britannian lives to remove the real danger looming on your very doorstep. Had we not, you would have already been killed and your kingdom would now be another Carthaginian outpost. For that help, we ask nothing further beyond the consideration of an ongoing trade relationship. As deals go, that seems like a very fair bargain and one that we lived up to. If you feel we haven't, then we can end our relations here."

"No," Conchobar said hastily. "No. I'm not suggesting that. I just hoped you'd continue helping me reclaim my kingdom and bring peace to this island."

"A noble goal and one we can admire, but it will cost yet more Britannian lives and treasure, which we will need for our ongoing fight against the Carthaginians. If you were a member of our alliance, you wouldn't have to ask for help retaking your lands and bringing the rebels under control, since you would have as much right to military security as the rest of us. The legions would be fighting for you the same way they fight for my people or the Romans on Britannia. We would protect you from future Carthaginian attacks, set up a branch of the praetorians whose job it is to maintain order and peace on the island, open up our markets to your people and give you full access to all of the new technological innovations coming out of the Empire. You would also still maintain autonomy to govern your people as you see fit, with the only check being the Imperial Senate, of which you'd have an equal voice with every other member."

"I don't like the idea of having to answer to someone else on how to rule my people. Even if we have an equal say, it still gives you and the Romans the ability to tell me how to rule my lands."

"That is up to you, Your Majesty."

Conchobar sat silently, staring at Llassar. Llassar looked passively back at him, neither challenging him nor backing down. He knew the king was in a no-win position. Before the Carthaginian's arrival, the Ulaid had relied on the other kingdoms fighting amongst themselves to keep control of their lands. All of the kingdoms that rallied to the Carthaginians were now working together and there was a chance they would continue to do so even after the Carthaginians were gone. Conchobar knew his only chance was to conquer the entire island, and even if the Britannians stayed and helped him do that, he wouldn't be able to hold those lands when the Britannians left. He needed the Britannians' continued support, but he wanted it on his terms. Which wasn't going to happen.

"So if we do want to explore joining your Empire, how would we do that?" Conchobar finally asked.

"You would need to go speak with the Consul, the Emperor, and probably members of the Imperial Senate. I wouldn't say negotiate, since neither my people nor the Romans would be willing to allow you to join the Empire on terms better than those under which we joined, but you could discuss it with them, and they could hopefully ease your concerns over the loss of independence. They are not unreasonable and will hear you out. It was made very clear to me when I was sent here that we were not invading your kingdom and want you as allies, not subjects. If you decide you do not like what they have to say, then you are free to return and govern your lands as you see fit."

"It is a dangerous time for me to be leaving my people," Conchobar said.

"Do you have someone else you trust to send to negotiate in your stead?"

"For this? No."

"Then you have to go yourself."

"Will you leave your legions here until I return? I don't want to go negotiate the future of my kingdom, only to find it gone when I return."

"We will. I will return with you to Britannia, since I don't think there are many there who know your language, and will leave Velius here with his legions. He still has to take the southern port, but that shouldn't take long. He will ensure the other kingdoms don't turn on you while you're gone. Your son has been working with Velius during the campaign. I know he's young, but this might be a good chance for him to get a taste of leadership while you are gone."

Conchobar looked doubtful. Llassar didn't doubt he loved and trusted his son, but there was a long history in every nation he'd heard of, including the Romans' current Emperor, of sons trying to usurp their father's power. In some cases, a king leaving his son in command during their absence returned to find they no longer had a kingdom.

Velius knew that thought went through Conchobar's head, but this situation was different. The Ulaid had no functioning military at the moment and were reliant on the Britannians, who could have taken his kingdom over already, if they really wanted to. Of course, perhaps he thought this was some form of elaborate trap, and he'd find himself in chains when he landed on Britannia. That wasn't unheard of, after all.

"I think that might work. Some of my advisors will remain to guide Cormac in this, as well as a good portion of my guard, to ensure he is well protected. I assume the legions will return here after they finish off the last of the invaders, to ensure the kingdom remains secure."

Llassar had no doubt the personal guard being left behind was more to keep the prince from getting ideas of taking over than for his protection, but if that's what Conchobar needed to feel safe enough to travel to Britannia, he wasn't going to argue.

"I will send a messenger to Velius at once, informing him of what's happening. I'm certain he will keep everything as it is until you return."

"Fine. Then let's go see your Emperor."

Chapter 23

Devnum

"Good morning," Ky said, looking down at Lucilla as her eyes finally opened. "How are you feeling?"

It wasn't, in fact, morning, but Ky found something humorous about putting it like that.

"Confused," she said, looking around alarmed. "What happened at the docks? There was a man coming at me. He had a knife and yelled something and stabbed me and then ... I don't remember."

"That's because Sophus put you in a coma ... uhh, an unwaking sleep, like the one I was in this past winter, so he could repair your body. He's kept you like that for almost two weeks while he fixed you. I rushed back as soon as you were attacked so I could help with your recovery."

"I was asleep?" she said, starting to sit up and wincing.

"Take it easy. You haven't used your muscles in a while and you're going to be sore. You also have some scar tissue that will take time for Sophus to remove, so it's going to hurt to move for a bit. He made sure all of the critical points were completely healed, or as healed as possible, before waking you up, but I'm still concerned there might be more internal bleeding."

"There won't be any bleeding, Commander. I am confident I have closed all the wounds and repaired all the damaged veins and muscle groups. The soreness should not last long and there is no danger of additional damage."

"You two have been arguing over me?" Lucilla asked, smiling weakly at Ky.

"The Commander has been unreasonably cautious on any topic involving your recovery."

"I just wanted to make sure nothing went wrong when we woke you up."

"I'm sorry to give you a scare," Lucilla said.

"You need to be more careful. I know you want to be there for the people, but you have security for a reason. I talked to Modius. He, and the rest of your guards, all said you ignored their warnings, allowing yourself to be surrounded by people you didn't know."

"They were mostly women and children. We're trying to convince their men to join us and man our ships. Treating their families as if they are lepers isn't going help us achieve our goals."

"But they aren't the only people out there. This isn't a legion camp where we know exactly who's around you, or even a Caledonian village where insurrectionists or Carthaginian agents would have trouble blending in. There are Romans who still hate us and blame both of us for the changes they hate."

"I've seen you walking through factories and even crowds. Why is it safe for you and not me?"

"An excellent question," Sophus added.

Ky ignored the AI and said, "That isn't the same. I have Sophus continually monitoring the crowds and my enhanced reflexes allow me to avoid attacks that you cannot."

"I have pointed out numerous times that I can only see threats in your point of view, Commander, and yet you continue to put yourself in situations where unknown individuals are directly behind you. Enhanced reflexes cannot protect you from attacks you do not know are coming."

"Fine, I don't take the care I should either, although my system also has a full suite of medical nanites, instead of the hacked ones Sophus has managed to create for you. I just worry about you, and don't want anything to happen to you."

"I know, and I appreciate that," Lucilla said, placing her hand on the side of his face and caressing his jaw.

"Just promise me you'll be more careful."

"I will try to not get stabbed again," she said.

"I find that answer vague and unconvincing."

"Me too, but I think it's as good as we're going to get."

"So I've missed two weeks? What's happened? Is Velius still fighting in Ériunia? Have you looked at the cannon? Did you see the ships? How about the refugee quarter and the merchant quarters that are being built? I want to get those people out of tents as soon as possible."

"Slow down, slow down. Yes, Velius is still in Ériunia. The last message we received said he was expecting to confront the Carthaginian army at any time, so that has probably happened by now. Yes, I've seen the cannon and you did an excellent job, and we should be testing the first cannon any day now. The ships are coming along well also."

"And the refugees?" she prodded when he stopped without answering all of her questions.

"Tensions are on the rise. The people, especially the Caledonians, are blaming the newcomers for your injuries. There have been some incidents."

"You need to make sure they're protected. We are still short on labor in every area and if these people start getting attacked, or worse, they might stop coming. Especially the Scandi, who are only here for opportunity and aren't fleeing anything. Hortensius says every day, how short we are on raw materials, and if they ..."

"I know and I've already ordered the praetorians to increase patrols in the refugee areas and have had the praecones add a warning into their latest public notices that violence against peaceful visitors of any kind will not be tolerated. Of course, that won't stop a lot of these people, but after some time, the outrage will decrease."

"I should get out of this bed and go out where people can see me. If they're angry because I was attacked, seeing that I'm fine should help calm them down."

"You aren't going anywhere. Sophus said you were healthy enough to come out of the coma, but you still need a few more days to give your body time to heal the rest of the way. We can keep things under control until then."

"Fine," she said grudgingly. "I've worked hard to try and get these people to stay and work with us and I know you have more plans in the works that will require more workers. We won't be able to meet that need if we let this get out of hand."

"Noted," Ky said.

She'd always cared about the people her family governed, but ever since her experiences with the Caledonians, who treated her as one of them and not an untouchable noble, she'd revised how she saw herself to be a champion of the average person. Even with the projects she was overseeing and the work she did with the Scandi and Germanic immigrants, she had still made time for random stops in less well-off sections of the city, talking to the people and trying to understand what they needed.

It's why there was outrage against those who people saw as her attackers had been so visceral, and not confined to just the Caledonians. Ky agreed she needed to get back out there and show the colors, as it were, but he was more concerned about her long-term health.

"But, if I wait here in this bed, once I'm up, I want to begin preparing for our wedding."

"What?" Ky said, surprised by the unexpected statement.

"You heard me just fine. I've already made it clear to you that I want to get married and I've waited while we dealt with one crisis after another, but I'm done waiting. We're going to be fighting this war for several more years at least, and I'm not willing to wait to marry you until we win."

Ky didn't disagree in principle. He loved her, both in the way defined by the people of his time in the future and in the more primal way people here thought of the word, but he didn't feel the need for some official title to express that love. Marriage as a binding contract wasn't a thing in his time. People were paired, and that was that. Of course, bondings were a lot less official there than they were here; where they required entire ceremonies and pledges of fidelity.

"I love you and do want to marry you, but I'm not sure this kind of distraction is what we need right now. We have a lot to do before this conflict is over."

"Which is why the people need a distraction. Now that they aren't under immediate threat, attention will waiver. Everyone's for high-minded civic pride and wants glory for the Empire when asked directly, but what people really care about is their day-to-day living experience. We are working everyone extremely hard, and that can take a toll, especially since there isn't going to be a chance for that pressure to let up until we get more people into the Empire to share the workload. They are craving a distraction."

"But ..."

"No. No buts. You may be from some far-off place with technology so powerful it looks like magic from the gods, but I know my people, and I know my heart. They are both demanding the same thing."

"I guess I have no choice but to agree then."

"See, you're already thinking like a husband," she said, putting her hand on his and smiling.

Southern Ériunia

"Are you sure about this?" Aelius asked, lying on the small rise next to Velius and looking at the medium-sized village below.

People were scampering everywhere, looking like ants running across an upturned mound from this distance, preparing defenses as best they could. Between the size of their army and the refugees from the night battle four days previous, the villages had several days warning to begin preparations, which now included a series of long ditches, not dissimilar to the ditches Velius had his legionaries dig around their camps that helped his legion defend itself during the night attack. Aelius couldn't help but wonder if they got the idea from the defenses that had mauled them so badly only days ago.

"Yes, I'm sure. The messenger we received a few days ago came directly from Ursinus's legions and had been present at the battle for Londinium. They faced a similar problem and addressed it in a similar fashion. It worked out well for them."

"Those ditches aren't the walls of Londinium."

"No, but we also don't have the same advantages they had there either. Until my legion can get reinforced and retrained, we're essentially down to two under-strength legions and street fighting there will play right into the Carthaginians' strengths. They can hold the alleyways and streets, forcing every attack to be a frontal attack. We can still take the city, they don't have the manpower to hold it, but they can make us pay to take it. Without being able to maneuver around them, our only recourse will be to hammer away at their front-line men. They're going to be surrounded so they won't break, because there's nowhere for them to run, which means we'll have to fight to their last man. If at all possible, I want to avoid that."

Although their last battle had been a stunning victory, it had come at a cost. His legion had stood up to a force close to four times its size for several hours and had come out of the fight badly mauled. He'd reorganized it as best he could to keep it field-ready, but he was only able to deploy five full cohorts, which was half the number of men he'd brought to the island.

This battle might finally secure Ériunia from the Carthaginians, but it wasn't going to be the Empire's last clash with them, and they were going to need as many men as possible to carry on the fight. Losing men with experience in a headlong attack was not what Velius considered a winning strategy.

"Won't they be spotted?"

"Maybe, but they're going to be Carthaginian ships flying Carthaginian flags, or at least ships of Carthaginian allies. Between that and the pressure we're going to be putting on them, they will hopefully be too distracted until we hit them to notice."

The situation was similar to the one they had at Londinium. The Carthaginians were again hemmed into a single point behind defenses and completely surrounded, which gave Velius some options. The countryside wasn't pacified like it had been around Londinium, but he had enough men that he could deal with that.

He sent half of Vibius's fourth legion west and half east to find fishing villages where they could commandeer boats for a landing force, and then he sent every mounted trooper he could muster, to cover the coast, watching for them. That had been two days before, and a rider had returned a few hours earlier reporting the sighting of a dozen small ships sailing towards the village from the east with Vibius's men aboard. There hadn't been any word from the cohorts he'd sent to the west yet, which wasn't unexpected. He hadn't been sure how many boats the men would find in either direction, which is why he'd split the forces in the first place, to increase their chances of finding enough to make a landing force.

He had to time the attack just right, however. Not because he was worried the Carthaginians might inflict enough casualties to break out, but because the most disorienting part of a fight was when the enemy initially engaged. Those initial moments were the ones where he'd have the most attention on Aelius's legion, which should allow Vibius's men to land and attack from the rear.

***

They'd been lying there for the past thirty minutes, Velius staring through his spyglass at the water to the east, looking for the sails. Finally, he saw what the scout had reported. The ships looked to be mostly fishing boats, some oar-driven and others with a single sail. The lead ship had strips of red cloth tied to the front of the boat, which was the signal the cohorts had been given to let his men on land know that they were on those ships.

"Let's go," Velius said, pushing back from the rise and returning to their horses and guards.

The legions were only a ten-minute ride behind, and they had to move fast. The ships would land in thirty minutes, and legions on land needed to be fully engaged at that moment. Thankfully, the legionaries were well-trained and had been standing ready while he and Aelius watched for the ships. As soon as they came over a small rise and into view of his men, the centurions had their men on the march.

The men already had their assignments and knew where to go, which saved the time of giving out orders. He'd released their Ulaid support to 'pacify' the countryside, keeping their unruliness from disrupting the battle plan. Although it would make ruling this area harder, since the people would have even more resentment after the Ulaid fighters savaged their villages and stole what few valuables they had, it was a necessary evil.

Velius hoped they'd distract the locals to keep them from harassing his legions during the battle, but mostly he just wanted the Ulaid fighters out of the way.

The buzz of action he'd seen in the village became a panic as his men marched over the rise and into sight of the village. Their line extended far beyond the village itself and wrapped around until both ends touched the coastline. They stopped their approach just on the other side of the wide trench filled with spikes.

The Carthaginians, who'd braced for the Britannians to try and charge across the trench, looked almost stunned when the Britannians instead stopped cold ... until the arcuballistas came up. The Carthaginians had helpfully packed themselves into tight rows, directly in the Britannians' path, and the Britannians took advantage of it.

Bolts began to tear into the Carthaginian lines, the distances short enough that they were able to punch through armor and even some of the shields. For a moment, the Carthaginians froze, unsure of what to do. Some started forward and even a brave handful tried to jump their trench, with varying degrees of success, while others began to break and run away from the incoming forces. Archers formed in the center of the village began to return fire, but it was sporadic and poorly aimed, since they didn't have a clear line of sight to the Britannian line. The few archers who had lined up behind the Carthaginian line were unable to fire as their own compatriots began pushing back, trying to flee the incoming bolts.

Velius couldn't see the beach on the other side of the village, but he could hear a commotion coming from the town. A few moments later, a Britannian trumpet blew two long and two short notes, the signal that they had made it ashore.

"Planks," Velius called out, and men from the back rows pushed past their compatriots to lay down planks of wood pulled from nearby buildings or even off their own wagons, strong enough and wide enough to allow one man to cross at a time.

The men ran forward and dropped the planks to span the trench. Normally, this tactic would be foolish, as his men would be vulnerable as they crossed and could only do so one at a time, which is why Velius had waited for the right moment. With a sudden attack behind them, the Carthaginian line had almost fully broken and chaos reigned, allowing his men to cross almost completely unmolested.

The legionaries formed quickly after they crossed and charged forward, cutting through the few Carthaginians who turned back to try and stop them. Within minutes, the first flags of truce went up, signaling men trying to surrender. Most were cut down by soldiers with their blood up until finally, the centurions were able to get the men under control.

The battle was the shortest Velius had ever experienced. It was over twenty minutes after his men first marched over the rise in front of the village with a loss of only thirty-two men.

With this battle, the Carthaginian power on Ériunia was broken.

Devnum

Hortensius had been better than his word and had the carriage system for the cannon built in under a week. Considering they'd never built something like that before, with its elevation mechanism and hitch to attach to a horse halter, which he also designed, and an ammo carriage that could attach in between the two, it was a miracle.

For the test firing, they met well outside of town away from anyone that might get hurt if there was a catastrophic failure. Hortensius came by carriage, where he'd stay for the entire test, saving him the pain of being moved in and out of it multiple times.

The manufacturer had wanted a true test of the entire platform, so the gun was hauled out to its position pulled by a team of horses, just like it would be in battle, unlimbered and pushed into position by a crew of workers. It was a slow process, but Sophus assured Ky that a practiced team could move artillery pieces in and out of position on a battlefield quickly. Although the cannon wasn't as good as the pieces fielded in the nineteenth century, the rest of the system was designed to those specifications, and it had worked well through several major wars, which meant there wasn't a reason it couldn't be practical here.

"We built the ammunition carriage as you specified, but it isn't large enough to hold more than a dozen shots. Are you sure we shouldn't have a larger carriage, or perhaps a second full-sized cart following along behind the cannon?" Hortensius asked as the men positioned the weapon so that the test firing didn't accidentally hit anything.

"I'm sure. As we scale up to steel cannons that allow for rifling, the cannon will get heavier, and having to add more horses will become a liability on the battlefield. Once we have enough cannons to form batteries of artillery, we'll have a supply wagon travel with them with additional ammunition and gunpowder, but we should keep it a little way from the cannon themselves. Every time we fire a round, there is a chance for a catastrophic failure and if that happens near an ammunition wagon, the results could be disastrous."

"I didn't understand a lot of what you said, but I get the point and I guess it makes sense. I just don't know how fast these can fire once a crew gets trained and experienced using them, so I don't know how fast they'll go through the ammunition on hand."

They'd reached the point that every other sentence required new words to be introduced so they could discuss possible advancement and tactics for using the technology, which was one of the downsides to skipping over hundreds of years of gradual development of each step. The language that developed around them didn't have time to follow suit.

"With the kinds of cannon we have now, they will probably max out at two rounds a minute. Anything more than that and the tubes will begin to heat up to the point where the metal could fail. Once we switch to an all-steel design, the rate of fire can increase to three and maybe even four rounds a minute, but that would be on the absolute outside edge of how fast they can safely fire. Anything faster would mean they aren't swabbing the guns out well enough, and a missed ember could set off the next gunpowder charge when it's rammed in, which no one would be happy about."

"I, of all people, should have probably thought that through, considering," Hortensius said, pointing generally at himself. "They're going to do a test with just the gunpowder charge first, but after that, I'm going to have them fire a test round as well. I know it isn't needed to check the pressure tolerances, but up until now, everything has been theoretical beyond seeing the small sample of gunpowder explode. I'd like to see what we're actually dealing with."

"That makes sense. Let's see if the gun holds up to firing first."

Hortensius nodded and waved to signal to the men at the cannon. After pushing in one of the pre-measured bags of gunpowder, one of the men lit the long fuse stretching out of a small vent in the back of the cannon, and then ran away from the cannon as fast as possible, trying to catch up to the other men sprinting across the open field the cannon sat in. Ky had directed them to cut a very long fuse, that would take over a minute to burn through, but he didn't begrudge them their caution. They'd all seen the wreckage of the destroyed gunpowder factory, and had a healthy respect for what it could do.

The men halted behind the carriage, stopping to peek around it. Ky suppressed a smile as the seconds ticked down, his enhanced vision allowing him to follow the progression of the fuse as it burned. Hortensius, at least, had a basic idea of how long it would take, but he didn't have an advanced computer in his head giving a countdown tied to a calculation of the burn rate, fuse length, humidity, and dozens of other factors that determined exactly when the gunpowder would ignite.

Which is why he and everyone else, except Ky, jumped as the gunpowder exploded, spewing a long tongue of flame out of the cannon muzzle. Hortensius had heard it before, but more close up, and Ky could see the manufacturer squint his eyes hard, probably as a flashback of his much more personal experience with gunpowder played through his memory.

The horses attached to the carriage, on the other hand, had never heard a sound like that before. In time, they'd be able to train horses to not spook at the sound, but there hadn't been time for that here. Hortensius had stuffed cloth into and over the horses' ears, but that had only cut down the sound. The men holding the horses had been shocked and almost lost their holds on the horses as they tried to bolt, sending poor Hortensius sliding sideways in the carriage. Ky's hand streaked out and grabbed the cart, holding it still until the men could get the horses under control.

"By the gods," Hortensius said, staring at the cannon.

"It is impressive," Ky said, letting go of the carriage and starting towards the cannon. "Let's see how the cannon held up."

Ky could hear the manufacturer's aides chiding the horses to pull their boss over to the cannon, and tuned them out. They'd make it over eventually, but other than visually inspecting it for obvious cracks, Hortensius couldn't really know how successful the test was, so his inspection was more of a formality than anything.

Ky circled the cannon, letting Sophus extrapolate the data as he looked over the cannon, examining it faster and more thoroughly than he could by himself. The long smooth surface, interrupted by raised ridges caused by bands added after the main tube of the cannon was completed, provided additional reinforcement at points along the cannon's structure.

"The structure is intact. No stress factors detected with minimal heat dissipation into the metal."

"Heat will be a bigger problem when we switch to steel, since bronze has less thermal conductivity than steel."

"Only by a small margin."

"Sure, but when blasting away as fast as the crew can work the guns, that little bit will matter."

"How does it look?" Hortensius called out to Ky as the carriage began to pull closer.

"It held up well. No fracturing, no warping at either the base or the muzzle, and no excess out-gassing through the vent. You did a good job."

"Well, your instructions and Lucilla's corrections did a good job. I merely assembled it."

"That's the important part though. So, you said you wanted to see what it will really do?"

"Yes. It's why I picked this spot. That building over there was abandoned several years ago. Could we ..."

"Put a giant hole in it? Yes, we can," Ky said.

Ky let Sophus work out the range and distance as he pulled the cannon into place with one hand, a job that had taken four men before. Looking down the length of the barrel, he adjusted the crank at the bottom, lowering the elevation until it locked onto Sophus's projection.

"You make that look so easy. If we had you manning the guns, we could free up a lot of men," Hortensius said.

"I'd like to think I had more important tasks, but if you think that's where I belong ..."

"Don't be so literal. I know you have a better sense of humor than that."

Maybe it was because of Lucilla's influence or maybe it was just that he'd had time to adjust to the different way people acted here, but he was finding himself being less stiff and more relaxed. True, a lot of his interactions had been with soldiers, which had its own formality that was not that different between his time and this time, but it actually helped him feel more comfortable, accelerating the process of acclimation.

Ky went around the gun and swabbed it thoroughly, clearing out any of the remaining embers before sliding in a charge of powder and tamping it down. Reaching into the ammo carriage, Ky palmed a cannonball and rolled it into the tube, using the ramrod to press it firmly in place as well.

"I think we're good. You should move the carriage back a little further this time and keep a better hold on the horses. Train your spyglass on the building. I'll stay here and operate the cannon, so you don't have to wait as long."

"Are you sure that's safe?" Hortensius asked.

"Yes. The cannonball won't be that much of a block and shouldn't cause pressure to build up too much before the cannonball is ejected. If it didn't blow up before, it shouldn't blow up now. Besides, I'm going to be asking men to man this cannon, or ones like it, very soon. If it's too dangerous for me, it's too dangerous for them."

"I guess," Hortensius said, sounding unconvinced, but following Ky's instructions.

"You should go too," Ky said to his four lictore, who remained with him as the carriage pulled away.

"We'll stay with you, Consul. Like you said, it should be safe," Sellic said, looking back at him defiantly.

"At least take a few steps back and to the left. When it fires, this whole thing is going to jump backward, and will crush anyone behind it."

The four men looked at each other and then took several steps out of the way, eyeing the tube warily as Ky cut a length of fuse and stuck it into the vent. Looking around to make sure everyone was clear, Ky lit a wick from a torch attached to a pole they had placed nearby and carried it over to the cannon.

"Fire in the hole," Ky said with a grin, before touching the wick to the fuse and stepping back.

The cannon leaped backward as flame shot from the muzzle, the cannonball cutting through the air, making a screaming sound that shouldn't have been heard for hundreds of years.

The men held the horses better this time, and the carriage then headed towards the abandoned building. Ky took a moment to look over the cannon again, happy to see it still held up. Eventually, one of these would fail and men would die, but that was an inevitability when gunpowder entered the picture.

Ky and his lictore left the cannon and made their way over to the building, part of which had now collapsed.

"It went straight through this beam," Hortensius said. "It's splintered like a twig and the one on the other side of the building is too."

"You should see what it does to men if you get it to skip across the ground properly. It will tear dozens of men apart in the same way."

"That's brutal."

"True, but so is gutting a man with a sword. War is brutal. The only thing different about this is its brutality is more efficient. Still, as tests go, I'd say this one was pretty effective."

"I'd say."

"We've seen what we need to see, your current mold and production work well. Get the production line started. You have directions on where to send the first batch, but the first four need to go to the docks. I'm also going to have some new designs sent over that I need taken care of. These shouldn't be that different from things you're already made, so it shouldn't be difficult for you. I'll also include where I need these designs taken. We need more cannonballs and as many gunpowder packs as possible."

"We've already begun training new workers to start in the factory. We'll get what you need delivered on time."

"I know you will," Ky said.

Chapter 24

Oceanus

"Signal those idiots to spread out," Kanmi said, pointing off the port of the quinquereme. "If they can't keep formation, I'll have them tossed in the sea and have someone else captain their ships."

His people had started as a seafaring people, and had sailed circles around the Romans, the Egyptians, and everyone else they had encountered; but that had been on the middle sea, which was a tame pond compared to Oceanus, with its giant waves that would come out of nowhere, swamping ships before they knew what happened to them. Already he'd lost twenty-two ships, nineteen of which were fully loaded with soldiers, sailing through the neck and around Iberia bound for Britannia. Even hugging the coast, the short sides and shallow draft made the ships unstable, and several of those lost had been caused by collisions, the oarsmen unable to get out of each other's way.

If he'd had his choice, he would have sailed the ships empty, and boarded them in Germania, from there it was a short voyage to the islands. There hadn't been time for that, since most of the forces on his ships had come from Africa, pulled out of the conflicts in Persia, and there hadn't been time to wait for the men to march across the continent to meet them. Apparently, the fool they'd sent to conquer the rest of that island had managed to lose the entire thing instead.

It had taken longer than anyone was happy with to get enough ships gathered and get the men loaded up, but the trip itself had gone well. Having sailed on Oceanus before, he'd already calculated an expected loss and had thought he'd actually have lost more ships than had occurred on the voyage. His annoyance with the captains was more an inborn personality trait than a feeling that things were actually going wrong.

What he cared about was getting to the destination on time with as many men as possible. Once he landed the army, their commanders would take over and his job would be done, but until then, he was in charge and he wanted word of his deeds to reach the emperor, whose favors could elevate a man's family for generations. What he didn't want was a disaster like the former governor, whose family was even now being rounded up and sent into a lifetime of slavery to pay for his incompetence.

It would still take another week to claw their way through the waves to the island, and then none of this would be his problem anymore.

Devnum

It was late in the evening when a rider found Ky at one of the semaphore stations close to the city, finally giving the design a once over. The messenger informed him that Llassar and an entourage from the Ulaid, including their king, had arrived. The Caledonian had sent a message ahead notifying them of their arrival, but that had been received just the day before and Ky had thought they'd have a little more time before the group arrived.

What they needed was a way to get messages quickly between the islands, but even the shortest points were almost forty miles across and even the large, mounted telescopes he'd had Hortensius design and set up could only see about twenty miles and still be clear enough to read the other towers' signal. They didn't have the construction materials to stand up to a mid-ocean station, which meant they were limited to messenger boats for now, which were too slow by comparison.

That was a problem for another day, but it occupied Ky's mind as he raced back to the city to greet the visitors. The men were gathered at the palace and waited in the currently empty forum, both because it could house the king, his aides and guards and because it was an impressive structure, both in size and design, which hopefully added a sense of awe that would play into the Britannians' favor. Ky wasn't sure he went in for all the psychology behind negotiations, not that the people of this time would define it as such, but the Emperor did and was a firm believer in holding most meetings there or in the throne room, depending if he wanted to highlight the might of his rule or the democracy and equality of its legislatures. Today's meeting fit the second need better.

Ky wished the Emperor was there, but he'd ridden out two days prior for Londinium to see the captured city for himself, leaving the management of the Empire to Ky until Lucilla was out of bed, which thankfully would be any day now.

"I'm sorry to have kept you waiting," Ky said entering the forum and coming down the steps to the corner where the king and Llassar were seated. "I thought you'd be at least another day away from arriving, and was outside the city when word came."

Ulaid guards flanked the top row, watching over their king and each was paired with a palace guard, all of the men looking as anxious with each other as they were over their charges.

"So you're this messenger from the gods I keep hearing about," Conchobar said, looking Ky up and down. "I hear you can throw a man clear over a building and fire green flame from your ass."

"Unfortunately, I can claim neither ability and I can promise you I have no divine origin. I was from a far-off land, but I am now a citizen of the Empire who the Emperor saw fit to name Consul, and that's all that matters for the moment. I understand from Llassar's messages that you are interested in joining our alliance and becoming part of the Empire."

"What I'm interested in is protecting my people. Ever since Fergus fled and I was given rulership, we have been beset by smaller kingdoms that constantly try and chip away at our lands. When it was simply raids, we could manage it ourselves but now they have seen fit to ally themselves with the most powerful empire the world has ever known. It is my duty to find a way to keep my people free, which means not subjected to either the Carthaginians or anyone else who would rule us. Unfortunately, it has been made clear by how close we came to destruction that we are unable to do that alone. Llassar has told me what your people are offering, but I wanted to hear it for myself."

"Having been involved in negotiations to create this new Empire, Llassar is far more than a messenger and knows firsthand what we are offering. His people wanted the same thing as yours, to build the strength to remain free without having to give up those freedoms in return. The Romans felt the same. As you pointed out, I came from neither people, so had no vested interest in either group having the upper hand over the other. We're offering you the same deal. Does it mean you give up some of your sovereignty? Yes, but everyone else in the alliance gives up the same thing and you will have the same say in what powers you give up, just like all of us."

"Will that include helping us gain control of the rest of our island?"

"Yes, although from Llassar's last message, how that happens might not be how you would do it. Some of the minor kings will need to be crushed to keep them from trying to regain their old power, but the smaller villages don't care who governs them. They just want to live their lives and feed their families. Armies marching through and taking everything they own, killing their sons, and raping their daughters will make them into rebels, not subjects."

"I've heard this speech from your men," Conchobar said.

"That's fine. I'm not trying to lecture, just giving you an idea of what you can expect."

"And what do you expect to get in return? You're letting us mostly retain sovereignty over our lands, have a say in those laws we do have to follow, and will use your armies to bring my island to heel. You aren't making this offer out of the goodness of your hearts, so what do you want from us."

"A fair question," Ky said. "Primarily, manpower. We're facing an enemy who conscripts men from across the known world. We've killed thousands of them, and only now are we starting to be considered a threat. Just freeing the islands isn't enough. They already have a large army sailing this way to retake the land we liberated. I think it's easy to see they won't stop there. We have to take the fight to them, and to do that, we need soldiers. Once you join us, we'll offer any of your people who want to fight a position. They will be paid, just as any worker is paid, and we will make sure they are taken care of while they fight for us, and they will be taken care of afterward. Our manufacturing base is also growing extremely fast to support both our war effort and to create the new technology we've begun to produce, some of which your people already have their hands on, and our needs are outpacing the number of workers available. Beyond manpower, we also need crops to support our armies and natural resources to build the weapons of war, all of which you can provide."

"So you want our resources," Conchobar said, sounding hostile.

Ky didn't blame him. What he was suggesting wasn't a model that existed in this time. In this time, if a weaker kingdom had resources a stronger kingdom wanted, the stronger kingdom would bring their armies and take them, sometimes leaving after they got what they wanted and sometimes staying, making the weaker kingdom a vassal that had to pay tribute to their overlord. What Ky had introduced with the alliance between the Romans and Caledonians, and hopefully with the Ulaid, was a novel concept that the people of this time would find suspicious.

"Yes, but not in the way you are thinking. We are not asking for it as tribute or just taking it. For one, there couldn't be tribute, because you will *not* be a kingdom we control, you would be part of us. Although the borders would remain, they are more delineations of responsibility, not a separating of our lands and yours. All of our people are one people, allowed to move freely between all parts of the Empire. The land with the resources we need belongs to whoever owns it now. If it's not owned, how it's disposed of is up to you, as it's in your territory. You could mine or grow the resources yourself and sell them to the people that need them, or you could sell or rent the land. If local entrepreneurs take the opportunity, it generates jobs for your people and tax revenue for you, to help pay for local services you choose to provide. It generates goods that you could trade within the Empire or with people outside of it. Your people gain wealth, we gain materials. Everyone gains from the arrangement."

"It sounds too good to be true," Conchobar said.

"We thought the same thing," Llassar said. "But it has worked out like that. There have been some rough patches. Our people have mostly been farmers, unexposed to things like contracts and business deals, but the Romans have been good about working with us to correct those problems when we find them. It isn't perfect, but most of our people are better off now than they were before the alliance. Fewer people are going hungry and they have more opportunities than they had before."

"Are a lot of your people moving to Rome? Doesn't that leave you with fewer subjects working the land, hollowing out your kingdom and leaving it poorer?"

Although the Caledonians weren't exactly a kingdom, Llassar took the question as it was intended.

"Yes, a lot are. Because we sent a force to fight with the Romans, a lot of men ended up joining the legions. Others moved for opportunities in the factories, but it didn't hollow out our lands. A lot of Romans have also moved to our lands, and while there, they are subject to our authority and taxes. Again, there have been difficulties, but on the whole, it has worked out to our benefit. We have access to markets to sell goods that we didn't have before, although a lot of that is goods being bought up by the Empire itself to support the war effort. We have better internal protection thanks to the imperial taxes paying for praetorian patrols which cut down the number of bandits, and some of these new Roman inventions have been making our lives easier. We aren't weaker than we were."

"I understand you're hesitant. You don't want to give up being your own kingdom, but you know you can't repel a second Carthaginian invasion and you don't have the power to conquer your rivals and pacify the island under your leadership. What we're offering is as close as you're going to get to having both. It's up to

..." Ky said, and then stopped as motion caught his eye by one of the entrances.

Lucilla was leaning against the door frame. Her skin was pale and she looked weak, a byproduct of the nanites dominating her body's resources to repair the damage it had sustained and one of the reasons he wanted her to stay in bed while she recuperated.

"Excuse me for a moment," Ky said, giving Llassar a look for him to take over and then rushing to Lucilla's side.

"She's supposed to stay in bed," Ky said to Modius, who was standing behind her looking equally concerned and ashamed.

"We tried, but when she found out where you were, she insisted that we'd either need to tie her to the bed or let her come here."

"I'm not a child," Lucilla said.

"You're still injured, though."

"You and I both know I'm going to recover, even if I start moving around. It might be a little slower, but that's it. Besides, I've stayed in bed long enough and you need help with this."

"We're doing fine."

"Has he agreed yet?"

"No, but he will."

"Probably, but we don't need him to just agree, we need them to want to be members of the alliance. Anything less than enthusiasm could plant a seed of resentment that will eventually weaken the alliance. You're good at a lot of things Ky, with amazing ability and knowledge, but this kind of thing takes experience. You did great with the Caledonians, but they saw you fight and you fit into their mythos, giving them a reason to trust you, or at least believe in you. This is a different situation and requires different skills. You grew up learning to fight. I grew up learning to do this. Let me do it."

"Fine, fine, but after it's done, you are going back to bed."

"Of course," sounding as if she wouldn't dream of being a problem, before becoming more serious. "There's something else."

"What?"

"There was a messenger reporting to the palace guard captain on his way to see you. Knowing how important this was, I asked him to give me the message."

"And," Ky said as she paused.

"One of Valdar's ships sighted almost a hundred ships sailing up the continental coast towards us. They're mostly oar-driven or a single sail and the captain said they were having trouble in the high waves, so Valdar's ship was able to get back here quickly, but they think it'll only be a few more days before they get here."

"Do they have any idea where the fleet might try to land troops?"

"No."

"Which means, we're going to have to intercept them before they get to the coast," Ky said, looking back at the Llassar and Conchobar.

"Go. I'll take care of this. You're going to need to get on the water now if you're going to hit them before they make landfall. I already sent a messenger to Hortensius to make sure he got everything loaded that you will need."

"Good. Right. I'll see you when I get back."

"Of course you will. You have a promise to keep!" she said, giving him a smile before taking Modius's arm and going into the forum.

Chapter 25

The Kushor

Kanmi watched the last bit of shoreline disappear as they passed the last part of the continent, continuing on towards Britannia, hoping the god of the sea that his ship was named for, was watching over them. Normally they would travel further along the northern part of Gaul until they got to the shortest span between the two landmasses, but that required traveling between the northern part of Iberia and the southern coast of Britannia.

They'd already encountered a handful of merchants and fishermen since passing the corner of Iberia, and the closer they got, the more likely the Romans would be able to guess their destination. Unlike the ships of the Northmen, their quinquereme was too heavily loaded to just pull up onto any beach. If they only had the triremes, they could have found one of the shallow sandy shores to pull onto, but they needed the quinquereme to carry all the men and equipment they needed for this campaign.

The larger boats' deeper drafts meant that they needed some kind of port. Although it would be preferable to have an actual built-up port with a functioning harbor, the governor's loss of the island kept that from being an option, leaving only the natural harbors scattered along the coast, where they could get close in and use smaller boats to ferry everyone ashore. It would be a slow process, however, which meant it was important to not attempt it under fire, and that they needed to keep the Romans guessing about where they would land until enough of their force was ashore to form a beachhead.

Luckily they had a series of surveys of the southern half of the island going back twenty or thirty years, so he knew what his options were. Which is why he was forced to cross as soon as they could, heading straight north once they hit the corner of Iberia, even though it meant a long stretch without the visibility of land they could follow.

Although the waves didn't get to the heights they would if he moved directly away from the continent, he still had his ships pull into a tighter formation, which was a problem all on its own.

The Victoria

"Knowing where you are and if you've traveled too far north or too far south should keep you on that line," Ky said, handing the circular metallic object he'd had Hortensius work up, back to Valdar. "At night, you can also use the North Star to do the same thing."

"That's basically how we've been doing it, getting direction from the North Star or the sun, but I never imagined it was anything more than a general guide of which direction we were facing."

"Which is probably pretty effective. If you have the right maps, showing you the seas broken down in sections that match the degree marks on the astrolabe, you can always know exactly where you are, at least when going east or west. There are ways to tell where you are north and south as well, but that will take more time; so for now, this will have to do."

"I don't suppose you have one of those maps handy?" Valdar asked.

"As a matter of fact, I do," Ky said, handing over a rolled piece of vellum, the prepared animal skin was expensive but able to hold up to the constant humidity on the ship.

Valdar unrolled it, looking at the burned-in lines and shapes of the continent showing the known world. Ky had another version he'd hand over later that showed North America and the Pacific, instead of stopping partway across Asia. He needed to lay more groundwork before he revealed what the entire world looked like and he didn't want them trying an Atlantic crossing in the ships they currently had, as they wouldn't stand up to it. As it was, this would go a long way to revolutionizing sea travel, especially once they finished with this invasion force and he could get Hortensius to produce compasses. The two together would be enough to allow vessels to break from the coastlines, creating more efficient trade routes and opening up new lands to them.

"You realize the value of this? Your enemies would be able to do a lot with something like this."

"I do, and they're our enemies now," Ky said. "And I suggest you keep it close, although eventually, I expect it will get out. All of our ship's masters will need something like this if we're going to continue our expansion and become self-sufficient. We can't let the fear of our enemies getting this keep us from using it. We'll just have to come up with new advantages once these get out."

"None of which helps now, since knowing where we are doesn't tell us where their fleet is."

"Between the ships you have circling the area and the fishermen we asked to keep an eye out, we have a rough idea where they are."

"Rough being the key word. A few mille passus this way or that, and we could completely pass their entire fleet. And it's costing me a fortune to have them circling the sea between Iberia and Britannia, instead of running back up towards Asia now that the northern ports are starting to lose their ice."

"Rough is enough and we've already agreed to cover your losses while they help search for the fleet. As long as we can get within thirty or forty mille passus, I'll be able to direct our forces to them. Besides, I have a good guess of where they're going to land, especially if your last captain was right about seeing them head straight off from the coast."

"He was a pretty far distance away, but he's an experienced seaman. If he said they held a northern course, then they did, so unless it was a feint and they suddenly turned east to head up the channel, then yes, I think that's right."

"Good. Then our course should get us close enough that I can bring us to the target."

"Then we only have to hope those monstrosities are worth your men carving up my ship. With the wind like it is, I'll be able to outrun any of their oar-powered ships, but I'm not going to be able to fight them," Valdar said, pointing at the forward-mounted cannon pointing out on either side of the bow and then to the symmetrical pair on the other end of his ship, pointing off its stern.

"They will," Ky said, looking past the guns at the open sea.

"I hope so. Now, can you explain to me again why we had to give my boat a silly Roman name?" Valdar said with a smirk.

They'd had this same argument every hour since Ky had come on board, although he was pretty sure the shipmaster was now doing it as a way of messing with him, since he wasn't a fool and could understand all of the reasons why Ky thought the ship should be Britannian, not just borrowed from a Scandi merchant.

Ky was pretty sure the man just liked to argue, as he started to list all the reasons for the hundredth time.

The Kushor

Kanmi was tired as the sun came up across the water, showing they were still heading more or less north. They'd have to adjust their course once they saw land again, but all in all, he was happy with their progress, especially considering he had more boats under his command at one time than any other sailor in the history of the empire. It looked as if they'd lost another five ships during the night. Two he knew for sure, seeing them collide and hearing the screams. The rest was based on word passed from ship to ship when he called for a status check of the fleet, which meant it could have been a few more or a few less, but either way, the numbers were acceptable. He'd probably lose another handful before the journey was over, but they'd still land with an army large enough to crush whatever the Romans threw against them.

"Sail, my lord," the lookout leaning against the prow of the boat called out, pointing north.

Walking past the exhausted rowers, Kanmi stared over the water, trying to make out what the lookout was seeing. The young man had been picked for his excellent eyesight and even with his help, it took several minutes for the Kanmi to find what he'd seen. The ship was still coming over the horizon and only the single sail was visible from this distance, although that was enough for him to identify the ship.

The sail was too large to be that of one of the fishing boats they'd seen and even a Roman trireme's sail would be masted closer to the body of the ship than this was, with the ship up higher along the mast, which meant it was one of the Scandi. The quarrelsome merchants didn't venture into the middle sea often but they were all over Oceanus and far down the coast of Oceanus. They paid their tribute and looked different enough to keep from having their ships seized when they came into ports, but they had a stark independent streak that Kanmi hated.

There'd been word that the Scandi had been more active in the area since the island fell to the Romans, taking advantage of the breaking of the Carthaginian control of shipping. The emperor had made comments that suggested their willingness to trade with the Romans was enough to change their status with the empire, making their ships open season for all Carthaginian captains, but as of now, that hadn't happened. The Scandi had a healthy sense of self-preservation, though, and the several Scandi ships they'd seen had turned and run as soon as they'd seen Kanmi's armada. This one seemed to have less sense, continuing on towards him, the body of the ship coming into view.

"If he keeps coming at us, send one of the unloaded triremes to intercept it. It can't carry enough men to stop even one of our ships, but there's a chance they're working for the Romans and if they're suicidal enough, they could set their ship on fire once they are in among ours."

At their current speed, the small boats they used to pass messages as well as offload men and supplies couldn't make it back and forth between them, which meant they had to use a message line with a waterproof pouch attached to a shot with a line thrown by the strongest man on the boat. It sometimes took several tries, but eventually, they made it.

Then something happened that Kanmi didn't count on. As the ship closed the distance, two plumes of smoke appeared at the front of it, partially obscuring it from view. Kanmi was just starting to think about what could have caused the smoke to suddenly appear, when two booms like the sound of rocks falling from a great height onto a stone bottom, sounded several seconds apart, one after the other. Then the unthinkable happened.

There was a crashing sound on the ship to his left as wood planks shot into the air just above the waterline and men began to scream. He couldn't see the ship on the other side of it, but the way the mast started to twist, something had happened there too.

They were in the middle of the ocean, so it wasn't possible that they'd struck anything. The way the boards shot out, it was almost like when a catapult shot crashed into a ship, except that happened with a stone falling straight down, and that hadn't happened here. The explosion had been at the water line and the boards had shot out horizontally, as if they were struck directly on. Which was impossible.

"Signal the fleet to slow," he yelled as the other ship began to sink. "Prepare to rescue the men in the water."

He hadn't ordered the fleet to stop specifically to help. He'd left the other ships that had gone down during the voyage to fall behind in their wake, but he wasn't sure what had caused the damage to make two of his ships begin sinking. Ramming the rest of his fleet into whatever it was, would just create more disaster.

Although he'd been looking at the ship in the distance, it wasn't until it again let out a puff of smoke and a set of booms that he realized whatever had hulled his two ships had come from the Scandi ship in the distance. It boggled the mind that the ship would be able to do anything at this extreme distance, but he saw two streaks this time, as whatever the projectile that sunk his first two ships passed across the canvas of its original victims before ripping through his next two boats. He could see one of the ships that was hit and noted that the tear was higher and went at a steeper angle than the first ship had been, tearing a long gash down the front and out the side just at the waterline, letting sea rush into the boat, already causing it to list.

No catapult he'd ever heard of could do what he was seeing! Firing at that distance, at that angle, and with that much power? It was plowing through thick ship timbers like twigs. Except there was clear evidence that this one did. The crashing sound didn't make sense, especially one so loud it could be heard over the sound of waves, but it didn't change what he needed to do.

"Get us moving. Rowers to the double stroke. We need to get to that ship. Archers on deck. Order the fleet to follow and take that ship."

With his ship taking off like it was, it would be hard for them to throw a message line or yell to the next closest ship, but they'd see him moving and figure it out. As the largest of the quinqueremes, it was unlikely that even with his extra set of rowers they would be able to catch the nimble Scandi ship, but once his smaller biremes got into the chase, especially the unloaded ones he'd planned to use as flankers and scouts, they might have a chance of catching it, especially if they could chase it closer to shore where the cross winds would slow the sail-driven ship down.

The Victoria

"They've figured out we're the problem," Ky said after the cannons fired a fifth and sixth time, sinking two more ships. "Turn us around."

"I've given up asking how you can tell," Valdar said, turning to yell orders at his men.

"You men move to the stern cannon," Ky said to the loaders Hortensius had loaned him for the battle.

They'd at least trained on how to properly reload a cannon, which is all Ky needed. Only being able to bring two cannons to bear at a time and the number of ships he had to sink with limited gunpowder, Ky had taken the task of aiming and firing them upon himself. Even with a full bank of guns, learning to aim guns on a ship that was constantly raising and lowering with the waves took hundreds of hours of gunnery practice and a significant amount of gunpowder, neither of which Ky had in great abundance.

What he did have was a tactical computer capable of tracking thousands of variables a second and plotting continually adjusting firing solutions. Eventually, Ky was sure he'd miss, but so far he'd managed to down six ships with six cannonballs. It helped that these ships weren't built like the ships of the age of gunpowder and sail, their overlapping boards being much harder to patch than the fitted boards on later designs, which could potentially be planked over to regain a water-tight seal.

He'd also taken the time to fire a few shots the day before, so the crew would have some comfort with the booming canon and could continue doing their jobs without panicking. He'd actually hoped the Carthaginians would panic more, and gained a grudging respect for their admiral, who'd only needed two volleys to figure out what was going on. Ky had hoped they'd be paralyzed by fear for a little longer, allowing him to pick off a few more ships before they got their act together.

Still, phase one had done what it needed to do. Now it was time to start phase two.

The Kushor

Sweat gathered on Kanmi's neck in spite of the cool early spring weather. The chase had been going on for the better part of four hours and it wasn't going well for him. The demon-spawned ship was faster than his larger, more durable ships and could sweep away his smaller ships as easily as if the gods had stabbed a mighty finger out, sending them to the depths at their whim.

After those first few minutes of confusion, he'd actually thought they might be able to end this early as his smaller ships began making headway as the sail-driven Scandi ship fought against the wind during its turn back north. They weren't. As soon as the ship turned, sailing away from his armada, it began spitting the plumes of smoke again, sending its projectiles tearing through the ships that had been closing in on it.

A few of his larger ships actually managed to take several shots before sinking, but they still sank. Any ship that the Scandi vessel decided to single out was destined to rest at the bottom of the ocean. After losing a large portion of his smaller, faster vessels, it became clear he had nothing that could get close enough to the Scandi ship without sinking, so he'd tried to disengage. He was already losing more ships than he could afford to lose, sending not just sailors and boats to the bottom of the ocean, but hundreds and hundreds of well-trained soldiers needed for the battle once they made land. Kanmi decided it would be better to ignore it as he would a buzzing fly and go on with his mission.

Unfortunately, the fly had a bite. As soon as he got his ships turned away from the chase, it too turned and began picking off the back of his fleet, two ships at a time. It was clear there was no way he was going to get away from it before it managed to sink his entire fleet. His only hope was to push it against the coastline and hopefully hem it in so that they could board it.

That last turn had been hours before, and the damage it inflicted was incalculable. Several dozen more ships had gone down and his overall fleet was now almost half the size of what it had been when he'd watched the sunrise that morning. The only good news in the entire debacle so far was that the gallows damned ship's destruction had greatly slowed. That morning, its noise and smoke announced destruction every few minutes, but as the day wore on, that had slowed until now it only destroyed a handful of ships an hour. Still much faster than his fleet could take, but at least not at the rate that he would run out of ships before he reached the coastline.

He just had to hope that the rate of destruction continued to slow enough that he would still have even part of an army left to put on shore.

The Victoria

"Why have your ..." Valdar started to say and then paused, searching for a word.

"Cannon?" Ky said.

"Yes, cannon. Why have your cannon stopped firing as fast? As deadly as those things are, you could have destroyed the entire fleet by now, if you'd kept firing at the same speed you were going at this morning."

"Not enough ammunition," Ky said, pointing at the now greatly shrunken stack of supplies he'd had loaded onto the ship during their hurried departure from Devnum. "We could only bring so much gunpowder and cannonballs. It's fine. We've shown them we're a threat and forced them to follow us a little longer. We need to keep them on the hook, though. Pull in a little more sail, let's let them start to gain a little ground on us."

"That's risky. If we get a bad wind and they're close enough, they could overtake us," Valdar said. "That'll become a real danger once we get closer to the coast."

"Just do your best. I need them to stay with us until we pass that point," Ky said, pointing at the map.

The Kushor

The sun was low in the sky as the cliffs of the southern shore came into sight. Kanmi hadn't sailed this close to Britannia before, but if they kept this heading, after catching up to the damnable Scandi, there was a port he could use. It would at least give him a chance to offload what soldiers he had left and try and repair the damage to the ships caused by running through their destroyed fleet mates.

The ship's destruction of his fleet had continued to slow, but he was still losing ships and men he couldn't afford to lose, with just over forty ships left on the water. Enough soldiers had gone to the bottom that he wasn't confident the army he had left to land would be able to go up against the Romans.

At this point, it would be smarter to turn around, head to a friendly port on the continent, and try again another day ... or at least, it would be smarter if that wouldn't lead to his head in a noose. The amount of resources put into this force meant the emperor would be displeased if it was unsuccessful, more so if he lost most of the ships and men in the process. And the emperor's displeasure was usually only placated by deaths.

The only bright point was that he had started to close on the Scandi, who'd started to pull in sail as they got closer to the shore. It had taken hours to make up the ground. Hours where he kept losing ships, but he was now just outside of arrow range. At the rate they were gaining, it would be dark by the time he got close enough to drop his boarding hook, but there was supposed to be a full moon that evening, which would be enough to let him board the smaller ship.

"Archers at the ready," Kanmi called out as they turned west to follow the coastline, the distance closing a little more, putting them into extreme arrow range, or at least extreme range on the water.

"Is something burning on that cliff?" one of the sailors near him asked, pointing up towards a cliff to the north, interrupting the order to fire.

Kanmi looked up to the cliff as the first projectiles screamed down on them from above, a cloud of smoke already obscuring whatever had fired. It was a trap. All of it. The Scandi ship had stayed in range, slowing their fire to keep Kanmi chasing them, allowing him to get a little closer every hour, to make him feel like they almost had the battle won, in spite of the damage it had inflicted, all to keep him sailing into their trap.

Kanmi started to yell for the men to turn hard away from the coast when a cannonball tore him in half before plunging deep into the ship.

Chapter 26

Devnum

Ky waited on the temple steps, his mind racing. The battle of Mare Britannicum had been the most one-sided anyone had ever heard of. The Britannians had lost three men, two accidents on the Scandi boat when men fell overboard and one on a lucky shot by a panicked archer when a Carthaginian ship tried to make it to the cliffside. The Carthaginians, on the other hand, had lost tens of thousands. Two boats looked like they got away, although even with Sophus's replay, it was hard to tell in the chaos.

They'd used a lot of their gunpowder in the process, but the cannons had worked beautifully, and word of their new wonder weapons was already spreading through the legions and beyond. The attack on Lucilla proved that there were still Carthaginian, or at least Caesius, sympathizers in their midst, which meant the rumors would get back to the Carthaginians eventually. If some boats did escape, a smart man would put two and two together and they'd be able to figure out what he'd done to their fleet. That was going to happen, eventually.

Lucilla was recovering much more slowly since she refused to go back to bed, even after she concluded the negotiations with the Ulaid. Still, it was good to have her back up and moving again. Although they hadn't gotten the deal signed-off, she'd done an excellent job leading Conchobar through the process, and his agreeing to join the alliance was now a foregone conclusion. Ky wondered at a rebuilt British Empire thousands of years before it happened in his time, and if their joining as one political unit was inevitable. Of course, the Britannic Empire wasn't the same as the historical British Empire, with a different makeup of people without the Vikings or Normans, but it was something to think about.

It wasn't complete, either. In addition to needing a finalized agreement between the Empire and the Ulaid, Velius still had to deal with the Ériunian kingdoms that had sided with the Carthaginians, but it seemed inevitable at this point. They also had the Isle of Man, or as the Romans called it Insula Manavia, and its Carthaginian garrison to deal with, but that should be doable. That was the last of the low-hanging fruit. Afterwards, they would need to decide how to take the fight to the Carthaginians so they didn't continue to send fleets and armies to retake the islands. There were a lot of options, but none of them were good.

That was tomorrow's worry, however. Today was set aside for the celebration of their victory both on Ériunia and on the seas, and Lucilla had already decided how to kick off that celebration.

As if his thoughts had manifested her, Lucilla arrived at the bottom of the steps to the temple carried in a chariot, stepping down carefully in her ceremonial robes. Ky had been forced to wear a ceremonial toga of his own, but it was at least more functional than the miles of fabric that seemed to wrap themselves around *her* body.

She didn't even seem to notice as she mounted the stairs and made her way toward him. The dignity and elegance she seemed to bring with her every step was just another reason he loved her. He hadn't considered marriage beyond assigned pairings when he'd been in his time, but now, looking at her, he couldn't imagine **not** marrying Lucilla. She was practically radiant as she passed the last step, standing beside him and looking down at all the people gathered to wish them well.

"Let's go make you mine," she said, a twinkle in her eye as she took his arm and led him into the temple of Zeus.

To Be Continued...

About the author

Travis writes science fiction, fantasy, and thriller novels (and the occasional coming-of-age story), with the hope of transporting and enthralling readers. Publishing novels since 2015, Travis's passion is creating worlds and characters that live and breathe, and experiencing the joy of those stories with his readers.

When not writing, Travis enjoys connecting with readers and other writers, managing the popular Complete Marvel Reading Order website, where he works on his other passion for comics and graphic novels, and spending time with his family.

If you have enjoyed this book, please consider taking a moment to rate or review it wherever you found your copy, as it helps new readers find my works and ensures I can continue writing book into the future.

Find out more at:
amazon.com/TravisStarnes/e/B072YBDC3S/

Or visit
https://tstarnes.com

Maps available at
https://tstarnes.com/book-series/imperium/

Signup to get free previews and notifications of upcoming books at

http://tstarnes.com/preview-notification-newsletter/

Other Books

John Taylor Stories

Rebirth
False Signs
The Wrong Girl
Burying the Past
Family Ties
Election Day
Danger Close
Extraction
Designated Target
Border Crossed
Desperate Rendition

Country Roads Series

Playing by Ear
Fanfare
Dissonance
Elegy
From the Top
Center Stage

Imperium Series

Shattered Lands Series

False Start Series

The Veilguard Saga

Stand Alone